BURNT TREE JUNCTION

THE ACCLAIMED HISTORICAL FICTION SERIES

· VOLUME 2 ANTHOLOGY ·

DAUGHTERS

LOVE AND A LOCOMOTIVE

JOANN KLUSMEYER

innovo PUBLISHING

Published by Innovo Publishing, LLC
www.innovopublishing.com
1-888-546-2111

Providing Full-Service Publishing Services for Christian Authors, Artists & Ministries:
Hardbacks, Paperbacks, eBooks, Audiobooks, Music, Screenplays & Curricula

BURNT TREE JUNCTION: HISTORICAL FICTION FOR ADULTS

VOLUME 2 (ANTHOLOGY)

DAUGHTERS

—

LOVE AND A LOCOMOTIVE

Copyright © 2022 by Joann Klusmeyer
All rights reserved.

ISBN: 978-1-61314-678-1

Cover Design & Interior Layout: Innovo Publishing, LLC

Printed in the United States of America
U.S. Printing History
First Edition: 2022

—

Has God called you to create a Christian book, ebook, audiobook, music album,
screenplay, film, or curricula? If so, visit the ChristianPublishingPortal.com to learn
how to accomplish your calling with excellence. Learn to do everything yourself, or
hire trusted Christian Experts from our Marketplace to help.

CONTENTS

Sudden widowhood left her totally unprepared, just as most things in her life had done. It had not been her fault, but it would truly be her fault if she condemned her daughters to the same life. And she wasn't going to let that happen... no matter the cost.

Lennie M. Marshall was named after Grandad, Leonard Marshall. By age 12, Lennie could shoot a rattler at 50 yards and was as fearless as a badger. Reading, writing, and thinking fast came easy, and Lennie was fleet of foot, strong and able, and looked out for others too. And boy did Lennie love trains. In fact, Lennie decided to become a security guard on the Mountaineer and ride the train all the way to Memphis and back, taking care of all the passengers. There was just one thing...Lennie Marie Marshall was a girl! And no girl had ever been a security guard on the Mountaineer.

PART I

DAUGHTERS

THE NOTE

For months the note had been pinned on the wall. The day she received it had been a day of fear and indecision, but the words of the note lifted her up to the joyous point of humming a tune and then breaking out in song.

And why? She hadn't a clue!

Neighbor,

I'm afraid I find myself in need of a daughter for a day. Could you come and talk with me? Sophie McKinzey

The note had been written in shaky print, and 8 year old Emma had presented it to her mother, jabbing her elbow in the direction of their nearest neighbor through the trees.

"It was her, Ma, and she had it sealed up so I couldn't see what it said."

Belle peered fondly down at her firstborn. "Yes, and that's as it should be. The note is to me and I decide if you should see it." Whereupon she handed the scrap of paper to her daughter.

Emma read it at a glance. "Mom! She can't be thinkin' on a daughter! She's so…well, she's…wrinkled!"

"You think she is too old, is that it? So tomorrow I go see her and then we'll know what she wants. Now do your chores."

Emma firmed her lips and shrugged her shoulders...just a little. Turning on a heel, she headed for the clothesline to bring in the dry sheets and towels.

Belle Burk attached the note to the kitchen wall as a reminder and began to prepare the evening meal. There was so much to think on these days that reminders had become important. Nay, they became absolutely essential!

It wasn't always that way. There was the time, barely a year ago, when her days were easy, with difficult decisions passed on to Jake who was happy to make them.

But now Jake was gone. Decisions were all hers. Not only for herself but the five little girls to whom she had become the only parent. Belle was absolutely not prepared for a life like this. Her meager life training had been aimed toward her being a southern lady to whom life was simple and easy.

It started out with Adam and Isabel Breckenberry who lived in Eureka Springs, Arkansas. Their plan would have been to produce children in their younger years but that had not happened.

Isabel was past 45 when the doctor who was asked to treat her indigestion told her, incredible as it was, that she was pregnant. He'd had trouble believing it himself, and had actually given her a stomach settling preparation and told to come back in two weeks. She came back. Still pregnant.

So, when she returned no better, his examination proved his first diagnosis to be correct. This lady, already graying and producing wrinkles was, indeed and unmistakably, going to also produce a baby. That, or one or both of the persons involved would not live through it.

Then, there was Amos who was speechless and unbelieving. Long ago they had given up hope, and had settled their minds to a peaceful and adequate period of 'later years.' The small savings would last well and they could look back on having done their best for their Maker, and they gave the matter no more thought.

The protective angels having charge over humans were having none of that...as that was clearly not in the agenda of the Boss. So, on schedule, along with the first spring robins, there came a little girl. The local midwife had been notified, but she was an unbeliever even as she felt movement. Then the little thing was born, cried and waved her miniature arms just as any little girl would do. Leaving no more doubts.

Hmmm, well…. It was hard to be a doubter in the face of all that.

The parents had given a lot of thought to a name. This little belated 'once in a lifetime' gift must have a name worthy of her status and one that would make certain she would be remembered. There were two names in the running, Hermione and Mehetabell.

Mehetabell won out, and the two parents devoted their days to making sure she continued to breathe. Their time was wasted, however, as the child was 'healthy as a colt' according to the doctor… though he couldn't say as much for the mother. At her age, it had been a severe drain on her system.

Then, in three months, the stomach trouble returned, and resulted in another little girl to use the second chosen name Amos and Isabel had picked out. The midwife shook her head in dismay and predicted that neither of the girls had a shadow's chance of being normal.

It might have been said that if she'd done her duty, they'd not have been permitted a first breath, but she just couldn't do that with such robust lungs as the babies had exhibited in announcing their entry into the world. If they had been sickly…well…who knew….

Little Hermione and Mehetabell were eleven months apart and Isabel had paid the price. Her aging body had gone through a strain from which she would never fully recover, but that was not fatal for another thirteen years.

Amos was left with two healthy, normal teenage girls for whom he was not emotionally equipped, but he did his best. Hadn't they been gifts from God? So it was up to God to make the meager pension be enough to keep them fed.

For a fact, though, the unworldly parents were to blame for the money shortage. Feeling inadequate to train the girls themselves, an expensive teacher/governess had been hired and paid with money they could not afford.

At ages 4 and 5 the girls began their instruction with the promise that Miss Hortense Brittingham would teach them everything they needed to know to be a correct 'southern lady.' That was reading, spelling, penmanship and a smattering of numbers. A lady must be able to count stitches in her embroidery and to add well enough to know if they were cheated by merchants. Hence the necessary knowledge of numbers.

She also forbade the girls calling their mother 'ma' as did others in the town. If they had been born in England, they would have said 'mum,' but they were in the colonies and 'mom' would be more appropriate. She did not explain where she received this particular insight. One did not question a governess, and the parents had enough to keep them busy, anyway.

She also read extensively from the old English classics to teach sentence structure, and at ages 7 and 8 had demanded Bibles for the girls as that would be their next reading assignment. The King James Bibles were expensive, but if Miss Hortense said they were necessary, Amos and Isabel would get them. They did.

They were also schooled in 'thank you' notes, letters of request and expressions of sympathy to send to acquaintances. Their perfect penmanship gave class to these simple communications. A lady was surely known by the round smoothness of her letters…wasn't she? And never an ink spot was permitted. .

The unwieldiness of the girls' names began to be unbearable, and young Hermione announced that hereafter she would be called 'Minnie' and refused to answer to any other name.

The older daughter sighed and looked at her name. Finally, passing over the obvious 'Mattie,' she settled on Bell…adding a final 'e.'

The girls were 13 and 14 when their mother's body just gave up from strain and the resultant effort of rearing daughters. Old Amos held out as long as he could, but joined Isabel three years later.

On a piece of advice from a neighbor, and with the help of the postmaster, the practically penniless girls managed to sell the house, retaining the right to live there for six months to let them 'get their bearings.'

Hermione (Minnie) put up her hair and acquired shoes with heels. She became '18' in a day, and, taking her half the proceeds of the house sale, headed to Fayetteville. Hiring herself out as a 'kitchen helper' in a diner. She existed until rescued by a well-to-do customer. Her letters to her sister said she was 'doing well,' whatever that meant.

Belle, however, had no such answer for the rest of her life. The sale of the house had not included Missy, the young filly used for pulling the aging buggy, and today Belle had driven down to the banks of the river to let her pony munch on the tall grass. That saved on hay that had to be bought. Missy must be healthy to bring a good price.

She liked Missy and was dreading to part with her. After four months (leaving only two more that the house was hers), she had become very money conscious. She had decided that her only option was to hire herself to someone needing a scrub person (what all did that require?) or maybe a dishwasher down at the diner.

Amazing that she had never before realized that people must do something to earn money. All her life, as she knew it, had seemed that money came in an envelope every month, and it must be made to last until more money came. She had, during the last years, come to realize that there was never quite enough of it, but what could one do about that? Nothing…apparently.

Since her mom died, she had learned a lot. In the last four months she had learned a very great lot more. Somehow, she was going to have to have what was called a job, and it had to produce something called wages.

Missy had munched down her fill of the grass and was now wandering around pulling the light buggy nonchalantly behind her and continually getting it caught on something. And she didn't want to back up to get untangled. Belle was not proficient in speaking 'horse,' and the animal did not listen to Belle's correct English.

The last confrontation of animal and object was with a tree root and getting her straightened out had created an alarming crunch, but the buggy still rolled. Belle's mind returned to the problem of money as she pulled back onto the cobblestone street and headed for home.

It was at that exact moment that one of the wheels had laid gently over onto the cobbles with a screech and a few splintery cracks and the buggy tipped and settled into a heap of boards, seat pads and pieces of torn roof. Belle herself had slithered down among the wreckage to the stones of the street and found herself sitting on the ground.

Missy was scrambling for a footing, and when she was again standing, she turned and looked scoldingly at Belle. Later, looking back, Belle shook her head sadly at what had been the worst moment of her life, and it put her in a position that no 'southern lady' should ever find herself.

That's when she heard the wonderful voice. "Lady! Are you hurt, Miss?"

And now almost nine years later she shuddered as she poked a stick of wood into the stove. Precious wood, it was, and it was not burned frivolously. That would be like burning money. Money was one of the burdens currently hanging over her head.

Young Emma pushed her way back through the kitchen door with the washing, clean and smelling of lye soap and mountain air. She heaved her load onto the table and began folding the sheets, towels and pillow cases.

Dora, almost a year younger, emerged from the bedroom in her 'work' dress and lifted the wire basket from the wall. Eggs. Her job. Those wonderful white globes had become very important to the family in the last year. One had to eat and eggs were adaptable and forgiving.

Joy, 6 years old, was heard screaming, "Stop, Nettie, stop. You'll get hurt!" followed by feet running across the wooden boards of the porch. Two-year-old Nettie knew how to run, but not to obey, and went flying off the end of the porch. Big sister Joy was just steps behind.

And 4-year-old Eva pointed accusingly at her younger sister. "Lookie at what you done! You got blood on your stockin' and Mom's gonna be mad with you."

Belle turned back to the wood and the preparation for supper. It seemed that her daughters had their day under control, and she could now return to wondering what old Miz McKinzey wanted with her. As if she wasn't busy enough as it was.

But there was the truth in it that a 'southern lady' does not fail to answer a request such as this. Miss Hortense had been firm about that. "Treat folks like you want to be treated. Besides, you may need help some day."

OLD MIZ MCKINZEY

The next morning, with the three older girls fed and on their way to school, she loaded Eva and Nettie into the little wagon she rescued from the shed and headed through the woods on the well-worn path.

She was met at the door. "Oh thank you for comin', Miss... Burk, is it? I was sure the little girl would get there with the note. Come right in and I'm makin' the tea."

Belle painted a smile on her face and followed. Tea? Who could ever think she had time for tea this time of the day? But politeness ruled, and Belle obeyed.

More instructions. "Just have a seat. I know you been puzzlin' over my note, but there wasn't much way to write it down. You gotta be showed, and we can have tea first. You bein' my best neighbor, we need to get to know one another."

Finally seated, and with the steaming tea in the delicate, old fashioned cups and the plate of cookies before her, the old woman began. "First can I give cookies to the little ones? I didn't know about them. I just thought about the three I saw coming home from school. Five little girls! How fortunate you are!"

Without waiting for an answer or response, she handed Eva and Nettie a huge cookie each. Then she continued, "There was a time that I didn't need no one, but then the rhumitez settled in my joints and now I don't move so good.

"My son, over past Eureka, almost to Siloam Springs, has him a ranch where he grows sheep for wool. Does good for himself, and brings me all I can make up, and it's all cleaned and ready for usin' and it keeps me busy makin' socks and scarves and such for the youngens'a the family.

"That was before I got all stove up with the rhumitez. We'll have our tea and I'll show you what the note was about."

About time, Bell thought. Work was piling up at home, and Belle was getting behind on her worrying. Miss McKinzey began again.

"How are you doin' over there? I was friends with the old folks 'afore they passed, but then it was empty. Been wonderin' who it'd be to move in. I hear you be a widow lady." She paused. The last statement was clearly a question. Belle's turn to talk.

"Yes, Miz McKinzey. Been goin' on about six months now.'

The old woman shook her head in sympathy. "No good. But then us women folk, we do what we can with what we have. The Good Lord'll look after you, just like it says in the book."

Then it was time to unravel the puzzle. They entered a room with sacks of wool neatly stacked about, a spinning wheel near the wide window and other implements, totally foreign to Belle, were lying all around.

"I can see this here is not somethin' you're used to seein' so I'll explain. There's this here is wool that gets pulled into pinches the size'a the yarn you're wantin' and gets twisted in your fingers to make a string. Then that wheel goes round and round and the yarn strings get wound up on the spindle."

She looked at Belle, and decided her explanation was being comprehended. Maybe. "The trouble now is, that wheel takes a push on the pedal to make it go, and I could do that while I worked, like a body's 'sposed to do, only I can't. The rhumatiz in my ankle has got it too stiff to move. Now most folks'd have a little daughter around to push the pedal, but all the little girls in my family are miles away. Do you see…??"

Belle was beginning to. The wheel was the job of the spinner's foot unless it didn't work. In that case, there was a need for a little girl with 'push' still left in her foot. Now how did she think Belle could help, considering all that was to be done at her home?

Miz McKinzey was reading her thoughts. At her age, she'd had a lot of practice deciphering expressions. "What I was thinkin', really, was for a little help until I could do better. If you could loan me the little girl maybe just an hour or two on her way home from school…? I see you can't be sparin' her on a Saturday. I can't pay much, but if I could have her for a little while so's I could fill the spindle with yarn, then I could knit the next day. It'd take maybe a hour and a half…? It'd be worth a nickel a day, makin' up a quarter a week."

Belle listened. Money was involved. Not much, but every penny was squeezed till it squeaked. "An hour and a half, you say? That'd be enough to help you out?"

"Oh, yes, Miss Burk."

Belle butted in, "Just call me Belle. We're neighbors."

"Then call me Sophie. Thinkin' it over, a hour and a half… maybe two hours of a afternoon'd be better. Little girls get bored. I remember that. But I know little girls get hungry after school, and I'd be certain to have somethin' for her. If you'd think on it, I'd surely be beholdin' to you."

Little Eva was yanking on Miss Sophie's dress demanding another cookie and a cookie. Holding up the index finger on each hand. It was obvious she was looking out for sister Nettie as well.

Belle promised to think on it and see her tomorrow, as she put the two girls, plus cookies, in the wagon. Well, at least the puzzle of the note was solved.

It was a busy day with one thing after the other. It was amazing, however, how much help the four year old was. Eva would hardly let Nettie out of her sight and Belle could hear them giggling and squealing, and sometimes Eva scolding her. Well, she'd take what she could get and Eva was big enough to scream if things got out of hand.

The school girls came rushing in and searching for a snack, maybe leftover cornbread or something. Changed dresses and grabbed their chores. Gathering eggs. Polishing shoes. (Miss Hortense had insisted on the importance of that). Sweeping up the ever-present dust. Always something and the girls were getting better at noticing what.

Dora was attempting to patch a hole in the fence of the chicken yard. Wires crisscrossed to cover the hole. Anything was better than nothing until they could do better. Couldn't have their egg-producers getting out and being nabbed by varmints.

Emma faced her mother. "Mom, what did she say I had to do?"

"You have to put your foot on a pedal and push. Then let up and push again."

Emma giggled appreciatively at the joke. "Really, Mom. What is the job?"

"I just told you."

"I don't have to milk the goat…or pull weeds…or…? Sure 'nuff, just pat my foot?"

"No. You pat your foot on a pedal. That's it. You work for an hour or maybe two, and then you come home. For that you get a nickel."

Emma's dark, piercing eyes bored into her mother's. She demanded, "What does a nickel buy?"

Belle felt a flash of pride. She'd never have asked a question like that at age eight. Emma deserved an answer. "Let's talk about five nickels paid every week. That'd be a quarter and it would buy a large sack of cornmeal. It would buy two jars of honey from the junction. It would be very important to us."

But, later, as she stretched her weary self out on the bed, she felt a pang of shame that her eight year old daughter was going to be 'hired out.' She'd have worried a lot more if she hadn't fallen into exhausted sleep, dreaming dreams of horror that were almost a reality.

JACOB BURK - THE FIXER

Missy, the pony, had tangled herself in the tree roots due mostly to an untrained driver. She had ruined the buggy which was no great loss except that it was all Belle had. And there Belle sat on the cobbles with a shattering of debris over and around her, and the concerned face of a young man peering in at her.

"Miss? Are you hurt?"

Belle sought for an answer. Finally, "No. Just a scratch, but I don't know what to do."

"Can I take you home to get your pa…? Or…."

No southern lady should be caught in a mess like this, but what could she do? She decided to be honest and wing it. "I ain't got no pa. I ain't got nothin' 'cept this horse and a pile a junk, and I don't even have a house to go to that's mine."

The young man frowned in disbelief. "You mean…uh?"

She nodded deeply so he would be sure to understand. If he had any ideas of where help was to be found, now was the time to share them with her. So she nodded again. "I got nothin' nowhere."

Might as well get the worse out.

Looking back, she hardly remembered what happened next, but she found herself seated on a wagon buckboard while Missy was unharnessed and tied to the rear of the wagon. Passersby stopped to help with the junk that could be lifted and put in the wagon, and the rest was pushed aside off the cobbles.

She heard the young man chatting with the helpers but she had no idea what he was saying. She was busy thinking what to do next. One couldn't expect a stranger....

But what was she thinking? She had no one else.

That was how she met Jacob Burk.

He dropped her off at her house and promptly left. Said he had things to do but would be back.Somehow she believed him...a total stranger.

She dropped into the house's only 'easy' chair and looked up at the clock. Noon. Where had the morning gone? What was there to eat? Crackers and cheese, it seemed, and she gave herself 30 minutes to eat and then she was going to get busy. At something.

For one thing, her clothes and a few small mementoes would need to be packed, and then she would clean the house (Miss Hortense would have insisted) and she must prepare to be serious about what to do with the rest of her life.

Cleaning took the rest of the day. It was barely daylight the next morning when the stranger was at the door. He walked in as if he had been there many times before, sat himself down at the table and motioned her to a chair.

"We got to talk, Miss Belle."

"I'll get tea." (Miss Hortense, again. A lady must be proper no matter what the circumstances.)

He decided not to argue and watched her fill the cups with steaming brew. Peppermint. He blew away the plume of steam, sipped, set the cup down and looked at her.

"Miss Belle, we got us a problem...both of us. You got only weeks to find somethin' to do, and I got no time at all to help you.

I stayed up all night thinkin', and I come up with somethin' that'll work if you let it.

"Now me, I got a real nice piece'a land up on the bench of Echo Mountain. Faces the sun in the mornin', good grass and a big house. They's things to be done, but I can do 'em. The thing is, it'll take up every hour of every day for the next few years, and one thing that house don't have is a lady. That makes it a very lonely house for both it and for me.

"Now you...you got no house and you're about the nicest, prettiest lady I've ever laid eyes on. I got my wagon here, and I loaded on the wheels of your buggy to take 'em away...bein' no way you could ever use 'em anyway. I got room left for whatever boxes you want to take, and maybe a chair or two if these belong to you.

"Not only that, I got room right there on the seat beside me for a lady about your size. And it looked to me like the answer to both our problems was right there starin' us in the face.

"Only one thing stoppin' it, and that'd be you sayin' 'yes.' Another problem I got is that I ain't got no time. I gotta be on the way before the hour is over to get back to the farm and see to my animals. Ain't safe to leave 'em alone too long and help ain't easy to get.

"So I can give you two choices. One is, I load you on the wagon and take you with me. When you see my house then you can say yes or no, and I'll take you to wherever you want to go. Or the other choice is we can go down to the judge and he'll marry us in about fifteen minutes and we'll be on the way. You decide which."

Belle sucked in her breath until her lungs were bursting and then let it out slowly. Married! A place to go. A stranger. Echo Mountain sounded like the other end of the earth. All of these certainties were frightening to the core. But what else was there to do?

She grabbed for the nearest question. "Wouldn't there be papers to make out if we were to marry?"

"Got 'em already. Told the judge I'd be back in a hour or not at all, dependin' on what you decided." In one motion, he emptied his tea cup and returned it to the saucer. Casting his eyes around the room, he saw the boxes tied with cord and a very large suitcase.

"But, Jake…is it? I don't know how I can take that much from you when I have nothin' to give."

Jake's shoulders shrugged away the objection. "Sure you got somethin'. That smart little filly'a yours. I'll put 'er in the stall for a while. Seems she must'a been kept in a pasture with others and she got herself bred. That makes two animals you got to even up the trade." He studied her silent reaction. Time was wasting.

He indicated the row of boxes with his elbow, "These here go with you?"

At her nod, he suggested, "You got time to pack up these dishes and whatever else you want while I hook the filly to the wagon." With that, he walked out the door.

Belle shook her head to wake up her senses. She had apparently committed herself, and that must be good. Decisions were so hard to make. Taking the only unpacked tea towel, she wiped the teacups and put and put them in the last unfilled packing box. She scanned the bare room for something missed.

Oh, the chairs. He wanted them, and there were two more in the bedroom. She lined them up by the door, and picked up one to take to his wagon when the door opened in her face. There he was.

"Miss Belle, I know this is goin' all wrong against what you wanted to happen, but I promise nothin' bad'll happen to you while you're with me. Can you believe me?"

What could she do but nod?

She signed her name before the smiling judge, saw Jake hand him a silver dollar and pick up a sheet of paper. He folded it and put it in his pocket, reached for her hand and led her away.

She was helped to the buckboard of the wagon under a canvas canopy and Jake seated himself beside her, smiling and whistling, and clicked the two mules into action. Missy, tied on behind, whickered her puzzlement, but followed docilely along.

Belle was in almost the same position. She had been taught that she would be told by someone what she should do next. It would be 'her place' to wait. That is what a 'lady' did. Then, whatever happened, she must be ready to make the best of however it turned out.

Jake rode happily beside her. He chatted about this and that. There was the pig that would make winter meat. They'd put in a garden. She would be able to preserve all the beans and tomatoes they needed.

"But Jake, I really don't...I mean I've never done anything. I wouldn't know the first thing about...."

But he turned to her with a wide grin. "Don't you be givin' that another thought! Them ladies up on Echo'll be linin' up for the privilege'a helpin' you."

"But they...Jake, I really don't know nothin' about what you're talkin' on. That about takin' care'a the honey...ain't that got somethin' to do with bees? I never really saw a bee...up close, that is. I'll be ashamed and the ladies you're talkin' about won't like me."

Jake paused and with a calloused hand he turned her chin toward his face. "I tell you, my lovely wife, Belle, that by helpin' you it'll show you how smart they are and they'll want to share their smart with you. There's a lot of 'smart' up there on that mountain... more'n Eureka and Wishbone put together, and a few more places throwed in. They'll help you with whatever you need to know with everything they know, and you askin' 'em about somethin' is better'n givin' 'em a present."

Belle tried to believe him, but how could that be? Why didn't she know all of this, if, indeed, it was true? That there were girls (ladies) who wanted to help her...What he said couldn't possibly be what she thought she heard. She sat and listened, and, in spite of herself, she enjoyed the ride. So much to see! She'd never been anywhere.

In early afternoon he guided the team into a shady grove. Opening a box he lifted out a generous wheel of cheese and a metal box of crackers. Belle saw crackers and cheese. And apples. Four of them...rosy and crisp.

Carefully cleaning his knife, he sliced off a generous slab of cheese and extended it to her. Lovely picnic it would be. And apples!

Munching the food he explained, "I know we could have eaten on the road, but the animals, they needed a rest. It's going to be a lot rougher from here on home."

Home. He said it so naturally it sent chill bumps racing down her arms. Could it possibly be…?

The sun was setting behind the mountain when she had the first glimpse of her home. He pointed up against a forest of trees. "See right through there. That patch'a white in the trees? That's our house. Problem is, we'll be a lot'a time getting there."

And they were. Darkness was falling fast when they came into the sound of animals…mooing, baaing and likely cackling. All of the farm buildings were just shapes in dusky darkness as he stopped the team before a wide gate.

"Miss Belle, I wish I could stay and help with the unloading but the animals are suffering. I'll take the box'a dishes and you decide one other box and I'll come back for it."

She chose the box of towels and followed him into the house. Empty. Dark. He lighted an oil lamp, picked up a bucket and lifted a wire basket from the wall. "You need to rest, and I'll be in with the milk as soon as I can."

Rest? What was he talking about! She gazed about the spacious kitchen, the large stove…recently polished. No table. A large wooden slab on kegs seemed to be it. More kegs for seating.

Opened the cupboard. Hmmm. Two cans of pork and beans. She knew what to do with them as soon as she saw the slab of bacon beside the sharp knife. Two remaining apples.

She poked the stove full of the dry wood and lit it from the lamp to save matches. An onion. Good. Chopped and mixed with the beans. Into the oven.

Cornmeal? Yes, here it was. And eggs. A whole bowl of them. Leftover apples sizzling in bacon grease the skillet, then drizzled with honey. Eggs in hot water then peeled. Still no Jake.

Feeling her way through the darkness she, she managed to lift two chairs from the load and get them to the kitchen. Taking dishes from her box she laid the table and took up the beans and bacon. Then the sweet, tender fried apples, boiled eggs halved and spread with mustard. A skillet of quick cornbread. Butter? Likely, there was some but she couldn't find it.

Sound at the door. Jake managing two buckets. She rushed to hold back the door. He brought milk…a whole bucket of it! Enough to fill glasses and put them on the table. Should she? Dare she?

Wire basket of eggs he hung on the wall. If one had eggs, they had a meal. Belle gazed fondly at the eggs.

Jake stared at the lovely china dishes and the steaming bowls of food spread out on the plank table and stood silent, wiping his eyes. Belle watched, hand over her mouth. Had she done the right thing?

Apparently she had. "Miss Belle, have a seat, will you, while we thank the One above for this feast." Whereupon he bowed his head and did so.

When he raised his head, Belle made the firm and brave decision to do something on her own. She arose and took two glasses from the cupboard…glasses she had used all her childhood. From a drawer she took her well-used dipper. From the milk bucket on the stand, she dipped the warm milk into the two glasses and took them to the table.

Jake smiled and tipped his glass to take the first drink. Then the two hungry strangers ate their first meal in almost total silence. There would be time later for words.

Dishes washed and put away in cupboards that had been empty for months. Jake told her, "I want you to look at the three bedrooms that have a bed and choose the one you like. Go in and close the door and I'll see you in the morning."

Puzzled she looked at him. "Jake, I know what married means."

He nodded. "So do I. We'll talk about it tomorrow. You are worn out from decisions and riding and creating this wonderful meal. You must go to bed and sleep as long as you can. Everything will still be here when you wake up."

She chose the smallest room with the wide window. Lifting the window, she felt the instant breeze off the mountains. Striping to her under-slip she stretched out on the bed and the next thing she knew was the crowing of the roosters.

THE FARM ON ECHO MOUNTAIN

Belle stepped from her bed into a new world. Birds were singing into her open window. Animals were mooing, baaing, whickering and squawking in their usual morning serenade…one Belle had never heard before.

After reassuring herself that she was actually in the right place, she walked tentatively down the short hall to an empty kitchen and faced last night's milk in the crock. Shouldn't something be done with that?

How about putting it into a pudding with all these eggs? There'd likely be more milk tonight. She loved pudding sweetened with molasses. And there was the molasses.

She attacked the huge iron stove like an old friend. Never mind that she had never seen one quite that big. While the stove warmed up, she stepped outside and saw what it had been too dark to see last night. She could see that the house was way up the side of a hill with the ground falling away on three sides. She saw blue mountains on top of blue mountains in the distance. The blue of the mountains faded with distance until they were the same hue as the sky.

She saw a red barn flanked by several sheds. Fenced pastures and gardens. Stalks of corn…dry now but still holding fat ears. An herb garden by the house and a pecan tree in the yard. And this could all be hers just to live here with…that fellow (?) who rescued her. Seemed like a good trade! Perhaps they could get acquainted today.

Back to the stove. She found the bacon and sliced it in the skillet. She'd wait on the eggs. Best when fried fresh. She knew that much. Biscuits in the oven, and there was the butter in a box close to the floor…to keep cooler, of course. So many surprises to find. Like when Miss Hortense hid Easter Eggs for the girls to find.

She'd measured out the milk and molasses for the pudding when Jake came in with a shiny pail. She startled, slightly. This would take some getting used to. He spoke and set the milk bucket on the work table. Belle looked in.

"But we…have…We still have…milk…?"

There was that happy smile on his face… like when he found her twisted among the dying buggy. She kept forgetting how fetching his smile was. A twinkle in his dark eyes. And a little bit wicked… was her afterthought.

"Yes, milk, and there'll be more tonight. Now you have a puzzle on how to use it all. What you absolutely can't use, we feed the pig and eat it later in pork. I'm going to ride up the road to the Corbin's and tell them about you. I'll ask Jesse Lee to drop in on us tomorrow to answer questions I can't. I do know, though, that cottage cheese is made from milk, and that should be started today."

Belle cringed, "Company…? Coming here…?"

"No, not company. Help. I knowd you'd need help gettin' started. Jesse is your closest neighbor and she's the best kind'a help you'd ever want. She's not much older'n you. How old are you, anyway?"

There was a lot of talking to be done that day for a pair of strangers who were suddenly partners for life.

Jesse Lee Corbin was all Jake had promised. She stepped inside the door and enveloped Belle in a hug. "I'm so glad you here…and living so close!"

And that began Belle's education. Being a 'farm-wife' seemed to be a full time job. Jesse knew all the neighbors, when to pick the seasoning herbs from the little garden. How to make the cheese and reconstitute the dried meat. ("You'll need to do this when you learn to can the meat in jars.")

She helped Belle find the clothespegs and sort out the wash and rinse tubs. Jake actually had lye soap that his mother had sent, but Jesse had brought a sample. Later, Belle would make her own. Jesse Lee promised.

"I can make this…? Really…?"

"Uh, yes. You sorta have to if you aim to get the clothes clean. Hair, too. It makes shiny hair."

Then she began to examine Belle things, particularly the contents of the two large wooden boxes Belle called chests. There were fancy embroidered pillow cases and dresser scarves. Padded pot holders and tea towels. ("Oh my heavens! You can't use these! They'll be ruined.")

"But that's what they…were made…?

"No matter. They're much to pretty to use and wouldn't last long enough anyway. You'll need to come over to my house and see what you need on a farm. I think Jake said you were from Eureka Springs? I think things might be different over there. Out here a girl is known for how much she gets done, not how purty her towels are."

Then the discussion went to babies. "You'll need to meet Granny Murphy. She don't like to wait till the last couple'a months. She acts like the babies was her own toys till they get born. Checks on them about once a month. I've already had my third visit."

Belle stared at her new friend in a semi-daze. So much to take it. A bit scary.

But then Jesse's eyes lit up like a couple of candles. "I know what! We'll have welcome party for you. The others'll want to meet you and that will get it over with."

"A…p…p…arty…?"

"Oh, don't be scared. I'll be here, and I'll come over to help you get ready."

"But the food. They might not like…."

"Who cares! Maybe they'd like to learn somethin' new. 'Sides, they'll all bring somethin' and there's always left overs. I'd say maybe next week…?"

Belle nodded. What else could she do? Actually Jake had said this would happen, but she hadn't believed it.

"You ever ride a horse? I though not. I know you got a buggy but there's the time wasted on hitchin' and things. Back on our trails there likely won't be anybody to see, and if there is she's likely to be on a mule. I'd guess Jake has one and'll teach you to ride. Or you can use a saddle if you want to. Who cares if someone sees your knees?"

And the ladies came. A whole eleven of them and Jake had to scramble to make bench seats for them. Four chairs didn't go very far, but there were plenty of nail kegs that were just the right height… with a cushion, of course.

As they entered…laughing and talking animatedly…Belle watched with excited apprehension. She'd never had a party and had hardly attended one after the 'birthday parties' with Miss Hortense.

Jesse Lee was first, of course, with her gift of 6 new towels from sturdy by-the-yard kitchen toweling…un-decorated, tightly hemmed with course twine and each one was a whole yard long! Instantly Belle could see great value in that length.

The gifts were not wrapped. Jesse arranged a place on Belle wooden chests to display them. "They'll want to spread 'em out so's everyone can see what they brought. That's part'a the fun of a party like this."

First was Maggie McGee, across the road and just north of Jesse. With a mischievous grin she placed her gift next to Jesse's. Six more towels exactly like Jesse's…could have come off the same bolt. Any lady in the midst of summer canning would need a minimum of a dozen towels. Certain to.

With her was Kate Simpson, a dimpled blond, proudly carrying a jar of beet pickles, the glass of the jar sparkling against the sight of ping-pong sized globes…brilliant deep red and decorated with a ribbon and sprig of mint at the top. Kate had a flare for the fancy.

Turning the jar to the back, she pointed out the glued, penned directions for making them. A note at the bottom of the directions said "I make 3 kind of cucumber pickles. If you want help next spring, let me know."

Belle shivered with excitement. Pickles of any kind had not been in the budget for years.

Caroline Hempstead, lean and muscular, eased down from the mule's back and untied a wicker basket. Swinging it proudly, she displayed it beside the pickles, leaving the bars of lye soap visible. Tied to the handle with a piece of string was the recipe. "Don't try this by yourself the first time. There's directions to my house on the back. Let me know when."

Gladys Gordon, petite and plumply pregnant, came by buggy, a tiny one-seater. Folded and tied with a ribbon was a clothes-peg apron with a bib and long ties. It had been created from a course and long-wearing canvas sack that had contained cow feed. No clothes-pegs in it, because Belle would have them…of course…but aprons wore out. The gift took its place with the soap. Being from Eureka Springs, she wouldn't have had one.

Maurine Jones and Evelyn Fields, sisters with a head full of blazing red curls, came together in a buggy of a slightly larger size. They lifted a rather weighty object from the boot of the buggy which turned out to be a box, about 1 foot by 2 feet with a strong wooden handle. It was built as a berry carrier but was packed with jars of jelly. Many kinds of jelly.

Maurine explained, "This here's a berry carrier made for them little square boxes, but we use ours for gatherin' garden stuff. See the open slats in the bottom…? Let's the dirt out if you dump a bucket'a water all over the greens and taters. We thought you'd be able to use it next spring."

Then Evelyn. "But it made a good carrier for the jelly. Don't bother to get the jars back to us. They're just mustard jars and we use a lotta mustard."

They set the carrier on the floor beside Belle's wooden chests. Made an impressive gift. All together the gifts created quite a collection. These ladies loved parties and in addition to gifts, there came cookies, candy and caramel covered nut kernels.

Among the gifts were a half a dozen small herb plants, a flowered printed bag of popcorn, unpopped. A dozen envelopes containing flower seeds, a number of thick hotpot holders. A wicker coffee-pot holder for the table. A roomy shelf made of wicker (and Belle instantly saw her alarm clock perched there.)

It seemed someone was late and the ladies were concerned. Harriet Mobley, the preacher's wife, hadn't made it yet. Schedules were hard for her to keep as there was always an emergency or something pertaining to the church, but there she was! Her buggy turned in at the gate.

The man with her helped her down. Pregnancy sometimes upsets balance. A small girl followed. A 4-year-old boy was next. And Harriet gathered her skirts in her hand and headed for the door, seeming to carry no gift. The toddling girl followed, holding to Ma's skirt.

At the door, she was greeted with a round of clapping. "You made it!" came the shouts. Pleased smile and a nod. It wasn't that she made it to the party. It was much bigger than that.

While digging into her sizeable bag, she withdrew a book. "Up all night, I was, and burned two candles down to the puddle'a wax. Got 'em all here, though."

She handed the book to Jesse who explained. "Miss Belle," she began, "This here little book has more'n sixty recipes that come from all of us. We gave her ten each, and she sorted out the duplicates and printed 'em all in here and put our names by our recipe. We figgered a girl from the city might not know what grows in the mountains or how to cook it. Our names are there so if you got a question, you'll know who to ask."

Belle took the book and nodded her thanks. Opening it, she saw the words were printed in the school-girl print of square letters taught by teachers in the mountain schools.

Belle, schooled by Miss Hortense in Elizabethan script, flowing, connected and flawless, sighed with admiration as she looked at the letters. What would have been the action of a day, to her, was a week-long labor of love from this woman with two children (at least) and a rounded belly…with a husband constantly on call and herself held to a rigid schedule of being available and still rearing a family.

To some, it might have meant recipes, but to Belle it represented an intense effort to make life easier for the newcomer. A newcomer she had never even seen.

Somewhat overcome, Belle eased back and sat down on the nearest keg. With the book on her lap, she leaned forward and thoroughly embarrassed herself as her tears welled up in her eyes and flowed through her fingers.

Jesse grabbed up one of her new kitchen towels and hugged Belle, sopping the tears from her hands, then her face. She rescued the book from the deluge and thrust it into the nearest pair of hands. Her guests stood respectfully silent until the sobs died down to a sniffle and a snub.

Finally, "I just don't know that to say. Nothin' like this ever happened to me. Jake said you were like this but I didn't believe 'im. Nobody'd do this for a stranger."

Silence. Small movements. Then Harriet Mobley. "But, honey, you're not a stranger. You're our neighbor and friend. We thought you'd need to know that if you were going to live on Echo Mountain."

Then Caroline of the lye soap. "She's right, Belle. This here old mountain…it has a mind'a its own. Seems like."

There were times, years later, that Bell was to remember Caroline's words. But on that day, tears were dried, talk and laughter happened, food was enjoyed, and Jesse insisted on showing everyone the fancy items in the wooden chests.

Kate, of the pickled beets, summed up the wonder of it all. "Law, sakes, honey! How'd you ever have time to do all them stitches?"

Belle had no answer that would have been believed. All she had experienced in her whole life was time. Nothing but time and the need to fill it with something.

And the party continued until the sun had cleared the top of Echo Mountain. They gathered children and belongings and prepared to go.

Evelyn Fields, of the tight, red curls, brightened. "Oh, yes! We were gonna let you know, you not bein' here for very long. You got windfall apples out there on the slope. Both kinds. Mostly Ben Davis but they's Jonathan's ready to fall. Them Jonathan's make really good jelly."

Belle let the strange word 'windfall' go by, but zeroed in on the 'jelly.' "Real apples make jelly…?"

She had all eyes and a few gaping mouths turned her way. Jesse hurried to the rescue. "Come on, girls, Belle here ain't had a chance to make real Jonathan apple jelly. I'll show 'er. Be no trick a'tall."

Aside to Belle she promised. "Day after tomorrow I'll be over here. We'll get them apples 'afore the coons and possums do."

Nodding encouragingly she had parting words with the community of young ladies, thrilled with the success. If there was anything a young Echo Mountain lady loved it was to get to show someone how to survive on the mountain or use an unusual plant.

And here was Belle, her neighbor, an empty slate! Such a gift!

BURK'S FARM ON ECHO MOUNTAIN

There was the huge barn painted barn-red. A group of utility sheds circling the barn like satellites surrounding a planet. Animals of various kinds populated the many pens and enclosures.

White-painted fence around a generous yard. The mountain arose sharply behind the house and descended just as sharply past the flat place beginning the hay pasture. Bench land, it was, and Echo Mountain had a lot of it. Echo Mountain also had landslides that were continuously reshaping the hulking pile of dirt, rock and trees.

For Jake, it was a kingdom that was his responsibility to rule during all waking hours. Jake was made for the farm, and the farm was what molded a complete life for him. Everything was now in place.

The ruler of the kingdom had selected and brought home the queen of his empire, and that had furnished the last piece of the mosaic of his life. Belle was here, his, and beautiful. She also seemed to love the house. The remoteness of it could have been a problem for him, when it came to finding his mistress. And now, he had not had to spend days and weeks in locating and courting, and the wonder of it was, she was a marvelous cook. Possibly better than his ma!

And, like his ma, she quietly went about the duties within the house but evenings were filled with talk, dreams, songs and readings from the Bible, their only book. He was highly impressed with the beautiful, clearly expensive Book she had brought with her. Paper thin as a butterfly's wing and her name in the front. She had been nine years old. What a gift from the parents for so young a girl!

Together they filled out the part about her marriage and noted fondly the spaces for children. An attractive woven willow shelf had come with her house-warming gifts. It just fit the Book along with the clock. Life was perfect.

Eleven months later, Granny Murphy brought her emergency bags and moved into a spare bedroom. The next night a little red-faced girl yelled her way into the world. Jake just couldn't seem to get the grin off his face.

So Emma Burk's name occupied the top line in the 'Children' column of the Bible on the wicker shelf. Granny Murphy laboriously filled out the legal papers required of a midwife, trained or not. Midwives were valuable persons…like the horse-doctor and the minister.

In due time the sketchy mail system found them and presented them with a copy of the Birth Certificate. A special place was found on the wicker shelf for that important document.

As Jake was made for the farm, Belle was made for motherhood. The girl who had never been around newborns or children of any age, tucked the little girl into the crook of her arm as though it was created for her. Maybe it was.

Jake came in from the outside, washed up, and picked up the little girl. He held her until food was ready, and reluctantly put her into the wicker basket his ma had insisted he take. He talked with Belle telling of something or other around the farm which meant nothing to her, but she loved his voice.

He talked with Emma and told her what he and she would be doing and she answered with squeals and coos. She also loved his voice.

Almost twelve months to the day, Emma's little sister made her appearance. Granny Murphy already had the important papers made out because names of the parents would be the same. All she needed was the weight, sex and name of the child.

Dora Burk occupied the second line in the Bible, and inherited the wicker basket bed. Emma was graduated to a solid box on the floor which she soon learned could be crawled out of quite easily.

Emma Burk was showing signs of inheriting her father's dark completion and eyes, hair line and chin dimple.

Dora, on the other hand, was round faced, soft chinned and possessing eyes as blue as the distant mountains. She also refused to take her blue-eyed stare from her father's face. She watched intently as he talked to her, smiling and nodding, telling of the wonderful times they could have if she would just learn to walk. When his voice ceased, a faint grin appeared as though she understand and would immediately put her feet to work.

At 8 months, Dora turned herself over, pulled dimpled knees under her round belly and pushed herself to a sitting position. From this height she could see a lot more…made her sister giggle…and made her father laugh his wonderful happy laugh and lift her to the ceiling so she looked down onto the top of his head. The experience was so exhilarating that she determined to demand it again. Often as possible.

The sisters created their own play games consisting mostly of passing their toys back and forth and tasting them. A favorite item was the hard-rubber baby doll, about 6 inches long and totally naked. From her sister, Dora learned to get a firm grip on the doll's head which positioned the fingers and toes of the doll in perfect position for chewing.

The doll was actually passed down from a cousin, now twenty-three years old and living in Bentonville. It had actually assisted in the teething of a number of small persons, and now had duty with the Burk babies.

When the long summer evenings stretched out before them, Belle, again plump with pregnancy, read in her trained voice favorite passages from the Psalms. Jake, cleaned up and fed, watched his daughters as they played on a quilt on the carpet. He smiled and often shook his head with the wonder of it all. What had he done to deserve such a life?

Then when the daughters began to rub their eyes with droopiness, he sat with a daughter on each arm until time for bed (because morning came so quickly!)

Granny Murphy had already made eight quick visits to the Burk's to visit Lily (or maybe Jake Jr, but likely not). The old woman cared nothing for adults or parents, caring for Belle only as a container for the next baby.

And now she came with her overnight bag. It was not surprise to Jake and Belle. The labor pains had been increasing, but they had no concern…Granny would come when the time was right. The community had ceased trying to figure out how she knew.

Granny Murphy brought her overnight things and the important papers she must send to the 'state,' whoever that was. That was no concern of hers. The important paper was already filled out with her heavy-handed printing, letters straight up and down and easily readable.

With only minor difficulty, Lily came whimpering and squirming into the world and immediately inherited the wicker bassinette. As soon as he was permitted to see her, Jake looked into the face of yet another beautiful creation of himself and Belle.

He shook his head humbly and was heard to wax poetic, humbly muttering, "Once again God has sent us joy. A perfect specimen of His love."

Granny ignored his sanctimonious words, printed the name, weight and time of birth as required. Packed her bags, received the huge fee of $5.00 (roughly the price of two bull calves that Jake had sold, preparing for this moment) and closed the door softly behind her. The Good Book said that a workman was worthy of his wages, and she felt certain she had earned hers.

Lily was a 'good' baby and content to examine her toes or suck her knuckles until someone came with whatever she needed. She learned to squinch her eyes tightly when a small hand reached into her bed. She rather liked to have her feet held by these small hands as they massaged her tiny toes, the size and shape of the field peas that were a staple in the Burk family diet.

It was about two months later that their copy of the birth certificate found its wandering way to the Burk farm on Echo Mountain. Knowing what it was, it was set aside as 'canning season' was in full swing. Lily was three months old when the envelope was opened and the paper smoothed out and added to the previous two.

It was Jake's sharp eye that caught the word "Joy" where "Lily" should have been. Hmmm, well….

When accosted by the mistake, Granny's faded eyes peered from the sheath of wrinkles and told the parents, "There ain't nothin' wrong with my hearin' or my understandin'. I stood right there and heard him say God sent him Joy, and it ain't none of my business what folks name their youngens. Her name is Joy."

And with that, Granny turned her head toward the door, fitted her walking bonnet to her head and strode out of the room.

The parents stared after her until she disappeared into the nothingness of distance and then they stared at each other. A full minute later they burst into laughter with Emma joining in the fun. Dora stared at her father, trying to learn why he was acting so strangely.

Finally, the laughter ceased and Jake took down the beautiful, expensive Book that occupied the wicker shelf. He handed the queen of his kingdom a sharpened pencil with an eraser.

Belle contemplated the next activity and, refusing the eraser, carefully crossed through "Lily" and wrote "Joy" above. Smiling at Jake, she closed the book and returned it to the shelf. Her name was Joy. What was wrong with that?

But when it came time for Eva, Jake stood over Granny while she printed in the name.

Emma was now five years old, and the closest mountain school was three miles away. This was going to present a problem of how to get her there and back without taking too large a chunk of Jake's time or leaving the younger girls unattended. It would have to be faced, of course, but in a year Dora would also be ready for school, and they'd figure something out.

Then, in the middle of the night Belle jerked upright in bed, startling Jake who, from habit, crammed his shoes on his feet and reached for his robe and gun. Anything could happen on Echo Mountain, and a homeowner had to be ready.

"No! No!" Belle insisted. "Nothin' wrong. I just got a good idea. I had a really good teacher, and I remember everything she taught me. I know how to teach readin' and writin' and numbers to get Emma started. I still got them books...remember?"

So Emma began to be homeschooled between weed pulling, bean shelling and potato peeling. She recited her alphabet while stirring the clabber milk for cottage cheese. She made the long-handled wooden spoon make a complete circle with every letter as she printed it in the clabber curds.

Dora loved the new game of sounds and she repeated her vowel and consonant sounds just like Emma. She then recited them to her father making him smile with pleasure, laugh with joy and swing her around and around.

Problem solved...for the moment. But still the specter of it appeared like a thunder cloud above them. Eventually an answer had to be found. Belle was so lightly educated herself, she would never be able to continue as far as they had planned for their daughters.

But the days went by and became months and years. It was a constant worry when Emma turned seven and Dora a bright and happy six. The younger girl's greatest pleasure was to follow her papa as he went about his duties. He insisted she was good help and found things for her to do. He was a fountain of farming information, and his second daughter was empty pool...eager for whatever he wanted to tell her...which was practically everything.

When he brought in wood from the wood lot, she rode on the sled as the mules pulled. When repairing the shingle roof, she nimbly climbed the ladder with nails and shingles. When checking the fence line, so important in the mountains, she was along, carrying the tack-hammer and the staples for re-attaching loose wires.

Emma preferred the kitchen and its possibilities so it worked out well. When Nettie was born, Joy was almost four and a great help in watching out for her and keeping Eva from piling all their toys into the basinet with her. She could check on the dampness of the diaper, and was adept at folding the cotton squares correctly to fit her sister's tiny bottom.

Jake's kingdom, all 80 acres of it, consisted of flats and steep sides, a lot of rocks and rich soil tied together with the roots of sumac and Virginia creeper. Some of the rocks were as big as a house, protruding from the small bluffs. There was no knowing how much was hidden within the mountain.

Mighty oak trees, eager for the minerals and moisture in the rock fissures, thrust their roots deeper and deeper and it became a contest of sorts. God's new and strong creation, the oak trees, against his older and more granular creation, the solidified lava of centuries ago. This activity was hard on fences. It took a lot of checking to make sure the livestock were enclosed as rocks were broken apart often damaging the protective enclosure wires.

Dora filled her bag with staples and slipped in the tack hammer. It was sure to be needed. Jack picked up the roll of wire that was certain to be required and put it on his shoulder. It was a beautiful day in April and the farm was blossomed out in many colors and vegetation contained at least twenty shades of green. Every bird in the world was competing for nesting space and father and daughter trudged along happily together.

The fence to be checked ran up the mountain about 20 feet and straightened out toward the west. Sure enough, a large rock had rolled against a post and it was leaning precariously.

Jake stood contemplating the damage and Dora put her bag on a nearby stone and was examining some small flowers. Should she pick them (they'd surely wilt) or....

She felt a small tremble under her feet and darted her eyes toward her father who stood like a statue below the damaged fence. Then, out of seemingly nowhere, a stone the size of a water bucket flew down the mountain and slammed into his shoulder, knocking him down. He had hardly hit the ground when he knew...absolutely knew...his life would end that day.

He screamed with his last breath to his daughter. "Run Dora! Run as fast as you can!"

"Where to Papa?"

"Hush! Run! Away! Go far...." and then the sharp piece of broken rock hit Dora's leg and she stared down, horrified at the instant blood.

Papa again! "Run Dora...now!! Go!! Go!!"

Dora ran. Leaving her hammer and staples and ignoring the blood running down her leg, she headed into the direction of the house. Once she glanced back, but kept running. Papa wasn't usually so mad at her as he now seemed, and she didn't want to make it worse. One quick glance did not locate him, but he had to be back there somewhere. He wouldn't leave her.

Besides, a storm must be brewing up Echo Mountain. She knew about storms from the rumble, but the storms mostly had black clouds. She pushed it from her mind, running blindly, stumbling and skinning her knees and elbow, but the 'storm' became louder and louder and seemed to be chasing her.

When she reached the painted fence around her yard, Mom and Emma were staring toward her and Emma was crying.

Her mom grabbed her up (and her a great big almost 7 year old!) and hugged her so tight it would have hurt if she hadn't been so scared. Here first thought was that Mom was going to get blood on her nice clean apron.

Her second thought was, "Where is Papa? He was right be...." and she looked toward the still rumbling and shaking high pasture.

"Shh, shh, darling. We're going to the house now."

Belle forced her feet, one foot after the other, toward the lovely house of her dreams. Inside, Joy, almost 5, was trying to hold Nettie from reaching the doorway. Eva had her hands full of Joy's dress, trying to help.

Belle, her entire insides shaking from what she knew was the truth, looked at her daughters. Three pairs of eyes, different as the days of the week, were looking at her...wide eyed and helpless. She drew in a deep breath and squared her shoulders. She would be brave and strong. She had five small persons counting on her.

"Emma, honey, poke up the fire and put on a kettle. Then bring me warm water from the reservoir. Joy, take Nettie away and amuse her. Eva, go with Joy. Dora, sit here and we'll look at your leg."

Bleeding had stopped. Shoe ruined, certain to be. Stockings in ribbons, the torn edges trying to adhere to Dora's leg in the drying blood. Dora, steadying her lower lip under her front teeth, sat like a stone statue as her mom eased the sock away from the wound, tearing scabs when she had to.

About four inches long and not deep, but a wide furrow of skin and flesh had been carved away with the flying lava sheet. Why wasn't she screaming with pain? Belle glanced up at her daughter's eyes…glazed over like the winter freeze-ups that coated all surfaces with a layer of ice.

Not good. Little girls cried when hurt. Of course they did! "Emma, put on the cocoa kettle and heat the milk and then put in 6 extra spoons of sugar in the cups. We're all gonna have chocolate milk."

"Even Nettie…?"

"If she wants it. Joy, bring me the Vaseline and the bandages. And bring another stocking. Dora, sweetie, this is going to hurt, but I have to do it."

No response from Dora. Eva sat down on the floor so she could get a better look at Dora's leg. Nettie whimpered, so Eva pulled her down beside her.

Emma, with efficiency above her age, had the painted mugs spread around the table at the usual place of everyone. Nettie's small cup beside Mom's. She stood now, feet planted firmly, eyeing Mom's face for whatever would come next. Milk on the stove beginning to steam.

Belle forced her hand to be steady. Miss Hortense would not have approved of her 'letting go.' A southern lady remains in control under all circumstances. Small leg cleaned and dried, the petroleum jelly smoothed over the bandage rather than the leg, as Miss Hortense had done ones for a skinned knee. Less sticking to the scab, that way.

Carefully lifting the clean sock over the bandage, she hugged her daughter quickly and whispered 'good girl.' She saw Dora flick her glance toward the door. Still no Papa.

Bell nodded to Emma, and the steady hand of the seven year old poured the fragrant and tasty liquid into the cups. Hot chocolate was expensive and hard to get. Special treat. For some reason, Mom had been insistent. Emma took it on herself to make enough extra for at least another ½ a cup all around.

Belle helped Dora to her chair and whispered. "Drink, honey. It's something you need." The little girl, eyes flicking occasionally toward the door, obeyed woodenly. She was told to do it and she would do it, her heart fighting with her mind to make something that happened into something that had not happened. It was a fierce struggle. As she drained the last of the drink, her mind won the battle and the tears began to flow.

"Emma, lead your sister to bed and cover her warmly."

Surprised, Emma obeyed. Belle felt a thrill of pride in her eldest. She knew that Emma knew that would have been Mom's job, but if Mom had left the table, likely Eva and Nettie would follow, puzzled and whining. This was better.

Leaving the sister with a soft cloth for the tears, she returned. Eyes wide and uplifted, questioning brows ready for the next duty. Seeing none, she took the kettle from the stove and poured the remaining chocolate into the remaining cups, removing Dora's cup as she did so.

Belle gathered her thoughts. Something must now be done. She should notify someone, but how...? But then the sound of galloping hooves from outside announced Ed Corbin and another near neighbor, with a young man of about 15 years beside them. Belle met them at the door and stepped into the yard.

Nettie reached for Mom's mug and lifted it to her face. The weight of it was too much for her small fingers, and the brown fluid was poured down the front of her pink flowered dress. Nettie puckered up to cry, but Joy rushed to hug her while Emma grabbed up a towel.

Sopping the worst of it away, Emma picked up Nettie, though she was told not to because she was too heavy, and carried her away so Mom couldn't hear her if she cried. Dried and in a clean dress, Nettie drooped with weariness from the activity and the very sweet drink.

Emma carried her to her bed and patted her to sleep. She returned to the kitchen and Joy had mopped the chocolate from the floor. Eva had pushed the mugs together (she wasn't to lift them) and watched, silently, for Emma's return.

Outside Belle listened as Ed explained. "Rock slide. Really big one, at least 25 feet deep. Uh, Belle, we…."

"I know, Ed. He's gone and I wouldn't want him dug out even if we could. The girls and I have gone through enough for today. Tomorrow we can think better."

Relieved, Ed nodded. "Jesse wanted to come, but there wasn't time to see to the youngens. I'll send her over quick as I get back. I'll be here for the chores, and round up some help. I got Nathan here ready to take a message to Wishbone. You got kin over to Bentonville, I hear tell."

Belle nodded.

Ed again. "They got that Marconi machine in the train depot that'll tap out a message. Nathan'll see it gets done."

Belle nodded toward Nathan. Handsome young man, just like his preacher father, and he rode a heavily muscled stallion. Should stand the 5 hours it would take to get there.

Jesse came, and they wept together. Not for the first time, because there were always things happening. One of Jesse's daughters had lived for six hours. Reason for weeping. They spent most of the night talking and neither of the neighbors could have remembered a word that was said…only the comfort of nearness remembered.

Harriet, Nathan's mother, came the second day, bringing her two youngest to play with Eva and Nettie. Belle well knew the sacrifice of a whole day for the ladies on the farms. Harriet was not a weeper…she was made of stone. Words of encouragement, strengthening thoughts and love were her weapons against whatever came. Belle would survive just as she had been meant to. Certain of it.

On the third day, what came was three men on fast horses. The three brothers-in-law from Bentonville. Abe, Luke and Jonah, all much older than Jake.

Belle didn't know them well, but they were the three she would have picked to come to her if she had been given a choice.

AFTER THE ROCK SLIDE

Decisions needed to be made. Short term ones, and then long term ones. The men were ready to pack her up with the five little girls and get her to Bentonville with the 'rest of the family.' After that, decisions could be made more sensibly. Belle would have ideas and there would be family to help.

The need for a burial did not exist. Obviously. And the nearest thing to a funeral had already happened over the last two days. Now the future must be faced. What would she like to take, and did she have neighbors who would....

But with wide eyes and gaping mouths they listened when she said she really didn't want to leave. Surely there was a little place over on Ridge Road, or somewhere, that she could stay in while she 'got her head together.' If the fellows would just see to disposing of the animals and selling the farm, also finding an empty house for her, she'd really appreciate it.

"But if we took you...."

"Please. My little girls were born in the mountains their daddy loved and I want them to stay here if they want to. I've been thinking, and that's what I'd like. This farm should bring some money, and that would keep us until I...well, until I could plan something. I'd like close neighbors that I could see from the house, and a place to get a message to you if I had to."

Abe and Luke, who had spent miles of thought and talk, had decided what would be best, as Belle would be in no shape to...well, she would be just as would be expected of family. And now, Belle had just erased their plans and they stared at each other shaking their heads in dismay.

Jonah, the youngest of the first seven siblings, had not been a welcome privy to the discussions, but now he came forward. "Abe... Luke...what about Pa's house? It'd be perfect while she made up her mind. We could have her moved over there in two days, and we could get back home while she thinks."

"Hmmm...well, I don't really see why not," was Abe's sensible decision.

The old folks had passed on last winter. The flu, likely. Really nice house right there in Burnt Tree Junction. Once a week mail delivery, close neighbors, and even a little place that sold food...of a sort. The fellows didn't know about the message tree that would be become such a part of her life.

As for the three family men, intent on doing their duty, yet having lives and duties of their own, finally nodded at the sense of it.

Jacob Burk had been the surprising last of their parent's eight children. The first seven had been going or gone when he had made his appearance. At that time, life was easy for the old folks, and a time which Jake's ma, older though she was, pulled through in fine shape, it was as though the old couple now had a live-in grandson.

Huge house, necessary for the family size. Eight rooms below and a lot of attic room. Would have sold for a good price, which would have been divided among the eight families. Unexpected money, even in one eighth quantities, would be welcome. Not to be.

However, there was this, as it was pointed out by Jonah. Taking her to Bentonville would tax their own resources to assist her as would be needed. As for remarriage, they could hardly expect any young man to take on a family of five girls under eight, no matter how desirable the lady. And face it, lovely and easy going as Belle was, she was no beauty as a lot of men would see her.

However, she liked the mountains (that was amazing in itself) and asked only for a place to be, while she thought, and here was an answer. The animals and farm equipment could be moved, and all her household furniture would be an effort, but two days...three at the most...and she'd be there. And she was not actually acquainted with the family so well that Bentonville would have been a comfort. Distance and age could not be gotten around.

So the brothers-in-law nodded their heads and bowed their backs into what was expected of a family. Moving was heavy work.

Belle herself had actually been to that house only three times, on special occasions. Weather, small children and farm animals were a tight tether for a farm family keeping them at home. However, what she had seen of the house she really liked. Maybe not as well as her own, but it was roomy, close to at least two neighbors, and best of all, Ridge Road and the civilization she would now need were there.

She worked herself down to a frazzle to make the move. She could cry later but now she didn't have time. Nor could she afford the spend the strength. She sent ahead a load of furniture keeping only the cook stove and a pair of feather mattresses, along with the wooden chests that held her girlhood fancy things.

The wagons returned.

She climbed aboard for the last time on a sunny day in April and left the lovely farm on Echo Mountain. A catastrophe had brought to her Jake and the mountain, and another catastrophe has now taken him and the lovely mountain away. She faced the west and braced herself for the at least 6 hours it would take for the slow, heavily loaded wagon to make the trip.

Jonah directed the team and the family as his brothers packed everything they could on the remaining wagon, buggy and carts and followed along. A neighbor bought the chickens, except for a dozen laying hens, and another wanted his plows and some other equipment. The goats were small enough to move, and Belle would need the milk. The men, practically strangers to this lady with a mind of her own, made the best decisions they could.

In the space of the three days and their limited time of joint conference, they came to the decision that maybe a situation had fallen into their hands that would benefit everyone.

If he had lived, Jake would have been entitled to a share of the home place, so now, if they just turned it over to her to do with what she pleased, that would likely be all she would ask...being so independent minded as she was. They nodded together, pleased with the decision.

Belle, still in a semi-daze, also agreed. She was gone from the destroying mountain. Her little girls were safe. She had no decision facing her in the near future.

The huge iron cook stove from Echo Mountain had been unbolted into its six heavy pieces to be moved, and was now bolted together again and in place under the rock-lined chimney.

The morning sun saw the three men from Bentonville on their rented horses and heading back to Eureka Springs for the Firefly express that would take them home. They had feasted on a royal breakfast of flapjacks and honey and had time to talk of the brother they hardly knew and his horrible death.

The brother himself had known from the first falling rock what the immediate outcome would be. The stone that had slammed against his shoulder and ribs had been a burst of fire, but there followed a flow of peace and assurance. After using his last painful breaths to scream for his beloved daughter to run! run! run! he had no memory of sorrow and pain, because where he was where was no such thing as sorrow. It was a transfer so hard for humans to get their minds around...until it was experienced and at that point, they had no memory of sorrow.

Belle wandered from room to room. So many rooms. The old folks had left furniture, but, like many of the tools and farm implements, much had been pilfered from the empty house. Still, there was plenty left.

The bleat of the goat called her attention to the barn. Milk. Had to figure this out somehow. "Dora, honey, grab up the milk bucket and let's go take care of that goat." The sound of her voice was cheery to her ears, but a dread everywhere else. She had never touched the udder of an animal. There'd been no need. Now... however...there was a pressing need.

Dora watched as her mom tried to determine the amount of feed to dip. "Mom, Papa used a can like pork and beans come in. Not quite full."

Bell dipped up the estimated amount and poured it in the trough. Daisy knew what to do, and Belle moved the three-legged milk stool into position. The full udder of the goat reached almost to the ground. How in the world was this to work. She stooped low and squeezed the fleshy teat and nothing happened. Daisy, chewing a mouthful of grain, turned to look at her.

Dora knelt beside her. "Mom, could I try?"

Belle shook her head. "You're too little."

"Papa didn't think so. He said I was just right for the goat. But he had her get up on the little table."

"Hmmm. Do you see a table?"

"I think that's it," and she pointed to a platform hanging on the barn wall. "I'll get it." The seven year old arms reached up and brought it down. Dust and straw chips flew. It took a bit of wrestling to get it in place, but Daisy knew what it was for.

"Mom, please let me try. I think Daisy will have to have more feed but I can hurry." The attempts were a bit awkward, but at least there were a number of splats in the bucket, and eventually about 2 quarts of milk. Daisy was let into a new pasture, and after a few assertive baa's, she began to investigate.

Mother and daughter walked to the house. "Maybe we'll have to do this together. Twice a day. Think we can do that?"

Dora grinned, her beautiful oval face a wreath of lovely pale skin. So beautiful, Belle thought. "Mom, I think I may be able to do it by myself. You got so many other things to do." And that was the truth.

There was the whole summer to learn how to exist, and there were many delightful discoveries. One was the mineral spring. Belle vaguely remembered it. It had been the pride of the old couple, and many travelers stopped regularly to fill their water bottles.

And the tree house. The old man built a tree house for young Jake and the boy had spent hours in it. It was still there, roomy, solid and cozy…wrapping itself completely around the massive trunk of the oak tree and enclosing some of the limbs. There was room for a full sized bedroll…in fact, several of them. It had windows with real glass panes. The shingled roof was watertight and the ladder was still solid, made of oil-treated oak limbs.

Dora was first to climb. Papa had told her a lot about it. It was one of his favorite toys, and now she was usually found there, times when not needed. Maybe she needed to be close to Papa, though she never cried. Belle reasoned, if it made her happy…well, then… maybe it would be sort of a goodbye.

Emma pushed the extra furniture around, like a robin adjusting the feathers in her nest. Eventually she got it where she wanted it. Joy made it her job to keep up with the younger sisters. Their best fun was to run, madly, along the long porch and jump off the end.

Belle arranged the glass jars, both full and empty, in the 'fruit cellar.' Nice and roomy it was. Moving so much glass had been heavy and laborious for the fellows as well as herself, but instinct told her she'd need everything she had. She even found a few empty jars the pilferers had missed.

She surveyed the garden. Nothing had been planted, of course, but there were volunteers among the vegetables. Potatoes, carrots, okra and a scraggling patch of onions. There was the herb garden that had been so strange to her at Echo Mountain, now she only noted that it needed weeding and trimming. That was one thing she could do.

This winter she'd have to give thought to it all. The enormity of the task made her sigh and slump her shoulders. And there was goat feed, chicken feed, and firewood to think on. There was a small amount of leftover wood now but winter would take much more. That would take money.

In her scanty education, she did learn a bit about money. Miss Hortense wanted her pupils to be able to see if they were being cheated by employees and delivery persons. Ha! What a laugh!

She left the garden and strolled toward the house. She'd put off the chore, but somehow she was going to have to figure out how to make the small amount of money it would take last until…until what…?

She boiled water for tea. At least there was plenty of that. She blew back the steam and sipped, then propping elbows on the table and chin firmly in her hands she made a decision.

The necessity had been niggling around in her brain for some time, and this catastrophe formed it firmly into a head. Her aging and unworldly parents had done the best they could, but times were different now.

Something must be done and she was the only one there to do it.

THE DECISION

Belle sat at the table in the house just off Ridge Road, possibly at the same spot where Jake had sat as a child. Her tablet was before her and a cup of fresh peppermint tea steaming in the mug.

Today would be the day she wrote the proper 'thank you' letter to Jake's siblings. She had just received the precious document that made her the sole owner of the property.

Dora sat at the table and fidgeted her hands, hesitating to interrupt her mom. Belle looked up, giving her a chance to speak.

"Mom, I think I should go to the pasture and find Daisy. She may not know the way back to the barn."

Belle hesitated, eying her seven year old. She was so small and the pasture so large…should she….

"Mom, Daisy likes me and this pasture is new. If she had trouble with her bag full…? Papa said it would hurt her, and might cause a lot of trouble later. Please let me."

Belle's first thought was, 'how did Jake manage to impart so much knowledge to her?' and that was followed with 'what if she was right?' The goat was a valuable asset.

She nodded. "Yes, and on one condition. You take that extra cowbell from the barn with you. If you get lost, ring the bell until someone comes."

Dora's face lit up like a sunrise, and she threw her arms around her mom. "Oh, thank you! Thank you!" And on a twirl of her toes she was gone.

Back to the letter. This was something she knew how to do.

For all members of my family,

For your speedy response to the disaster that befell your brother and his family, I sincerely thank you.

For the effort, not for just a day, but until I was truly settled, that was given to my move. It was a grueling experience and the men gave help so willingly. For that I sincerely thank you.

For the offer of Abraham to deal with selling the farm, I am extremely grateful as it would have been an unbearable sacrifice to leave Jacob's children with neighbors and try to do it, and impossible to take them with me. I humbly and gratefully thank him for that.

For the sacrifice you each made in transferring this property to me, I am speechless to say what it means to myself and the children. They will greatly enjoy the lovely yard, the swing in the hackberry tree and the treehouse that was made for their papa. I can only repeat, inadequately, that I am humbly grateful.

To those who sent, with unnecessary apologies, the lovely package containing dresses of all sizes and the lovely coat that just fits Emma. They are a very thoughtful gift at a time when they will be sorely needed. For that, I haven't words adequate to thank you.

And lastly, and certainly not the least, I appreciate the offer of help in the future if I should need it. As I am essentially a stranger to you, the offer is truly generous and precious, though I pray that I will not need it. Your kindness has set us up so well, and we are all children of the same God, so that I am sure there will be a way for me to rear these five girls in the manner that would have made Jacob proud.

Belle Burk and daughters.

So easily and smoothly the words of Miss Hortense came back to her, and she was grateful this moment for that fact. Her family. It was clear that she had been given a gift that only they could give, and it was given quickly with no strings attached.

She might have added the wonderful fact that she now had a postal box and it even had the right name, BURK FAMILY. She had only to walk less than an eighth of a mile to the road and put the letter in the box. She could lift the red flag and the postman would take it. That miracle happened every week. If she had no stamp, attaching three pennies assured it to be accepted.

Carefully folding the letter so the corners touched, she slipped it into the matching envelope. This was the first letter she had written on the stationery she had brought to the mountain.

Pushing back the letter and lifting her now-cool tea, the door burst open and a flushed and smiling Dora flopped into the chair beside her. "I did it, Mom! She was down where the greener grass grows by the stream. I just told her it was time to milk, and she walked beside me."

And she followed with, "Mom, she walked slow and sort of waddled. That means it's time to milk her. I know you have things to do, so could I try to milk her all by myself?"

"But Dora, you're so little...."

"But Papa didn't think so. Was he wrong?"

Put like that, what could Belle say? "Go ahead. If you need help, come and get me."

"Oh, thank you! Thank you!" And she was gone in a whirl of braids and skirt tail. Twenty minutes later she was back with a bit over two quarts of milk. Wordlessly, she wrapped the straining cloth over the bucket brim and poured the milk into the crock.

In a flash, she was gone again. Belle turned to watch, and saw, through the window, the edge of a skirt tail and a pair of worn shoes as her second child climbed into the treehouse sanctuary of her father. Not an unusual sight. At times, when she descended, her eyes were red rimmed. Belle shook her head sadly. *We all deal with sorrow the best way we can.*

Now back to her decision. There had to be some changes, and Belle must figure out how that would happen. The protected 'southern lady' was tossed, within minutes, into the rugged life of a 'farm owner.' How could this have happened, and what could she have done to change it?

She, of course, had nothing to do with the rock slide. And, thinking back, she had nothing to do with any other happening in her life. Could that have been the problem?

It was not her fault that she and her sister were not born to younger parents. Nor that the parents unwisely trained the girls to be what they could never be. Nor, with limited means, they had hired a governess, rather than a public school teacher, using money they could not afford.

It was not the girls' fault or the parent's fault that the couple were not prepared to take on two little girls. They did what they thought they should, not knowing how times would change.

Miss Hortense did what she was hired to do, and did a marvelous job of it...the difficulty of it being that she trained them for another time and another country. Belle had no idea where her sister was, and likely never would know, only hope for the best.

The two girls were not made privy to the family finances as that was 'not proper to bother children with.' Absolutely no effort was made to give the girls a way to support themselves…because that would never be necessary. Well, it didn't happen that way.

So now Belle was faced with the education of five little girls, and she was no better prepared than her parents had been. Also, her situation was not her fault…as not had been her parents'.

Belle pulled her tablet toward her…not her precious stationery. In firm letters, she printed:

MY DAUGHTERS WILL NOT GROW UP LIKE I DID.

How this was going to happen was something to be figured out, and it must be done quickly. Tapping her pencil thoughtfully against her teeth, she watched Emma as the girl reached to the high shelf and brought down the book so laboriously printed by Miss Harriet during midnight hours and the burning of precious candles.

Emma thumbed through it, nodding here and there, and turning another page. At one point, she frowningly studied the words.

"Mom, here's the directions for Potato Dumplings. I watched you make dumplings and I can do it. I'd have to have a half a cup of the sausage grease. Could I try it? We got potatoes trying to grow that we need to use."

Potato Dumplings…? What could that taste like? But Emma was right. The potatoes needed to be used up. Sausage grease was precious, but they had to eat something. Why not…?

Emma was watching intensely with her father's dark eyes under his dark brows. Strange how his masculine features were so feminine on his daughter.

"Yes, my dear. If you need help, I'm here."

"Oh, thank you! Thank you!" And she grabbed up a bowl and headed for the cool cellar and the grease.

Belle watched, thinking. Two hugs from her daughters with nothing from her but permission to step into higher duties, not go to play in the yard. Seven and barely past eight. She and her sister had been reading *English Fables* written by a fellow named Grimes when they were that age.

Back to her thoughts and the blank page.

The mountain school house was about a half a mile from the postal box, and in two weeks, Emma and Dora would be going. Emma had just made the case for letting Joy go because she was almost six. That would be permitted if the teacher had room.

Emma had asked, adding, "…unless you need her to watch the little ones."

Since when had five year old Joy become the official guardian of her sisters…? Because she had taken it on, that's why! And why did four-year-old Eva play baby games so that Nettie could play. Because she was permitted to and thought it necessary…that's why.

Alright, Belle, she reminded herself. There's something hidden in these incidents. Figure it out. She watched Emma snap off the sprouts from the potatoes, peel and dice them, then consult Harriet's directions. Poke up the fire and melt the grease, put in the potatoes but don't brown them. Take off the skillet and heat water in the soup kettle.

Add the potatoes and put on the lid. Now for the dumplings. Slowly and a bit awkwardly, Emma's small hands stirred the batter, rolled it out and cut strips.

Back to the boiling potatoes she tested for doneness, nodded, lifted them out into the skillet and dropped in the dumplings, a portion at a time. She studied the kettle contents, bottom lip caught under teeth.

Checked with Harriet's book. Nodded. Lowered the potatoes back in the kettle, shut down the fire and pushed the kettle back.

"Smells good, Mom. I'll heat it up before we eat."

Such confidence. *Please, God, may the mixture be tasty. She's so proud.* Belle shook her head slowly. She herself had not been permitted near the stove until she was almost fourteen.

Joy appeared. "Mom, Nettie's cranky. I think she's sleepy."

Belle nodded. "You may be right. I'll come along in a minute."

Joy, with her green/brown eyes, looked sternly at her mom. "I can do it, Mom. I just wanted to be sure it was all right. I'll sing about the lost kitty. She likes that song."

With a skip, she disappeared to the strains of, "Oh, where is my kitty? My little gray kitty? I looked…." and the door closed behind her. Belle stared for a long minute after her third daughter. Then shook her head clear of this thought and turned her attention to the tablet and pencil.

Money. Almost ten years ago she had been in the same predicament. Money. Money that was not there. Hortense's teaching presumed there would be.

Now, however, there was money but not enough and there must be ways to stretch it. She began her list.

1. Wood for the cook stove, and later the potbelly heater.

2. Oil for the lamps. It wouldn't take much.

3. Flour. Would that be from Wishbone? How could she get it home?

4. Soap. The recipe in Harriet's book, but it took valuable grease.

5. Sugar. Honey was available at the Junction. Less than a mile.

6. Help to butcher the two hogs.

7. Chopped corn for the milk goat. Where could she be bred again?

That seemed to be enough to start with. The list was sure to grow. Not the money, though. There was the small amount that Jake kept in the barn. She counted it carefully and returned it to the quart fruit jar. It had seemed a great lot, over at the mountain. Now, it was almost nothing. $107.28. The extra horse brought $17.00, and she could sell the mules, but they were taking care of themselves in the pasture. She'd wait on that. One cow had been moved. She would calf soon and Abe thought she could either butcher the calf or swap it for service to help butcher the hog. How would she find someone to swap to?

The hay mower brought $22.00. Jake had been so proud of that. She might wish it had been moved. Oh, well….She had swapped most of the chickens to Ed Corbin for the service of showing the farm to prospects. He'd assured her that the rock slide would not hurt the price. Slides happened, and anyone living on Echo Mountain either knew it already or soon would. Mostly the slides were not so big, and mostly there was no one standing in the path that could not get away. Dora had told her that Papa was knocked down by a big rock and couldn't get up.

Enough figuring for today, and she put away the tablet and pencil.

The day was gone and the room was becoming dark. Emma lit the lamp. Matches. That needed to go on the list.

Emma began to set the table for supper, and Dora came through the door. She headed for the milk crock and dipped a cup of milk for everyone. Not much left, but there'd be more in the morning.

Emma, face flushed with excitement and apprehension, set the huge serving bowl on the table, and placed bowls for everyone. She handed Mom the dipper.

The aroma was wonderful! The milky gravy had thickened around the dumplings and potatoes. The sausage grease had flavored the gravy giving it a meaty aroma. And there was so much of it! It seemed to have swelled while waiting to be served!

The first bites were tentative, it did look strange, but it was not strange very long. Emma couldn't keep from smiling, her mind racing to look at the book again. There were over 60 pages!

The note at the bottom of the Potato Dumpling page said leftovers were even better than fresh.

UNCLE JOEL SHARPENER

Not really his name of course, but like the ancient English names, a person was best known by what he did. Painter. Farmer. Butcher. Carpenter, and so on. Only made sense, when one took a look at it.

Uncle Joel was well known on Ridge Road. He was almost as necessary as the midwife, because all tools and implements eventually became dull with use, and the residents of the mountains used their tools. Dull tools made hard work, and no one needed that. Not everyone had equipment for sharpening.

He owned a long wagon on which he had built a cover of sorts with windows down the sides. A canvas sheet could be let down to cover the windows…or when he was traveling…and the letters painted on the canvas announced:

U N C L E J O E L
SHARPENER

Knives, shovels and plow points, etc.

Uncle Joel loved explaining what the 'etc' meant. Sort of a talking point to new customers as he plied the Ridge Road all the way from Berryville in the east to Eureka Springs in the west. He had a house in Eureka Springs, but he didn't stay there much.

A fellow didn't make money if he was not on the road, and the road was so difficult that Uncle Joel had a monopoly on practically all the sharpening business. He had his favorite places for 'over-nighting' where kind residents allowed Cricket and Skeeter, his mules, to rest and graze. His covered 'van' had a bed. A bit crowded, but Uncle was a thin, drawn-out sort of a man and the bed needn't be very wide. He also kept easily prepared food, but when necessary he could build a fire in his brazier. It also served as a forge when welding was required.

Made a good living, he did, and he'd been on the road continuously since his young wife died of the pox. Just couldn't stand to stay around the house after that.

Uncle Joel tried never to miss anyone no matter how remote and inaccessible their dwelling, and he headed Cricket and Skeeter down just about every little trail and lane that led off Ridge road. There just might be a cabin down there and someone who needed him. That was how he found Dan'l McElroy.

It wasn't that the old mountaineer needed his services…more like they were 'two peas in a pod' and had become fast friends. So comforting to be with someone who remembered the same things you did…and maybe had gone through similar family losses. Dan'l's two sons were killed in a fire in a logging accident, and his wife caught the consumption and 'coughed herself to death.'

The two old mountaineers could sit on Dan'l's porch, chairs tipped against the wall reminiscing. Dan'l could make a mean cup of tea and Joel might have brought a handful of jerky sticks he'd bought at Uncle Burley's Bistro. Jolly good jerky, actually.

So Joel reluctantly hitched up the 'insects' and headed out to Ridge Road. The obedient mules, replete with Dan'l deep green grass, pulled the van up to the road with ease while Joel thought.

There was the situation with the Burk place. That was another friend he'd hated to loose, but the house being empty did not keep him from stopping over to 'see to things.' Of his favorite places to overnight, old Burk's was his pick. And today, he'd push the 'insects' the last half mile to get there.

He'd been going there for decades, drawn, at first, by the wonderful spring of icy cold mineral water. All frequent travelers on Ridge Road knew about the spring and freely helped themselves. It was near the road and easily accessible. Joel became a devoted fan of Burk's Spring, and consequently the Burk's family. Soon he was turning the insects into the calf pasture and spending a restful night in the van while the animals filled their stomachs.

He had been in a positon to watch as the family grew to seven active youngsters, and the construction of the housing additions necessary to contain them. The last addition was a two-roomed 'ell' with a large screened-in porch designed for entertaining noisy friends. Away from adult ears.

Seemed like there was now nine rooms plus the porch and two roomy attic rooms. An immense lot of house for the mountains. And Joel was there as the children moved away, mostly to Bentonville. The old couple, well into their forties, were then surprised by the 'fall crop' of children in the body of little Jacob.

If the boy had allowed it, he would have been pampered and spoiled beyond redemption but the little fellow had his head on his shoulders. Whatever new gadget that came along, Jacob got one. His biggest toy, however, was the treehouse which took his pa a month to get built.

The boy and his friends had a blast pretending this or that, but one thing bothered him. Joel had asked him if he was permitted to spend the night in it, and the boy had sadly shook his head. He was scared to be there alone. No problem, Uncle Joel assured him.

The old family friend agreed with him that it was scary, but that he just needed an adult to spend the night with him and tell the 'scary' to go away. He added that he, Uncle Joel, had met the scary a lot of times, and had always made it go away and stay away.

So man and boy climbed the generous, sturdy ladder with their bedrolls. They sat in the dark while Joel told stories about his adventures on the road, and then noticed that his listener no longer listened, but was fast asleep.

Smiling to himself, the old tinker stretched out and lay back on his huge pillow, his arms crossed behind his head. Such luxury! Cool breeze through the open windows…no biting bugs…whisper of the limbs and soft songs of the nightbirds. So after that, he often spent the night there, boy or no boy, and continued to do so long after the 'boy' had gone, found himself a wife and created a family.

In view of the history he had with the Burks, it seemed normal to 'see after' the old place whenever he was in the vicinity. Then he heard on the gossip grapevine that a rock slide had killed 'little Jake' and left a family of small girls. Whispered voices and frowned foreheads wondered what would become of the family. Maybe go to Bentonville…?

But then when he stopped by, he saw Abe, Luke and Jonah, who remembered him well. Joel learned that Jake's widow and the girls would be given the house because she needed to be closer to neighbors. Made sense, and was something old Burk's sons would do.

After losing an argument with himself, he decided to stop in and see how things were…after all, he was a 'friend of the family.'

Belle heard the sound and pulled back the curtain. A peddler's van. Certain to be. Now if there was anything she didn't need, it was something to buy. She was thinking up words to get rid of him then he tied his animals to the gatepost and made his way in.

She met him on the porch. Joel wasn't born yesterday. He quickly knew he was facing a lady bent on sending him on his way. He was ready for her.

"How do, Miss Burk. You must be Jake's pretty wife I've been hearing about. Haven't time to stop. I was just needin' to fill my waterbottle, on account I've got that little run down to Blue Lake.

Thought I'd check in first, thinkin' you might have a dog that took exception to me walkin' up to the spring. No dog…?"

Belle shook her head, and prepared to offer her speech, but this old man held up his canteen bottle with a friendly smile. "Reckon I'll just go fill this. Less'n you'd rather I went away. The old folks always let me get water and even rest my two friends out there. They liked his grass." And tipping his well-worn straw hat, he turned toward the spring, whistling, then remembered, "Good day to you, Miss."

What could Belle do but watch after him while he filled the bottle, turned toward his team, and, lifting his arm in a friendly wave, climbed aboard the van. To Cricklet and Skeeter he muttered, "No good grass tonight. We'll have to go up to the junction, but we'll be back here. Don't you worry."

He did, indeed, make the precarious trip down to Blue Lake and Turner's saw mill and put a keen edge on a couple of saws. They kept extra blades so they wouldn't have to shut down when one went dull. Work quickly done, he climbed up out of the hollow up to Ridge Road and drove to a vine covered lane by the postal box saying, "Polly Patrick, Persimmon Jam and Pups."

That just about told it all. Somehow a clever city girl managed to scrape a living with her half-breed pups and a spicy jam made from native persimmons. Her pups were half bloodhound and half the gift of a traveling salesman from the local wolf pack. Good dogs, and she got a good price. Worth every penny.

Joel nodded as he agreed with himself that it would be worth it in the end. So, with a pup (loose, wrinkly skin, velvety flopping ears and alert eyes peeking from under the skin folds already forming on his forhead) tucked in a box beside him, he instructed Cricket and Skeeter, "Get on away, you lazy insects. Make tracks."

To the mules, these words were sounds of endearment, and for the sound of those words, the insects would take him anywhere.

It was late two days later that he again tied up to the gatepost. Holding the pup in plain sight, he passed a trio of interested small girls with only a smile, and walked up to Belle. "Miss Burk, please pardon me bein' so forward, but I wouldn't be feelin' right to old Burk and little Jake if I left you without protection. I been watchin' after this house, bein' it was empty and they was both my friends, and now you're here without no dog."

Belle and her daughters looked on with interest at the man and the darling, and unbelievably ugly, face of the pup. "Now this here dog, he ain't much but these dogs grow fast. Can't beat 'em for sniffin' out trouble. This little fellow ain't a toy for the girls. He's a bodyguard for the family, and he should owe his best feelin's to you, Miss Belle. It must be you who feeds him for the next month, and you must talk to him and touch him so he'll know you. He was bred to guard and track, bein' bloodhound and wolf. Can't get a better mix. Now his name was Harry Barker, but he's little enough that if you don't like it, change it now."

He looked to each one to be sure he had their attention. "Now for the first month, you little girls must not pick him up. You can touch him, and pet him with one finger. Then after that month, you can play with him like any other dog but he'll know he belongs to your ma, and you are just his play friends. Do you understand?"

The lengthy speech won Belle's heart. That someone would care for her safety…bring a gift that did not belong to the girls…and his sensible speech about safety. Who could resist?

"Mr…uh, Sharpener…? Would you come in for a cup of tea?"

"I would ma'am and be grateful. Could I turn my mules into the calf pasture for a few minutes? They're eyein' that grass like a wolf eyes a rabbit."

When he returned, the table was set for tea and the aroma of peppermint was temptingly strong. The biggest girl was preparing a box with a blanket. Perfect timing. "Honey, could you get a pair of shoes or maybe stockings that belong to your ma and put 'em in the box? The scent'll help 'im to be comforted, it will."

While Emma held the box, Joy dashed away and came back with a pair of felt house slippers. She looked up at Joel with her papa's face and her grandmother's unusual eyes. Joel told her, "Very good. Just tuck them in the box and let your ma put him in it."

Through three cups of tea, the young mother and the little girls heard more about their papa's family, and about the little boy who had lived there, than they'd ever expected. Treehouse and all. "Much obliged for the tea, Miss Belle. So if it'd be alright with you, when I'm close and it's evenin' I'll just pull in and tie up. The mules know not to go too far, and I'll just make my supper and go up to the treehouse if you're sure it's all right…?

It was certainly all right, and Belle slept better that night than at any previous night in that house. Here was a connection to the outside world, and he apparently already knew her.

Not only that, he had been vetted by Jake's parents and been found harmless.

Later, when the children had left the table, he had confided, "'Nother thing, Miss. It ain't just for me. News gets around in hurry, and it'll be known by everyone and all the birds in the trees that there's a purty lady here with no man in the house. Not only that, she has possession'a one's the best pieces'a property on the Ridge. Add them things to that spring'a water you got, and you'll know right off you're likely to get company you don't want and certainly don't need.

"I'm well known all up and down the Ridge and it won't hurt none for folks to know I'm still 'seein' after' the Burk family. I'm bound nothin's gonna happen to little Jake's family, and that's a promise."

BACK TO THE NOTEBOOK AND PENCIL

She had a smattering knowledge of money, of course, by the teaching of Miss Hortense that was strongly within her. Belle knew about income and outgo, and that the later must not overtake the former.

Sure, she could slow down the outgo, but the years stretched out before her. There was Nettie, barely past two. How long would it last?

It was a rainy day in October that Belle, tired of the house, put the younger girls down for a nap and donned Jake's slicker and boots and trudged to the postal box. Most days there was nothing, but at least she got a view of Ridge Road, beautifully graveled with chips of flint rock, multiple shades of grey and tan.

At a far distance, she could see the group of oaks that marked the cluster of civilization called Burnt Tree Junction. Such a comforting sight…people…help…and certain specialized foods.

Sometime when money was not so scarce, she'd try their pork jerky that was so popular.

Mr. Harry Barker trudged after her, snorting the raindrops from his sensitive nostrils. Duty was duty, and if his human wanted to make this trip in miserable weather, who was he to argue? One thing was nice, though, if he got really wet, she would rub him down with a towel. That was enjoyable…partly because she had such a good smell.

Belle stood for a full minute looking both ways. Echo Mountain was lovely, but Ridge Road and Burnt Tree Junction was…well, maybe just comforting. There was an actual burnt tree, of course, but the important tree was a tall and spreading oak with a trunk bigger around than the biggest barrel. There was a message board attached, and it was usually full of interesting items…more informative than a newspaper. And all of local interest.

In addition there were thumb tacks in the bark attaching scraps of paper with notes. Everything that was on the notes was to be bought, sold or maybe just information to be passed on.

Sometimes she went there just to see what was going on, but today it was raining. She checked the box and there it was…the letter. Someone cared enough about her to say something to her. It was a good day!

It was addressed in ink so she tucked it quickly under her slicker and hurried home. Abraham Burk. Brother-in-law.

My loved Sister in Law,

We have succeeded in selling the farm. Ed Corbin earned his chickens. The amount was less than I wanted but more than I expected. A Church Group wanted a remote piece of land for a retreat and for a summer camp for children. They thought it perfect and were authorized to pay only $400.00, so I took in your name, showing Jake's Death Certificate as authority.

I could not send the money to you safely through the post, and I also know how gossip goes in the mountain. If I brought it to you, someone would figure out that I had sold the farm and that you had the money. Then someone would decide to find it. That would make it unsafe for you and the girls.

Incidentally, Jake's hand gun from the barn is in the bottom of the chopped corn barrel. When you can reach it, I know you will keep it in a safe place. I wish he had taught you how to use it, but he didn't intend for you to need the skill. The rifle is wrapped up in the horse blankets. You'll find it when you need to blanket them against the cold.

I opened an account for you in the Wishbone bank, located in the Land Office building, as I presumed that you did not need funds immediately. I arranged that when you went to take out some money, you would be sure to take a copy of this letter with you as proof of who you are. The bank will expect it. After the first time, they will know you, but you might keep this letter in a safe place anyway.

We think of you often, and we admire your strength and trust your decisions which are a great comfort to all the family.

Your family.

Belle firmed her lips and nodded, folding the letter and slipping in n the envelope.She must manage, somehow, to not need the letter for years. She now had money, a little, and she was determined she would never again be without it. How she would manage, she hadn't a clue, but manage it she would.

Putting it on the high shelf, she reached for her stationary with matching envelope.

Dear Abraham and family.

Words fail me to tell you how much I appreciate you all. A load has been lifted from my mind, and now I can go on to other things and plan for the future. I am confident we will be fine.

Thank you for information about Jake's weapons. I hadn't given them a thought. He took care of everything. Uncle Joel Sharpener came by and told me a lot about you all. He will be stopping often, he says, and loves to stay in the treehouse during the summer. Perhaps he will help me learn about the gun, as I think you believe I should.

This house is going to be such a comfort in the winter, as it is so large and comfortable. The girls have such wonderful room to spread out.

I am hoping you are all well and happy.

Belle

There. That was taken care of, and she must work toward never being a burden on these helpful people. They have their own concerns.

Now that Emma, Dora and Joy were got off to school every day there was time to think and puzzle out her future.

Emma was totally taken in by her 'job.' Apparently Miss Sophie had allowed her to 'card' the wool she used to make yarn. Whatever that was, apparently Emma did a good job.

There was the day she raced home, to be sure to be on time 'so Mom wouldn't worry.' Miss Sophia had insisted, so her ma would continue to let her come. Well, the silver quarter always equaled 25 cents, and it bought 2 jars of honey, the girl's favorite sweet.

But that wasn't the best of it. Emma had 'great news.' Miss Sophie said she couldn't pay Emma more money to stay over, but if Emma wanted to learn to knit with the sticks she called 'needles' she could have as much wool as she could knit up into scarves. Free. Scarves were the easiest to make, but there could be hats and then socks if she got good enough. Hmm, the nickel a day and even more training.

"Mom, it might take extra time until I learn. Then I can bring it home to work on because the sticks will be mine. She said one of her daughters used them to learn on. Can I, Mom?"

Belle studied her daughter. Flushed pink tints shone through the light tan of her face. Dark eyebrows seemed thicker, and she had a way of slanting her head and looking at her. For all the world, she was looking more like Jake. It was enough to burst Belle into tears of loneliness, and then hug her daughter in pride. She did neither.

"You say scarves and hats. Do you think you can learn?" Almost nine, but still she seemed a little girl.

"Of course, Mom. If Dora can learn to milk the goat, surely I can learn to use the sticks…the needles, I mean. She said she was paying me for an hour and a half, and if I wanted to be taught, it would be on my own time."

Bully for Miss Sophie! Her opinion of the wrinkled old lady jumped up a notch. Nothing was for nothing, and her daughters needed to learn that. The fact seemed to have escaped the almost nine-year-old Belle two decades ago. So sad!

"Yes, we'll try it. I think you can do it, and you three girls need warm scarves for school." That was settled.

By Christmas, when the real winter arrives in the Arkansas mountains, there were six scarves in various colors. Miss Sophie also knew how to make certain colors from plants. Imagine that!

Now for the hats. Heads must be measured from lower ear lob over the head and to the other ear lob, then two inches added. Also measured cheek bone to cheek bone. Size was computed from these measurements, and Emma was good at numbers. The patterns had numbers, and all she had to do was follow!

Belle had actually made the trip to Miss Sophie's house to be reassured that her daughter was correct, that wool would be given free as long as Emma converted it into something useful.

Miss Sophie, delighted for the company, explained her supreme pleasure in Emma's help, and also her progress. Hinted that she would be making 'tube' socks (whatever they were) next.

Belle went home contented. Emma was not paid much and was missed at home, but at least she was learning something that Belle could never teach her.

BARNYARD ACTIVITY

As farm animals go, Buttercup was considered a beautiful cow. Well-proportioned and the color of rich cream, fading into tan and light brown around her eyes, nose, hooves and tail. Pure Jersey, she was, and had been pampered and petted. She was also even-tempered and she obviously liked Dora. That was a help because that made her patient with inexperienced and small hands.

Of the four cows, she had been chosen for the laborious trip from Echo Mountain by high-sided wagon and not only for her beauty. She had recently been bred, and the fellows thought Belle's family might need the meat…if not the money. Calves were one of the most important dividends of farm life.

Dora knew that Buttercup had been bred (whatever that was) so she could have a baby. She thought nothing more about it, and Belle knew nothing of the event. Why should she? Papa took care of all that.

Occasionally Buttercup mooed for attention, but generally went placidly about the pasture, enjoying the wealth of greenery. Then there was that night in early December. A sprinkling of snow was falling, and a fierce "norther" was bearing down along Ridge Road.

About midnight, Buttercup set it up, roaring as though her legs were being chewed off by a wolf. Dora shot out of bed, crammed feet into shoes and grabbed hat and coat. She slammed the door behind her just as Belle had scrambled for the hand gun in the closet. She was not a good shot but maybe the noise would scare away the varmints.

She reached the corral gate just as her swift daughter disappeared into the stall where Buttercup was waiting out the storm. A quick glance proved no wolf was present. Not even a coon, but something was bothering the cow. She was snorting uncharacteristically and trying to circle in the small stall.

Dora climbed up the wall out of the way and tried to puzzle out the problem. Belle caught up, and peeked through the slats of the wall. No answer except for Buttercup rolling her eyes and contorting as though saying, 'what took you so long'?

63

Mother and daughter, hearts pounding, could do nothing but stare at the obviously demented cow.

Then, after a considerably larger twist, Buttercup flung her head to see behind her just as a soggy lump of something hit the hay of her bed. The cow turned quickly and began to attend to the lump, turning it into a miniature version of herself. Rich cream and tan color, legs, tail and all. Wet from ears to stumpy tail.

Then a pause as Buttercup looked up at Dora, and another splat. Another baby just like the first! Buttercup edged herself around, carefully protecting the baby from her hoofed feet, and began to attend to the second lump.

The audience watching from the sidelines had no way of knowing a crisis had passed. Flighty animals, as Buttercup might be considered to be, were known to often reject a second calf as not being hers. Buttercup, however, generously claimed them both and in less than an hour had the pair sucking contentedly.

Duty done, she turned her head to the hay, actually dry grass raked up by mother and daughter, and began to munch contentedly.

Mother and daughter, fingers and toes frozen from inadequate wrapping, hurried to the heated kitchen. Warm tea with honey. Fingers warmed on the thick mugs.

Dora wondered, "Mom, do you think they could both be girls?"

Mom sighed and took a sip. "I wouldn't know, honey. You know a dozen times more than I."

The girl did not argue. Facts were facts. "Well, Papa said if she had a little girl, we'd keep her because Jersey cows usually gave more cream in their milk." After sharing that bit of information, she sipped and set down her cup. "Mom, they might both be girls. I think Papa would say to keep them both."

"We'll see, honey," was Belle's wise reply, "but now you need to get back in bed. School tomorrow, you know."

Later the next day, Uncle Joel stopped in and let the insects into the pasture of dried, but still nutritious, grass. He worked on items in his van, but was invited insistently, into the house for supper. Beans. The perfect winter supper.

"Two little heifers," he assured them, nodding his head with approval. "Some farmers would consider it a present from the Almighty."

Dora, spooning bean soup into a hungry mouth, agreed. "Papa would have. Uncle Joel, I got a question. When you drive around, do you ever see someone who has a broody hen they would let go?"

"Hmmm, well…folks don't usually discuss their broody hens with me but I could ask around." He turned to Belle and saw from her face she wondered what was a 'broody' hen.

Dora again. "Papa says that some chickens just like to be mamas and some don't. While they're bein' a mama to babies, they don't lay eggs, and hens that like bein' a mama, keep on likin' it. Said sometimes folks got tired of it and wanted to get rid of her. Sometimes they ate her."

Belle, Emma, Joy and Eva turned fascinated eyes on the girl, as she studied Uncle Joel's face to determine whether he would go along with it. Uncle Joel turned to Belle, "She's right. Dora, if your ma agrees, I'll do some askin' around."

Contented and reassured, Dora returned to her bean soup. Then she'd go see if Buttercup was all right. While she was there, she'd look ahead to the broody hen Uncle Joel would surely bring. She'd already seen the little A-shaped brooder house in the barn loft. She'd get it down and be ready. Such fun to have baby chicks! HER baby chicks!

It was in February that he was visiting in the Garland community that the rotund and smiling Mrs. Carmichael admitted that, yes, they had a broody hen. "It's that old Rhode Island Red that we've been trying to break up for years. She's so insistent that we've begun to admire her so much we can't bear to put her in a stew. It would likely make everyone sick as her last revenge on us. She's just scooped up a nest under the feed boxes and scrounge some eggs. The youngens tell me she's got 5, but who knows if they'll hatch. They may be old or even rotten.

"So if that little girl wants her, she can have her. I even have a box to send her in if you want to bother with her right now." As they transferred the eggs, Mrs. Carmichael chucklingly admitted that three of the eggs might not be from hens, but old Granny Redhead took what she could find.

Granny Redhead jabbed her beak at the hands that tried to move her, and grumbled in the new box until she saw the eggs were coming with her. She was fairly content for two days, only leaving the box to poop. (In the van, of course.)

Dora fairly exploded with excitement. "We can put her back under the feed box if that's what she wants. I'll put water in there with her."

It was in March that the eggs pipped and out stepped two fluffy yellow balls on legs slim as a toothpick. The other three chicks were tan and humpbacked with shorter legs. Uncle Joel was called in as an adviser.

"What happened, Uncle Joel?"

"Nothin', my dear. You now have three baby guineas and Granny Red Head is going to have a tussle of a time raising them. They can fly and she can't."

"Really...?"

"Sure enough. Guineas are almost wild. They like to sleep in trees, as a rule. But they really make good watchdogs. They squawk at strangers."

Uncle Joel had helped in another important way. He located a source for chopped corn, and also a fire wood supply. The wood lot was just on the next farm, and they delivered. Those two things were absolute necessities.

He also brought flour and matches, along with salt, pepper and sugar from Wilkerson's Market over in Wishbone. Took a load off her mind, it did, and he convinced himself, and her, that he had a responsibility because of his friendship with old man Burk. Could be true, actually.

DAUGHTERS FOR A DAY

A round of birthdays brought Emma up to a solid nine and Dora a scant year behind. Joy happily turned seven. Their mother was settling in nicely, though very busy. How would she ever have made it without the girls?

There were others she could do without. Uncle Joel had warned her about the male attention she was bound to attract. So she wouldn't have been too surprised to know that Richard Glover (called Red because of his red curly hair) and Spike Wilcox (so called, because he was slim as a strip of beef jerky) had spent more than one hour at the picnic tables at Burnt Tree Junction.

"Say, how far does that Burk farm stretch back in the woods?"

"Don't know, Spike. Hear tell, though, that there might near 120 acres, all told. Has that good spring right up by the road. If that was mine, I'd charge for the water." Red Glover picked his teeth thoughtfully with a cedar twig.

"That widow, she couldn't be very old, bein' married to old Jake. Maybe thirty five…six…?"

"Naw. She don't look like…well there's the youngens. One is goin' on ten, I heard."

"I'll bet she got a lotta cash from that farm she sold. Would it be worth puttin' up with youngens to get land and cash?"

"Some folks'd think so."

"You…maybe…?"

"Could be."

The fact was, he'd already dredged up a plan to make an acquaintance. Tomorrow was when he was going to put it in operation…if he didn't back out. Thing was, he thought the lady was right pretty, whatever age she was. And how much trouble could little girls be?

So he got himself a hair trim and a clean shirt, and made his way to the Burk farm. Knocked on the door. Took a few minutes, but she finally answered the door, stepping out on the porch to speak. Mr. Harry took a strong whiff to get the man's scent. Who knew if it would be needed? It just seemed to be something he should do.

"Ma'am…Miss Burk, is it…? Bein' your neighbor down the road, I thought it'd be neighborly to offer my services. Find myself goin' in to Wishbone for this and that, and wondered if you needed something I could get for you. Maybe corn chop for the cow…or somethin'?"

Belle looked him up and down and remembered Uncle Joel. "No, thank you. I'm doin' fine." And she edged back through the door.

Red was disappointed but not totally crushed. At lease she didn't sic the bloodhound on him. The dog sure looked like he wanted her to.

Back in his wagon, he let the horses mosey along while he thought. All was not lost…maybe she was just shy of taking favors. Two days later he again showed up at the door.

"Miss Belle, how are you today?" he began brightly. No answer. She just looked at him, but he plunged on.

"Picked up a extra bag'a corn, thinkin' you might'a changed your mind." He smiled his best, and he was thought by many to hold his own in looks.

She looked him in the eye. "Mr…uh…Sir, if I'd'a wanted you to get somethin' I'd'a said so. Mr. Barker, come on out here."

Harry Barker squeezed his generous frame through the doorway and eyed this person. His beloved mistress had not said 'sic 'em' so he just stood his ground and barked. Twice. The sound reverberated through the rafters of the porch and doubled back.

Thunderingly!

The unfortunate Mr. Glover stepped back suddenly, missed the edge of the porch and slipped to the step, lost his balance and landed on his backside on his clean overalls. Wordlessly, he gathered his legs together and stood, keeping his eye on Mr. Barker. Carefully he retraced his steps to his wagon and left.

He had occasion to meet Spike on the road. "How'd it go?"

Red shrugged off-handedly. "Close up, I'm guessin' she's past forty. I thinkin' I don't need that."

Spike noticed the bag of corn with its flowered covering. "Thought you just got corn."

"I did. Is there a law agin havin' two bags? I gotta be goin'."

Spike watched, stroking his chin of day-old whiskers. "Forty, huh! That can't be. But there's that mineral spring…hmmm, well…."

Miss Fennella Carter, third generation manager of Carter's Caramels, stopped at the Burnt Tree Junction roadside stand for a refresher. Their apple cider was not to be beat for rich flavor, and the road was long and dusty.

She had been to Eureka Springs to solidify the contracts for candy with the local stores. She had left her buggy and team at Wishbone and taken the train, and returned, bringing the buggy and successful negations home. Long trip. Heavy pull up that last hill and the poor animals needed a rest.

To amuse herself, she read the notices on the Message Tree while she sipped. Amusing, puzzling, desperate and imploring…they ranged the entire gamut of human emotion. She read on, chuckling, until a thought hit her.

She really needed a candy wrapper. The summer was the time to stock up on the famous Carter Caramels. Problem was, each had to be individually wrapped in the small cellophane squares. Tedious and boring. She'd done her share of the wrapping as did the other girls of the family. There were other jobs for the boys, but then the whole birth rate took a decided turn to male children.

She needed a sharp young girl with small fingers who would work for five hours for a small amount of money and all the candy she wanted to eat. Little girl…that would be best. Maybe she should put her ad on the tree!

With that, she chuckled merrily. Imagine, a Carter being forced to use the Message Tree! She returned to the picnic table and watched her ponies munching the spring grass. But the more she thought, the surer she became that the answer was in there somewhere, if she could just ferret it out.

Then she remembered the interesting bit of gossip about old Miss Sophie McKinzey and her 'daughter for a day.' Feet too arthritic, she persuaded a little school girl to press the pedal for her. The word was, it was working out famously, and she was even teaching the little girl to card, spin and knit the wool the McKinzey family brought her.

Hmmm, well…where does one find a school girl?

Wait! Didn't that young widow in the Burk place have several daughters…? How old would they be? Apparently she let them be hired out, so maybe…. It would take some thinking about.

The ponies had pulled the buggy about as far as they could go through the tree roots when Miss Fennella stepped aboard, mind reeling with thought.

Wasn't it the Burk place where water was taken to make the caramels because of the unique taste the minerals gave the burnt honey/sugar preparation? Of course it was! But the job of collecting water was given to one of the many Carter Boys. She's just have to check it out herself.

The matched ponies drew the single 'lady's buggy' into the lane by the postal box marked Burk Family. She made her way to the porch and was greeted by the lengthy flopping ears and velvety face of a canine.

Mr. Barker lazily arose, shook himself within his loose skin, and looked up at the stranger with eyes gentle and benign, but with every muscle tensed. He relaxed slightly when she walked softly around him and tapped gently on the door.

She was allowed into the house, so Harry settled himself on the porch again, but was far more alert than he appeared to be.

Miss Fenella drew in a careful breath. She was not accustomed to having to do this sort of thing. So she began as she was trained to…something to set the other person at ease.

"Miss Burk…is it? My name is Fenella Carter. I've come with what I feel is a belated 'thank you' for the decades your family has allowed the community to visit your unique spring. My family makes Carter's Caramels, just down the road and many feel that it is water from your spring that makes them special. I feel they may be right."

Belle smiled slightly. What was this REALLY about? "Won't you have a seat and a cup of tea? It's our pleasure to give the community something of value." Miss Hortense's instruction were very helpful.

Dora had already set the decorative mugs in place and was pouring the tea from the matching pot that had been brought to Echo Mountain on that first memorable trip.

"Miss Carter, this is my daughter, Dora. So tell me, how are things going for you today?"

"So kind of you to ask. I actually had another reason for stopping by. Carter's Caramels is a very detailed operation, and in the spring we gear up for summer trade in the nearby towns. That means a lot of wrapping. Customarily, the wrapping was done by the young girls of the family, only everyone seems to be specializing in having boys. They tend to be clumsy and slower, and can't master the special twist that keeps the cellophane wrapping secure. While asking around for help, I heard that your daughter was helping Miss McKinzey with her knitting. They tell me that she asked you for your daughter to be her daughter for a day. So kind of you, I'm sure.

Belle listened, nodded and sipped her tea. Waiting.

"So I wondered if you might have another daughter you could spare for a few hours on Saturday until school is out, then maybe 2 or 3 days a week. She would be paid, of course. We offer 20 cents for the day she works and all the candy she wants to eat." This last was said with a depreciating smile.

She had cast an eye toward Dora. Maybe nine years old. A good age. "Would this be the daughter who is Miss McKinzy's daughter for a day?"

Belle mind was whirling, trying to put the pieces together, and still be pleasant to the visitor. "No, Miss Carver. This is my second daughter. It is Emma who is being taught to knit by our neighbor." She stressed 'being taught'.

Miss Fenella brightened. "Oh, then perhaps this young lady would be interested, with your permission?"

Belle nodded pleasantly. "Just a couple of questions if I might. I would assume she would be in the presence of your family at all times, as I am extremely careful for her safety."

"But the other question is most important. Emma is learning a valuable skill that will be a help to her all her life. Already she has made hats, scarfs and socks for herself and her sisters. That is very is very important to me. I am pleased to share my daughters if and when this happens. If my Dora agreed to help you, would she be doing anything besides wrapping candy in cellophane?"

Taken back, Fennella grabbed for an answer. "Uh, well, there would be the pay, of course. Also, she would be treated kindly."

Belle paused, as if in thought. Miss Hortense's training had not been lost of her. "Then, if that is the case, I think I would have to refuse."

Fennella cast a bewildered look around the room. "Well, I...."

Dora caught her. "Mom, I wouldn't mind helpin' till she got someone." Fennella cast a relieved look at the girl…then at her mother.

Another silent moment as Belle looked pleasantly at her visitor. "Well, I've always wanted to help folks in a tight. There's times I've been helped. So if my daughter wants to help you for a while…."

The business transaction seeming to be completed, Fennella was properly appreciative. "Thank you so much. You're very kind. We're quite close, about a half a mile through the trail. I'd be glad to take her to our factory to look around and bring her back. You could come too, if you'd like."

"I think no. This would be my daughter's decision, and she is capable of makin' up her own mind." Belle silently complimented herself with this negotiation. Conditions needed to be clear.

So Mr. Barker stood by Belle and watched the buggy with the matched ponies as they circled and left through the driveway. He did not entirely approve, but his mistress seemed to be all right with it. He sauntered back to his favorite place on the porch and settled skin and ears comfortably.

Belle went back to the kitchen and warmed the tea in her mug. Well, another one gone. But the 20 cents would be welcome. Still, there had to be something better for her.

Dora uncomplainingly continued through the summer and fall, mindlessly setting the block of caramel onto the cellophane, gathering the ends, and giving it the final tight twist (the way boys cannot seem to do).

"It's not too bad, Mom. I can do it without thinkin' and it gives me time to think about all the things I want to do here. You know, Mom, those guineas won't come in the shed even when it snows. Uncle Joel said they used to be wild in India, and I think mine still are."

Belle had to smile, indulgently at the word 'mine.' Dora, behind the beautiful oval face and clear blue eyes, was her papa's girl through and through, even though she looked like an angel. Could do worse!

Then in November, Dora came down with a severe chest cold. Belle put her to bed and sent Joy, going on 8 now, with a note to the

Carvers. Joy's parting words as she skipped out the door, "Mom, if they'll let me, I'll stay and wrap candy."

Belle had no time for a reply and as she saw the brilliant red knit cap and flying red scarf disappear into the trees, she could only sigh and warm her tea. It was going to be a busy day, and what would she have told Joy if she'd had a chance?

Nibbling on the last of a jelly biscuit (made by Emma) she thought for the millionth time. At age eight, would she have gone tearing confidently into the wooded timber excited at the prospect of doing something important…and having all the candy she wanted to eat?

No way to know.

What was different? It always boiled down to one thing. Her daughters did what they did because they COULD, while she had been given no opportunity to see what she would have done if she could have.

She was not really happy with Dora, obviously bored out of her skull, using nine to twelve hours a week on a job where she learned nothing. Well, maybe she learned patience, and had acquired a pride that she was 'helping out.' That was something…wasn't it…?

With Joy gone, there was wood to be brought it. Unsettled weather in the winter, and wet wood just didn't work out well together. She'd killed one of 'Dora's' roosters yesterday, and hot noodle soup would be good for her patient.

Later, when she peeked in on her patient, instead of resting, the girl was propped against pillows with her arms behind her head. Far from boredom, she had an excited, almost smiling, look on her face.So like her papa…the few times her father had been ailing, she could get the 'body' to bed but the mind traveled 'ninety to nothin' as they said in the mountains. Like as not he would dream up some new way to make his beloved farm work better.

Pulling her from her reverie was Joy, bursting through the door. Rosy cheeked from the wind and laughing at life in general. "MOM! They say I can come with Dora every day if you let me! Then THEY gave me a sack of candy to bring home."

Belle felt her shoulders slump from the news. Joy, seven, excited and laughing at some sudden new thing in her life. Singing about her work, excited with life. Loved her 'toasty warm' hat and scarf. Then the words seeped in to her brain!

Candy...? Sack of candy...? "Joy, where is the candy?"

"Kitchen. Eva and Nettie took it away from me." Laughing, she yanked off her red hat and scarf, folded them carefully and put them away in their drawer. Joy loved red!

"Kitchen...? Eva and Nettie...."

Turning toward the kitchen is her best 'Mom' voice, she yelled. "EVA! NETTIE!! PUT THAT CANDY DOWN UNTIL AFTER SUPPER!!!"

BURK FAMILY FARM

Fortified by a bowl of chicken noodles, Dora was persuaded to allow her mind to get some rest. Little girls heal quickly. Fortunately.

Later, she was allowed to come to the table for tea and toasted biscuits. "Mom, I've been thinkin'. Buttercup is actin' different like she's tryin' to tell me somethin'. I looked all over for sores or somethin' and I think know what's wrong.

"Posie and Violet have been weaned for a long time. I asked Mr. Collins over at the Junction about what to do. He said no trouble, just bring her on over 'cause he has a bull he kept to keep the varmints outta his apple trees. I think I remember that it's gotta be done soon or we'll have to wait a long time. I sure would like to have a lot of calves like Posie and Violet." A pause as she studied her mom's face.

"I can do it, Mom. Really I can. I wish Uncle Joel was here, but I don't think we can wait. I'll be well tomorrow. You'll let me, won't you?"

"But...all alone? By yourself?"

"No, Mom. I'll have Buttercup with me. Mr. Collins said he'd see that she was milked but I told him she already quit."

Belle was once again brought up shortly, facing life square on. Tell her daughter she could not let 'her' precious cow come ahead of her health...That her beautiful daughter would be taking the cow to be...*Dear Lord, what can I do?* Well, there was no other way. Emma was scared of the cow. Belle looked into the beautiful, expectant face.

"Yes, my dear. We'll see how you are tomorrow, and you must ride the horse and lead the cow. You'll be safer that way."

"Sure, Mom. You won't make me use a saddle, will you? It hurts. The blanket feels a lot better."

Belle nodded permission.

"Anyway Mom, we sorta forgot about Daisy and Poppy. You know how we didn't think about them last time? Well, I think we did it again, and Vi's pregnant. I think. Wonder whose billy it was." For a minute she was contemplative.

"I remember Papa sayin' that the only reason a billy goat stays in a pen is because he wants to. Suppose we could let him find our ladies every time? Makes it easier on us."

Belle groaned inwardly.

"And, Mom, I really wish we had the hay mower we had to leave. It takes so much time for you and me to cut and bring in the hay...and Emma can't help. She's right about it making her hands too rough to knit. Maybe we could rent a mower from someone or swap them a young billy. I know I could get it hitched up, and mow down the meadow in two days. The mover rakes the hay into rows and it's a lot easier together up."

On this, Dora did not ask permission. She already knew what she was going to do. Then came the big one.

"Mom, have you thought about lettin' Joy take my place? I think she'd be better'n me, 'cause she wouldn't be dreamin' about the farm."

Enough of this talk! "We'll talk about it, honey. I want you in bed early if you plan to take Buttercup tomorrow." Belle walked out onto the porch in the brisk wind without a wrap. Shivers and chill bumps, but it cleared her head. Clearly, what she had to do was let Joy promote herself and get Dora back on the farm before the whole thing went down the drain. She stepped back into the kitchen as Dora drained her tea.

"Oh, yes, Mom. Something else. We got watercress greens down from the spring. Papa showed me some on the mountain but the water wasn't right for them over there and they were bitter. These are peppery and crunchy. I'll bring some in. I'll bet Emma'll love 'em."

For two springs, Belle and Dora had barely 'scratched' the garden so they could plant, but without much luck. Uncle Joel said it needed something called a turning plow every spring. He and Dora discussed it like two old farmers, which neither of them had ever been.

"Uncle Joel, I want to put a sign on the message tree for someone to help butcher the calf and then plow the garden for half the beef. Would that work?"

"Yes, but for the half beef you should also get the old cornfield plowed. You could grow corn. I saw a grinder in the shed that would make your cornmeal."

And the conversation went on and on.

Belle, armed with advice from Uncle Joel, had fended off the attentions of several residents from Eureka to Berryville. Her mirror reflected that she was 'passable pretty.' Pleasant features and abundant hair, slightly wavy. Hard work had kept her slim and well rounded, but she had no illusions that something else overshadowed her appearance. Possession of the farm.

And there was that frightening specter of a grown man in the house with her daughters. An outcome not to be imagined! Sure she was lonely at times. Years passed and she was thirty-three.

They had moved into the farm before it had a chance to run down completely, and Dora's interest and the hard work of both of them had built up the most important parts. Prioritizing, they had managed to live fairly well, using sparing amounts of the ready cash. It was amazing how the nickels and dimes paid for a day with her daughters had filled in the cracks of the money flow, and so far the account in Wishbone had been untouched.

She had a little trouble convincing Butch Doughty that she meant business and he was not going to be a part of her household. At one point, she had lifted Jake's Winchester and fired into the trees, just to convince him. It worked for a while but Butch was determined. She knew she hadn't seen the last of him.

Uncle Joel had been assisting Belle with the gun for a while, using spare times when he was camped in the yard. She could now, as the saying goes, 'hit the side of a barn,' but she would never be accurate. She could, however, LOOK skillful and make a racket.

Finally, Uncle Joel suggested that as soon as Dora's wrist would hold the gun steady, she might should be permitted to learn. SOMEONE in this household should be able to fire a kill-shot if necessary.

With a little help from the left hand on her right wrist, Dora began to practice. What a determination in that compact little body and angelic face! It was not long before she could do well enough to fend off an invader with two legs, four legs and no legs at all.

Sent an egg-stealing rattler off to his next life, and then sliced open his body to retrieve the two eggs from his insides. HER eggs.

Summers were hard and hot for Belle and Dora, but food must be planted, grown and canned in the Mason jars. Emma took over the kitchen, and Joy skipped happily off to wrap candy.

Uncle Joel came oftener and stayed longer, making himself useful where he could. He was invited many times to set up camp in one of the empty rooms but he staunchly refused. Winters in his warm van…summers in the cool treehouse. No deviation.

He was there when Dwayne Carpenter, a well build 16 year old with sun-streaked light brown hair answered Dora's message for someone with a 'breaking plow.' The young man had naturally gravitated toward the old man as the one who would be negotiator, but Uncle Joel pointed to Dora.

"Over there's your boss. That lassie'll tell you what she wants."

Dwayne turned to face a small figure…maybe eleven or twelve, in worn overalls and a shirt several sizes too big. Her straw hat, obviously made for a man and adjusted down, still failed to fit, attempting to hide the smooth face, determined mouth and eyes that met him head on.

Young…was his first thought, *but won't she be a beauty.* He certainly didn't expect this. Pa had said to him that the lady down at the Burk's place needed help. Told him to take the breakin' plow and throw on the harrow…she might need it.

"Do her a good job," he said. "If we'd'a knowd she needed help, we'd'a already offered." Those were his exact words. Christian duty was one thing, but they'd'a done it anyway. And for nothin'.

Take the tools on down, he'd said, so's to get a good early start. Might finish in a day. Don't hold 'er to the butcherin' but see when she wants it done. You and me, we can fix her up. Glad to.

The thing was, Pa didn't know who they would be working for.

Dora greeted him with a smile and motioned him to follow her. "The garden first. We want to plant vegetables and can't get a good row. Then that pasture that used to be a corn field. I'd like it good enough to plant it all in corn."

"You're…gonna plant it?"

"Thought I would. That and the garden. If I had a smaller plow, I'd'a had the plowin' done."

"Uh, miss…I don't think you'd get a small plow through there. Been let go too long but I got one that'll do the job. I'll leave my tools here and…."

"But you need to see the calf we gotta butcher." Leading him out into the knee deep grass, they found the young jersey bull. Good butcherin' size, Dwayne told himself. "Who ya got helpin'?"

Dora pointed to her chin. "Me."

"You…? Are you certain…?" He knew it was a stupid response but it just slipped out.

"Yep, I'm sure this is me, and I'm the helper. You get half. Do we have a deal?"

"Sure do. I'll start early in the mornin'."

"I'll be here. And thanks."

The astounded young man swung aboard his horse and waved to Dora. "Man, oh man! Wait till Pa hears what happened here!"

Pa actually did come for the butchering, but might not have needed to except for lifting the heavy side of beef into their wagon. The girl's ma had the table ready for cutting up her part. Obviously done it before.

Pa inspected his son's work and noted that he had given 'over and above.' 'Course it wouldn't have been because of this little doll he was working for. Shame she wasn't 2 or 3 years older. Said she stayed with him all day, bringin' fresh water from the spring out to the field.

Dwayne found himself doing a number of chores the ladies had found impossible. He also found himself at the table at dinner time, and that dark haired older girl was a winner of a cook.

Uncle Joel stroked his chin and looked on. Couldn't'a worked out better if he'd'a thought it up himself. If they could just keep that young fellow on the hook for a couple'a years he'd be a goner. He was already eying the bait like a hungry trout after a fly.

It was two years down the line that Pa warned. "Watch what you do around that girl, son. She ain't old enough to know what she wants."

"You're wrong, Pa. She knows exactly what she wants and it's that farm. She ain't gonna give two words to the fellow that don't love it with her."

Gave Pa something to think on.

Dwayne was there when Dora and Belle cut the corn stalks after the harvest. Hot, hard and heavy job, but those ground up cobs made goat feed or hog bedding. Didn't pay to throw away anything.

He was also there when they butchered the young billy goat and ran the meat through the grinder. Tedious job. He was also there when the goat meatloaf was served. Right tasty food, that goat made!

He made sure he was there when Dora turned fifteen.

MISS HOLLY CHAMBERLAIN

The Chamberlains named their fifth child Holly. How could they avoid it as she arrived on Christmas morning…a noisy little package, waving pink fists and toes at her four excited siblings.

Holly loved pencils just as soon as she learned not to poke them into her eyes, and she loved that they made a satisfying mark on walls, bedsheets and occasionally on paper.

School was a holiday every day, and she determined early that to continue the holidays all her life, she must become a teacher. So she did.

At age seventeen she completed her examination for a teaching certificate. At age eighteen she was assigned to a rural school called Ridge Road Academy. Accredited teachers who would accept rural assignments were rare, so she was considered a gift from above,

Because of her young age, she was assigned a local family who, for a pittance, agreed to be her on-sight protector and the provider of supplies she might need.

She was given the key to the one room cabin outfitted with stove, bed, table, two chairs and a storage cabinet. She was assigned a pony and single buggy for her own use, and a corral for the pony. The corral would be shared by the day with others as the distance to school was prohibitive for some unless they came by horse and dog cart.

Holly Chamberlain was thrilled. Seventeen students for grades 1 through 4. The enrollment three years later rose to 20 students when the Burk girls enrolled.

There was Emma Burk, dark eyebrows shaped like raven's wings. Dark, serious eyes. School assignments prim and perfect.

Dora Burk. Beautiful child. Gorgeous blue eyes that darted swiftly, taking in every detail. Questions like: "How does the baby chick know when to crack the shell?" and "When a Guinea egg is hatched by a Rhode Island Red hen, who is its mother?"

Then Joy Burk. Round face and laughing. Quick with assignments. Loved by all other students. Unusual green eyes when serious, but flecked with gold on the playground. Her only problem being her propensity to break out in song at any moment. The first note got everyone's attention as notes and words were made up at the moment, like "One and one are two…two…two. And Summer skies are blue…blue…blue! That's why I love you…you…you!" Disruptive, but they certainly made her memorable.

Then a couple of years later….

Eva Burk. Dark eyes and brows like Emma, but more outgoing. Positively the 'mother hen' type, a trait very familiar to Holly who considered every student to be her own child. It was due to Eva's persuasiveness that her sister, Nettie, was allowed to attend when barely five. Eva promised to 'watch out for her and make her mind.' She did. Eva loved helping younger students when Miss Holly was busy.

Nettie Burk. A loveable little splinter of a girl. Eager to learn, and much of her 'learning' came from her sister. It was in Nettie's first year that the school experienced a horror that the community would never forget, and that gave Miss Holly frantic moments. But more about that later.

The Eldridge family across the street were the ones selected to 'see to' the young and attractive teacher. They must see that she had food and other necessities bought from Wishbone Hollow stores. They must see to her laundry as she had no facilities. They were not required to include her in family occasions, but they did.

The pony assigned to her must be kept in the Eldridge barn, fed and cared for, and hitched to the buggy when she requested. No problem. Stephen Eldridge loved animals and called the pony 'Peanut' because he obviously preferred peanut hay.

The meager stipend allowed for this service hardly covered the time and services, but the community prestige was a social perk money could not buy. To be chosen to 'see to' the young lady who held one of the most prestigious positions in community was a social 'plum' to be proud of.

The fledgling Arkansas Board of Education would have preferred middle aged, hopefully not too attractive, spinster ladies who had no prospect of changing their status, but these were in short supply, and they generally preferred cities. Then, eventually, they passed onto their reward.

Hence the assignment of Miss Chamberlain. They had no reason to regret this decision, as she seemed to be the darling of the parents, a blossom to the community and made no demands on the Board. She dealt with what was issued and clutched the children to her like a mother hen. In addition, her expectations were high and she felt it was her duty to see that they were met. By every child.

Therefore, when it reached the ears of the Board that possibly young Steven Eldridge was even more helpful to the teacher than his family was paid to be, they waved the thought aside as they would a bothersome fly. What would they do about it, anyway? Replace her? With whom? Perish the thought!

So when the later news filtered through the human grapevine that Miss Holly Chamberlain was now legally Mrs. Eldridge, they ignored it as she was still Miss Chamberlain on the records and her wages were paid to Miss Chamberlain. The checks were deposited in the Wishbone Hollow bank in the account opened by Miss Chamberlain.

Who cared if it was Mr. Eldridge who furnished transport to Wishbone, and took her to dine in the local diner afterwards. He also escorted her around town with her proudly attached to his arm like a precious jewel.

The Board also believed they did not hear that Mr. Eldridge had spent his nights in the teacher's cabin, and that he had also built an unauthorized room off the tiny kitchen.

It was when Eva Burke was in grade four that the school was promoted to a six year school, so Eva had two more years…though she still wrapped caramels at Carters, and had long ago brought Nettie along. No big surprise. The Carters were pleased and Miss Fennella Carter decided one of her best days when she plucked up the courage to ask for one of Miss Belle's daughters 'for a day' that turned into years.

With the school grades raised, there were more students, and the Board, aware that catastrophes occur with children, and more often occur with more children, their valuable Miss Chamberlain must have help, even if it was not 'certified.'

Perhaps a former student??? Or a parent with a modicum of education???

So it was when Eva was almost twelve, and had already spent a 'free' year just because she couldn't bear to quit (Miss Holly handed her a few coins) so now she could be 'legitimate.' Miss Holly told the Board that, yes, she had a very bright student who was available, and MAYBE would consent to help out for half the teacher's salary.

What could the Board do? They could face a law suit or, much worse, a possible 'walk out' by Miss Holly. Belle swelled with pride that one of her own was actually recognized for what the world should be able to see.

Miss Holly acquired books to loan Eva and dredged from her memory what she could of the test for certification. This 'wonder girl' must take the test.

What happened next should have anticipated, and actually the timing worked out beautifully. With minor alteration to her wardrobe, Miss Holly managed to hold onto the 'secret' that was not a 'secret' until 1 May when the school session ended. Mr. Steven Eldridge III obligingly remained in-utero until mid August, then appeared in time for his ma to be ready for the next session.

Eva Burk was then thirteen, had spent the summer in the treehouse studying the books and the test questions.

Young Steven Eldridge was ably cared for by his grammy and his ma went to the school to her job. Eva was ready and eager to pick up the major part of the load.

When Eva turned fourteen, Miss Holly insisted she turn in her request for the certification test, leaving her age blank. She appeared for the test and handled it comfortably, then confessed that she had made an error on her application, and could she now correct it?

She might not have gotten away with it, except that Miss Susan Eldridge was not as obliging as her brother, and insisted on being born at Christmas. Holly stayed on the job as long as possible, obvious to everyone that she was 'in a family way,' but what could they do?

All the Board had was the falsified application and an undeserving certificate belonging to a highly qualified applicant who was a native of the Ridge and likely would be there…long term…? After 'learned heads' passed many words back and forth, a solution of sorts was found.

The job would be awarded to the applicant who was too young by a year to even be a 'helper' and the qualified Miss Chamberlain retained as a 'helper' until other arrangements could be made.

Eva moved into the 'teacher's cottage' still under the protection of the Eldridges, and surveyed her class of 24 students, feeling her heart expand with pride. This was what she had been born for!

Miss Holly helped when she could, and in any emergency, but the bottom line was…Miss Eva Burk really didn't WANT any help. The classroom was now hers, earned by hours in the treehouse, and it was only her love for her teacher that she accepted any assistance at all from Miss Holly.

At one point during this period of time, Mr. Eldrige, Senior asked the whereabouts of his second son, David. Whereupon, David's mother answered in a whispery voice. "He's gone over to help the new teacher put up a wall shelf."

Pregnant pause. "Do you think we might get lucky and snag this teacher as well?"

And Mr. Eldridge merely shrugged, winked and smiled… and walked away.

But all of this came later. There were a lot of happenings back at the Junction…specifically the Burk Farm.

BACK AT THE FARM

Emma continued to go Miss Sophie's house. Though the old lady's arthritic fingers were no longer able to draw the wisps of wool from the bag and give them the twist that created yarn, they could still knit. Old fingers do not forget easily and they continued to knit and purl. Emma could take care of the yarn preparation.

Mark McKinzey still came with his older cousin to bring wool, though it was dwindling in its use. The trip was mainly instigated by the family to check on their old relative. Not really very good.

Seemingly the stringy old muscles still remembered their duty and when she must practically be lifted to her wheelchair, the fingers still manipulated the needles and turned out garments without fault or flaw.

Until she couldn't.

The McKinzey family made a trip up Ridge Road with a sad request. They could either take the old lady down to Eureka Springs to a 'rest' home…or they could try to find some kind person who would make her last years as comfortable as possible.

They were fully aware that she had been 'renting' Belle's daughter for a pittance. Embarrassing, actually. She should have at least 50 cents a day, and more if the old lady became bedridden. If that happened, then a move was inescapable. And Auntie didn't want to go. She wanted to stay in her home, no matter what. She insisted she could 'die just well in her home as in the rest-of-her-life home where no one knew her.

So here was the plan. If Emma, who the old lady loved, could 'look in on her' a couple of times a day and see that she ate something, they'd see that she was paid what she was worth.

If she became totally bedridden, and remained that way, would Emma come and stay with her…? That, of course, would be worth more money.

Emma was fifteen and a half. She listened to the negotiations going on around her, with her mother being mostly silent. Finally she could stand it no longer. She stood, faced the adults, drew in a breath and began.

"Do you know what Miss Sophia means to me? I've seen her every day for almost seven years. She has baked cookies for me and my sisters. She made a double chocolate birthday cake for me. She gave me knittin' needles and taught me every stitch she knew.

"Last year Mark brought me her first spinning wheel that she wanted me to have for a present. I've used it ever since. She gave me a confidence I might have spent years a'gettin'. She liked me and talked to me like I was a grown up. Told me stories. I may know more about your family than any one of you do. Sure, I need to earn money, but we're sittin' here talkin' about a grand lady who has given her skill to a child, and her companionship to an almost grown up girl of the mountains. She actually liked me.

"My mom doesn't have to answer for me. I will stay with Miss Sophie as long as she wants me to, and you let me. If she passes on, I'll get a message to you as soon as possible and I'll stay with her until you come. What you pay me is up to you."

Belle watched the emotion on the face of her firstborn and never was more proud. Her precious Emma. The image of her father, and a young lady who would have made him swell with pride. She felt she needn't add more words. Enough had been said. Sure to have been.

Depreciatingly, she stated, "Just a moment and I'll serve tea to everyone. I believe we also have cookies made by the recipe Miss Sophie said was a family favorite." And with the dignity and pride of a queen, Belle left the room.

Emma also left the room. "I have a few things I need to gather, and I'll be ready to leave with you after tea."

Young Mark, who was present during this discussion, watched the departing figure, her shinning black hair pulled to the top of her head, and her hand-knitted cardigan fitting her slim shoulders.

He nodded. The sweater was much like the ones he had taken to the shop in Wishbone where they were sold to 'summer people.'

Mark McKinzey could plainly see that it would be up to him to make regular and frequent trips up Ridge Road to check on his great auntie. It would be well to stay on good terms with the neighbors at Burnt Tree Junction, as it was a firm plan of his to buy the 'old family place' when he had saved enough money. It wouldn't be long.

He was doing quite well learning to be a wheelwright. The country ran on wheels, and there were a lot of them on Ridge Road. There needed to be someone to keep them in running order. Why not him? And Emma already knew her way around in this house.

UNCLE JOEL AND OLD DAN'L

The two old men sat on Dan'l's porch with their chairs tipped comfortably against the wall and a corner post. Things were getting serious and some discussion needed to take place that would hopefully end in firm plans.

Uncle Joel was becoming more tired than usual before the end of his self-appointed schedule, and spent his days behind the insects, Cricket and Skeeter, dreaming of the comfort of the treehouse and the persons close by.

Even Mr. Harry Barker was a comfort. The dog only lifted an eyebrow creating four above-the-eye wrinkles instead of the usual three when Uncle Joel arrived. He knew the score. This human was safe.

There was that other human, though, that raised both eyebrows and lately, even his head. There were many people who stopped at the mineral spring for water…filled their canteen or bucket…and moved on, often whistling happily.

One person, however, came very often, sneaking through the trees, and lingering over the water. He stood, tall with thick hunching shoulders, his hands in his pockets and his eyes on the Burk house. Mr. Barker didn't like it at all, but his mistress did not seem disturbed, and she had never told him to 'sic 'em' to this person.

So he turned toward the man with his cap pulled down on his forehead and watched, scarcely blinking. He'd like to do something, but he didn't know what. There had been no one to train him in any particular duty, though he seemed to know there was something that could (and should) be done by him…somewhere….

The man at the spring was not entirely to blame for his actions. While he spoke well and could work hard when given specific directions, his social acumen seemed to have ceased development at about age four.

There were not many things that Butch Doughty really wanted, so the social problem was not generally known. But when there WAS something he wanted, he felt that it should be his, and tried with patience and all the ability he had to advise others of his desire.

His latest torment was the Burk farm and its mistress who seemed oblivious to his wishes and ignored him. When he came close to the house, she asked, not unkindly, what did he want? How could she not know what he wanted? He should not have to explain himself. It should be evident.

Not only that, there was that dog that stared at him, and lately, might leave the porch and advance toward him, stopping about 20 feet away and rumbling his growl from deep inside that huge body. Then he'd shake his head, flapping those enormous ears so that he sounded like a gaggle of geese…or maybe a flock of crows all taking flight at one second. Unnerving, at the least. He was not sure how long he was going to be patient and he sat himself down to think about it. There had to be a way.

He had to let the ruler of the house know that he could be a help. Why had she not invited him in?

Belle had noticed the man, but considered him harmless. She knew that Mr. Barker disapproved, but so far had not attacked. She did wish, however, that he would get his water and go.

Mr. Barker watched his mistress stand on the porch and look toward the spring with irritation. He could always tell. The way she stood. The aroma that wafted away from her. He would like to do something, but what…? If she could only tell him…what…?

There were others that came for one reason or another, like the young fellow called Carlton Martin. When he came, he always brought sticks cut from trees, and they were eventually taken into the house. This person was acceptable, and often invited in the house. If Joy happened to be home, she helped him unload his wood from the sled, laughing and talking as she always did. Acting normal. Nothing for him to be concerned about.

And Mr. Barker was right.

At first when Carlton and his older cousin, Eugene, brought the wood Miss Belle had ordered, he had seen Joy rush to help. Hmmm, something familiar about her. She looked up at him, squinting and studying his face.

Those green eyes. It was a cloudy day, and her eyes were green as cedar branches in the winter. "Joy…? Is that really you?"

Joy laughed as merrily as a robin on a limb. "Carlton! I didn't know you could cut down trees! And you've got a lot bigger!"

Carlton shrugged, "Couldn't help it. I think the birthdays were the problem. You got bigger, too."

Joy giggled. "I remember you from Miss Holly's school. You were a big boy but you played with everyone like you had fun. You used to 'drop the hankie' behind me and let me catch you even though I couldn't run very fast. And you used to push me higher in the swing than anyone else."

Carlton grinned at the fond memory while Eugene stared at the two obviously daft people. Carlton's grin was wide and familiar, and the seven year old looked at the twelve year old. "You got a lot prettier when you got bigger!"

At that, Carlton turned pink and Eugene laughed until he lost his breath, coughing and patting his knee in merriment.

Joy, who had only seen Eugene on the delivery trips, wasn't sure what was funny, but laughed merrily. Such fun to see someone after so long a time. "Do you cut wood all the time?"

Carlton shrugged good naturedly. "Seems like I'm goin' to. My cousin, here, got 'im another job and now this'n is mine."

"Then you'll be comin' here every time we need wood?"

"Sure will," and in a stroke of bravery he asked, "and will you run out of the house to help me unload?"

"Sure will. It's a promise." And it was.

But that joyous reunion did nothing to solve the problems of the aging residents of the Ridge. Strange thing about life.

When it seemed to be finished, sometimes it just strung out day after day, meaning nothing and going nowhere. Just sort of 'being' with no particular reason. The thing was, the two old fellows down by Kings River could be no help to each other as they were in the same boat…and seemingly the oars didn't work any longer. Too many birthdays…for a fact.

It was going to take a lot of talking. They sat on the porch of Dan'l's little cabin set conveniently by the Kings River. Many's the hours they had spent fishing in the water that almost seemed to toss the fish onto their hooks. No more. What was the use? Catch a fish…eat it…and live another day. Another fish, another day. What was the use of it?

At daybreak, Joel hitched up the insects, well fed after a day of rest, and pulled his van up out of the Kings River valley and onto Ridge Road.

As he reached the lane to the Burk farm, both Cricket and Skeeter turned as one to enter, but Uncle Joel pulled them back. NO! He was not going to the treehouse. He was going home to Eureka Springs and do some serious alone thinking. He had come to a turning point.

Dora no longer needed him for advice. She had Dwayne and Pa Carpenter for anything she needed. After all, they had actually been farmers, and Joel could pass on only what he had learned from conversation. He was not even a 'has been'…he was truly a 'never was' as far as the girl was concerned. At least that's the way he felt.

And Miss Belle owed him nothing. Mr. Barker did a better job of 'seeing to' the farm than he ever could. No one needed an old man, not even the old man himself.

The insects, having been told no different, followed the road down through Garland community and on through Enterprise. Wishbone Hollow was just ahead. It was a long, sorrowful pull to get back to Eureka Springs where Uncle Joel had nothing left but a soundly built four rooms with a leanto.

He had married and bought the little place, perched on the side of a hill as were most homes in that town. Some homes were on ledges, some were jammed against the mountain and held there by, as folks said, the grace of the Good Lord. Maybe they were right.

The small tree behind his house was now a massive oak with exposed roots that wrapped around a submerged stone ledge like the tentacles of an octopus he had seen in a picture. Hanging on for dear life, it was, but it had grown massive and furnished protective shade for the house.

He could sell for a good price. Certain to, the way summer people were moving in. He'd give it a thought as soon as he figured out where he would go. Could one actually live in a salesman van? That's practically what he had been doing for decades.

And his tools. What would they be worth? Maybe he'd check in on young Adam Bentley. He was operating the town's only tinker shop, and seemed to make a go of it. Yeah, he'd do that before he settled down to the painful decision.

"Hey, fellow!" he was greeted. "Get yourself on in here and drag up a chair. Tell me what you've been doin'. I'm about to go crazy inside these four walls."

Joel nodded, grinning. He'd been there, too, before he decided to hit the road. He learned quickly that having no wife meant having no home. So to speak.

There was the weather chat, and the neighborhood gossip. The amount of business and general health.

"How's the misses? How many youngens you got?"

The dreaded silence filled the shop as Adam just looked at Joel, slumped shoulders and drooping mouth.Joel shook his head in knowing sympathy. "Not you! How long back?"

Adam slumped into a chair. "Diphtheria. Two years back. Took her and the boy." When he was able to speak again, he added, "And whoever she was a'carryin' at the time."

Joel had heard about the epidemic, went through town like a goat through clover, leaving deaths by the hour. Joel had wisely stayed on the road.

Adam went on. "Joel, I'm here to tell ya, I ain't stayin' around here. 'Thout Bonnie and the boy, there ain't no home. Got my place up for sale and I'm goin' somewhere. That's what you did, wasn't it?"

Adam closed up the shop and the two men walked to the diner. It took two huge cinnamon rolls and a gallon of coffee, but a deal was struck...maybe. Adam would make a round of Joel's customers and see if he wanted to take over the route. Maybe a few years in the country, rolling up and down Ridge Road, would clear his head.

Anyway the two men, three decades apart in age, had a lot in common. At least, they'd be sympathetic company for the couple of months the tour would take.

Carlton Martin, now age 15, flung the rope over the tree limb and hoisted himself up. It was a perfect tree, an oak with huge limbs and a twisted trunk. Fastening his halter carefully to the limb above, he began to saw, thoughts keeping time with the zizz-zaw-zizz sound as the saw-teeth cut into the sappy wood. Pa was going to like this one with all its twists and turns the grain would have really good curves and wavy lines.

Below him were the bushy small limbs and top branches of unusable wood scattered liberally over the dead leaves. He knew he should have piled the scraps out of the way, but it took so much time. Now the limb he had almost severed would fall right on top of the brush, and he'd have to stop, gather and pile.

Should'a done it first 'cause he had to do it anyway, heaping the ends and twigs out of the way. Ready for the one to fall. Now it was all twisted and piled together.

"Ker-ack!" and the limb fell away, right in a mess of scraps and a few shrubs. He'd be at least two hours trimming this limb. Something had to be done if he was going to make any money.

A couple of years ago he been sat down by his pa and great uncle. They had a lot of words that didn't mean much to a twelve year old, but the old fellows were insistent that they were giving him a chance of a lifetime. Maybe they were, but a twelve year old has trouble realizing it. He was now older, and understood a lot more, but the job still seemed endless.

He selected a spot with a stump where he had just cut a tree. He'd pile the scraps there, and they would be decayed by the time the stump grew another tree. Thought whirled around in his head. Some change had to be made.

But right now, he needed to chop up medium sized limbs to make a load of stove wood for Miss Belle. The chance to see Joy created a small smile. He'd schedule the load for late in the day when she'd be there to help unload, and maybe they'd invite him in for… maybe hot chocolate! At the least, there'd be tea and cookies.

That green eyed Joy! She'd be eleven now, goin' on twelve. She sure was good help…chatterin' and singin' and the time just flew. He could use her right now!

Dropping the busy twigs he held, he shouted, "I COULD USE HER RIGHT NOW! Folks been rentin' the Burk girls for years, why couldn't I?" The thought gave him so much energy that the brush and sticks flew. He grabbed up his ax and severed the small limbs from the big one he had just felled and heaped the wood on the sled.

He'd do it! Just watch and see!

Emma had returned to her home bringing her spinning wheel and all the loose wool. Where Miss Sophie now was, she wouldn't be needing it, and what's more, her joints wouldn't hurt any more. Somehow, though, Emma just couldn't seem to pick up where she had left off. Her fingers rebelled, and she had to take out rows of stitches to correct a mistake. She hadn't done that in years. What was going on?

With a dreary sigh, she put down the knitting and moseyed out to the kitchen. She could start supper. That's what she could do. What to cook? Well, there were lots of choices. Dora's chickens created more eggs than they could use. Occasionally even Mr. Barker got a plate of the golden scrambles.

He was happy to oblige, though he might have preferred them uncooked. Couldn't do that, though. Country dogs can't be given raw eggs lest they decide to get them for themselves. From the nest.

So Emma set out the eggs. Maybe a big, spicy bread pudding that created good leftovers. Very popular snack. Then sausage and gravey…with potatoes and…. Hey, there was Dora's watercress! Those juicy green leaves were so good wilted with bacon grease and garnished with boiled eggs. Maybe Dora would go get…but no, she'd said something about a leather harness that need to be patched…or something. No telling where she was right now.

Well, perhaps she could find the cress by herself. It was in the stream below the spring she knew, so how difficult could that be? With large pan in hand, she headed out. Mr. Barker lifted his huge head and watched, accessing what he should do. If she left the yard, he'd go along.

Yes, there she went and that other person was sitting by the stream looking toward her. Stepping quickly to her side, he turned toward the man and flapped his ears sharply. That not only made a satisfying noise, it stirred up the scents that floated around. The scent of the man was very strong, and then he tested the change in Emma's scent. She was scared…maybe. Humans were puzzling.

The bloodhound drew in a breath and let it out with a low growl that made his velvety lips ripple. The person stood, turned and hurried away. Good. But he'd follow along with Belle's girl anyway. She didn't go in the woods very often.

And there she was! About to step on that rattler!

Harry leaped forward with surprising speed, grabbed the scaly body and flung it around like a lasso rope, as Emma cowered back against a tree. When Harry thought it had enough flinging, he dropped the reptile and it landed, stomach up. He stare for a few seconds…sniffed the corpse…snorted noisily and looked up at Emma.

Emma, heart pounding, reached out and smoothed Harry's head. "Thank you," she told him. That was enough for him, and he wagged his stump of a tail as a reply and stepped ahead of her, leading her to the place where Dora had set rocks to be able to gather greens without stepping in the water.

He waited and led her back to the house. Now, he should get to do something like that more often. It was so satisfying to be useful.

At the supper table, Emma commented, "Mom, that man was out there again staring at the house. Harry ran 'im off. Wonder why he does that?"

Belle nodded. "I know. I wonder, too. I' m not sure he's…well, I'm just not sure." And the meal proceeded.

Butch Doughty hated that dog. When he was master of the Burk farm, that dog would be gone. That was a promise he made to himself.

ANOTHER DAUGHTER FOR A DAY

Carlton Martin rehearsed his speech most of the day and in his sleep. Tomorrow he would cut the right amount of cook stove wood for the sled. He would bring Slugger along. He was possibly the world's most disagreeable mule…when he wanted to be. Otherwise, he was much the same at other mule, just hard headed.

Some folks thought a mule could not understand sometimes but that was likely not true. The mule likely didn't obey instructions because he just didn't want to…not that he didn't understand. Maybe Slugger would have a good day. If he knew he was going to the Burk's, maybe he would remember the potato, or something, that he always got.

Slugger did not understand much of the language so it was impossible to inform him. What a shame.

Carlton had thought and thought, and this negotiation, if successful, would be the immediate answer to his bottleneck of work, so why could he not do what others had done? Somehow, he expected a fair amount of difficulty with Joy's ma. He got it.

He was invited in for chocolate. He had discussed this with Joy, first, as would be proper. Now her mom.

"Miss Burk? I got something to ask you."

"Yes, Carlton. Ask away."

"I heard folks talkin' about the way you let your daughters do things for other people. Maybe for a day at a time. Well, I've got myself a job that's goin'a be good if I can just keep up. I don't mind hard work, it's the scrappy little easy work that's gettin' me down." He paused, summoning his courage.

"What I'd like is to rent a daughter from you for a while. I'd…."

Belle turned to Carlton with a tolerant smile. "Son, I might let them go but not to just everyone. I'm very particular about where my daughters are."

He nodded rapidly. "I know that, Miss Burk. And I can guarantee you'd know where she was, every minute, and could almost hear her if the wind was from the north. It's in that woodlot right to the north. That's where I'm workin'. I been workin' on my own for two years now and never had an accident. Shot a few small varmints, though, and scared off a wolf.

"What I need is someone who can gather and pile up the scrappy ends of tree limbs so they'll be outta the way for the big limbs to fall, and then for the whole tree to come down. It's a good easy job, but I ain't got time for the scraps. I gotta cut the big ones or I don't get paid much."

"You don't get paid by me when you bring wood?"

"Oh, yes! But that's not much compared to the big trunks I cut for Pa and my great uncle. They need a special kind'a wood and I know just how to find the right ones. The thing is, there's waste limbs that I cut up for fire wood, and it leaves a lot'a tiny limbs and scrap. Part'a the deal with pa is that I keep the scraps piled as I go, so's it's clean under the trees." He paused for breath.

Fascinated, Belle decided to play along. "Who tells you what to do?"

"It's my pa and his uncle. Land belongs to his uncle and he's old. Says he'll pay me to bring him the right logs for what he does and if I save my money I can buy the land. It's that acreage right across the fence from you to the north. Good place. Has a good, flat buildin' spot."

"And you're buying land already?"

"Yes, ma'am. Been at it for nigh onto two years."

"Does your uncle cut up the logs you save for him?"

"No, ma'am, I cut 'em. He wants 'em 40 inches long and straight grained. Sycamores is good, and hickory is straight but the wood ain't right."

"Not right? For what?"

"Fiddles, ma'am. He makes fiddles and sells 'em in the cities. Folks write to 'im and say what they want to sell in their stories and he sends 'em if he has 'em. If he don't, he makes what they want. Folks really like his fiddles."

"He makes…fiddles…?"

"He does, for sure. Particular, he is, though. I get what I can for the wood like I brought you, but he pays a lot for special logs. When I find a good tree, I cut it into pieces and roll 'em down the hill into the little stream. Gettin' wet is good for 'em.

"Then when the winter rains come, the stream fills up and the logs float on down to the ponds where he catches 'em and piles 'em up to cure."

"To cure…."

"Yeah he's got to know if there's gonna be a split somewhere when they dry out. It's the sap inside and it's gotta dry so the wood is in the shape it's gonna be, 'afore he puts in the time sawin', trimin' and sandin'. He's always got fiddles started, partly done, middle way done and finished. Then when they're finished they're either alright or good. He gits more money for the good ones. The others is mostly for youngens to learn on."

Belle had almost forgotten what this conversation was all about. "So, why do you want one of my daughters?"

"Not just one of 'em. I want Joy. Her and me, we was in the school playground together. You knew that. She was just a little mite but it was easy to remember her. Happy all the time. All she'd have to do for me is gather the twigs and pile 'em on a stump where another tree just got cut."

"Carlton, I think you need a fellow for that. Maybe one of your friends."

"I tried, ma'am. I really tried. The little fellows don't know how to work, and the big ones, like me, want a real job to make money... same as I do. I really, really tried. The thing is, it's a easy job not worth as much money as a hard one. I have to pay for help if I get it, and I have to make money."

"If you have to pay, won't it cut into your share?"

"Oh, no, ma'am. I can cut really fast and I'm good at bein' up in the trees. That's where the money is. But I can't gather twigs any faster'n a little kid could. Takes up time. D'ya see?"

"Yes, I see. You seem to know just what you want. I hope you find someone."

"Ma'am, I don't want someone. I want Joy. I been figgerin' to pay her 15 cents a hour for four hours, three day's a week."

Fascinated, Belle asked. "You can pay that much?"

"Oh, yes. Pa and Uncle pay a lot for what they want, 'cause they charge a lot when they sell it. Pa says that's good business. Time used to be the follows got their own trees, but it's cheaper to pay me."

"Your pa works with his uncle?"

"Oh, no, ma'am. He makes chests. Some of 'em are like those over there." He jerked an elbow toward the wooden chests where her fancy work was still stored. "Pa has to have a'nother kind'a wood. He has to have straight lengths for at least five feet and he likes curly and wavy grain. Some trees have the lengths and they're the easy ones. Maybe three cuts on one tree. I can work fast if you let me rent Joy for the day."

Belle looked from the boy to the chest to her daughter who, for once, was not singing.

Then Carlton again, "Ma'am, you thinkin' my money ain't as good as other folks'? It's the same kind and it'd spend for the same things. Joy'd be safe with me. I used to swing her high in the swing, but I'd never let her fall. Any varmints in the wood's gonna be took care of with my gun. As for me, if I hurt any girl, my pa'd skin my head and then kill me. He wouldn't stand for no shame comin' on his family." He paused, and a slight smile appeared on his face.

"Fact is, Miss Burk. If'n I was to grab 'er to hurt her, she'd likely twist loose 'afore I got a good holt. And in these mountains, I guessin' she could out run me." That brought on a smile.

"'Nuther thing I was gonna say. If she'd go ahead and pile the wood on the sled that's comin' here, that'd save me time so's I could afford to charge you only half as much. Time is my problem, not wood."

Belle thought...*and this is a product of the Ridge Road school and a pa who gives good training? Hmmm, well....*

"Carlton, if I let Joy go, where would she find you?"

"Oh, I'd be by to get 'er. If we didn't have a sled to load, I'd be on the mule. Lots'a room on his rump. I'm workin' just through the fence, here. Someone a long time ago put in a gate. Covered over with possum grape vines."

"You're a good talker, Carlton. I'll let her go one day as a trial. Then we'll see."

"Yes, ma'am. I understand. And if she can find a job payin' what I can pay 'er, that she likes to do, she'd be right to go to it."

So Joy rode the sled down through the woods and through the gate he had liberated from the vines. She worked for him off and on for the next three years, and stopped then, because he had cleared the whole mountainside of perfect trees. New ones were growing from the stumps. Take years to be big enough to cut, but there was a huge pile of both kinds of logs piled by as a house waiting for the uncles to use up.

Toward the end of the three years, Carlton moved on to his next project, a house. It would be mostly logs, his most available building material, and he'd start with 4 roomy spaces. He even had plans for the new bow-windows that were so attractive and could be made with short lengths of logs.

Another wonderful accident was that the new house would be only a quarter of a mile through the woodland path and the reconditioned gate to the Burk farm. Close neighbor. Amazing how things worked out, sometimes.

Joy spent a lot of time looking over his shoulders watching the house plan develop, but about this time there had been a totally new discovery. Quite accidentally Belle got what she wished for all of her daughters…that they learn something of value that she had never had a chance to do.

With the pride of a relative, Carlton took Joy to meet his pa and Uncle Eben. Uncle Eben was putting the finishing touches on his latest instrument…that he insisted already 'had the music inside it.' Joy looked at the beautiful creation that had emerged from the trees Carlton had been bringing down. Incredible! Totally unbelievable!

But there it was before her 14-year-old eyes. She was smitten. The three men watched with interest as she approached the instrument and caressed the grain of the wood with a delicate forefinger. Couldn't seem to take her eyes away.

"Is it real…?

"Of course it is!" Carlton told her. "I told you all about it."

"I know, but I couldn't see it in my mind."

"Come," he told her, motioning her away to another room.

She stared, transfixed, at the rows and rows of beautiful fiddles. "All those are from trees I picked for him. He learned from my great-grandad. You know…I told you that day at your mom's."

"I guess. I wasn't listenin'. I was crossin' my fingers to give you luck with Mom. Now I see. I gotta have Mom see what we've been helpin' to happen."

"Any time. Uncle likes to show off."

Back in the work room, she couldn't take her eyes off the fiddle. "How long does it take to make one of those?"

"Oh, maybe a year and a half."

"That long?"

"Yes. But of course, it ain't worked on all that time. Fiddles have to rest between what's bein' done to them. They can't be made to hurry. It takes about that long to make one, but the same length of time can make a dozen or more."

Joy made a sad face, strictly unusual for her. "I sure wish I could learn to make one."

Pa looked at Uncle Eben and Uncle looked at Carlton. Carlton looked back at each of the men and nodded. Pa took over. "Joy, Uncle Eben has agreed to teach you as much as you want to know. All you have to do is be here when you can. It takes a long time to learn and you might change your mind…and that would be alright."

Joy looked at Carlton and then at Pa, then came forward and hugged the old uncle. Another strictly unusual thing for her. "I will. I'll ask Mom but I know she won't care."

Then added, with a wry grin, "Anyway, I've lost my job of piling twigs."

Belle was more amazed than Joy, but time would tell whether she would stick with it. Anyway, no experience, good or bad, is totally lost.

All this, while Joy spent hours cross-legged at the feet of the old man or perched on a chair nearby absorbing every word he chose to tell her. What better gift would there be for an old and lonely man in his later years?

And Carlton…he loved it. He smiled to himself as he worked on the house. Joy was right where he wanted her. Tucked safely inside his family.

MEANWHILE, BACK AT THE BURK FARM

Emma was alone. Not only without people, but alone inside. She wandered aimlessly from room to room…like the albatross or the petrel that flew the thermals on the seas knowing there was no place to pause.

Joy was at the fiddle-makers'. Eva was being an assistant to Miss Holly. Dora and Mom were…somewhere. Nettie was on her third year with the Carters. She was now the one who instructed other girls on the correct wrap-twist to make the cellophane papers stay intact.

Nettie also helped with the delicate chocolate that could be sold only in the winter months. Not only that, she had invented a hard, sweet mint made from sugar and a speck of cornstarch and flavored with the peppermint from the Burk herb garden. Another valuable summer candy that did not melt.

While Emma, woodenly performing household duties at hand, refused to pick up the knitting needles. She also refused to open the door to the room that held her spinning wheel.

One thing held a minor interest…the watercress. It appeared at many meals prepared in various ways. As Dora was always elsewhere, it became up to Emma to go gather it.

She didn't mind, actually, after the first scary trip. It was rather nice to sit on the flat rock that was wedged against a very large oak tree. She could sit on the rock and lean comfortably back against the tree. No one needed her, so she was never in a hurry to fill her pan with the fresh green leaves. So peaceful. So amazing how a plant could grow in the constant flow of the mineral water, anchored only by thread-like roots attached to the soil under the gravel bed of the stream.

Butch Doughty also seemed to have nothing to do, but that would be misleading. His mind refused to hold to many ideas, but when one attached itself, it stayed and often grew.

He had spent hours in thought over a single idea such as the best food for his chestnut stallion, Chester. He'd also spent time deciding how many hickory nuts it would take to fill his hat, and finally gave up because he could not decide whether the nuts should be removed of their hulls…or not. Also which hat would be the measuring container.

Sitting by the Burk's mineral spring was his favorite thinking place, and for the last several years, he had been working on a plan. It was a difficult one for him, and every avenue down which his mind had wandered seemed to have a block at the end. One thing Butch had, though, was patience. Also strong was faith that at some time he would work it out.

The kernel inside the plan was to somehow manage to acquire the Burk farm and the person who ruled it, Miss Belle Burk. The direct approach had failed, and he had not the courage to do away with the dog or to use the dog within his plan.

The plan he eventually decided on was to be able to return to Miss Belle something that she had, but had lost, and he had been able to find and return to her. Reason told him that she would be so overcome with gratefulness that she would beg him to be her partner in the farm. Now he had to decide what that object would be.

He should have been able to use the dog, but the animal was just too big and furious, and he had a very un-dog-like stare in his dark eyes under all those wrinkles of furry skin. A look that seemed to bore right into him. Upsetting, to say the least.

He'd also thought of nabbing the youngest girl as she left school, but and he had scouted out the possibilities, but she was never alone. There was always the next oldest girl with her. Now, either girl would be acceptable if she was alone, but, big, strong and powerful as he was, he knew he could never manage two kicking, squealing girls.

At one point he'd actually attempted the abduction. With a bandana tied around his face below the eyes, like the pictures of gangsters in the newspapers, he had hid in the bushes near their trail.

He'd strung a light cord across the path the girls took and waited in a thicket for them to pass. If he jerked the cord at the right time, one of the girls should stumble and fall, and it would likely be the little one. So that left him to grab the older one and tie her hands and feet, then the little one would be simple to catch. He hadn't figured how he would get them both to the hiding place but hoped the knowledge would appear once he had the prize.

As expected, the girls had come through the woods, talking about something or other. The little one was ahead, as he had hoped for. He held his breath for the cord to juggle, like the fishing line juggled when attack by a hungry fish. The problem was, it kept on not jiggling and he couldn't see clearly why.

Then the girls started singing one of the silly songs girls sing, and before he could decide what to do, a strange animal…maybe two of them…jumped out of the bushes behind him and he knew the best thing for him to do was RUN! And he did! Even more important than acquiring the Burk farm was saving himself.

So he put rapid distance between himself and whatever animal it was, and was relieved when he easily out-ran it. A cave about halfway down the hill was the destination of his choice, and it seemed best to use it now. So, breathless and shaking from the run, he crouched in the silent darkness of the cave for the rest of the day. He was fortunate, though, because the animal did not find him.

The 'animals,' however, had returned to the path, snickering behind the hand over their mouths. One had seen the cord and stopped silently. The other had clasped her hand, retreated back down the trail and circled around. Such fun! They snickered all the way home and didn't bother to tell a soul about it. Why would they? They took care of it, didn't they?

So the poor kidnapper was back to square one.

Later, he would have been interested in abducting Nettie on her way to Carters, but she was always on a horse. Eva was seldom alone because she often stayed at the school.

There was Dora, but she carried that bag on her back and from the shape of it, he was certain she carried a gun. Big gun.

Guns scared Butch, so the idea of Dora was discarded. Emma was never considered, due to the shortness of the distance between her house and Miss Sophie's. So, back to the mineral spring, the flat rock and the dog that stared at him.

And the days passed.

Mark McKinzey, who should have already moved his wheelwright business to the empty McKinzey house, had a project that had delayed him for days…actually several weeks.

He needed a gift. Not candy…or lacy handkerchiefs…or a book of poetry…or even a letter of his intention. Nothing so ordinary. As it turned out, he made a trip to Bentonville expressly to find this usual item. This meant visiting the fancy store that sold expensive woolens and the implements to create them. Needles, dye, buttons, hooks and books.

BOOKS! YES! Thumbing through them, he didn't know one stitch from an ant's trail through sugar, but he knew how to ask. Where would he find the very best book to tell knitters how to make impossibly intricate stitches? Could they tell him?

Sure. The store actually had a copy of such a book but it was just to look at, not to sell. Yes, they could order one for him. He could pay now and it would be sent to him, or it could come to them and they could notify him when they had it.

He chose to pay. He still had a lot to do getting his equipment ready to move, and finish his apprentice agreement at the shop in Eureka Springs. A couple more weeks should do it and then here came the book. He held it to his chest, tilted his face upward and pled with the Powers above him to make the book say what he could not.

Finally, his possessions loaded aboard and the precious book wrapped in white paper and tied with a silver bow lying beside him, he clicked his team into action. It was a long way to Burnt Tree Junction, and Mark had hours and hours to become petrified that his gift would not be right.

Then more miles and hours to chide himself. "Mark, you asked for help from Above, now where is your faith?" His trembling reply was that he didn't know.

He spent the night in the nearby town of Wishbone Hollow, and got an early start the next morning. He would head east on Ridge Road and it would take him to the front door of his new home and place of business.

Back in Eureka Springs, Adam Bentley had merely locked the door to his shop and put a sign on the door: "Closed until further notice. Interested parties inquire at the bank." With a duffle bag of his immediate necessities, he boarded the van with Joel. They moved out behind the insects and settled in for a long ride.

Uncle Joel had successfully convinced the young tinker that he needed to take a month off to clear his head, and that a trip up Ridge Road and a visit with Joel's customers would do the trick. However, the old man had added silently to his own head, the trip would either clear his mind or make it worse. No promises.

But anyway, the old tinker now had another person to talk with and that was worth all the effort he had put forth for Adam.

At the Junction, Butch knew he had the right plan.

He sat by the spring and beside him was the equipment he thought he needed. He'd spent hours of thought, going through every eventual need and then he spent days of sitting by the spring waiting for the exact right time.

Any minute the oldest daughter (and certainly the eventual heir to the farm) would be coming out with her pan and walking down to the place where that green stuff grew in the water. He'd sneaked, quiet as a puff of smoke, down there to see what took her so long, and had seen her sitting on the rock, eyes closed a lot of the time. Having only these thoughts to think on, he had thought it through and through until he was dizzy.

Miss Emma was not very big, not quite as tall as Dora. She was also skinny. Carrying her would be no effort at all…not nearly as much as a sack of chopped corn. Very important was that she must never see him or hear his voice. That would spoil it all and after the months…even years…he had been working on a plan, this one had to work.

Butch was accustomed to walking silently in dry leaves. A successful woodsman had to be. Carefully, each footstep placed with absolute precision, he made his way down toward the spring. He knew she would be looking the other way, but he mustn't make a sound.

Over his shoulder was the thick wool quilt, and in his left hand was the eight inch length of sticky tape he had carefully removed from a package. It must still be very sticky for the plan to work… and it was.

When directly behind the tree, out of sight, he purposefully snapped a twig. As she leaned forward to look around, he moved quickly around the tree and slapped the sticky tape over her mouth, careful to miss her nose. If she couldn't breathe, she would die. He knew that much, and if she was died it would spoil all his plans.

With his strong right arm he flung the heavy quilt around her head and shoulders, quickly tying it down to hold her arms against her sides. He could deal with kicking feet but not with arms and scratchy fingernails. He'd thought of everything. This time.

Flinging her over his shoulder, her knees at his chest and her shoulders and head hanging down behind him, he started off. He knew, from observance, that this would not injure or kill her. Wounded hunters were rescued this way…and he knew he needed to hurry.

The cave was not far away, actually on the very next piece of property to the Burks. It was a good cave, perfect for his purpose, and he had outfitted it with the items necessary for the rest of his plan.

Practically running to the cave, he entered its dimness but he didn't need a light. He sat her down on the arranged rock and caught her kicking feet in a length of metal chain and clicked the padlock closed.

So good so far. Then he pulled on the slipknot of the rope around her arms and fled in seconds through the cave door. He knew she would have the quilt off her head in a shake and the sticky tape removed moments later, and that was part of the plan. She must be alive and able to assist in her rescue.

She must yell for help, else why would he have reason to be so close by to hear her? He grinned with pride at the way he had thought of everything. The cave was cool, almost cold, but she now had the warm blanket and she could never get her foot loose from the chain.

Now he must stay at least a quarter of a mile away until he heard rescuers coming.

Belle and Dora returned from their chore tired and sweaty, certain that Emma would have food ready. It didn't happen. Not good news.

"Emma? EMMA, where are you?" Belle actually screamed at the woodland around the house.

Then Dora. "Wait, Mom. I know where she goes," and she leaped from the porch and was gone. Belle waited breathlessly for the next minutes, until Dora returned with the pan but no Emma.

Fear wrenching her whole insides she turned to Dora, unable to speak.

"Mom, sit down and don't fall. I'll get Mr. Collins." She dashed to the calf pasture and swung aboard Rascal, her lively young just-broken-to-the-bridal stallion. She disappeared in a cloud of dust. It was supposed to be unknown, but the whole of Ridge Road knew that Mr. Burley Collins was a deputy constable. Carroll County was so long, and divided by Kings River, that it was necessary to have several deputies scattered about.

In minutes she was back, and hardly seconds before Uncle Joel and Adam Bentley pulled in, expecting tea and a welcome. What they got was Dora's frantic voice, "Uncle Joel, Emma'a gone. Lost or stolen. I just been to get Mr. Collins and I'm gonna go find her. Can you help Mom?"

The old man called after her, "Wait! You must tell me just where you're looking so I can tell the others!"

Dora leaped from Rascal and pointed in the general direction of the property fence line. She shouted, "Caves down there!" and was gone, her satchel bouncing on her back.

Joel turned to meet the anxious eyes of Adam. "No worry. She's got her gun in that satchel."

Minutes later Deputy Collins appeared in a cloud of dust followed by three neighbors also on rearing horses.

"More are comin'," he announced to Belle. "Where's Dora?"

Joel waved the direction and the deputy dismounted and took off on foot in another direction.

Another animal galloped in and Dwayne leaped to the ground, and saw Uncle Joel. The old man pointed, "She went that way-away and she's alone with her gun." Dwayne sprinted in that direction.

Mr. Barker was very confused. He knew what caused the problem, but something inside him said he should get directions from the humans before assisting. He looked from Joel, whom he knew well, to the stranger he did not know. Raising his huge head and lifting his furrowed brows, he looked closely at Adam Bentley, his sensitive nose drawing in his scent. He was not the problem, Mr. Barker knew, but maybe he was part of the answer and no one had told him.

Adam looked at the bloodhound that was seriously trying to tell him something. He wondered why the dog was not in on the hunt. A bloodhound, of course! No one had trained this dog or told him who he was!

"Miss Burk…is it? Could you get a sock or something your daughter has worn?"

"A…sock…?" What was that stranger try….

The stranger demanded, "Get it quickly. Please. I have an idea."

The distraught mother woodenly obeyed, returning with Emma's knitted scarf and handing it to the strange man."

"Perfect!" he complimented. "What's the dog's name?"

She just looked blankly at this person, so Joel answered, "Barker. They call him Mr. Barker."

Quick nod from Adam and he advanced toward the bloodhound extending the scarf.

Harry watched. He knew that scarf. He extended his thick neck toward the man that carried it. He touched the scarf with his nose, sniffed and snorted…then sniffed again.

Adam walk past the dog and called, "Let's go, Mr. Barker. Let's go find her." And he again held out the scarf.

Harry's genetic background kicked in. Now he knew.

He must tell the humans where the person was who smelled like the scarf. That was something he could do. He knew exactly who was the problem and he certainly knew what HE smelled like. Down the path he trotted with the strange human following close behind and calling him by name.

"We can do it, Mr. Barker. I'm right here. Good job, Mr. Barker."

Harry stopped momentarily at the site of the watercress, but then moved on. He flapped his ears noisily to freshen the scent. He waved his head from side to get a direction, and off he went. The trail he followed had scuffed dry leaves. Easy to follow.

Adam saw the scuffed leaves and his heart beat faster. It looked like it might work. At lease someone had been this way. Maybe the girl was just lost…but being lost in one's own property did not make sense.

It was commonly known on the Ridge, that in a hunt like this, a gunshot would be a signal. It would mean either the lost was located or the thief himself was spied. So far…no signal.

Dwayne Carpenter, scared spitless about Dora, made breakneck speed down the mountain and caught her. Grabbed her into a relieved hug, kissed her cheek and demanded, "Where to, now?"

Dora pointed. "Caves on the Martin place," and the pair plowed through the trees.

Someone was close by.

Stopping and ducking behind trees, they advanced toward the person, Dora's gun at the ready. Cave just ahead. Stranger standing by. Then came the petrifying sound of Mr. Harry Barker's joyful accouchement. He had done what he was born to do, and it made him so unspeakably happy, he howled again. Just for the sheer pleasure of it!

The stranger, with cupped hands to his mouth, called out, "Found! We have her!"

Dora and Dwayne slipped and slid on the slick dry leaves down to the cave. There was Mr. Barker rapidly wagging his stump of tail. By him was the strange man.

"I'm Adam Bentley. Just part of the hunt. But now we have a small problem. She's chained to the mountain and I have no way to break the lock."

Dwayne reached for Dora's gun and marched into the cave. "Hold your ears, Emma. It's gonna be loud."

It was. It echoed and reverberated through the depth on the cave, even shattering a few pebbles from the roof and a puff or two of dust from the sound waves. Smoke cleared and on the floor of the cave was the mangled and twisted remains of three of the chain's links.

Emma stood and looked at Dora, and their arms entwined as they sobbed on each other's shoulder. Fear, excitement and relief were just too much. The sisters had not done that since, at age 4, when Emma had fallen and skinned her knee. It was Dora who had screamed for assistance, then helped her sister cry.

The 'found' blast from the gun had stopped the rest of rescue party who were now converging at the cave. Mr. Barker, excited for the praise from the humans, decided to carry it a bit farther. Trotting into the dense trees, he found what he knew was there.

Stalking calmly up to the overalled man, he stared into his face. The human was petrified with fear and did not move a muscle. By doing that, he did himself a favor.

At the slightest move, Mr. Barker was prepared to take a bite from somewhere below the knee. A big bite. However, the loud growl was sufficient. All the humans at the cave surrounded him, and the man with the silver on his clothes put the big man in handcuffs of fabric.

There, plainly hanging from the hammer loop in Butch's overalls was a bolt cutter easily capable of severing the chain.

What would happen to him now was unclear. He would not likely be imprisoned, knowing who he was. Also, he had not hurt her and had every intention of being the rescuer. Why? No one could guess and he seemed incapable of explaining.

One thing for sure, though, was that all of Ridge Road would hear and know what Butch was capable of, whether he intended to or not. It was important to know, and thereby be prepared.

The weary, excited and relieved rescue party trudged up the hill, through the trees and slick fallen leaves, to the Burk house. Tea and cookies for all served by a joyous mother, still red-eyed from weeping.

Dwayne Carpenter had barely dismounted his horse and tore down the mountain that Mark McKinzey had guided his weary animals into the yard of old Miss Sophie's place. Through the trees he saw Uncle Joel's van. He heard the snorts and nervous whickering of horses. Something was going on.

Losing his saddle horse from the loaded wagon, he leaped aboard and thundered down the short trail. There was Uncle Joel and Emma's mom. Trouble for sure. But then the shot rang out. Success!

Uncle Joel filled him in. Emma was safe or there would have been more shots, calling for help. He thought of the white-ribboned gift on the seat of the wagon. Better it be left there. After all, he was now a resident and there would be time.

Mr. Harry Barker accompanied the excited humans. For about the first time in his life, he, also, was excited and he loved it. He'd tried before to talk 'human' but without much success. Now here was a human who talked 'dog.'

Could life ever be better than that! Not likely!

ADAM BENTLEY

Uncle Joel and his guest were persuaded to stay over. The old man even allowed himself to be forced to occupy a room in the house. Lots of rooms. Empty rooms that echoed from footsteps. Two of them now had humans for three whole days.

Difficult as it was for Adam to discuss his personal life with strangers, these hospitable people deserved to know. They were good listeners. Life happens to everyone, and each person has a story to tell. Belle's story about Jake could wait.

It was a gorgeous spring day that Mark McKinzey pulled Aunt Sophie's 'lady's buggy' from the shed. It had been carefully protected by its cover, but the years had eaten up the grease from the wheel bearing and dried the softness from the leather upholstery of the bench seat. Wheels needed a bit of adjustment...nothing that a skilled wheelwright could not take care of.

Bringing the buggy up to present day was a labor of love and he whistled while he worked. Anyway, the Burks had house guests, and he was still a stranger except to Emma. He had time to unload his equipment and get acquainted with the household furniture. Looked good. Smelled of mint and lavender...still.

He'd loved the old aunt and was relieved when the family said he might stay a year, and if he liked life on the Ridge, he would be permitted to buy it from the family. By then he would have his business going...if it was ever going to be 'going.'

He was now twenty-two, and time to be looking to the future. As he had prayed that his gift would be accepted, he also prayed that his future would be right here on Ridge Road. After all, wasn't it said that humans should ask and then they would receive? He wasn't sure he understood it all, but he liked the sound of it.

Back in down the trail, Adam Bentley was being introduced to country life. How fun it was to 'show-off' farming and survivor skills now that they had mastered them. Now here was someone as green as they had been, but he was game for everything. He even climbed into the treehouse, insisting that 'someday' he was going to spend the night there as had his friend Joel.

When possible, he eyed the lovely lady who was their hostess. He watched her go about duties, making everyone comfortable if she could.

Widowed with five young daughters, and what a job she had made of it!

The rescued daughter busied herself in kitchen. The third daughter, Joy, was delivered home by a young man who had transported her there, seated on the rear of a mule. No, he couldn't stay. Had to nail a few things together at his house. Could be a storm, he said.

The girl was excited, her eyes dancing and her laugh like silver bells. It had been a wonderful day. For the first time in the whole two months she had been observing the fiddle maker she reached a turning point. He let her touch the wood, and even scrape and sand the fiddle-shaped board that was to be the back of the next instrument. He'd thumped the board and listened to the sound and said he thought this one had music in it.

Just yesterday he'd let her help with the glue. Sweet gum sap, it was, to start with, and some kind of powder was added, and it was heated until it smelled burned. He'd said that was the kind of glue that, once being part of a tree, became actually part of the two pieces of wood and didn't 'rob its music' like some other glue might.

The youngest daughter came home on a horse, ladylike and proper. Excited about her job. Passed around the candy that she said was her own 'invention.' Said she'd demonstrated how three of the peppermint mints could lay on the wrapping paper and be twisted together just like the caramels.

The second daughter, Dora, had a bit to say about Rascal. One of the neighbors wanted to 'borrow' him. No problem as long as they watched out for his habit of nipping sleeves just for the pleasure, and sometimes he got more than sleeve fabric. She didn't want anyone blaming her for Rascal's bad behavior. He was young yet, and she'd take it out of him. Also she mentioned that Dwayne was coming Monday to help with the pig. A little fresh pork would be welcome.

On Saturday, the fourth daughter, Eva, dropped in for a few hours. She was a teacher, and excited that her certification had come through, and now she could get full pay. In addition, she had plans for a Christmas play put on by the students. Hadn't been done before, but she thought it would 'go over' nicely. Adam nodded to himself. It most certainly would.

Daughters! What a wonderful creation!

On the third day the men took their leave, armed with a blackberry cobbler from the berries picked by Dora and baked by Emma. They could drop off the pan on their way back up Ridge Road.

Adam gave a lot of thought to the lady. Past thirty-five as he was, he would notice her. Did she ever think of changing her status? He couldn't actually ask Joel.

He met the customers. Most had some little thing they wanted done. Some didn't but still treated him like a welcome guest, and wanted particulars about the kidnapping of the Burk girl.

The weather held well, and a bedroll on the grass was a new experience. Night birds, insects. The sparkling trail left by fireflies as they signaled for a mate. The steady crunch and shuffle of the hobbled mules as they worked on the fresh grass.

The one night it rained, the two men spent the night in the van talking. Neither actually heard the other as their discouragement was put into words, but both were relieved to be able to talk about it to another human being. One who clearly understood.

By the time they had reached the Burk's again to deliver the cobbler pan and spend the night, Adam had decided a country route was the one for him. By the time they again reached Eureka Springs, they had made a deal. He would sell his home and buy Joel's rig, animals and equipment. He would put up his own business for sale to be handled by a local. There had to be something to do besides what he had been doing.

Details took him a long, boring six weeks to accomplish. He'd look for a small place on Ridge Road for his headquarters. There were five months of summer and fall and he should be settled by then. Excitement that he had not felt for years set him to thinking. Sure, unattached ladies were scarce, but not totally annihilated. He'd start his search for a new direction by getting better acquainted with Miss Belle Burk.

After all, he should thank her for the wonderful three days as her lodger. Then, with a grin, teased himself with the thought that she might let him spend the night in the treehouse!

He'd like to take her a gift, but couldn't, for the life of him, think what would be welcome but not pretentious. Not flowers…or sweets…or a book…or…what did she not have? From appearances, she had everything.

Mark McKinzey had waited a whole week before seeing Emma. Any sooner after the abduction might seem rude, any later would seem to be an afterthought. He harnessed his saddle horse to auntie's miniature buggy, wheels turning properly and silently now, and laid the wrapped package on the bench beside him.

Stepping aboard, he signaled the horse down toward the Burk house, his heart thumping wildly. Nothing must go wrong. He'd picked early afternoon as the time she might more likely be alone. She was.

She answered the door, looked at Mark and smiled. She hoped he couldn't tell how utterly glad she was to see a human face, especially his. She'd been wandering from room to room, wringing her hands from boredom. She even considered asking Dora for permission pull weeds in the garden, but she'd probably even mess that up. And here came the knock.

"Miss Emma! So glad to see you. I hope you're all right after that abduction."

She practically pulled him in the kitchen and sat him at the table. She poured tea and tempted him with warm apple cake left over from lunch.

Finally he got to the reason that he thought allowed him this privilege. "I've just liberated auntie's buggy from the spiders and dirt dobbers and thought I'd take it for a spin. I'd certainly like to take you along if you have time."

Time? What a joke! That was all she had! "Why, Mark, I'd love to. When?"

"Maybe tomorrow? Or even right now if you can."

She could. A quick note on the table that she would be gone for a while with Mark. She didn't want the posse called in again.

Lace shawl and hat in place, she was assisted into the buggy as though she was a grand lady. A sizeable package lay on the bench. It was wrapped in shiny white paper and tied with a silver bow. She delicately moved aside it enough to sit.

Mark stepped in the other side and took the package. He'd practiced words to say, but they suddenly disappeared. "I wanted to bring you a gift. You were so good to my auntie and all. But it wasn't just that. I thought this was something you could make good use of."

The silver bow came apart easily. Carefully Emma pulled back the paper without tearing it. A box. Inside the box was the most beautiful book she had ever seen. A vase of flowers had been embossed in the soft white fabric that covered the book.

She lifted back the cover and read:

Advanced Designs and Patterns
for the
Skilled Knitter
Below the words he had written:
"For my friend Emma as thanks for her
friendship and the care of my beloved
Auntie Sophie.
Mark"

Silently she turned a few pages and looked at the beautiful and intricate stitches and remembered how the simple stitches had seemed so unreachable about seven years ago. Now she could do them in her sleep.

Another page. Her fingers itched to feel the shape of the polished wood of the needles and the gentle tension of the thread. She could do these stitches. She absolutely could. It would take time, but it would be worth all the time it took.

The enormity of it all tumbled in on her and her tears began to flow. Mark startled in alarm, then realized that girls did not usually weep when they were angry. Someone had assured him of that. Girls shouted when they were mad.

"Emma…?"

"Oh, Mark! These are so beautiful! I want to try every one of them."

Mark actually sighed with relief. That 'someone' had been right! She liked the gift.

"Then let's see how this old buggy works. Git on up there, Dancer!" And they were on their way. Two hours later he assisted her from the buggy in her yard. No, he couldn't come in today, but maybe in a day or two?

Emma nodded understanding. The fact was she really didn't want him to come in that very minute. What she wanted was to grab up her needles and a spool of yarn and try out some of these new dips and turns and whirls. Mark would be back, and she'd have something to show him.

Belle saw her firstborn enthroned in a chair at the kitchen table where the light was good. A beautiful book lay open beside her. She said nothing. There would be time later for words but Belle smiled to herself. God was good, and wounds can repair themselves if human's let them. A good friend might also help get the healing started.

Uncle Joel had certainly been there when she needed a friend.

AND LIFE GOES ON

It was at the breakfast table that Dora announced to the world in general, "If Mark needs any milk, he can borrow Rosie for as long as he wants her. If he only wants milk once a day, he'll need to take one of her kids."

Then the afterthought. "Emma, there's an awful lot of eggs. Take some to Mark if you want." With a jelly biscuit for the road, she was gone, hurrying somewhere to do something. Mostly her family didn't ask where.

An early cold spell had set in…the thing they used to call 'squaw winter,' a reminder to the earlier inhabitants that the summer of plenty was about over, and if they needed to increase their winter cache of survival items, they'd better get with it.

A few leaves were turning, and a shower of hickory nuts had fallen overnight. In late afternoon, Carlton pulled in with an unexpected load of stove wood, and came shivering to the door. "I know you didn't order wood, and this one is a freebee. I just wanted an excuse to beg a cup of hot chocolate. Also, to say the hickory nuts came down with the leaves and if anyone wants them, today's the day. Tomorrow at the latest. Remember the squirrels."

Joy nodded. "I just thought of somethin'." She walked to the wooden chests her mom had brought from Eureka Springs to Echo Mountain and now to Ridge Road. Very attractive. She removed the vase and the embroidered scarf and lifted the top.

Pushing the contents aside she exclaimed, "Just as I thought! There's an 'LM' printed on the side. Lemuel Martin. Carlton, your grandpa made these chests."

Carlton, his cold fingers around the warm mug, shrugged his shoulders. "I know. Figgered it out the first time I saw 'em. His chests are all over Arkansas and I don't know where all. So are Pa's. Pa's been after me to get started. About talked me into it. It'll be the only way I can git 'im to shut up."

Joy returned to the table with a smugly satisfied look. Belle looked at the pair of chests and reminisced. When the chests were given to her and her sister, she had no way of knowing they'd been much too expensive. Their Pa had wanted his girls to have the best, even if he couldn't afford it.

Then her sister had traded with her for something, Belle couldn't remember what, but she ended up with the pair. And to think, her daughter was friends with the maker's grandson. The earth goes round and round and so do the things in it.

Joy helped unload the free wood, grabbed the bags for the nuts and planted herself on the sled. She'd get those tasty little fellows! 'Get 'im before the squirrels' was the expression. Nothing like hickory nuts for flavoring winter baking.

Belle thought about Carlton…weather tanned face, eyes that looked straight at hers like an equal. Strong and ambitious. Cutting trees was just a way to get to the place he wanted. Seemed that maybe making beautiful chests was next. Maybe even designing new ones. And there was that day so long ago that he had to talk her into letting him 'rent' her daughter for the day!

Eva showed up for a few hours, bring David Eldridge along to meet the family. Something was surely going on there.

Emma was knitting fast and furiously and being visited by Mark as often as he thought was proper. That wouldn't last. He was obviously working up to moving her into Aunt Sophie's house!

The sign in the yard was bringing business, and his probationary year was almost up. Of course, he would buy the house. Was there ever a doubt? And he would win her daughter...never a doubt there, either.

Just last night Nettie had proudly announced that she was made 'boss' over the wrapping of caramels and mints. She would keep the books and figure the profit, and if more girls were needed, she would be the one to do it. And she was only fifteen. Clear to see, the smart people of Carters knew an asset when they hired one!

Then they would all be gone. Thanks be to the Good Lord for giving her the sense to bank the $400.00 from the sale at Echo Mountain! And not use it and possibly deprive her daughters of... what....

THE SPREAD DOWN BY KINGS RIVER AND OTHER THINGS

Dan'l McElroy was a lost soul wandering here and there...to the river and back...up the lane and down again. Joel was expected any day now and they would make final decisions. None of them good, especially, but necessary nevertheless.

Joel Davis, whom he had met decades ago from the route, had, in fact, sold his van. Dan'l was surprised. Thought all that talk was just talk, and then here he come drivin' in with that new man. Young fellow. Wanted the young fellow (Adam, was it??) to know where the place was so he could call on the new owners.

And now the new owner had already bought Dan'l's livestock and moved in some of their own. Good grass down here by the river. The folks ought'a do good. Certain to. He had.

Now where was that Joel?

'That Joel' was making his last trip down Ridge Road while Adam, back in town, attempted to pull the ends of his life together. This was not really a sales trip for Joel, more of a farewell to his favorite people and a stop at the Burk farm. He had business to conduct, and the outcome would go far to shape the rest of his life.

He directed the insects, now belonging to Adam, into the well-known lane to the Burk farm. No one knew the way better than Cricket and Skeeter.

Belle was home alone. Perfect. Now if he could just get thoughts straight and make his words come out right.

She greeted him with the usual smile and quick hug. Something was different with him. He looked different...not something a body'd put their finger on...but different. She braced herself for bad news. He lost no time.

Seated at the table before a cup of tea, he began.

"Got a friend, I have, by the name'a Dan'l McElroy. He's had a spread down by the Kings River fer a few decades. We struck up as friends way back, both'a us havin' the same sort'a background.

"You're rememberin' I lost my wife a long time ago, and he did, too. Not only that, he lost two sons in a fire. Left 'im all alone... like me.

"We got to thinkin', him and me, that a couple fellows that had a good life, and now was nearin' the end of it, ought'a be thinkin' on how that'll be. We was never ones ta let life carry us by...more like wantin' to paddle our own canoe, so to speak.

"Both'a us ownin' a home place, and bein' a savin' person by nature, we got to where we are by not owin' nothin' to no man nor beast. Bein' thankful to the Good Lord for what we got didn't keep us from thinkin' on what we didn't have...that a lot'a folks like us do have.

"We decided that down by the river wasn't no place to be left alone when the time comes, that bein' better done in a little house in town, like I got. So he put up his place and got a buyer right off, just like we expected. And there's plenty'a room in my little house for two old men to rattle around in, 'thout getting' in each other's way. There's always that if we can't do no better.

"We've looked around and see old fellows dwindlin' down to tha end like us, and they got a place to go. Chances are they'd'a had a family that included a daughter in a position to care about 'im.

It ain't that son wouldn't…it's just that fellows ain't made that way. Mostly.

"So we thought, him and me, if need be, we'd start lookin' around to see what could be had. I been tellin' 'im about you and your daughters and what you went through. Mostly on how things seem to be turnin' out.

"One daughter a skilled knitter, another a school teacher, and there's Joy, startin' to put together her own first fiddle. Gonna make more, I wager, and'll make you proud. And there's that Nettie, just a slip of'a tot when you come here, and now she's helpin' to run Carters Caramels. That's got'a make you proud.

"Then the last…your Dora, steppin' in where you'd expect a son to. Usin' the little she picked up from her pa to build a whole lot'a smarts in her head. Knows 'nough about farmin' to write a book, she does, if she just wanted to and had the time. She's made this place as good or better'n it was when her granddaddy was runnin' it, and I'm the one that'd know that for sure. Grandaddy did what he did 'cause he had to. That Dora'a yours, she does it 'cause she wants to… and demands the right to do it. She's gonna latch onto that young fellow, Dwayne, who worships at her feet like she was the princess'a the land. Good match for the both of 'em.

"Now I said all that to say this, you done a good job and it wasn't so much what you did but what you didn't. You done lost your man, but you didn't let that make you keep those little girls under your wing. You let 'em go so'a they could find a place that fit 'em good…a place that you might'a not ever of thought of. I know you thought about what Jake'd like to see. I can tell you a fact, knowin' 'im in his young years like I did. Why, he'd'a be 'bout nigh onta tears to see them girls.

"So see, daughters are wonderful. Old Dan'l and me, we know that, but we didn't have no chance. We'd'a liked a daughter, but it just didn't happen.

"We done our service in the big war and now the gov'mint sees fit to hand out a thing they call a pension. It ain't hardly enough to make a difference, 'cept to savin' type fellows like Dan'l and me."

Belle had watched him intently. A lot of this he had already said at one time or the other, but this was put differently. Serious like.

She stepped to the stove to refresh the tea. Old Joel had some to say, and he's say it…eventually.

He continued. "Seems we two old codgers find ourselves in the spot to try and find what we should'a already had. A daughter. Like the folks that took your daughters for a day or a month, we're particular about who we get. We gotta have someone special, and we can afford to look around…havin' money to make up for what we'd'a give a daughter if we'd'a had one. The gov'mint shook loose with $8.00 a month for each of us ole soldiers, and that makes $16.00 for us together. Every month.

"Both of us bein' a savin' sort, we ain't needin' that $8.00 to get along on. We done prepared for that. It's just the daughter we didn't get. One who'd'a put us up in a room, or even put up a cabin for us to spend the rest'a our days in.

"So, the daughter Dan'l and me gets, she wouldn't need ta do much. Two meals a day, or maybe access to her kitchen…time, she didn't feel like cookin'. Both'a us know our way around a stove pretty well. And then we need clean overalls, not too often though, and the bed sheets washed ever so often.

"So I got me an idea. It might not affect me and Dan'l, but it's a idea that might get you to thinkin', you with no old pa to see after. Could you come with me?"

At this point he stood and walked toward the end of the house, turned east into the 2-room 'ell' that old Burk had added to get noisy boys away from the rest of the family. The 'ell' consisted of two large rooms with a narrow hall between and hooked onto the side of the main house. The hall led to a generous screened-in porch. The new rooms held two beds each and he'd stationed his four sons in them and gave them room make whatever noise "they was a'mind to," Joel explained.

Uncle Joel had been there when the rooms were built. Smart thing for old Burk to do, Joel had thought at the time.

"So see here, Miss Belle. Time come you need a little cash money to carry you through after these youngens leave, you got this. There's a lot'a fellows gonna get that $8.00 a month and few of 'em gonna find they ain't got no daughter…or the one they got don't like 'em.

"You puttin' out a sign, you'd get the pick of the lot to let have one'a these rooms and the use'a the porch. It'd be my advice to board in that porch and put up a pot belly stove. That'a'way those fellows'd have privacy and so would you. They could heat up a spot'a tea, if they was a'mind to. You could set the rules how you wanted 'em to act and they could take it or leave it. Believe me, the most of 'em gonna take it.

"Now you seen this, let's go back to that nice tea."

Thoughts whirling in her head, Belle followed the old man back to the kitchen and freshened his tea. She set out the remains of an apple cake Emma had baked and hoisted a generous slab of the cake into a saucer. Her mind had leaped far ahead of his words, and she now knew where he was taking her. She'd wait and let him finish his thought.

"So now you see what could be done, come time you need it. Your Dora ain't never gonna leave this farm this side'a tha grave, so you'd have food to feed 'em and chances are, the fellow'd find little things to do around the farm. Maybe pull weeds in the herb garden. I wouldn't know about that.

"But now Dan'l and me, we'll be picky about choosin' a daughter the same way you'd be in choosin' a person for your 'rest home for old soldiers.' I wouldn't take in any others, if I was you, that hadn't put in time for the gov'mint. They might say they had $8.00 a month to spend, and they might or they might not. Safest to stick with ones that has pension money, like Dan'l and me.

"It's our plan to make a list of possible names quick as Dan'l gets down to Eureka Springs with me, bein' we don't know any one down there yet. But first off, we'll be quick to say that if we had an actual daughter, our first choice'd be one like you. One that's proved herself and knows a daughter gotta be left alone. Like you done.

"Like, if we was to be picked for livin' here, we'd stay down in our room or maybe out and about in the woods for exercise. We'd know to stay out'a the way of the family. We'd be able to stoke our own stove and if there was to be fellows in them next two rooms, they'd need to do the same. We'd know that sometimes, maybe a lot'a time, there'd be no need to cook for us. We know how to fix eggs and taters. We could take a tray to our rooms keepin' out'a the way.

"Miss Belle, I keep thinkin' on what Jake missed, but if he'd'a lived I'd'a never got to see his family. Ain't that a selfish thought on my part? True, though."

The kitchen was quiet as Uncle Joel worked on the apple cake. That little dark-eyed girl, that looks so much like Jake, sure knows how to put food together.

When the last bite was speared on the fork and lifted to his mouth, he sipped the last of the tea and stood up.

"Well, now, that was mighty good. But now I got'a go down to Kings River so old Dan'l and me can make plans. Folks that bought his spread find themselves wantin' to move in."

He reached out and patted her arm as he often did as a farewell. She caught his hand, palm calloused from work with metal, and knuckles knotted from arthritis. She held his hand in both of hers and asked, "So, Uncle Joel, when are you gonna bring your friend here with his clothes and all? If he has a pot belly stove that didn't sell with the place, you might bring it along."

Old Joel Davis stepped backward and sat down in the chair he had just vacated. Tears formed and ran embarrassingly down the wrinkles of his cheeks. "Oh, I just can't believe it's true."

"Why not? You're family and there's certainly room for your best friend. It seems you two have already found out you can stand each other. But there's one thing I must insist on."

Concerned, red eyes looked up quickly. "What? Anything you say...."

With a twinkle in her own eye, Belle warned, "I don't want to see either of you ever goin' up in that tree house. Do you hear me...?"

A chuckle wiped away the tears. With another slab of the cake wrapped in paper, he stepped aboard his van to begin the last trip with his name painted on the side.

It was two weeks before Uncle Joel was back. It was a matter of two old men telling 'good bye' to an 'old friend'...the fast-flowing river current that roared down the valley. The temperamental Kings River, rising and falling suddenly, but never failing to provide fish and sometimes turtles for the table. Cool in the summer but bad about drifts on the few time it snowed. Good friend, was that river, and deserved a proper farewell, one last afternoon of fishing.

Then the end.

Beautiful and private was Dan'l's place, but sometimes private is another word for lonesome. Rather than a congenial parting, the two men considered it the funeral for a friend and life goes on. The river would go its way and so would they.

The potbelly stove had to be moved. There were small versions of that historic stove, but to know its full value, one had to have the large one. It provided much more heat for less wood if kept going constantly, and would be still warm in the morning. Coals for the next fire.

It did, however, require dismantlement. It came in five molded and embossed pieces of iron. There was the four legged base, the lower half of the belly, the upper half of the belly with the opening, the door to the upper belly and then the top. If one counted the removable lid, there were six pieces.

The base and the belly parts were very heavy on their own, and it would have been a struggle for one person to actually take it apart and put it back together. The dismantlement took six hours, and the next three hours were spent on the river bank disturbed only by a fish jerking the line.

The next day they were loaded in the van and Cricket and Skeeter were brought in. They had been hobbled to make sure they did not wander to the back pasture. Ready to move out at first light.

They stopped at the Burk farm and when they stepped down from the van, Belle's first impression was that of a ball and a bat. Long, lean stringy, weathered-skin Uncle Joel and Dan'l, short with a round middle, round pink cheeked face, shiny bald head and a smile from ear to ear.

Belle met them with her own smile, modifying her first opinion to visualize an exclamation point Miss Hortense had told her, with a rare smile, was sometimes called the 'ball and bat' punctuation mark. The exclamation point.

They put the stove together and settled in, each in his own room. Took the whole day.

The next day they left in the van for Eureka Springs. Uncle Joel would rent out his house for a year or so, just in case something didn't work out with Belle. Perish the thought!

They left the van with Adam Bentley, transferring to Joel's buggy that would be their future transportation. Adam's saddle horse would pull the buggy back to Burk's farm, and from there on, there were horses aplenty available.

It didn't take long for Belle to understand that Dan'l would be glad to 'help out' in the kitchen any time. Not long after that, she realized that he would just as soon have the kitchen to himself, but Belle held her own. Maybe in a tight...she told him. After all, that had been Emma's domain for the last decade.

A few days later, Uncle Joel approached her with a pair of printed signs he had acquired in Eureka Springs. He shyly showed them to her...as it was her property...for goodness sake!

The signs were just alike and proclaimed:

OLD SOLDIER'S REST HOME

He wanted to put one on the far end of the house where it could be seen from the mineral spring, and the other was to be put near the postal box on the road.

"Two reasons," he told her. "It don't need to be noised around the Junction that you was forced to take in a couple'a tramps. Everybody knows about the new pension the gov'ment set up, but they might not know Dan'l 'n me put in time with a gun. 'T-other sign is for the postman to know where our checks gotta go. That'd be a concern to him...bein' gov'ment, and all."

Made sense to Belle. So now she was officially in business. Not only that, there were two more empty rooms if she was so a'minded, and if another 'old soldier' came along that Joel liked, she could put him up with very little more effort.

Wayne Carpenter had fairly well taken over one of the rooms with his wet-weather gear, his barn boots, leather gloves and an extra pair of overalls. Also, dress pants, shirt and jacket...just in case he needed them.

So when he and Dora announced to Belle that they were 'goin' to see the preacher' and would she like 'to come along,' no one was surprised. It would make very little change in the farm's routine, and Dwayne would be a lot handier. Actually, Uncle Joel begged to come along...to see the first of Jake's daughters get hitched.

Dwayne's addition to the household relieved Belle in a number of ways. Strong, competent hands took over for her own, often inadequate ones. And now, she had nothing left to contribute to the running of the farm.

If she was not diligent, she would lose her place in the kitchen. Dan'l could back up his claims in a wonderful way. He left no doubt that he 'knew his way around.'

Carlton Martin took Joy to Eureka Springs for a holiday, and brought her back with a new name. The family didn't see much of her after that. Every moment was used to watch the old fiddle maker. It would be two years before she managed to complete an instrument, so particular was the uncle with his directions.

Not exactly a show specimen, it was, but her first fiddle was no slouch either. It took its place on the wall like any other show-piece. She was now looking for a teacher who could help her learn to play. Uncle refused, but agreed to continue teaching her to make the instruments.

Mark McKinzey had been squiring Miss Emma to the Sunday services so when she announced her own wedding, it was no wonder that it would be the social event of the month... maybe year. Dressed in glittering white, she wore a shawl just as white and made from a pattern from the book Mark had given her.

The wedding party was at Aunt Sophie's house where dozens of their friends spent the afternoon, the girls admiring her knitting skill. Aunt Sophie would have been amazed and proud if she had been there.

Emma's departure from the kitchen left a possible vacancy that Dan'l was breathless to fill. Belle considered, and then told him 'maybe for the mid-day meal' and he was ecstatic. It grew from there.

The two old men loved the herb garden and kept it weeded. They proved they knew what they were doing (at least, Dan'l did) and Dora permitted them the privilege. Nothing must happen to the source of their favorite drink.

Changes. Gradual but added together, they mounted up.

TEN YEARS HAVE GONE BY

The biggest change had happened when Emma took her personal possessions and moved the eighth of a mile down the lane to the house where she had spent so much of her life.

Belle turned over in the bed, surprised that dawn was breaking. Such a long night. She glanced toward the Carter's Calendar that Nettie furnished each year. Clever advertisement...that calendar! Could get looked at by the whole community every day.

Her heart thumped...as it did every time an anniversary was passed but this time was different. Ten years. A complete decade. Emma and Joy, gone. Dora had taken possession of the farm. These were happenings she would have asked for if she had gotten the chance. But still, they left a strange emptiness.

Eva still dropped in on Sunday's quite often, and always with David Eldridge. She could hardly have made a better choice. And there was Nettie. Little Nettie. Now a grown-up fifteen. Making her own decisions. Carter's Caramels was her second home...maybe her first.

Nettie had a lot to say about a young man at the candy factory. An important young man just three years older than she.

Miss Fenella Carter, who had first asked for a 'daughter for a day' had, indeed had all four of them for a short time, but Nettie was different. Eva had persuaded Carters to let her come along before she was even out of Miss Holly's school and she had dug in...maybe for life.

The old man Carter, the actual founder of the factory was given the hardly manageable name of Cassander...seemingly the name of a French soldier in a novel his mother had read. The cumbersome name was no hindrance, though, and was quickly shortened to Cass.

While still in his teens Cass had experimented with caramel candy, eventually wrapping bits of it in waxed paper and selling it to 'summer people' in the nearest shops in the small town of Wishbone Hollow.

This was not his eventual dream, and as he sold a bit at a time, he worked on his recipe. More of that… less of this… longer cooking time. The addition of the mineral water. By his mid-twenties he was able, with minutes stolen from his 'paying job' to perfect the recipe so it stayed soft enough to chew in the winter and did not melt out of shape in the summer. Quite a feat, and he wasn't telling how he did it.

Gradually the candy took over and the 'paying job' was left behind. It hadn't been easy at first…as the outlets for selling were so few and far-distanced. Long trips to Eureka Springs and Berryville, and later to more distance towns. But it sold well…especially after he found the kind of wrapping that showed the candy through the cellophane, in all its golden-tan goodness.

The specially cut cellophane squares were well worth the price and by the time his son was born, Carter's Caramels were known all over northern Arkansas and Southern Missouri, and were shipped out in a quantity that required a special driver to haul the product to the railhead in Wishbone.

His son, Cass, Jr., grew up in the factory and worked along with Fenella and two other siblings. Cass, Jr., became the president, but Fenella did the work of the day to day operation. She forewent romance and a family as they would take up too much time. She was inventive and got the work done…much like the time she forced herself to ask the widow, Belle Burk, for a daughter as the Carters seemed to produce mainly sons.

Then Cass, Jr.'s son, also named Cassander, was funneled into the business at age 12, and showed great promise. This young man was called 'Cass Three' for convenience sake. Nettie explained this to her mom when she began to speak of 'Cass Three' this…and 'Cass Three' that. Made sense, actually, when one thought about it.

The family heard a lot about Cass Three as the years passed and thought nothing of it, but at age thirteen, she spoke of his 'sixteenth birthday celebration' where he was given a department to manage. The Final Wrap and Pack department.

That was when business reminded Cass Three to cast an eye on fast-fingered Nettie Burk with her good ideas and who worked with singleness of purpose.

Now, no one would ever refer to Nettie as beautiful. She was pleasantly round faced, good teeth, quick smile and eyes that seemed to twinkle. She was like the caramels in the wrappers…sweet, nice to have and kept well. She was, in fact, a very junior version of his aunt Fenella. Cass Three was no dummy. Someday he would run the factory, and a 'Nettie' would need to be by his side.

He knew, of course, that he was at least three years away from possessing her, but it didn't hurt to accept the invitation to her mom's house for Sunday dinner.

So Belle, in her early morning reverie, was certain—sure that Cass Three would eventually be part of the family, as was David Eldridge. Nettie could do worse. At least, Nettie and Cass Three would know each other so well that there would be no unpleasant surprises later in marriage.

She lay back lazily in the bed. There had been times when this would be a luxury, but now it was just something to do. The aroma of cured ham in the skillet drifted into her room. That meant Dwayne and Dora were being fed by a skilled hand, and there would be no need for her to get out of the bed until…well, maybe forever!

Mr. Harry Barker lay on the porch as the ham flavored aroma wafted over his sensitive nose. There'd be gravy for him, and it was a favorite, but he knew it was not his human at the stove. It was not even Emma. His sharp eyes noted the change. Good or bad…he'd wait to see.

The canine drew in a breath and let it out slowly. He stood and shook to re-position his loose coating of skin, settled back of the porch flaying his ears out so he could hear every sound. He knew his duty…such a little bit of it that there was. His person was not up and about yet, and that could be a reason for concern.

A lot of miles to the west, Adam Bentley had severed all ties to his past. He had cleaned his shop and locked the doors, leaving the key with the agency who would attempt to sell it, and it shouldn't be hard to do. The only well-outfitted tinker establishment in the town. It had been good to him, but Adam could no longer stand the thought of what he had done for the last almost eight years. Sighed with the futility of his life. Moved on.

The work had been good for him, after the loss of his family, but then it changed. When a broken leg is well enough to walk on, who needs a crutch? So what if the leg healed up a bit crookedly? It still worked.

So now, with his special saddle horse tied to the rear of the van, and the pair of mules in the harness, he turned his face toward Ridge Road and his future. His neighbor, Joel, had survived it, so why wouldn't he?

He had a niggling doubt in the recesses of his brain that told him he 'was not Joel' but he paid it no mind. He was leaving the past and going into the future, and he'd take it one day at a time.

That first day, he got as far as Wishbone Hollow, a tiny town on a road that led off Ridge Road. Wishbone was straight down from the ridge, and the mules knew to strain their necks and stiffen their legs so they would not be run over by the weight of the van behind them. They'd been down this road before.

Wishbone, as a railhead for the Mountaineer train engines, had a quite grand hotel and a diner that was locally famous for its food. Adam had decided on this stop there as a 'PERIOD, NEW PARAGRAPH' of his old life, and a beginning of his new one.

He would look around town, maybe pick up a few last minute items, eat at the diner and spend the night in the hotel. He stationed his three animals in the local livery where they would be taken care of. Why…he might even stay another day. He'd see how it went.

The thing was, grand as the hotel and diner were, it was as dawn broke that he held the reins and encouraged the 'insects' onward and upward out of Wishbone and onto Ridge Road. At the top of the road, Cricket and Skeeter turned, as one, toward the east. They knew the drill. They had been fed well, and had hay before them all night. Now it was time to move on.

They did what mules do. They ate, they waited and they pulled. What else was there to do, and that seemed enough. Through the community of Enterprise, then Garland, and there was the Ridge Road Academy. The Burk farm would be very close, and there it was.

Belle leisurely dressed and reached for her hair brush. She needed no mirror. Here she was, going on thirty nine and her hands knew what to do with her hair. They should… they'd done it enough.

She made her way into the kitchen, pulled ahead by the enticing aroma of fresh coffee. Coffee entered her life as a regular item with the arrival of Dan'l, who brought his own. It made an instant hit with Dwayne and herself. Good for starting the day.

With a wide smile on his rosy pink face, Dan'l held a chair for her and when she was seated, he poured the steaming brew into her decorated mugs. Echo Mountain. The mugs always reminded her of Echo Mountain, and usually it was a good memory. Not today.

She cast the memory from her mind and blew the steam back from the coffee, sipping gratefully. Just what she needed. No, Dan'l, she didn't need eggs or ham, maybe just a biscuit. Dan'l's biscuits were a thing to write home about, if she'd just had a home to write to.

Butter. It was Uncle Joel who shook the jar of buttermilk to make the butter form a golden lump. He'd begged for the job, and had a rhythm that might be the envy of a drummer. Ker-chunk… ker-chunk…ker-chunk…. Said he needed 'somethin' ta do.' Likely he was right.

She was beginning to feel that way herself. How did one lay down a burden (however precious or heavy the burden) at some time and walk away?

She watched, from the corner of her eye, as Dan'l began to prepare for lunch. Dan'l understood food, and it apparently understood him. He was a true artist. The kitchen was his palette, and the food his paints. It was on the large table that he created his masterpieces, regularly and without fail. He whistled, tunelessly, as he worked and treated each carrot with loving care. Each potato as a jewel.

Food was not just food, it was his life. He had meat a-plenty to work with. Meat of all kinds… beef, pork, chicken and what do you call young goat? Anyway, he had that, too.

He loved Sunday dinners when other family members came. Whoever came was just more of 'his' family. When Eva and Nettie could be there at the same time, they had their heads together, interrupting each other's sentences and giggling as they had when they had been ages four and six.

Dora took what came, as she had all her life, and Emma occasionally asked Dan'l a question and he beamed with pride while he answered. And Joy announced shyly that she and Carlton had 'something to tell.' There had been silence at the table, smiles all around, waiting for what was surely coming. They were not disappointed.

The first grandchild!

Of course it would be Joy who produced it. Carlton, the planner and business man, had completed his log house and now had joined his father in making beautiful chests from the trees on his paid-for land. But now he blushed like a maiden at the excited congratulations from his wife's family. All a part of the plan. Just as his plan to acquire Joy had been made possible by buying her services. One did what one needed to do to acquire what one wanted. No grass grew under the feet of Carlton.

Belle looked around the table, at these gatherings, and felt pride and a sense of accomplishment. Her daughters had been given options, and they had made the best of them. She had been given no options…she was just tossed into the stream of life to swim or die. She'd swam. Had to.

But now, today, her happiness was confined to the momentary joy of the buttered biscuit. Jelly picked from the blackberry plants down on the bench-land by Uncle Joel.

Biscuit and coffee breakfast completed, she arose and went out onto the porch. Mr. Barker lifted an eyebrow. Something was not right, he could tell by her smell. Humans told so much by their smells, why did they need to use words all the time?

Belle stood for a while gazing at nothing, then returned to the house. Mr. Barker shook his head to once again test the smell. Not good. He'd have to keep a watch on her today. He knew his duty, and it usually gave him pleasure but this day it was not good.

In a short time, his human again came out on the porch, knelt beside him and stroked his velvety hide and the rows of rippled skin over his eyes. He leaned toward her to encourage her to obtain whatever comfort she could from stroking him. If he only knew what else he could do….

She stood and stepped down from the porch. Going to the postal box? He stood and shook his loose skin into its natural folds and waited. She just stood there instead of walking on, so he stood and watched.

She started across the yard, and he lumbered his ten-year-old body after her. He was carrying a few extra pounds, mostly acquired after the arrival of the new person with Joel.

Keeping a respectable distance, he followed as she headed toward the treehouse tree. He'd never seen her show any interest in the treehouse. Joel had gone there a lot. Dora took her turn way back when he was a puppy and she was smaller. But after that…?

After that it would be Joel, but now the old driver slept in a room like the other humans.

He watched Belle lean against the tree. Huge, huge tree it was, and she would be safe there, but it was something she had never done. He was certain of that. And then she began to climb the ladder. He shook his huge head and flapped his ears nosily to get her attention. Maybe she didn't know what she was doing.

About half way up the ladder she stopped. Good. Now she would surely…but no, she started to climb again. He watched as she pushed up the trapdoor entrance and climbed through. He saw the trapdoor being adjusted back in its place and she was gone. Out of sight.

What could he do now? He couldn't reach her…he couldn't even see her, but he went to the base of the tree and waited. What if she never returned? What would he do with himself if he let his assigned human be damaged?

Then he heard the sound coming from above, and it made his skin crawl with anxiety. He'd heard the girls cry over disappointments or skinned knees, but the sound was always short lived. Sometimes he could shorten the length of the sound if he went near them, and maybe offered comfort with his tongue.

He'd do that now, but he couldn't reach her. Maybe she would stop, but she didn't. He strained his ears for a better sound. There were no better sounds…just the awful horror of…what…?

He shook his head fiercely to assist his wonderful hearing, but it didn't help. He looked upward until his neck hurt, sniffing the air, but there was nothing new to smell.

Hidden away in the treehouse, out of sight from any human, Belle had crouched into a corner of the little room. No one could hear her and it was safe to agonize. From the depth of her being there dredged up the bleeding rags of her loss and her loneliness. It was as though the massive rock slide must roll over her again and again, and there was no room to get out of the way. No way to push it back.

Her daughters had come first. She was all they had and she must make herself be enough, and it left no room to grieve. As she had all her life, she attempted to fit her emotions into the room provided to her.

Now she was left with open spaces. Tears flowed like they had never been permitted to do. It was as though her inmost soul and perhaps her whole body was converted into the salty moisture that dropped to the floor and seeped into the cracks of the treehouse floor.

Leaning down she seemed to desire to push herself into her tears and dissolve away. Then there would be no more pain. Her heart begged, *Jake, my love, my darling...my all. I know you didn't want to leave me, but nevertheless, you're gone. Never to return.*

She was never going to be able to leave this treehouse, as, for certain, there would not be enough of her to manage the ladder. The walls closed in, cradling her, and carrying her away. She was deep within the pile of rocks and dirt that had taken her love away.

The lap of her dress was sodden and her feet and legs were numb from crouching.

On the ground, Mr. Barker waited, trembling in his anxiety and the futility of his efforts. What to do....

He'd just decided to lie down, as the wait might be a long one. What else could he do? But his ears began to quiver with the excitement of a message. A good message. The sound in his ears, inherited from his bloodhound mama, and the wary alertness and wild intelligence he received from his papa, the leader of the Ridge Road wolf pack, joined together and he shivered excitedly within his loose skin.

He turned his gaze toward the road, some distance away. He knew what would be appearing soon, but wondered why, when he knew the driver was safely out back in the garden. But, surely as he had known it would happen, the two mules and their burden appeared in the distance, heading his way. He waited, trembling with anticipation.

The van stopped and a man stepped out. Not Joel, of course. This was even better. He already recognized the smell of the man who could speak 'dog.' He could help. Certain to.

He had helped rescue Emma, but Mr. Barker had always known where she was. What was wrong now with his human, he surely did not know, but this man could speak 'dog' so he'd go meet him and ask for help.

Lumbering heavily out to the gate where the mules were tied, Mr. Barker approached the man. Head lifted, eyes trained on the man's face, he pled silently. Flapped his ears.

Adam greeted the dog with a pat on the head? "How're you, old boy? Folks been treatin' you alright?"

Words. Mr. Barker, stub of a tail motionless, listened. Not the right words. So he flapped his ears again, and that meant he was looking for a particular smell or direction. A question.

The sound made the human's face wrinkle above the eyes. He knew what that meant...he now had the man's attention.

Adam frowned in puzzlement. The dog had something to say, and it was highly important...at least to him. "What's the matter, old boy? You got a problem?"

The dog was still a bit puzzled, but the sound was better. He'd take a chance. Lifting his head in one resounding bark, he turned and trotted toward the treehouse. The man followed.

At the treehouse he stopped. He stood by the ladder and looked up, shook his ears sharply to hear the sound from above, and it was still there. Quieter, but still there. Surely the man must hear it.

With great effort, he lifted his paws up to the third step of the ladder, leaned heavily against them, and looked up at the bottom of the closed trapdoor.

Adam watched. So unusual for the dog to do that. Something was going on in the treehouse that worried Mr. Barker. Well, likely a squirrel and he could tend to that later. He walked on toward the house, and the canine hurried after him. Ran...actually, and Mr. Barker never ran if he didn't have to.

Adam stopped and looked around, and the dog stretched his neck and reached toward a leg of Adam's trousers. Carefully mouthing only the fabric and not the leg, he pulled back gently. Then sharply. That should be enough. He turned and loped back to the tree. It was difficult to converse with humans, but it was all he had, and this man just had to listen.

Adam returned to the tree and began to climb the ladder. He looked at the dog, who had now sat back and watched, a distinct expression of reassurance in his features. Then Adam heard the sound. Crying. Certain to be...but why?

Quietly, step after step, he climbed. Then slowly he lifted the trapdoor. There, at the far side of the roomy treehouse, huddled on the floor and leaning into a corner was Belle. In her huddled position she appeared to be no bigger than one of her daughters, and she was weeping, sobbing broken heartedly into her scarf.

Climbing the last few steps, Adam pulled himself up onto the floor of the room. What now? Does one intrude on grief such as this, especially when the this one had expressly and obviously sought solitude in the treehouse? Adam knew grief, and this seemed more than the lady could bear. He knew about that...too.

Mr. Barker sighed loudly. While on the ground, the dog knew the dreadful sound had continued but he had done the best he could do for her. Now it was up the man.

Adam, having finally made up his mind that, for the dog's sake if nothing else, he'd see if he could find out what was the problem. Quietly, on hands and knees, he crawled toward her. They were practically strangers, actually, so what actions would be considered proper in this instance? Should he climb down and locate Joel?

With another and fresher burst of sobs reaching his ears, his mind was made up. Good or bad, he was going to find out what had happened. He sneaked closer, drew in a breath to bolster his courage, and reached out a hand to her shoulder.

She startled at the touch, turned suddenly facing him with red and swollen eyes and sodden cheeks. Her carefully brushed hair had escaped its combs and hung damply around her face.

Adam sought for words. "Belle, my dear, what can have happened so dreadfully? Can you tell me?"

She couldn't, but she did something better. She turned and held her arms toward him. He pulled her close and rocked back and forth as though comforting a child. Maybe it would help. He had plenty of time. No one was expecting him to be anywhere in particular, and likely never would for the rest of his life. So he waited. At least she wasn't pulling away.

Finally she found a voice. "Sorry! It just hit me all of a sudden. Today is ten years." Sobs and more tears. Snubs and a ragged breath. She continued.

"Ten years. The rock slide...exactly ten years ago today. It just...." and words failed her.

"I know, Miss Belle. Some things just got no answer." A quick thought. Should he or shouldn't he. If he added his grief to hers would it make hers lighter...or not? Well, here goes, and he'd try.

"Miss Belle, no one knows more than I what you mean. It was eight years for me, back in November. Anniversaries are dreadful. Sometimes we just have to cry and deal with it. We didn't cause what happened to us, but we're the ones expected to go on."

She looked up, nodded understanding, and again dissolved into her tears. He held her more closely and was amazed when his own eyes began to water, and a tear flowed down and fell against her hair.

Mr. Barker, at the roots of the giant oak, heard the periods of quiet and was encouraged. Humans could talk with humans better than he could, and he had done the right thing for her. He'd sent the man to her, and now he'd just lie here until he knew everything was alright.

Then he heard quiet human words, both those of his human and the other one. He recognized the tone of the words. Good. Very good. Still he waited, eyes drooping, ears spread to better catch any sound from above.

It was considerably over an hour later that they came down. When her sobs died away, and when his own moist eyes were dried, the words had begun.

These two, essentially strangers, had poured out their hearts to each other in a language only learned by great loss. The pain of the loneliness and the seeming inability to get the courage to start looking around again for a preplacement to their loss. Their burdens so similar yet so different. A woman alone with five daughters, firmly intent on her duty…and he, totally bereft of his reason for living, and it happening within the space of a week. Epidemics steal their victims rapidly and permanently…just as do rock slides.

While Cricket and Skeeter squirmed in their harnesses, eager to get to the calf pasture, and the saddle horse switching the flies with her long tail, the two talked. And talked.

In an hour and a half, the pair knew each other better than if they had 'courted' for six months. Courting so often showed only the best side in the most appropriate circumstances of two people, but grief and agony strip away pretenses and the real person, hiding inside, is revealed. Quickly. Efficiently.

Without words being said to that effect, both of these persons, ages nearing forty, knew they would be together. It would be just a matter of time, and the merger only made sense.

Later that day, somehow they found time for whispered words. They decided, due to circumstances and when all was added together, a month would be long enough to wait. During which time he would make several 'business' runs to reassure his new customers that they had not been deserted. This would give them both time to discover any hesitation they might feel at the suddenness of this relationship. Until then, Adam would spend his nights in his van.

He managed to be back on Sundays to escort her to the services, establishing an open courtship relationship. He could also be present at the dinners lovingly prepared by Dan'l. It was during one of these dinners that Adam became acquainted with Mark, the neighbor and wheelwright. A lot was said in a few words.

Yes, Mark was very happy except for one thing. Running a business alone meant someone had to be there every minute. Customers expected that. Adam listened to the young man walk boldly into the 'trap' he was planning to set. The sharpening business and the wheel fixing business were first cousins from any way a body looked at it. Two owners would mean time off when desired or was necessary.

Besides, Adam had never planned to spend the remainder of his life on the road…as Joel had. Adding his advertising sign to Mark's, and financing a building large enough for both businesses, came out of an after-Sunday-dinner-visit. *Hang in there Mark. Another month should do it.*

The wedding party consisted of family. Mark and Emma, Dora and Dwayne, Joy, plumply pregnant, with Carlton protectively close. David was happy to bring Eva, and Cass Three was present with Nettie. He was determined that nothing happen to her for the next 2 or 3 years. He was a business man to the core, a true Carter, and she was certainly made for his business. Love was easy, but a business partner must be sought for and courted.

Uncle Joel was on hand to give his blessing…wouldn't have it any other way, but Dan'l chose to stay and prepare the celebration dinner. Who would have thought otherwise?

Mr. Barker snoozed on the roomy porch, as was the due of any old bloodhound. Among the thoughts that roamed around in the mostly-unused canine brain was the assurance that the household addition of the man who could talk 'dog' was entirely his own idea and he had brought it about while lying at the root of the oak.

When Adam again resumed his route, beside him was a comfortable addition of a chair, handy for conversation with the driver, and occupied by the lady of his dreams.

With a smiling sense of freedom, Belle waved goodbye to the family, accepted a hug from Uncle Joel, and gave a head and neck rub to the faithful dog. Mr. Barker submitted to the treatment, knowing she could not speak 'dog' and that was all she knew to do. He also knew he was right to let her go without a fuss, as he might have done had it been with someone other than the man.

The talk along Ridge Road was interesting. The bride going along on the van…?

But if that was the way a couple wished to spend their honeymoon, who were they to make a comment…though they actually did make many comments. News was often scarce and one gossiped about whatever they could. Even made some up when necessary.

Interesting it was to Belle, that as much as she talked with Adam, her mind also talked with Jake. Gone, suddenly without warning, had left her with much unsaid and she had hardly had time during the next decade to think on it…to say nothing of having someone to say it to. Who could possibly under the sudden and horrible finality of that day except Adam?

Finally, she knew she must write a letter. Oh, of course Jake could not receive a letter, but that didn't matter. It was the writing that was important. Totally essential to her sanity. She would do what she had to do.

Adam was notified that his business had sold and he must come and sign the final papers and pick up the few tools he had kept in reserve. Belle opted not to go with him. This would give her the time she needed.

On the decorative stationery that come with her from Echo Mountain, she began to write from her heart.

Dear Jake, my rescuer and my first love.

I know you cannot receive this note, and I also know that you had no way of knowing how I made out without you. If you had been permitted to know, it would have made you sad, and you explained to me that there is no sadness where you are now.

I have to tell you of the children. I let them do what they chose to do and not what I was taught, and it seemed to be right. The girls are married or are intended, to excellent young men, much the same as you were.

Your Uncle Joel has been a big help, but he was not able to work with me through the grief you left behind. So it was on the tenth anniversary that an answer came, and I know that if you could have provided it, you would have.

Since you could not, the next best thing happened on that day. You told me many times of the way angels are assigned to watch over humans, and to have charge over them if the humans will permit it. I only half believed you because it sounded too wonderful. If there had been an angel for me, why was I left alone to suffer as I had been when you found me, but then, on that day a few weeks ago there came the anniversary of your departure, I knew. I knew suddenly that you had been right.

My angel knew I would not have been ready to come away with you if my buggy had not broken, and if I had found a way to survive. You found me at the exact right moment, and that couldn't have happened by coincidence. I know you said you didn't much believe in coincidences. Also, if you'd not been so busy and not have had time to look around at Echo Mountain, you might have chosen another girl. Now I know there are angels.

There is another man in my life now, and I know he is my second love, as I am his second love. If he had come sooner, I would have turned him away as I did several who tried to see me. I did not have time to learn to care for another man when I had five little girls to care for.

Then the girls went away…one by one. I suddenly had time, and I climbed in your treehouse from sheer and painful loneliness. It was at that time the answer came in the form of a man who needed someone as badly as I. These things don't happen coincidentally. They are made to happen, and as you were not there to make something happen, it would have been assigned to an angel. That's what you taught me.

So now I have a second love and have been blessed. I know that if you were where you could know about me, you would have wanted this for me. This is the only way I have of telling you.

I'll love you forever, and I have room for another who needs me as badly as you did. He is my second love. So, until I see you, I remain,

Your loving first love, Belle

Belle rolled up the letter, carefully written on the expensive stationery and sealed in a decorated envelope. She inserted it into a shiny clean Mason jar meant for canning vegetables.

Taking the shovel from beside the garden gate, she walked resolutely to the massive oak that held the treehouse. With a determined thrust of her foot, she gathered clods of the rich soil of the Arkansas mountain. When the hole she dug was fully a foot deep, she placed the jar at the bottom and scooped the black dirt over it.

She smoothed the top and stood back, leaning on the shovel and surveying her work.

Mr. Barker, who had followed her to the garden gate and back, noted with relief that she did not climb the ladder. He had not expected her to, but humans are tricky. She had not smelled bad. She had smelled like she should have, and she was making the face humans make when they're happy.

So he was not worried, just curious. She had put something in the hole on purpose, and had covered it, on purpose, the way he would have buried a bone if there were another dog that might take it.

She nodded her head up and down, and that was another thing humans did that was not bad. She looked at him then reached down and patted his head. When her hand stopped, he moved over to where the hole had been and stretched out on it as though to keep whatever was down there…down there forever.

She knelt and gave him the head and neck rub she liked to do, and he stood and walked with her to the house. Everything was as it should be, and there was a chance that, being with the man, she might even learn a few 'dog' words.

Possible, actually.

PART II

LOVE AND A LOCOMOTIVE

IRON PONY

"But you're…uh…a girl!"

"Yes, sir," she answered decisively. "Always have been. I'm thinkin' it might be a mite harder'n bein' someone else…but I manage."

"But here on your application it says 'Lennie M.'? We naturally assumed…."

"Oh, that. The application blank said middle initial. Didn't know you wanted my middle name spelled out. It's Marie after my Gram."

"This is actually your name?"

The girl (young woman?) nodded, her red curls bouncing on her forehead. "Yes, that's me accordin' to the papers made out by the midwife. I was to be the last'a the grand youngens, and Grandad never had one named after him. It was really important to 'im for that to happen." She paused and studied the man's face. Had she said enough? If one talked too long, the listener might quite listening, or so she'd been told.

"I was to be Leonard 'afore I took a breath. It ain't never been a problem…unless there's a problem now."

The man at the desk fingered the application absently. Such a disappointment. It had looked so good on paper. Someone who fulfilled the requirement and wanted the position so bad that he'd sent it in a month before he (?) actually became 18. And now there stood before him a well-built young lady…maybe five foot seven. A no-nonsense cap on the bushy, red curls, and a dress made of red and blue gingham plaid.

"I regret to say it, Miss, but…."

"Wait, sir. What part'a the requirement do I not match? Nothin' was said about not bein' a girl."

"But the person would have to lift bags and…."

"Try me."

"And help old folks off and on and…."

"Try me. And I think the job would also be to quiet restless children, revive someone who fainted, take water to the thirsty, and maybe sweep out the debris at a rest stop…. Sir."

Mr. Andrew Hackett listened and nodded. In spite of the dress, this applicant looked good. Well, that wasn't everything. "This position requires a proficiency with…."

"A weapon? Try me. Granddad had me shootin' rattlers when I was twelve. Said it wasn't safe for me not to, livin' on Willow Bluff like I do."

"Well, certainly that is one thing we would have to know before anyone was hired." Then he realized what he had just said… sounding like he really could hire this determined person. He could just imagine what his superiors would think if he even suggested it.

"Sir? Could I say another thing? Somethin' I noticed."

"Why not?" Mr. Hackett shrugged. At least this conversation was entertaining. He couldn't wait to tell the fellows at lunch.

"Thank you, sir. It's over at McCafferty's Corner diner. It's located here in Wishbone where the train takes on water, and the fellows come over to get their six-inch buns. Even the leftover ones, they're so good. I hear 'em talkin' and sometimes I ask questions. I'm friendly, and love to talk, but I hardly get time to get to know'em, till they're gone and someone else is there.

"So, thinkin' it over, it seemed to me that you folks have trouble keepin' a qualified guard on that little stretch'a mountain line. Fellows with marryin' in mind…they gotta move on to better routes, I was thinkin'.

"But me? I want that little route that shoots over to Memphis and back to Eureka Springs. It goes right by my house and I could maybe wave to Grandad. He took me to watch this train go by since before I could walk." She paused. Had she said enough...? Too much...? How could one tell...?

"Hmmmm, well, you have a thought, I see. There are a few other minor problems, such as the overnight stay in Memphis... but.... Actually, there are other people you'd have to see. Let me think about it." It was meant as a polite dismissal. Of course she would understand.

"Thank you, Sir. Is there a place where I could wait while you think?"

"Uh, well, I meant a day or two. I'll have to explain this and that, and it'll take a little time. Can you come back in two days? Then there's the weapon.... You realize, of course, that the answer will likely be no."

"No, Sir. I didn't realize that. I have one question? Can you try me on a 9mm of any brand, or maybe a Winchester Rifle...? I'm thinkin' a fellow shouldn't be the only one hired if there was a girl that qualified. My school grades were good as any of the fellow's... and...."

"Wait, Miss Marshall. I haven't given up. You are very convincing." It took a smile and a friendly clap on the shoulder to reassure her. There was a chance. Actually, a chance for him to make history, and he'd never done that before. Likely never would, unless....

Lennie Marie turned and walked away, leaving it up to fate. The family had told her it would be this way. It was clearly Grandad's fault. Everyone agreed. But she stubbornly had to try. Otherwise what was there to do?

Not her fault at all...it was Granddad's!

All during canning season (the entire summer, actually) and at other times, the old man, Leonard Marshall, would be relegated to tending the current crawler, toddler or small child. What better to do than walk over to the tracks to watch the train come through?

Rambunctious, puffing acrid smoke, clanging its metal wheels on the iron rails, it came. Noisily rounding the base of Willow Bluff, it crawled in sight. If Grandad was spotted in time (holding crawler, toddler or child) the whistle would blast a magnificent three more times. If the crawler, toddler, etc, happened to be her, his namesake, she would be bouncing up and down in his arms crowing with glee.

The quarter of a mile walk to and fro, and the waiting time for the train would take the most part of an hour in which he had no other entertaining to do. Win/win situation for certain. For both of them.

For the next years, the train's passage never failed to make her pause and listen for the whistle, just for the pure pleasure of hearing her iron pony lift his voice in a joyful greeting.

The iron vehicle got its name at Lennie's age four. "What's he made out of, Grandad?"

"He, who…?"

"The train, Grandad! The train!"

"Oh. He's made out of iron, like what Gram's skillet is made of. It's called a special kind of metal, and is very heavy and hard to break."

"Oh. See how he has round feet so he can go faster and stay on the skinny trail. See how his knees make his hooves work?"

Grandad nodded, agreeably. "Where's his face?"

"Up front, Grandad! Can't you see anything?"

And that was the day the clanking, smoking traveler on the Memphis & Little Rock Railway, that swung through Eureka Springs on its way south, became a personality and acquired a gender.

It was at the little girl's age ten that Gran had asked, "What kind of doll to you want for your birthday?"

A thoughtful sigh, and a recitation of last gifts. "I have a teddy, kitty, dog and clown. Then last year you made Annabelle and she is just as new and pretty as when you gave her to me. I take very good care of her."

"I know you do. So what do you want this year?"

"What I REALLY want is to ride the train all the way to Memphis and come back but I know I can't have that."

Gran's head tilted in thoughtful silence, then, "Maybe not all the way to Memphis, but maybe to Berryville. Maybe your papa would be there to meet you some day that he has to go, anyway."

"Oh, could I? And you could go with me?"

"Hmm, well, maybe not, but I'd bet Grandad would go."

And he did.

Grandad and his namesake boarded the Mountaineer at the town of Wishbone Hollow and rode to Berryville where Papa (he had to make the trip anyway) met them.

Lennie got to lean her face against the window and wave at the spot where Grandad and she had stood and watched…too many times to count them. The car was practically empty so she was permitted to cross the aisle to enjoy the view from both sides.

Then the uniformed guard came strolling through the car, greeting passengers on both sides. Shaking hands with the men who offered a hand, and touching a finger to his cap at the ladies. Handsome rascal, he was, uniformed in midnight blue all the way down to his shiny black shoes.

He came close to Lennie and extended his hand toward her. She looked up into his serious face and knew he had not made a mistake. With a leap of joyful pleasure, she lifted her hand to him and he nodded, smiled and shook her hand…and when he let go, in her hand were two pieces of red candy. They were wrapped in the paper that shows the candy inside…almost like a coating of glass.

Without a word, he shook hands with Grandad and moved on down the aisle. Lennie looked at the candy in her hand and solemnly offered one to Grandad, who politely refused.

Untwisting the ends of the paper and popping the candy in her mouth, she smoothed the paper carefully and tucked it in her pocket. There were always uses for paper that could be seen through like a window and the sharp, spicy taste of the cinnamon candy would forever remind her of that gift.

The guard made a trip back through the car but did not stop. Lennie studied him and the proud way he walked, and the seed of an idea was pushed into the fertile soil of her mind. He was proud of his job, this man was, and why wouldn't he be? He practically lived on the wonderful train.

It was back when she was barely seven, however, that the children's games started. One person alone could not be an entire train, and her brothers were too old to play. Next door (actually farther than that but near enough to be heard if one yelled) were the Barkers, and Orville was almost nine, with sisters six and five.

Four persons could make a 'people' train. Engine, coal car, and two passenger cars. Orville did the tying…wrapping the rope around each one in turn and tying a knot. This train of two-legged cars, accustomed to mountains, bluffs and rivers, now traveled over yards, fences, leaning sheds and under the low limbs of bushes.

The engine could make the appropriate noises and the cars could join on the chug-chug-chug. When the engine ran out of 'steam,' the coal car (usually Lennie) could scoop 'coal' from her pocket to put on his head. After an appropriate pause to re-fire the boiler, the rope connectors became taut and drew the cars into line.

For the next pair of years, there seemed to be an endless number of variations to the game, until Orville was moved into more duties at home that cut unmercifully into his playtime.

And there was school.

The community of Willow Bluff was divided by said bluff into two levels. The Marshalls and Barkers lived on the lower side, as did the Johnsons. To get from below the bluff to the top of the bluff where the school was located, was an impossible, straight-up climb.

Though the homes and the school were practically within yelling distance, it was necessary to walk about a half a mile to reach it. Or one must somehow scale the bluff.

That's where the inventive mind of Wayne Johnson, age 10, came in handy. He scrounged pieces of rope which he tied together. Rope, being a valuable commodity on a farm, was of serious necessity well 'aged' before Wayne was permitted to have it. No matter that it was well worn; he valued it.

He strung together two pieces of equal length and tied one end to a massive chinquapin tree in the school yard. Tough lengths of persimmon sapling were tied about a foot apart down the length of the ropes creating a ladder that started on the lower layer and ended on a sheet of prehistoric granite near the school yard.

It was a wonderful invention, and Lennie insisted Grandad watch her climb. Grandad swallowed the fright lump in his throat as he watched his namesake shinny up the ragged rope ladder like a squirrel away from a hungry redbone hound. He held his breath as she safely descended, a happy grin of accomplishment spread across her face.

"Uh, Lennie? We're gonna make a little change before you climb the ladder again. Go change your dress into something prettier and wash your face. We're going to make a little trip to Wishbone."

Grandad would have swung her up on Duke's brown speckled back, but there was an important package to bring home. A very weighty package. In due time the pair returned with 200 feet of chain, its links made of strong, shiny steel.

To save the pride of the young inventor, Wayne's help was enlisted to create two ladders...one from the ground floor to a ledge about half way up, and the other attached to the Chinquapin tree. Grandad commented, offhandedly, that with two ladders, a fall (should a younger child loose his grip) would be unlikely to be fatal. Also, chain was heavy, and the weight would put a bit of a strain on the bark of the Chinquapin tree unless the length was divided.

Young Wayne, his eyes shining, immediately saw the value of the improvement. He had a few other things in mind to invent, and if Lennie's Grandad was going to be available, why not get help?

It was when Lennie was twelve and in the last year of her local school, a change of teachers came about, and Miss Dollie Carville appeared. Dollie was a docile appearing, sweet faced young lady with a mind of steel. She loved literature, both prose and poetry, and was determined that her students...at least some of them...should also fall in love with rhyming words.

After explanations to her sixth grade class on rhyming words and meter (the important te-dum...te-dum of lengthy of lines). The words should 'speak a song' and be fun to read. She read to her students from a variety of subjects, including a butterfly in the wind, the eyes of the tiger that glowed 'in the forest of the night.'

Lennie sat in adoring and rapt attention...elbow on desk and chin in hands. Eyes unblinking and fixed on Miss Dollie. The teacher was assigning a poem of at least eight lines written about the very favorite thing in her pupil's life, be it a dog or cat, a rainbow, fried chicken for Sunday dinner...or even the hoot of an owl in the darkness.

At the word 'hoot,' Lennie heard, in her mind, the long and mournful blast of the Mountaineer as it neared a wide corner. That whistle was meant to alert any stray razorback hog or mule deer to clear the track or get hit. And there was the 'toot-toot,' to alert the postal distributer of Willow Bluff that the mail sack was about to be tossed.

There was the high pitched staccato of blasts that notified Wishbone Hollow and other whistle-stop towns that the train was leaving and whatever and whoever was using the tracks was to remove himself. It meant the Mountaineer was on its way and any animal, human or otherwise, would be scooped from the tracks with the cow-catcher and tossed into the ditch.

That night, Lennie could not make her eyes stay shut for thinking of how the Mountaineer could be tucked into a poem. Finally she settled on one.

IRON PONY, CANNOT STAY

The Iron Pony on the track
Coat of mail on front and back,
A puff, a jerk, a mail in a sacs.
The Iron Pony on its way.
Rumbling, trembling on the rail
Smoke streams like donkey's tail.
Whistle screams a warning wail.
The Iron Pony cannot stay.
Shovels full on shiny coal
Steam to make the big wheels roll
Through valleys green to reach his goal
Beside the fields of golden hay.
The pony's hoof is like a wheel.
The path a double line of steel.
The Iron Pony shows his heel.
But Pony? He'll be back someday!
'Cause Iron Pony
cannot stay!

She read the words to herself noting sadly that some lines did not 'sing' the way she wanted them to. She frowned, but was not sure how to change them without losing what she wanted to say. So it would stay like she wrote it.

She gave a bit of thought to a title, but there was only one would really fit with the words. Miss Dollie wanted this assignment to be fun. It was kind of fun, but she knew someday she'd do better.

Maybe later Miss Dollie would have the class try writing something sad. That would be something to think on. When she had finally crawled from bed and lit a candle, her pencil had done the rest.

Magic. Correct title in place. Had to be.

She re-read it several times, viewing it critically in the morning light. Yes, it was only 'twelve-year-old school girl' good. But it was a start. There would be a time that she could…and would…write poems that were grownup, adult good, that people like Miss Dollie would read and remember.

Her mind told her, *Nothing any good can be this easy.* But when she read the words one more time and she could almost hear Miss Dollie nodding and smiling. It just felt 'right.' She couldn't change a word because each one described her feeling toward the great noisy, iron creature she loved.

Twelve-year-old feelings were different from grownup, adult feelings. Sure to be. But she'd learn.

THE TRAIN GUARD INTERVIEW

The interview was obviously over.

After Andrew Hackett had escorted Lennie to the door and given her a friendly pat on the shoulder, she walked away, her mind in a whirl. What had just gone on?

She climbed into the buggy and tapped her line against Missy's rounded ivory rump. With a toss of the head, Missy shook to settle the traces more comfortably on her back and sides, then stepped out onto the brick streets of Wishbone Hollow.

Mr. Hackett had to 'look into it.' Was that whether she could pass a test…or even be given the test? Was it whether she, as a girl, would be given the job…or even allowed to remain a girl? What was it, anyway? What was there to be looked into?

But then, of course, she had been warned. In addition to the family, both Wayne Johnson and Orville Barker had given her their frowned-forehead, squinched-eyed look. Sure, she was known for looking at things from a different point of view, but her actually getting a job as a train security guard…? Really, now…!

But she was Lennie, and she had to try. So now she was on her way home to think about what had happened. Would he contact her? Or would she just be tossed out of his mind? *Hmmm.*

Andrew Hackett had lived for more than five decades, and would never have thought he'd have a day like this one. He had a lot to think on. There was the determined…then puzzled…look on the young lady's face. Seems she actually thought she might get so far as being tested…? Certainly she spoke well, and he was sure she could 'take charge' of a problem. If only she had been a fellow…! Oh, well….

The TEST! That's what would save him! She was sure to pass the written test, but the timed foot-race, the marksmanship, and then, what would they do for a uniform for her? Good idea about the test. That was sure to take away the need for any more thought. He'd send her a note right now.

Dear Miss Marshall,

After serious thought, I have decided to go ahead with the test given to all applicants for Security Guard. In view of that, you may drop in here at your convenience and we will begin. Be sure to wear comfortable clothing and flat shoes.

Sincerely yours, Andrew Hackett

Three days later, when the note reached Willow Bluff, Lennie read 'at your convenience'! Needless to say, it was convenient the first thing in the morning.

Missy trotted gaily between the shafts of the small 'lady's' buggy. Lennie wore a newly made blue serge skirt, fitted at the hips and gently flared at the knee. Comfortable as could be. Her flat leather shoes tied snugly. The weight in her handbag was her gun. Surely they'd have the one she should test with, but she was determined to take no chances.

Mr. Hackett seemed surprised to see her. That should have tipped her off, but she excitedly presented herself for the test as though it was an ordinary, everyday occurrence.

Miss Dollie and the other teachers had done a good job with her. The written questions were answered clearly and completely, also neatly.

Papa and Granddad had also done a good job with her. If she'd been a girl who remained inside all the time, occupied with 'women's work,' she would likely not need to learn how to handle a gun, but outdoor girls certainly did. And that was Lennie.

She passed the short dash. There would hardly be a need for long distance running, as a guard, but the short dash was essential. Lennie passed without breaking a sweat…or becoming breathless.

When the marksman instructor came back and presented Mr. Hackett with a 'bullseye' sheet of paper, the supervisor groaned. All Lennie's marks were within limits and some were dead on. So… what's next?

Painting a smile on his face, he complimented her ability, and said that decisions were made in Fayetteville, and he would see that they received notice of her qualifications.

So she was being pushed off again. "Mr. Hackett, Sir? Can you tell me if I passed?"

The man thought a minute, considering his words carefully. "Miss Marshall, you seemed to have done well, but that is only part of the requirements. There are others who make a final decision. I'll be sure to let you know when that happens."

He longed desperately that he could say he would let her know 'if' instead of 'when,' but the eyes, the dusty blue of distant mountains, below the red curls bored through him in spellbound intensity. Why did he have feelings of guilt? He assured himself that he had done absolutely nothing wrong. Not easy to convince himself, though.

Lennie strolled to the diner and settled into the wire chair beside the tiny wire-legged table. This needed thought. Either they needed a guard, or not. She either passed, or not. She could look forward to the next opening, or not. What was this thing about 'thinking'?

After five minutes of puzzled thought, she treated herself to mincemeat pie and tea, neither of which were any help with the puzzle.

Mr. Andrew Hackett boarded the Mountaineer and betook himself to Fayetteville to consult with the other three who would help make the decision. The girl deserved an answer.

There was old Mr. Smithfield. Also the round-faced and rotund Mr. Canter along with the newly promoted young Mr. Stuart. Somewhere amongst the four of them there should be a way to conveniently and politely rid themselves of this problem. But it was not to be.

The men listened with interest about this young lady who dared to expect to be admitted into the ranks of male employment. It was decided the thing to do would be to have her come to Fayetteville for an interview. There might possibly be a place to put her that would be satisfactory. By all appearances, she was certain to be a good employee.

Dear Miss Marshall,

In regard to your application for Security Guard, you are requested to be present at Railway Headquarters in Fayetteville for an additional interview. Perhaps an answer can be given you at that time. Enclosed is a round trip ticket. Please be here on Thursday, next.

Sincerely yours, Andrew Hackett

Lennie picked up the tickets that had dropped to the floor, and read the short letter. Hmmm, well, this might be good news.

Grandad took her to the depot in the buggy. He had a lot of friends in Wishbone, and could easily spend the day visiting. She would be returning very late.

"Now, little girl, don't let yourself get your hopes up. This may mean nothing at all. It might be a useless trip."

But Lennie, not to be discouraged, pointed out, "But it's in Fayetteville with big stores, and there are a few things I need." Not exactly true, but it sounded good.

In spite of the seriousness of the trip, the ride was pure enjoyment. She settled into a window seat and gave herself over to the rumble and sway of the great mechanical monster that enclosed her. She glanced over at her fellow passengers, her mind inventing stories about them. Anything to avoid becoming apprehensive.

Mr. Andrew Hackett met her at the office door and escorted her across the room to a circular table.

The rotund Mr. Canter began, "Miss Marshall, so pleased that you could come to Fayetteville." (Hadn't she been ordered to…?)

"We have been discussing you and your most complete and informative application. You've done well on it, and your handwriting is exemplary. Also, we were all impressed by your marksmanship on a gun you were not accustomed to." (Huh…? Wasn't a gun just a gun…?)

"So we got our heads together, and are sure we have an acceptable answer for you. Would you tell her, Mr. Smithfield?" (About time, after all.)

The older man cleared his throat and stroked his grey beard, thoughtfully. "Miss Marshall, you actually did present us with an unusual situation that put us in a temporary quandary. It is certain that in our collective memory we have not had a young lady apply for Security Guard.

"We do, actually, hire certain young ladies for duties which they perform much more efficiently than the young men, and we are in position to offer you one of those positions. This particular position would be performed between Memphis and Wishbone, with two nights per week being a stay-over in Memphis." He paused and forced a pleasant smile, as though waiting for her enthusiastic acceptance.

Lennie had been attempting to process his round-about way of trying to tell her something. Trying to gift wrap it somehow. She looked at each of the four men individually, critically, assessing their expressions. What was going on?

Mr. Smithfield's painted smile remained, and the rotund Mr. Canter managed a small frown of concern. Mr. Andrew Hackett had slumped shoulders, as though he had given up, entirely…and not that he would be pleased to give her what she wanted. Young Mr. Stuart had flashing black eyes that twinkled while he sought to hold a serious expression.

A small hint of a smile played around the sides of Mr. Stuart's mouth, and his eyen narrowed to mere slits. His thoughts were as blank as a chalkboard that had been erased.

Hmmm. She moved back to Mr. Smithfield, whose smile was fading into a lopsided grimace. Mr. Canter had firmed his lips into a straight, hard line and had lifted his chin. Mr. Hackett had sunk lower but Mr. Stuart had held his own. The next move was obviously up to her.

Lennie stood up, carefully and with ladylike decorum. She managed a pleasant smile and told them, "Gentlemen, I thank you so much for the time you've given me, and your generosity in offering me a custodial job on the northern Arkansas run of the Mountaineer. So I will bid you good day."

Silently she turned and gracefully made her way to the door, her navy blue serge skirt swaying gently. She silently turned the door knob, stepped through the opening, and closed the door after her. Not making one tiny sound.

Her disappointment/anger/weariness immediately erased her painted-on smile and slumped her shoulders much the same as Mr. Hackett's had been. It would be an hour until the next train headed back, so she found a café that seemed to offer ice cream.

Chocolate. Slathered with chocolate syrup. The sweetness cooled her mouth and throat and helped her think. *All right. It's happened. They told me it would.* Grandad and Papa. Wayne and Orville. And all her brothers. *They said it would be this way, so what did I expect?* She finished the ice cream and paid her bill. Her feet took her, in wooden steps, to the train depot.

She'd lift her chin and smile. She would get over this, and do it right now. She didn't deserve sympathy. There was never a chance, and she should have known it.

She mustn't let Grandad feel bad for her. Sure, she could take a custodial job, and she might just do that, but it would not be on the Mountaineer. There were cleaning jobs in Wishbone she could do.

She was now eighteen and all the girls she knew were married or making immediate plans. In addition, she knew she would marry sometime, but first she wanted to do SOMETHING! Before she became a WE, she wanted to have been a ME. She sighed audibly and lengthily as the magic carpet made of iron carried her home on shining rails.

The rumble of the drivers under her and the scenery flying by the window soothed her. All would be all right. She had just come to a sharp turn in the road. She was not stopped...she was just turned aside. She would return to her comfortable world and regroup her forces. Then she would...well, she'd see....

There was Grandad at the depot and Missy in the shafts outside the door. "You were right, Granddad. It didn't work. So that means that it was not for me. I will find a job in town." She climbed aboard and rode the seven miles home to Willow Bluff.

She somehow found the strength to smile.

HEADQUARTERS, MOUNTAINEER RAILWAY

The young lady had risen and exited with the grace of a queen. Her smile had been pleasant, and she had made no complaint or asked a question. There was a round of relieved sighs.

Mr. Hackett resumed his upright position and the four men sat in silence for a long minute. There was a lot to consider since the attractive and poised young lady had stood and taken her departure.

Young Mr. Brian Stuart gazed sidelong at his three companions. He had recently been promoted to this position, and was being respectful of those older and presumably wiser than he. All four were aware than he was being groomed for higher positions, and could very well become their boss, so the groundwork must be carefully laid. Politeness above all and respect for elders.

Mr. Hackett sighed a great sigh of relief that, though the burden was not totally shifted from his shoulders, at least there were others to help him bear it. It had been his feeling that he had done his part…testing and not outright passing along to her that her chances were not only remote, but astronomical. Also, he did not take well to changes.

Mr. Smithfield had been the source of the employment offer under question. He had been in his position for decades, having grown up more or less with the new railway. The rules they had abided by so far were sufficient, and a girl (woman) was capable and able when attached to a broom, and there was no reason to change it. Granted, this one was obviously of superior quality, and the railway could always use that. Dealing with smoky grime was a constant job, and women did best at it.

Mr. Canter studied his cuticles, fingering a hangnail that must be taken care of as soon as possible. He resisted the urge to attack it with his teeth. For him, there was no major problem on the table. Mr. Smithfield had stated the matter accurately, so it was time to move on to other matters.

He was noticeably relieved when the door opened and a woman of indeterminate age entered with a steaming coffee pot on a tray with a number of shortbread cookies. This was something else women were good at. What was wrong that that girl that she did not see this?

Mr. Brian Stuart broke the silence. "Do we have an applicant to review for the custodial opening on the Mountaineer's northern leg?"

Mr. Canter startled and clasped his fingers into a fist. "But, Brian, we have just done that, and she has been accepted. Mr. Hackett will see to the arrangements."

A profound silence followed while Mr. Hackett cast his eyes about, begging for clarification. He'd see to the arrangement of what? There was nothing to be done.

More silence. The coffee woman turned and took her departure. The ornate clock on the wall continued with its 'plunk, plunk, plunk' marking the passage of the seconds.

Mr. Smithfield cleared his throat suggestively, helped himself to a pair of cookies and proclaimed. "Next item, please. We need to get through here before noon."

Mr. Stuart learned something. It seemed that discussing problems had a deadline which was not necessarily equal to the time in which they were to be solved. He began again, "I beg patience, as the newer person here, I must ask what we can do about the custodial position open on the northern leg of the Mountaineer? I feel we should keep up our reputation of cleanliness in our depots."

More silence. Mr. Smithfield adjusted his spectacles on his nose and lifted his head to better view this person at their table. Then he shifted his meaningful glance at Mr. Canter.

Mr. Canter came to immediate attention. "I believe, sir, that we have finished with Miss Marshall. Mr. Hackett will handle the details."

Mr. Hackett longed to retort, 'What details?' but held his breath. Better to be silent and thought a fool than to open his mouth and remove all doubt. It was an ancient rule he always sought to obey.

Mr. Stuart reached for a cookie. "Let's think now, gentlemen. We have just witnessed, not acceptance or retreat, but a strategic withdrawal of a proud and capable young lady with her weapons still intact. If you are of the opinion you will see that talented young lady again, especially on the handle of a mop, you are sadly mistaken. There are other worlds for her to conquer, and if not this one, there are plenty more. She is qualified in every respect other than being permitted to wear trousers. We may very well see her employed by a competing rail line.

"So I reiterate, do we have an applicant to review for that open custodial position before we are written up for dereliction of duty?"

Mr. Hackett and Mr. Canter gazed expectantly at Mr. Smithfield, who issued a resounding 'Harrump.' "I have stated that we will leave the details to Mr. Hackett. So let us proceed."

Mr. Stuart nodded agreeably and quietly pushed back his chair. "Then, gentlemen, if there is nothing more, I have duties to attend to and will be in my office."

Mr. Hackett and Mr. Canter forced into their lungs a sudden intake of air to temper their stunned reaction. Mr. Smithfield removed his spectacles and frowned, nearsightedly, at the departing person of Mr. Stuart, and at the closed door.

Looking at the two other men, he issued the command, "This meeting is adjourned."

The Firefly rapidly transported her from Fayetteville to Eureka Springs and she stepped down from the iron step to the gravel of the train yard. The Mountaineer was taking on coal and baggage. Lennie moved woodenly toward the puffing locomotive and climbed aboard.

The Mountaineer rumbled and whistled its way out of Eureka Springs with Lennie staring out the window as though her answer was somewhere out there among the trees.

From Eureka Springs to Wishbone Hollow, being seven miles and twenty-three minutes, she came to the knowledge that she had been right, and would make no permanent decisions for one month. Thirty days. Then the answer would be there.

She knew she had reached a fork in the road. The angels that were given charge over humans were on duty, of course. That was a fact she never doubted. Maybe she was being too headstrong and hasty, and must leave it to her future daughter to forge a path in the direction she chose. It was either that, or the other fork was right, and she must just wait and gather her courage. One way or the other must be the path.

She had now been home for the whole of one day (mostly spent in snapping green bean for the canning jars) when Orville appeared. Truly handsome, he was, with an appealing 'little boy' look about him in spite of his height of six foot two. He wondered if she could tear herself away from her duties.

He grabbed up a handful of the beans and began to snap in her pan. He had a hopeful look on his face, rather like when he used to come and ask, "Can Lennie come out and play...?"

It seemed that he had his eye on a tract of prime real estate just off Ridge Road...the best and handiest location. It was expensive, but with help he could swing it. Would she like to take a drive with him while he looked it over in every detail? Such a nice day, it was.

Lennie really, really liked Orville and they had such fun together. She was sorely tempted to leave the tiresome job with the beans. She wasn't exactly needed there, anyway. She did, however, know exactly the purpose of the offer of this trip. And if she was not intending to share the land with him, then she should not waste his time. She cared for him too much to do that.

Also, she had noticed the difference forming in their relationship. Lately there had not been much laughing fun, but serious talk of the future. It was talk that was only natural for a young man nearing twenty. Orville followed the rules and did things right.

So why did she feel the way she did about him? True, the girl who got Orville would get a gem. Why couldn't that girl be herself? She turned to him and hesitated, still holding the beans.

Orville was smart and did not need to be hit over the head with a fact. He knew Lennie too well. After a respectful moment, he nodded understanding (the beans must be canned) and appreciated the save of face that would have occurred with an outright refusal.

He smiled and said, "Some other time…maybe." And he was gone.

Lennie glanced up at his retreating back, sniffed and blinked sudden moisture from her left eye. She turned back to the beans with a sigh for the Lennie of only a year ago who would have been laughingly eager for a drive. She reached for another handful of beans, the crisp, green objects had come to her rescue. This time.

Later, as she blew out her bedroom lamp, she allowed herself a few tears for the knowledge that she had passed a milestone. Her life would never be the same. It would be good, of course, but not the same.

Gram, who had been snapping with Lennie, had watched with silent interest. As the handsome neighbor, Orville, passed through the door, she gave a silent thanks to the good angels.

IRON PONY, FLYING BY

It was on the second day after the green bean snapping incident, another childhood visitor appeared. Papa was digging a well in a lower pasture and well-digging was definitely a two-man job…from any direction one looked at it. So, there appeared the 'other man.'

The visitor peeked into the kitchen to pay respects to the women folk as was the expected act of politeness in a neighbor's house. Wayne Johnson saw the cookie dough spread out under the roller. The temptation was too great.

He entered, watched as circles were cut and transferred to the cookie sheet, and then he picked up a string of odd shaped leftover dough and transferred it to his mouth. With a wicked wink of his dark eyes, he whispered in her ear, "Too much salt."

He ducked away to avoid the soft kick in the shins he deserved, and would get, then whispered again, "Hey, when your pa and I get through, let me take you down to the tracks so you can wave at the Mountaineer. Bet you haven't been down there in a while."

Lennie smiled as she transferred the cookie pan to the steaming oven. She poked another stick of wood into the firebox and sparks flew as she hurriedly close the iron door.

Well-digging took two men. One in the well and one on the rope, and of the two, the man in the well had the easier (also dirtier) job as he filled the buckets with moist earth. The man on the rope needed to have well-developed muscles as bucket after bucket was pulled up, set on the ground, and an empty bucket lowered.

The full bucket would be taken a respectful distance away to be dumped and ready to be the 'empty' on the next 'draw up.' A six hour day of this took the dirt in the hole very close to the high water table. By then seepage would be turning the well bottom into mud, and it was clearly time to stop.

The sun was sinking over Ridge Road when Wayne re-appeared. Somewhere he had rinsed off the mud, changed his sweaty shirt and scraped his work shoes almost clean. Lennie had sacked a dozen sugar cookies and put a jar of water in a basket, her bonnet draped over the handle.

Wayne lost no time in addressing her disappointment with the employment.

"No luck, huh. Well, some grown men are still children and others are lunkheads. They think it can't be done if it ain't ever been done that-away before. I'd say you might think on not bein' in a hurry to do somethin' else. Never know what might happen once they get their thinkin' straightened out."

The he wisely changed the subject. "Your pa's gonna let me run my goats in that brushy strip in the bottoms. Willow Creek bein' there handy should make those ornery beasts happy in the heat of the summer. A day'a swap-out work on that diggin' was well worth it to me."

Lennie nodded. Wait, he had said. Well, he hadn't seen the look on the faces of those men. She'd wait, though, until she got strength to go on. She'd wait the thirty days she had promised herself.

She rode along, relaxed, and listened to Wayne recounting his hopes and dreams that had apparently nothing to do with a decision on her part. That was Wayne...always had been.

He had invested in those crazy looking goats that had ears lopping down on each side...the goats that grew that long, tough hair that had to be sheered like a sheep. There were places that paid good money for that goat hair...he'd told her. Along with a lot of other things. The sound of his confident voice recounting his plans was relaxing.

Sure it'd be a job sheering, he was saying, but a fellow had to do something with his time. And the hair wasn't all. The females...the nannies...gave a kind of milk that made a different kind of cheese. McCafferty's Corner sold a lot of double cheese sandwiches for workman's summer lunches. It didn't spoil like meat in the summer or get tough like eggs.

Cheese always stayed in the sandwich being chewable cheese, and Wayne had a very large cave on the property he had just bought. Didn't cheese like caves?

He grinned, causing dimples low in his cheeks. "It's gonna take a lotta practicin' to get that cheese just right. Gonna learn, though. I got it in my head I can make a livin' on the hair and the cheese, and all the little billies that I can eat."

The mare, stomach full from a few hours of good grazing, leisurely stepped along the newly trimmed trail. The buggy bounced and swayed, and Lennie kept balance with both hands on the seat cushions and the basket between her feet. Wayne talked on.

"I been plannin' to tell McCafferty's that goat meat makes the best chile, and that's what they sell in the winter. That might take care'a what I can't eat."

No more mention of the lost job, much to Lennie's relief. The western tip of Wayne's land touched the eastern tip of Papa's. But where most of Papa's land was low, down by Willow Creek, Wayne's stretched out on a bluff that extended toward the train track.

"Whoa, Bessie. This looks like a good place, huh Len…? We're high enough to see it comin' round the bend. That smoky mule tail'll show up past that grove'a trees just seconds a'fore the locomotive levels out on the track. I sort'a like that."

They sat in silence, munching the cookies, warm from the afternoon sun. A breeze swirled up from down under the bluff. Below them a trestle spanned the cheek, now just a gentle brook. One would have to have seen it in action to know what it could do in a rain storm. With a dozen tributaries, it could rise up to flood stage in minutes.

A rumble in the distance. Echoes seeming to come from nowhere, and a whistle shrilling as it neared the wide curve. The whistle had many uses, but this one was long and mournful…to hopefully remove any animals from the rails, two legged, four legged or no legs at all. Most of the time it worked.

As it neared, Lennie made a move to step from the buggy, and Wayne was there, elbow extended. They walked to the edge of the bluff and watched as the two passenger cars and six box cars rumbled by attached to the locomotive. The caboose held the brakeman who waved, as expected.

They watched it disappear into the distance and returned to the buggy. "I better get you home 'afore I get in trouble. Gitup, Bessie!" And the mare wandered leisurely to the strip of packed dirt meant to be a road someday.

At her house, he held an arm for her, and whispered, "Don't give up too quick. Give the lunkheads time to come to their senses."

Lennie could have grabbed him and kissed him…but she didn't. She just smiled, sweetly, tiredly, and nodded.

Two days later, in Fayetteville at Mountaineer headquarters, Mr. Stuart sat with chin in hand, deep in thought. A sigh, and a dip of the pen in the ink, he began, "Dear Miss Marshall."

A lot had gone on in his head before the 'Miss Marshall.'

Young Mr. Brian Stuart, new to his promotion, had given the matter a lot of thought. Just because something had been done a certain way, that did not mean there might be another way just as good. But how could he go about it, being the new guy of the quartette?

He spent a silent evening, and went to bed early. Julie, his bride, watched and wondered. There he was, leaning on his pillow, arms back and head on folded hands. She, Julie, lay beside him.

"What's the matter, Brian. Can't sleep?"

"Lot on my mind."

"Would you like to shove some of it off onto mine? I can't sleep with your mind going round and round like a pinwheel."

Brian Stuart hesitated a moment, then *why not?* "It was just running through my mind the times that a woman in the Bible either chose to, or was pushed into doing what was considered a man's work. At least, something that would not necessarily be done by a girl or woman, due to either strength, opportunity or strong motivation."

"Tell on...maybe I can help."

"All right. First to mind is the whole book of Ruth. A young Israelite girl who had been born in a foreign country was impressed by God to go back to her family's country of origin because her former mother-in-law needed her. And if she went, it would mean the total loss of her own family. She went.

"And there was the battle when Barak from Israel went against Sisera, a general in the army of the enemy. Barak was afraid, and went to the prophetess, a woman (Judges 4:4) who was also a judge. She bravely told Barak to go to war and he would win, but he begged her to go with him. She went. Not only that, it was another woman of Israel, named Jael, who chanced to see the enemy king come by her tent. She quickly saw that she had a chance to act as a double agent by inviting him in her tent to rest from the battle. She bravely fed him and let him go to sleep, then, even more bravely, killed him by driving a tent stake through his head. Her people sang a song in her honor." (Judges, chapter 5)

Short silence, then Julie, "I personally like the one where Abimelech, a brave warrior, was in battle near a tall tower. A woman saw him and threw a piece of millstone down on his head and mortally wounded him. He begged his armour-bearer to run him through with a sword so it would not be said that he had been 'slain by a woman.' And the armour-bearer did it." (Judges 9: 52-54)

"That's a good one! And there's the time when Nehemiah was rebuilding the wall of Jerusalem, and assigned various parts to his skilled workmen and their sons. A portion was assigned to Shallum who had no sons. His daughters came to work, and they completed their assignment." (Nehemiah, 3, 12)

"And how about Rahab, daughter of Bazaleel, who was an Israelite living in Jericho. When Joshua's spies came to the city, she hid them and let them down from her window with a red rope so they wouldn't be caught. She would have had to be very strong to let down a grown man, but she was determined to save the lives of her family when Jericho fell." (Joshua, chapter 2)

Julie had another to offer. "There was Moses' mother who defied the king who told her to kill her baby. It must have taken great bravery to leave him in the water, to the mercy of the king's daughter…and he grew up under the very eyes of the king! (Exodus 2, 1-10) Really, Brian, I'm sure there are several more."

"Right, but this is enough. I'm going to do a brave thing with a young woman who qualifies as a Security Guard, and the others want to give her a custodial job that she is not going to take. I'm going to see she has her chance."

"Huh, well one good thing! I am reminded of why I love you. Now go to sleep!"

And he did, and the next day it was time for him to write, "Dear Miss Marshall…."

By the time the note had passed through the hands of Mr. Canter and Mr. Smithfield, and had acquired their begrudging permission to send, it was forwarded on to Mr. Hackett.

With drooping shoulders of resignation, Mr. Hackett noted the signatures on the routing slip and added his own. He enveloped the signatures and the copy to send back, and folded the original. He put it among the envelopes and small parcels to be pitched off at Willow Brook.

It was a wonderful system, and it had been a long time since it took a horseback ride into each town every week or ten days to collect the mail…if any.

It was ten days from the time Mr. Stuart dipped his pen in the ink to the time Lennie slit open the letter, and read the words with interest.

Dear Miss Marshall,

We regret the delay in your receipt of this information. Our only excuse is that it takes time to break new ground, but without broken ground, very little grows! In view of your excellent test scores and your outstand skill with a weapon, we are pleased to extend to you the invitation to join our family as a Security Guard.

For the first month, we think it best for you to assist us only on the Memphis to Eureka Springs run. We would do this for every new employee, and hope it meets with no hardship for you. Mr. Hackett, there in Wishbone, will assist you in every way he can, and will be there to answer any questions.

We regret that we have no complete uniform for you. As you know, the jacket and cap are dark blue serge, and the shirt is light blue. We will attempt to fit you as best possible with currently available items, and request you wear the attractive blue skirt you wore to the interview. Black stockings and any comfortable black shoe will be acceptable.

We are working toward correcting these deficiencies in our organization and will appreciate your patience. Mr. Hackett will discuss salary and any other matter that concerns you.

Best wishes to you from the Mountaineer family,

Mr. Brian Stuart

Hmmm, so now what? Lennie slipped the letter into the envelope and went to her room. What happened when you get the present you want…right there in your hands…and it suddenly seems to be too heavy to lift?

But by morning, she was filled with vigor. She handed the letter to Grandad. She watched the wrinkles of his face realign themselves to his smile.

"You made it, little girl. You'll need to watch out your window when you can. I might be waving as you go by."

SECURITY GUARD, MOUNTAINEER RAILWAY

Wordlessly, she handed the letter to Wayne. She watched as his dark eyes moved from line to line, then from the top again. Then he tossed it over his head into the breeze that swirled up from the bluff and reached for her.

Arms clasped at her waist, he whirled her around, again and again. Then dizzy, he sat her down on the grass of his pasture and lowered himself beside her. "You did it! I am so excited for you. When you get time off, you must tell me absolutely everything."

Wayne had built a small shack to live in until he 'got things going.' A shed for the goats came first. Endless rails must be cut for a fence. Goats don't like fences, but they are needed to enclose property.

And there was the order he had placed for the massive steel vats he had located in view of a flood of goat milk that was to come. An act of faith, for a fact.

It had taken a lot of research and thought before settling on the Landrace breed of goats from Finland. That country depended heavily on goat milk and cheese for food, and developed an all-around breed that produced long, somewhat silky white hair, marvelous for combating the cold of a northern country.

The hair being white was the deciding factor for Wayne, but also the cheese making, hence the order that could be waiting for him in the post office. His new two-seated buggy would be adequate, and it happened that Lennie was being taken to Wishbone to start her new job.

"With me a'takin' you, we'd be savin' your Grandad a trip," he'd told Lennie. "I gotta go anyway. It's high time I was learnin' the secret of makin' that goat cheese called feta."

So, bouncing along the trail in his two seated buggy, brand new, he filled her in on the intricacies of this special cheese. "It don't make itself like you'd think. You gotta have a 'starter' like in making sour dough bread. That makes the special flavor that cheese is supposed to have, but after you get started, it makes itself."

Wide, mischievous grin, "Can't beat a deal like that!"

Lennie listened with interest, partly because it helped to quell her small bit of nervousness. She pictured him in the tent he had pitched inside his very large cave. He explained that the tent inside the cave kept dirt clods and spiders from dropping into the milk kettles. Certainly a thing to be desired.

There was the heating to a certain temperature (requiring a special thermometer) and the stirring into tiny curds so the starter culture could properly flavor every tiny speck of curd.

Then, would you believe, the curds were dumped into to brine for several days to harden and absorb salt.

Sounded simple, but it wasn't that easy. A whole lot of things could happen that would ruin a whole batch. He explained to his passenger that he really couldn't afford to mess up when he started using vats. Have to get it right from the beginning. Too expensive otherwise.

Then he had built stone shelves in the back of the cave and walled it off. Shelves for the wheels of cheese. The cheese was usable immediately, but better when aged…the directions said.

He determined that he was going to have a perfect product, and take over the market of the double cheese sandwich at McCafferty's Corner. Lennie nodded to herself. If Wayne Johnson had his head set on the cheese market, he'd get it. He'd invent a way. His invention skills dated way back before the ladder up the bluff to the schoolhouse.

It was later that day that the new Security Guard for the Mountaineer Run boarded the 'Iron Pony.' Then she met Joe Castille.

The young blond man with the wide smile approached her with an outstretched hand…just like she was one of the fellows. Lennie accepted it with a smile just as though it was a usual greeting.

"They told me I'd get to show you the ropes! Boy, was I lucky! I don't even care if your weapons skill is above mine." Then his happy smile dimmed. "But I don't want you to think this job's a snap. You'll be ready to hit the bunk whenever you can."

First were the boxes and suitcases to load. She started to lift a suitcase when Joe made her put it down. "Rule one is that we don't carry what can be put on two wheels…unless there's an emergency."

Baggage loaded, the passengers began to board. Lennie and Joe stood ready to assist. Old couple, but they seemed to manage it. Man, alone. Another man, alone. Woman with baby. Woman with baby and three children.

The mother paused, and the oldest child, a girl of about nine, turned to the toddler. Lennie glanced at Joe, who nodded and raised a finger meaningfully.

Lennie bent down. "Sweetie, will you let me carry the little one, so you can help your brother?" After a quick glance at her mother, the girl put down the toddler and took the hand of the boy, about six. Together they followed the mother to a double seat. The girl sat down, pulled the boy up beside her and reached toward Lennie for the toddler.

Lennie watched for a second, then turned back up the aisle, the scalp on her head tingling with admiration for the woman who had trained these children. She glanced toward the ceiling of the car…may the angels be there to help her to be that kind of a mother! Sometime!

Joe had most of the passengers aboard, and when the last one had stepped on the iron step, he took her down the tracks to where the two cargo-filled box cars were attached.

"Now, we got this ladder here, see, and with only two cars, it'll be easy. We just climb up high enough to see if we got a hobo or someone on top tryin' for a free ride. They'll lay down flat and grab onto the handholds so we can't see 'em, but we can. You can climb up and see what you can see."

Lennie climbed up until she was about waist high with the top of the car. It gave her a view on the entire top of the car and the one behind it. When she was back on the gravel on the track, Joe looked at her seriously.

"You wouldn't believe the fellows who slide off the car and get killed. Just 'cause they hung on for that first jerk, they think they don't have to keep holdin'. Even a bend in the road that ain't very much'll throw 'em off."

He nodded in agreement with what he just said, and added, "…and we got a lotta bends 'tween here and Memphis. Old Line. New lines cut off the mountains and push 'em into the valleys. Make the rails go straight over. Not for old Mountaineer, though," and he patted the iron side of the car with obvious affection.

Next she was sent through the four cars, just for practice. All was peaceful, with only a bit of movement while they settled in. She turned and came back, and Joe handed her several cellophane wrapped candies. "Put 'em in your pocket. For when you need 'em," he explained.

She learned how to operate the stove that made coffee for the engineer and others. She was introduced to the coal car, though that would not be her job except in an emergency.

She was shown the stock room where quilts and pillows were stacked, necessary against a drop in temperature. A first aid kit and a quick lesson on its use. There were several lanterns strapped to the wall on account of their full tanks of kerosene that must not be allowed to spill.

At one point he turned to look at her. "Sometimes there ain't nothin' to do for the whole trip. Then the next time, you'll wish you were twins. I'd warn you, except there ain't no two trips alike. What it comes down to, we gotta be ready to do anything any else does, and take care'a anything that goes wrong, answer any question like we know what the answer is.

"We even carry a quart of milk and a bottle, just in case a baby bottle gets dropped and broke. And a dozen diapers. I know there's a lot I ain't tellin' you, but there'll be a whole month 'afore you get someone else."

"Where are you goin'?"

"I'm getting transferred to the Hobo Run."

"Hobo…?"

"Yeah! 'Course it's really the Holiday Express goin' through Kentucky and Tennessee. They call it Hobo on account'a the hitchhikers they pick up in the towns. Hitchhikers wantin' a ride find a place next to the station where the train goes under a street. They hang on the edge'a the fence and drop down on the top'a the car 'afore it gets up speed. The Hobo Run's been known to have a dozen fellows ridin' up atop. Hard to know how many, though, 'cause they start droppin' off when we slow down for the next town."

Lennie shook her head in amazement. "But why are you leaving?"

"Closer to my home. I'm outta Knoxville."

Sitting down for the first time, Lennie felt the rumble of the rails beneath her, and vibration of the entire car. Of course, she had ridden before, but then she had sat on an upholstered seat. Now she was on a bench in the stock room.

The sun had lowered, and Joe turned to her. "This bein' your first day, and you may be a bit nerved up, I'll take the first nap. Come, let me show you your cubby."

And there it was, just ahead of the two boxcars. Just about the size of a generous clothes closet, it opened out from a center aisle. It contained a narrow bed, a shelf and a peg for hanging a jacket.

"Come midnight, you'll come wake me if I ain't already awake. Then you lay down and try to go to sleep quick as you can. Always rest or sleep when you can. Never know what'll happen next. If you need somethin', wake me up and ask…I go right back to sleep."

Lennie walked back through the cars, slowly and attentively glancing in every direction. Some passengers were already settled in against cushions, eyes closed. The mother of four leaned in toward the window attempting to relax. She had the baby asleep across her knee.

The nine year old girl looked up at Lennie, her eyes bright in the dim light. The little boy sat beside her, but leaned against his mother and the toddler was cuddled against the girl's chest with one of her sister's slim arms cradling her.

Lennie reached in her pocket and brought up three pieces of the hard candy. Putting her finger across her mouth in 'Shhh' position, she reached for the girl's free hand and tucked in the candy, closing the girls fist over it.

With a quick smile, she stood and walked on, remembering the time a guard did that for her, and how she had smoothed out the 'glass' paper. So long ago.

Also, so long ago, was the Iron Pony poem. Very good for a twelve year old, and Miss Dollie had praised it enthusiastically. But she had known then, as she knew now, there would be another one, and it would be a must better one. It would be from a grown-up girl remembering the twelve year old. She would not write it today…or tomorrow…but someday.

When darkness fell, the windows turned black, reflecting the interior of the cars. She could see her own reflection walking past the windows. Here she was, her first paid-by-someone-else job. The job she wanted more than anything else. Almost breathless to think on.

The interesting weight of the holstered gun, modestly hidden under her uniform jacket, brought her mind back. She must be ready for any intrusion…any disruption…any personal problem or distress by a passenger…any slip and fall. These were only a small fraction of the things she must notice and, if possible, anticipate.

Stay alert. Mr. Hackett stressed that point. Remember she was a GUARD and that was the responsibility of a guard. They guarded!

Now, she saw the little man on a double seat by himself had pushed his bony frame into the corner. Huddled against the window frame. Cold???

Stepping into the stock room, she took one of the wool blankets back to his seat. Touching him startled him from his doze, but he gratefully accept her help in tucking the cover around him. There! She had noticed the situation, and it might even qualify as a 'distress.'

At midnight she rapped on Joe's door, and he opened it immediately. Awake and alert. He told her again to get to sleep and forget everything else. He'd wake her if he needed her. That caused a smile…as though he would need her. She slept for five hours before he knocked on her door. They were in Memphis, and there were things to do.

In Memphis she watched with fascinated interest as her Mountaineer rode the 'roundhouse' wheel that turned it from going east to going west again. How clever.

The Hobo had come in with only one hitchhiker who managed to leap down and scuttle off. Let him go! Hobo's engine was turned and headed back east and three of its cars were hooked onto by Mountaineer. The heavy clamps on the connections screeched, jolted and jerked as the cars pulled into line behind the engine. It took huffing jerks that pulled the first car into place, another jerk to take up the slack in the next one. Amazing!

She and Joe were served sandwiches and coffee in the station house, and the passengers reboarded. Dark this time. Joe stood by the step with his arm extended to each passenger. "Watch your step, please." Lennie watched carefully. Later, that would be her, and she must appear strong enough to be of help, not a 'weak female.' No problem there.

Passengers in place, they settled quickly. Most of them had been awakened, and were ready to go to sleep again. There was no baggage to load as it stayed with the cars. The entire transfer had taken two hours.

The Mountaineer, with a full head of steam, headed back to Eureka Springs, the end of her shuttle run.

WAYNE'S GOATS

Wayne Johnson was in that mixed up position between a break from home to fulfill his dream, and the need for the security of home for a few things…namely, shelter when it stormed and Ma's biscuits.

And now he sat on his north-facing bluff looking out over his goat pasture. The track of the Mountaineer was stretched before him. Looking good! He was dirty from having planted a half a dozen small persimmon trees for future food and shade…mainly for all the fancy goats he would have. He knew, from the common Arkansas goats, that they were animals that needed shelter more than some others. They also needed variety of food.

So now he was planted on his backside on the grass, knees bent and elbows on knees, determining the next job. In the stillness among the crickets and bird calls, he heard the rumble of an on-coming locomotive. So it was that time…huh?

He turned his head toward the east watching for the mule's tail of white smoke to lift up over the trees. Strange how the rails rattled minutes ahead of the train's arrival. Then there it was. She would be riding inside. How had it gone for her? It wasn't really what he wanted for her, but he, above so many others, knew the pleasant ache of a dream inside and the painful possibility that it might not be fulfilled.

He watched until it was only an echo in the distance. She wouldn't have noticed his wave at the windows. No matter. He waved, anyway. Then he stared at the retreating Mountaineer until there were only empty rails and tall trees.

All right, Wayne, he chided himself. *Get your mind off that girl and onto some problems of your own. Problems that you can... and must... solve.* That expensive buck Landrace goat had been consuming Arkansas grass for three years, and the two females had their second round of kids. A small problem was looming in the near future.

The need was not yet dangerous, but it was coming. He must find another male Landrace and maybe arrange a swap...or perhaps just a loan. The trouble with having something unique, like the fancy, long-haired goat, there would surely be a unique difficulty to overcome.

Fact was, he needed another buck for breeding to maintain herd health. In addition, he needed the buck before the next round of kids would be produced. He grinned to himself, thinking it was rather like hunting easter eggs; the eggs were there...they just needed to be found. The Landrace buck was there to be found, and without doubt, its owner was needing a swap, as well. Or perhaps he knew who the other owners were.

Anyway, he needed to know. His crated animals had arrived addressed to 'Depot, Wishbone Hollow, Arkansas.' He, of course, would be easily found. So likely another owner picked up his animal at the depot, so...without a name...he was going to be difficult to find. There just weren't all that many long-haired, foreign born male goats being freighted in Arkansas.

Maybe he'd need to go back to Finland and buy another one... then sell this one. That would be the hard way. Oh, well, thinking about it was something to do.

Beside him sat his collie mix. A coyote had put in an appearance somewhere down the line, but that was common here in the mountains. Not being one to dwell on names, the animal had been called Ornery, as a pup, and the name had evolved into 'Henry.' Sometimes just Hen.

The collie was busily attempting to scratch where he couldn't quite reach, the same time that Wayne had picked up a stick and attempted to reach an itch on his own lower spine. He reached over and scratched below the dog's ear, sympathizing, "Chiggers, huh? This here bluff might be called Chigger Ridge for the itches it causes."

Grinning at the thought, he remembered, "Hey, Henry. Our folks back in the old country named their houses because there were no street numbers. Good idea. From here on, this little chunk of earth is named, 'Chigger Ridge'."

The dog registered his agreement with a wild wag of his golden plume of a tail. Good dog. Not much protection, but perfect company and he was happy to alert his master to danger. Chigger Ridge was fine with him as a name.

So as he planned his next job, the thought ran alongside. Why not? A sign would be rather fun and provide a bit of distinction. He'd do it...first chance he got.

So, where would he put the new sheds? Goats needed some protection...summer heat and winter-wet cold. The shelters could be just a roof, with maybe a windbreak on the north, especially for the Danish imports.

Sheds. Maybe one down by Willow Creek, one here on the bluff and one more somewhere. Decide later.

And later, when his herd reached fifty, he'd need more. To be self-sustaining, he figured that he'd need about three dozen young males to butcher, and twenty four constant milkers. Meat and cheese, two of the mountain's favorite foods.

Those two items along with the sale of shorn hair. *Wonder how difficult it would be to shear all that hair?* Reckoned he'd find out soon enough.

Eventually he'd need pigs for the extra milk. And so the dream continued, seeming to expand in every direction. The more he thought, the more there was to think on. It was like the balloons blown up by children. Every breath made it bigger until it couldn't grow any more, and then all it could do was bust with a loud noise and a shower of shredded rubber. He heaved an exasperated sigh.

That was just exactly what he was doing with his dreams and his business. "Gotta stop this thinkin', Wayne," he told himself, firmly. "Come on, Hen. Time's a'wastin'. We gotta go to the shed and try out those new kettles we brought home."

The working shed was cramped and stuffy, but it'd have to do, at least for now. Things would be better later.

ON THE RAILS

It was on the second week out from Wishbone Hollow that Lennie's training got a boost in another direction. It was mid-morning, and they had huffed their way out of the station.

The mail bags were lined up in the order they would be needed. Willow Bluff was the first to be passed. Their out-going mail, if any, would be in a bag hanging on a handy peg, ready to be caught by the train with their hook. The mail for Willow Bluff would be tossed in that direction in a waterproof bag. Worked really well.

Then all it took was a whistle, a short "toot" and a loud 'wail,' to say the mail had been dropped and the designated officer should come and pick it up. It also meant the twenty or so families would be spared the seven to ten miles to the Wishbone post office.

Lennie was tending the mail today. Joe was busy with the broom, sweeping up spilled popcorn, while the little boy's ma was sopping up the tears from the loss. Too bad! But just part of the job for Joe and Lennie, and a part of life for the little boy.

It was about twenty miles out that a flat stretch of track stretched before them, and it was often a good place to pick up speed to make up time. But not this time.

There in the distance was a human figure on the track waving flags, orange in one hand and red in the other. The first thing that came to mind of the engineer was damaged track and human disaster. He applied the break to the tune of a screech, and laid on the whistle in a dot-dash pattern. An SOS of sorts.

When the Mountaineer was stopped on the track, the engineer, fireman and three other men prepared to step out. Joe parked his broom and patted his pocket. "Lennie! Come here, please. You need to go with the men. You're a better shot than I, and it could be a hold-up. I'll stay with the train, and you don't let that engineer get… out…of…your…sight!" He emphasized every important word of the warning.

Lennie patted her pocket and felt the outline of her weapon. A chill shiver passed down her arms and spine, but she was not afraid. She was ready.

Joe repeated, "Remember! Eyes on the engineer. He'd be the first target. If someone seems to reach for a gun, you shoot at the ground. You have six shots. Use the first one. Then point at the suspect, and if a gun appears, shoot at him. Do it! Don't think about it." He was looking at her sternly and soberly.

While he spoke, she recognized that he quoted the manual perfectly. Short sentences. Easy to remember. She nodded and hurried to catch up with the train's officers.

The flagman lowered the flag and approached. "Trouble. Got a big rock on the track. Folks was doin' some dynamitin' and cracked a ledge. We was hurryin' to get it off the track 'afore you got here. Ran into a snag."

The engineer nodded and offered, "Maybe we can help."

"Only if you got a bunch'a liftin' jacks. We got it off one rail, but can't get it out from between. Rock too big. We can't seem to get a grab onto it."

The fireman spoke up. "We've got a jack. We'll get it."

Then the engineer, "Go on back and I'll pull up closer. Them jacks are fiercely heavy." With that he turned his back to the flagman, but Lennie stood watching the other man until he turned around and headed back. Then she followed a fair distance behind.

It took a while and a lot of jerking and clanging to get the cars started again, and by the time the Mountaineer chugged and puffed around the bend, the local crew was standing, helpless, the rock wedged securely between the rails. It was about the size of a dining table and at least a foot and a half thick, composed of the thick, heavy molten material from which the mountain had been created.

The brakeman broke out six of the jacks from their secured position on the wall and the men pulled them to the job site on a small utilitarian sled.

The engineer again left the train and stood watching. Lennie turned to him, trying not to be obvious. Being a girl/woman standing nearby was enough of a strange sight. Joe's words rang in her head. "Keep your eyes on...."

The brakeman dictated the position for the jacks, being disputed with a time or two. Instead of an argument, he stood... hands on hips...and stared. Then they returned to work. With a lot of pumping and heaving, the stone edge raised to their total height, then pushed toward the outside of the rails. It took several lift and push sessions to get the massive stone onto the grass.

The conductor walked toward the bluff from where the stone had fallen and examined the grass. He looked up at the engineer, who strolled over to him. Lennie had a shivery sense that something was wrong. She followed the engineer while looking back at the local crew.

A few nods but no words passed between the men. Then they walked back to examine the rails. The brakeman took a straight edge from his tool pack and ran it along the outside edge of the rail...then looked back at the engineer. With pliers he tapped a few bolts.

The engineer nodded. "Fellows," he addressed everyone. "Seems to be a bit of damage from that rock. The rock is out of the way, now, so you fellows are dismissed with my thanks for the flagman."

No one moved. Lennie shifted into a better position, her eye trained on past the engineer. She forced a breath. Mustn't be caught breathless in an emergency. Weapon at the ready.

The engineer repeated louder, "I said, you are dismissed with my thanks."

That was when one of the locals reached inside his shirt with his right hand, and the others were watching him, waiting for a signal, no doubt. Lennie, whom no one was watching, reached into her pocket, hand in position on her weapon.

As the man began to draw his arm from his jacket front, Lennie jerked out her gun, lowered the barrel to the ground and fired. First shot! Then she lifted the barrel to waist height and started walking toward the man. She felt as though her feet were taking directions from someone (something?) other than herself.

Past the engineer she stopped, raised her gun and fired over the heads of the locals. She still had four shots, but she didn't need them.

The five locals turned and fled into the trees, and the next sound was of horses galloping away through the brush. The train's officers stared after them, then turned to look at Lennie.

She felt herself shiver, and her gun hand begin to tremble. She shuddered from a small shiver of distrust. It made her angry. Why now, when her grip had been so solid just seconds ago? Her feet, that had marched into danger so bravely with, were now stuck to the ground like two tree stumps that had grown there!

The brakeman was first. "Good show!" he shouted. "A body'd think you shot a gun before!" Then he laughed uproariously.

And the engineer, extending his hand. "Now that's why we carry Security Guards out here in these hills. Problem solved…no bloodshed that required so much paperwork. Men, can that rail be fixed?"

The other train officials were bent over the rail. "Yeah, John. Not much damage but it'd'a throwed us off track. We'll have it patched in a little bit."

The brakeman nodded. "They was just wantin' to get us stopped so they could rob the passengers and run. Didn't seem to want us to derail, lessen that was the only way to stop us."

Next the engineer. "Seems they went to a lotta work for nothin'. I'll get on back and get fired up. I'm leavin' the security here with you, though I'm thinkin' they'll be a mile away by now."

Lennie, the security, had not said a word. She turned and watched the man walk back to the train, turning several times stare into the brush where the would-be robbers had disappeared. No sign of horse or man.

The Mountaineer built up enough steam for the whistle, then for the boiler. A chug and a puff, chug and a pull, then a jerk and a clang as the tension tightened the cars and the Mountaineer inched forward.

Lennie climbed aboard to the smile and sparkling eyes of her partner. "Good work!" and he grabbed her around the waist for a quick hug. "I watched! You looked like a veteran old-timer!"

Lennie found her way into the stock room, and settled onto the stool. She did it. Angels above must have protected her, for she knew that the act of moving her feet had not been done on her own power. The accurate shots were a gift from pa and Grandad, but a steady hand was a gift from Above. Had to be!

Then she saw Joe standing beside her with a glass of water. "Drink it all," he commanded. "Listen to the voice of experience. It helps. We've all been through that first shot, knowing we might kill someone. Drink the water."

She drank and it helped. She left the stockroom, and saw a number of passengers trying to see from the window what the hold-up had been about.Joe walked down the aisle. "No problem, folks. Just had to straighten up a spot'a rail." He was correct enough.

Lennie lined up the mail bags. Enterprise Community was next up. Life goes on. The incident would, however, be noted in the journal she kept. "Two air shots fired by security, Lennie Marshall. No injuries. Attackers fled on horseback. Bent rails firmed. Time lost: forty-three minutes."

They were delayed too long for the time to be made up entirely, but there were a couple of spots down the way where maybe a few minutes could be recouped. They would be late, but no damage to passengers of equipment had happened. Just another day.

It would be time for Joe's three days off, so Leon Barker came on. He'd be three days with Lennie, then three days with Joe, then Joe and Lennie would be on again. Ten days on, three days off. Seemed to work good, just took some getting used to.

Leon was shorter and broad-built, hair and eyes black as half past midnight. He was heavily muscled. It almost appeared that he had so many muscles that they must surely get in his way, but they didn't seem to!

He was particularly handy at the water tank. The water for the steam to run the engine was stationed in several places, one of them being a few miles past Willow Bluff. A huge metal tank was held up on strong legs at a height that gravity would carry the water into the locomotive's pipes. That worked well, but what was emptied from the tank must be filled again from the well by means of a hand pump. Couldn't ever leave an empty tank.

Leon loved to talk, and could converse on almost every subject while manning the long-handled pump with one hand. He was also good on the broom and Lennie cleaned fingerprints from windows while the train was being checked over and oiled.

As word got around, almost as though blown on the wind, Leon had heard about the threatened holdup. He had his own comments. "As many of them attempts happen, a body'd think the robbers'd get it through their heads these here guns ain't just to make us look purty. You showed 'em it wasn't. Good for you." And he pumped a few strokes with the long pump handle.

Then, grinning, he admitted, "That first time I was so nervous and a little scared I thought I was gonna upchuck. Didn't, though. Shootin' into the ground is a good idea…scares off the cowards, but they's some that'll still try. I had one of 'em shoot a chunk outta my shirt sleeve…burned my arm. Made me real mad!" More pump strokes.

"I leveled and aimed, took out 'is knee. Walked stiff legged after that, I heard tell. This here's a good job, though. I like the Mountaineer run. Mostly I have the Eagle up into Missouri."

Lennie was beginning to put together the family of trains. There was hers, and the Eagle, the Frisco, that went south. It was called the Firefly because of its decorative wings painted in red on the firebox. That was four. There were loops that were privately owned like the spur lines into the forests for lumber, and the loops that brought bailed cotton in season to Little Rock.

Lennie would not ever be put on the spurs and loops, only the four regular runs. The loops furnished their own guards…mainly being the brakeman.

The Fayetteville to Little Rock was a long run. In time, she'd have her turn on it. The Firefly made dozens of little mail drops, and whistle-stops for water and passengers in the little towns. It needed two nights on the road…sometimes three, depending on the passenger load and whether more cars must be attached. Also, with the traffic on that line, it often had to wait on the siding for someone from the other direction to get by.

Leon told her, "The Firefly is a good trip, a fellow not having a family countin' on 'im to be home. The thing is, when somethin' happens out there, you may not get home in ten days. Sometimes more like two weeks. Could be more."

Lennie was fascinated by the stories, and Leon loved to talk. Seems he'd been everywhere.

While the holdup had been in progress, it was lunch time on Willow Bluff.

Wayne opened the metal pail that came with Lucky Leaf Lard in it and set out his lunch. Biscuits with ham. Two boiled eggs, four fried-apple pies spreading their spicy cinnimony smell over everything in the bucket.

Henry lay with nose on paws, eyes on the food waiting for his share. Wayne had spent last night at his parents' house, and Ma had packed his lunch. Ma always did a good job. There'd be sure to be something in the pail for him.

Left on his own, Wayne's breakfast was usually pancakes (batter made without eggs), bee-tree honey, and coffee. His bed would have been a hammock in the shed. No matter. All that was temporary. He had a very clear picture of where he would be…someday! There'd be a time that his bed would not be a single-person hammock. That was a promise!

While lying in the luxury of his boyhood bed, he had thought about the little goats that would be sold for chile meat. Making trips to take the butchered meat to McCafferty's was going to be a bummer. Especially in the winter weather. Also, winter was when they would want the meat to make chile soup. There had to be a better way. Going into town killed a day.

Staring at the ceiling of his boyhood room, he thought. No answer seemed to be coming. He'd just mention it to Ma. A lot of times, that brought an answer.

Ma made chile, and it wasn't necessarily made at the time a goat was butchered. Ma canned the meat. She took chunks of cooked meat from a quart jar and chopped it up. Hey, why not can the meat for McCafferty's? If they had the meat in jars, instead of fresh, then they could use it when they wanted to, and even have several jars on hand.

At breakfast he'd told Ma. She'd looked at him and sighed, and said it was a good idea…a lot of work, but maybe less than any other way. He'd save time for McCafferty's, as well. More work for him. But then, he'd have the bones to boil for himself. Bone soup. Tasty! And Henry would have a share.

Once he'd asked Gram what was bone soup. He'd gotten a long lecture on the nutrition in the bones that helped make little boy have strong bones. He'd never forgotten. Now Ma had said the same thing and he'd have bones. Well, hmmm, why not?

He'd buy a dozen gallon jars. Maybe two dozen, and there'd be enough to swap out and pick up the empties. He'd sell only the contents of the jar as McCafferty's would have no use for the jar, anyway.

So around and around his thoughts whirled. He liked to keep his thoughts busy on his work, which he could control, rather than on red curls behind a blue bonnet, over which he had no control. It wasn't easy. The grin and the red curls kept edging their way into his head.

The Mountaineer was scheduled for a late evening departure. The Iron Pony sat in the depot…empty of crew and cold of boiler. They would head out with locomotive and coal car only and pick up seven coal cars in Berryville.

No passengers meant only one guard, and it was Lennie's turn up, though her training month had not been completed. Apparently that was not important.

She turned her attention to the gun rack. The upkeep and cleaning of the weapons was a duty of the guards…being the ones who depended on them. No matter. She knew all about that.

Taking her time with the duty, all guns were in the 'ready' rack by the time they reached Berryville. She watched the connection with the coal cars, fascinated by the controlled 'jerks' that pulled the couplings into place. The safety of the couplings was a duty of the guard. Every coupling checked on every trip.

Leaving Berryville was a downhill slope, always a hoped-for event. Then on to Memphis with the coal destined for a factory in the West Memphis town on the Arkansas side of the Mississippi River. The departure time was chosen for the fewest siding stops to let oncoming traffic pass. Coal was heavy and hard on the brakes. Minutes were valuable and siding stops were expensive.

Barely out of Berryville, Lennie began looking for something to do. Nothing seemed available. Joe and Leon had both mentioned the boredom of doing nothing and still remaining on alert. She sat in the stock room contemplating the soothing vibrations that flowed up from the floor, through the legs of the stool and through her whole body. Amazing, actually. She fought off getting sleepy.

And there was her personal notebook.

There were so many things she had not known when she had written her Iron Pony poem for Miss Dollie. And, of course, there remained her decision to write one that was good enough for a grownup. She was not yet ready for that, but she actually could write an interim piece…just for practice. *Let's see….*

MY FRIEND, THE MOUNTAINEER

Mountaineer, he cannot rest,
From blazing sunset in the west,
To sunrise o'er the mountain crest.
Seven cars of coal behind
What's in the cars, he does not mind,
Nor where the shining, steel rails wind.
Blind mountain tops and trestles deep
Pray that all the steel rails keep
For Iron Pony cannot sleep.
Wind and rain and icy steel
Creeping on…by touch and feel…
Pushed by steam and iron wheel.
Heat of summer, burning rail,
White steam making long mule's tail.
Open window, sacks of mail
Mountaineer meets journey's end,
Roundhouse wheel…and gone again.
Iron Pony feels no pain,
If he's not running, he might as well
Be just a pile of Junk.

Lenny chuckled at the last line. Miss Dollie had insisted that any subject or rhyme pattern could used as long as it 'sang' and the pattern was consistent. She read it over, and decided it was all right, for an amateur. She'd save it and see if she got any better with practice.

Surely she would.

CHIGGER RIDGE

Fall was on the horizon…easy to tell because of the multicolor leaves on the trees. Absolutely every direction he looked, Wayne saw the signs of fall.

His weary sigh told it all. Ordinarily he was happy for the approach of fall as the amount and types of duties changed. There were bad-weather days of light duty. Last fall he had just begun to accomplish his dream as he was caring for the buck, the three females and their seven kids was his main concern. Easy to do.

But there was now the Mountaineer in the mix of thoughts. To be more specific, the blue eyes and red curls.

Now his herd numbered eighteen, and the cheese experimentation had begun. Somehow, the time of the Mountaineer's return seemed to catch him on the north side of his acres, somewhere on the small bluff that furnished such a good view of the tracks. That meant he would have to stop and watch it pass. Somehow it seemed to be a requirement.

It the distance he heard a faint whistle and what could he do but stop and watch? Then came the plume of smoke and the vibration of the ground as the iron wheels hugged the curve on the steel rails. Locomotive with seven cars that would be loaded with goods from the east.

The tinted windows seemed dark, but he thought he saw a figure inside. Uniformed in blue (such a flattering color for her) and wearing a strawberry blossom completion. He suddenly remembered that he needed to set some strawberry plants on his bluff, if only for their blossoms of creamy white with just a mere touch of pink.

He grinned as he imagined angels with their paint brushes tenting the petals of the blossoms with the paint left over from Lennie's cheeks. Then there would be a mop of bright red curls that had resisted being tucked under the attractive cap, its rim being trimmed in gold braid. Maybe roses...clustered in a bunch?

She would not be looking...but he waved anyway.

It was going to be a long winter. Good that he had so much to do. The first of the little male kids was to be turned into chile meat. Ma had given him specific instructions, but then said she'd just come on over for the event. Canning meat in jars was touchy, and expensive when the jars didn't seal properly. Doing something for the first time was risky. Good old Ma!

This had to work. The whole operation depended on this and the selling of hair along with the cheese...rather like a three legged stool. Just two legs would not be enough.

He'd tried his fourth batch of cheese, and it was edible. He'd eaten a lot of it, and tried to imagine what would make it better. And uniquely different. Just a matter of time. Sure to be. He almost convinced himself.

The mule's tail of white smoke had disappeared beyond the bend, and the feathery substance of it was dissolving in the breeze. She would be getting things together for Wishbone, before going on to Eureka Springs. There was no reason for him to stand and watch any longer.

Wayne was not to know that she was not to be on the Mountaineer. It was decided that she was due to make the northern run up into Missouri to meet the cross country Santa Fe. A get-acquainted trip, so to speak, to be ready for a fill-in on someone's days off.

She had overnighted at Eureka Springs, the Eagle's home base, and had assisted in readying it for its shuttle run to Joplin. Sweep floors and clean windows, check the supply of blankets because they would be leaving at midnight and the weather was getting cool. If no housekeeper was available, Security Guard did it. The timing of the schedule set to allow a returning locomotive to pass by on the tracks up near the Missouri border.

The Eagle had picked up the name Screaming Eagle for the great number of tiny towns on the route that must be warned by whistle of the train's arrival, night, day or whenever. They were hardly out of sight of one small town when they were approaching another, and the whistle blasted again.

Some local artist had painted a stylized eagle on the engine.

Six passenger cars. The passengers, themselves somewhat dopy with sleep from dozing in the depot, stumbled aboard and seated themselves without much fuss. No children. Even before departure they were asking for their wool blanket so they could go back to sleep.

Her partner on this trip was Charles Cutler, on the last day of his ten day shift. He sank wearily onto a stool and sighed. She persuaded him to allow her to take the first shift. He was not hard to convince.

Checking her passengers regularly, she realized it was going to be an easy run. Ole Screaming Eagle was humming along, clickety-clacking on the rails and sending a soothing rumble of vibration through the cars. Some security guards insisted they couldn't sleep, but Lennie couldn't understand that. The humming of the rails was like a lullabye.

Hey, what better time than this to add the Eagle to her journal.

SCREAMING EAGLE IN THE SKY

Locked in stable…dark of night,
Guards with lanterns…only light.
Breakfast-ed on shiny coal,
Screaming Eagle set to roll.
Jerk of coupling…clang of chain,
Pick up slack, and jerk again.
Red coals in boiler…puff of steam,
Big eye shines its forward beam.
Into darkness, all is right
Screaming Eagle now in flight.
Mail bags sorted…whistle stop,
Just one hobo up on top.
By breaking of tomorrow's sun
Eagle made its shuttle run.
Turning on his roundhouse wheel

Back upon its rails of steel
Sails through small Missouri town
Children listen for his sound.
Every lad and every lass
Wave to let the Eagle pass.
Then snug into its stable tight
He'll sleep until tomorrow night.
For Screaming Eagle, all is right.

She poked the pencil under the edge of her cap to keep track of it, then she re-read her work with a smile. Not too bad. Miss Dollie would smile and nod...a poem should tell something. Should create a feeling of love, hate, peace, turmoil, anger, humor or extreme sadness. Lennie could read both humor and sadness in this one.

There were times that she thought of Miss Dollie with a feeling of loss that she was not near enough to speak to her. Miss Dollie knew so much about what was important to feel. Lennie had remembered, in an instant, how it was all right to add that last line on the end. It was the finality of the final.

Every grouping of the words needed a completion, and early poets often added a final line that was a completion of the whole piece. For her, certainly, the Eagle was all right.

After her three days, she would be back onto the Mountaineer. She missed seeing Joe, but sometimes got a glimpse and a word while the Hobo Express and the Mountaineer exchanged cars. Small problem with this guard job...no chance to develop friendships. Could that be done for a purpose? Maybe she'd ask Mr. Hackett.

And when she was on the Eagle the invitation to Orville's wedding party came. Laura Lee. She re-read it from somewhere past Devil's Canyon. Sooner or later she'd meet Laura, of course, but as of this minute, Lennie knew ten times more about Orville than Laura.

That would change, of course, and Laura would have reason to be happy with her choice. The choice that could have been Lennie's. She should have been happy with Orville, but it seemed not to be.

Wayne also received an invitation, and passed through his mind the thought that he might go. They'd been friends all through school. Knew each other well. But then he remembered the butchered goat and Ma coming to help with the first one…and he also realized that Orville would not miss him at the celebration. They'd see each other a lot, as the years went on, but not at this time.

His profound relief was that Laura was not Lennie. Wayne had known, of course, that Orville had offered to take her to "see his new place" and Lennie had chosen not to go. That didn't mean, of course, anything except that she was not Laura! It did not mean that she was his, or that she was ever going to be his.

Wayne was invited to supper at the Marshalls on Lennie's second day at home. Her ma had created a wonderful party, and had insisted that Lennie must spend the day with her 'friends.'

So they wandered about, even looking at the strange, long-haired goats. He'd invested in clippers and attempted shearing the adults last spring but had rather mangled the job. The first shaggy animals were even shaggier. By the fourth animal, however, he was getting the hang of it. (Feed the animal something it liked while he did the legs and belly.) He'd get used to it. He'd study the directions better.

The goat sheds were built low because goats are small, and that let the various younger animals consider the roof tops as an extended playground.

All the trees on Chigger Ridge (Lennie had giggled at the name) had lost their leaves except the oaks which kept theirs until they were pushed off by new growth of spring. Cardinals darted everywhere. When they were very small, the children called the brilliant creatures 'winter birds.'

There was a time that Lennie had said the cardinals were the red ribbons of winter tying the trees together. She had the most interesting way of seeing something different in simple things.

Lennie was so comfortable to be with. Wayne almost bit his tongue to keep from talking about the house he would put up where spring water would flow into the kitchen. Instead, he discussed the cheese. Safe subject. He was determined not to wear 'his heart on his sleeve.' If she ever wanted his heart, he had no thought that she would have trouble finding it, but he didn't want to risk driving her off by being too serious.

Also, Orville was not discussed.

He insisted she talk about her job. That took about an hour during which time he could watch her face without seeming to stare. Watched the touch of pink in her cheeks, brighter because of the chill. They sat in the buggy facing the sun, side flaps down. The sun's warmth spread over the isinglass windshield in a golden glow.

He watched her eyes, and there were pauses during which she seemed wistful. Not eager excitement, but steadfast persistence toward a goal. Much like the way she had attacked her arithmetic assignments. Not the sparkle like when she worked with words. What did it mean? He mustn't try to speculate.

She tasted the cheese. Hmmm, well...it was different. Of course she had never tasted the café's offering of feta, and goat cheese was not a farm staple. Maybe too much trouble, some folks thought. Too many kettles of something that required too much to be done, and then it had to 'rest' in its special compartment in the back of his cave.

She decided she'd be interested to taste the 'rested' product, but even more, she'd like to taste it in a casserole with tomatoes and other vegetables. All in good time.

And there were the six-inch buns Wayne hoped he was making the cheese for. That would make a difference. Why not? They currently sold no light bread buns, and neither did he...but there were cold biscuits. Oven-freshened biscuits and a generous wedge of cheese. Hmmm, well...maybe it should be toasted.

He had no good way to try it, like McCafferty's would have, and he couldn't ask to try it at McCafferty's until it was perfect. Too much was hinged to its success. Lennie watch the earnestness in his face, the determination to get it just right, and the confident expectation that he would find it.

So like Wayne. Like the ladder from Lennie's house up the bluff to the school house. He wanted to get it exactly right.

The afternoon created a lot of questions and answered a few. It was not the happy-go-lucky afternoon's play of children. More of an assessment of adults toward each other. A new chapter in the relationship. And then the day was over.

As she walked out with him to leave Chigger Ridge, the snow was filtering down, flakes glistening in reflected light from the stars. Then he drove away, still feeling the poignant touch of the farewell.

Wayne did, however, secure the privilege of returning her to Wishbone Hollow tomorrow to begin another ten day stint. He'd just have to be glad for what he got. And he really did have a reason to go. He had to send a letter to the American representative of the Finnish Double Landrace goats. It was time to work on it…might take all winter.

It was while he was spending a little time in Wishbone that he saw the hobby shop that was packed with Christmas toys. Hmmm, December already? He stepped inside, and saw that a woodcarver had been very busy.

Right there under a green artificial tree was a train. Carved in wood, it was, and each car measured about six inches long, with the rest of the set sized in proportion. Pullman cars, regular passenger cars, coal cars, and the most intricately carved engines. Stop signs and watering tanks. But most fascinating of all was the track.

In pieces, it came, with connections like a jugsaw puzzle, each piece fitting any other piece so the track had a variety of possible shapes. A toy, obviously. But he couldn't tear himself away. It wasn't cheap, but was in reach, if he really wanted it.

He drew in a breath, sighed and turned away. Not today. He'd give it the thought that was its due, and he'd be here again. It would still be here. Sure to be. But then he remembered that Christmas shopping had just begun, and there was no telling how much stock the shop had. What if there weren't many track pieces left, or maybe the engine? The set would be of no value without the engine.

He selected the engine, coal car and eight different cars, including three boxcars, and then a caboose. Ten pieces of track that made a circle, then he picked up three more. He paid for them, and left…a profound satisfaction enveloping him.

He went to McCafferty's and bought two pork chop sandwiches, removing the meat to eat and saving the buns. He'd SEE if cheese tasted different on the light bread buns.

He saw the vats of chile soup, now that the weather was cold. He took the old owner aside and told him what he had. What's more, he'd bring in two of his gallon jars next time he came, and leave them free for trial purposes.

Of the items he doubted, the canned meat was not one. That was something Ma had perfected. He explained to Isaiah McCafferty that the meat had been from YOUNG goats and thoroughly tenderized even before being packed in the jars. He pointed out the time and fuel savings that would be of great value as well as the wonderful shelf life.

He added that if Isaiah McCafferty agreed to try it, he, Wayne, would be back in a week to pick up the jars. No charge. He'd acted as though it was no big deal whether it worked out with them or not…there were others. Actually, there were. He could take the train on over to Eureka Springs, and if he got really big, he might…well, anyway.

Dream big, Wayne. It don't cost no more to dream big! So he rode home behind the filly, her feeling frisky in the cold, clear air.

He dreaded the cold shed where he would spend the night, but he had a lot of quilts. He also had two yeast bread buns and he'd have cheese sandwiches for breakfast. Toasted.

He WAS going to get there with his cheese even if he had to leave a wheel or two for free…but not until it tasted right. He'd take some home and have Ma taste it.

Then as he began to climb the hill to Chigger Ridge, he patted the reassuring bulk of the train pieces. Would there possibly be a way to paint 'Mountaineer' on the locomotive? Maybe not…Lennie could do a better job.

The full sized iron Mountaineer sailed past Chigger Ridge as Wayne was separating the filly from her harness and putting her in her shed. Silver flakes of snow were again falling. The animal was noisily consuming her chopped corn when the Mountaineer whistled a track warning as it approached the wide curve ahead.

"Animals remove yourselves," it said. In spite of himself, he stepped out of the shed and looked to the east. No trailing boxcars, but the donkey's tail of thick steam was rising slowly against the falling snow.

He swallowed hard. *Oh, Lennie, my beautiful dream!* And he sniffed…brushed the snow from his eyelashes…and headed toward the cold cabin with absolutely no smoke rising from its stove pipe.

A friendly aroma greeted him. On the cold stove was one of Ma's favorite kettles with a lid. He lifted the lid and sniffed the aroma of Ma's chile, still slightly warm. Beside it was a note.

Son, if McCafferty's has trouble with their chile, I'll be glad to instruct them. Ha Ha. I have an idea before you start another batch of cheese.

Mother

Wayne pulled himself together and poked wood into his dinky little multipurpose stove, meant for cooking, also heating, and set on the kettle. *Ma.* She not only wanted her son to climb into success, she begged to help build a ladder.

He thought of the snow down where the goats were, shivering at the wind coming through the slats of their sheds. But even then it wasn't as cold as their native land. Finland was up to its armpits in snow all winter, or so he had heard. The buck was teamed up with the filly and would help warm the small shed…and tomorrow was another day.

Lennie was dealing with her own concerns. For some reason, ten-year-old Mary Lou was riding alone. A belt and shoulder strap stating that she was an 'Unaccompanied Minor' stated such. The harness meant she was the special charge of the Security Guard… Lennie.

Lennie's partner to replace Joe was Roger Summers. He was almost as new as she, and was thrilled to leave little Mary Lou to Lennie. They had barely pulled onto the rails and were rounding Willow Bluff when Mary Lou's rolling tummy gave up the fight and deposited its contents on the seat, the floor under the seat and a liberal slosh onto her stocking and dresstail.

The girl, as well as dealing with motion sickness, was totally chagrined at having humiliated herself with an upchuck. Roger could hear Lennie chattering lightly to relieve the agony of the child by telling her that upchuck was not as bad as poopy pants and she'd dealt with that a lot. Not only that, rinsing a skirt tail and stocking was not nearly so bad as a shoe with all its crossed strings, and "Look, honey, there's not a spot on your new shoes or that pretty coat!"

Lennie used up half the trip's towels sopping around the legs of the seat. Fortunately, there was no one in the seat behind. When the floor was clean, and Lennie had cleaned herself, she sorted through the wrapped candy for a trio of peppermint pieces.

"Mary Lou, honey, I'm so sorry all this happened on your first trip by yourself, but next time you won't be scared. Now, I want you to suck on these, one at a time, and see if they don't settle your stomach. My Gram always kept them for me."

Then she brought a quilt and pillow. It was going to be a long way until morning and Memphis if the little girl didn't get to sleep. The dark had fallen outside the windows and the tiny candle-strength night lights came on along the sides of the car.

Maybe…

WINTER ON WILLOW BLUFF

The light powdering of snow turned the dry grass of the pasture white, but the goats didn't care. They nibbled on dry leaves and grass stems loaded with nutritious seeds and then nosed around among the icy grass blades for tasty morsels like the frozen dandelion leaves.

Wayne was, after six weeks of correspondence, successful in finding another owner of Finnish Double Landrace goats… primarily just for their hair. Perfect stuffing for sofas, it seemed, as it had strength to puff up after being repeatedly squashed.

It was down in central Arkansas in a town called Hot Springs that Glen Evans operated the farm. He'd been in business for six years, and had been obliged to send back to Finland for a buck, as the warm climate was producing kids with scantier hair growth. He was glad to hear of a possible swap with someone right here in Arkansas…not so expensive.

In a transfer of correspondence, it was decided to wait until late spring as the animals were set for the winter where they were. Maybe next May or June Wayne could bring his buck down to Hot Springs where he would be met and brought out to the farm.

195

Sigh of relief. That taken care of, he was left with the cheese. Ma had decided to help and, though he might not have asked, it was good news. Ma wouldn't put up with failure. It was not in her vocabulary.

"Son, bring over some of that cheese you've made up. I got a few ideas yesterday while hangin' out the wet overalls."

To Wayne, the statement was crystal clear. Like: "I've given you enough time, Son. Best you get your problem on over here so we can get you going." Wayne had no problem with that. Ma insisted on answers, and Wayne needed one right now. Besides, Ma had lived a lot longer than he, so naturally she was smarter.

He loaded two wheels of the cheese into a sack, tossed a blanket across Bessie's back and leaped aboard. One wheel would likely have been enough, but if Ma was on the road to success, he certainly didn't want her hampered by running out of the cheese that was 'OK' but not 'delicious.'

Ma set the two cheese wheels on the table amongst several small jars of dried leaves. "Now, Son, what we got here is rosemary, basil, parsley, and peppermint. Also powdered onion and garlic and dill seeds. We may try celery seed but I don't think…really, the tastes don't mix…to my way'a thinkin'. They's others we can try, but we'll start here. I'm thinkin' the makers of that little flavor pack didn't want you to have the best taste, wantin' to keep it for themselves. Maybe I'm wrong, but I've knowd women to give out a recipe and leave out somethin' important. On purpose. What I want you to do is slice up some really thin slices, spreadin' on a thin layer'a butter."

Now, that was pure Ma. She'd start with the first thing and give a body a job to do. To make him feel important, so to speak. So, with the cheese cutter, he began. Slices approximately the size of McCafferty's 6 inch buns began to pile up.

Ma dipped in the butter and smoothly spread the first slice. On top she sprinkled a layer of dill, and topped it with another slice of cheese.

"So, son, I'm gonna make the bites tiny, on account'a we gotta try so many. So now take a nibble and keep it in your mouth, sorta wallerin' it around."

Wayne obeyed, with Ma's faded blue-gray eyes boring into his face, absorbing every grimace while she did her own 'wallering.' "Hmmm, well…let's try the parsley." They did…and then each other flavor in turn.

On to Ma's next step. "This here next slice we're gonna sprinkle with this powdered onion. I'm knowin' this here is just to get an idea, bein' that when we find one we like, you'll have to put it in the milk 'afore it makes a curd."

Ma chewed the onion/parsley/dill cheese…her eyes squinched up in thought. Possibilities, for a fact. Wayne couldn't help producing a pleased smile. Ma did so love success…especially with one of her children being the audience.

"What'd'ye think, Son? Maybe this'n here ain't it, but it looks like a sign board sayin' we're headin' in the right direction. Think about a half a cup'a seasonin' in the milk, and lettin' the cheese age a couple'a months? I know it'll be a long wait, but I think…well, what'd'ya think?"

Wayne was willing to think anything Ma thought. "Sure, Ma. Why don't let's make sandwiches with some'a this and some' that and label 'em. I could pack 'em back in the cave for a week, and we could see what we get?"

"I do believe you got it, Son. We can make up a bunch and when you come home for Christmas, bring it along. We'll see what they say. Amongst the 26 of us, there might be a good opinion. What say?"

"I say you got yourself a good idea. You got a hunk'a paper handy?"

She did. She also had another piece of news. "I'm hearin' from Maisie Marshall that her youngen'll get her Christmas early, on account'a needin' to be workin' on Christmas Day. They're thinkin' on havin' the family dinner on the 20th. The other youngens're in favor, needin' Christmas Day for the other side'a the family."

Wayne nodded. "Not surprisin', her bein' new."

"The thing is, you're gonna get an invite…less'n you tell me you can't come. Don't reckon you'll be busy, do you?"

Wayne pretended to think a bit. "No, Ma. I'll just be herdin' the goats, as usual." He buttered another couple of cheese slices.

"'Course that don't mean I can't come here on Christmas Day, does it?"

Ma grinned pleasurably and she playfully poked her son with her elbow. "Now, just what'd'ya think, you ornery, head-strong lunk!"

Wayne packed his 'sandwiches' along with biscuits and a pink jar of blackberry jelly. He headed back to Chigger Ridge in a joyful frame of mind. Maybe he'd go on over to the Marshall's and show what he had for Lennie, and maybe he'd get the invitation then. Being taught that 'every good and perfect gift is from above' (James 1:17) he looked up. And he had certainly received two of them today.

He was positive Ma had the right idea on the cheese. How would the folks in Finland know what tasted good in Arkansas? And so his Christmas day was sewed up as neat as a hole in a stocking heel.

Lennie would be working on Christmas Day. Quite fair, actually. The holidays off were scheduled with families in mind. Children and length of service determined who had first choice. No matter.

It seemed that Leon Barker would be solo on the Mountaineer with a load of coal, and she would be on the Firefly. She would be third guard on a twelve car string, picking up and dropping off in small towns all the way from Eureka Springs to the state capitol of Little Rock.

The Firefly took three days round trip, and the Torch tagged along on the in-between days. This little tag-team resulted in the two locomotives meeting during their coming and going. Somewhere someone had to go on a siding. Fort Smith and Van Buren were the usual towns for this.

Little Rock was a very large town and naturally had a lot of coming and going. It also had another line going straight from Little Rock to Memphis, but Lennie would never be on it. That one belonged to a whole different family of locomotives.

The Firefly began its trip. Lot of families. Lot of small children. Sandwiches to be served and spilled drinks to be mopped up. Sure to be. No matter. It was all in the job she'd worked so hard for. The fellows did it, and so could she. In fact, she rather looked forward to a different route.

But regularly she and Leon had the Mountaineer. She really liked working with Leon. He loved to talk and they had so many things in common. One thing though, being gone for such long stretches, he was worried about his girl friend. Too many fellows at home, and Cassie loving to go places.

The hard thing of it was, Leon liked the job and it paid well enough to give him a start. Unfortunately it seemed that Cassie was not particularly interested in the future of his job. Or maybe it was just him.

Over on Chigger Ridge, Wayne loaded his test material into the buggy and put Bessie between the shafts. The numerous trips between his childhood home and Chigger Ridge had worn a trail. Bessie knew where she was headed, and it was a good thing. Her driver was in another world. Thoughts zooming skyward.

It was a good idea to pull Ma into this venture. What else did she have to do! But it was her idea to do the first canning of the butchered goat, just to get him 'started out right.' And now one of his next jobs was to take a test jar to McCaffery's. If they didn't go for it, it would mean going on to Eureka Springs. He'd have to do something with the wealth of meat. Couldn't eat it all.

And there was the new flavored cheese. Good idea to have the family test it at Christmas. His fairly large extended family loved projects, and also loved to express opinions.

In addition, there was Lennie.

He struggled, often unsuccessfully, to pull his mind from the smart looking uniform, the blue cap with gold braid, and most of all, the red curls trying to escape the cap and frame the most beautiful face in the world.

Later, he told himself. *You got things to do right now.* Bessie heard him and flicked her ears, but as none of the human's sounds meant anything she remembered, she continued to trot along the hard-packed path.

Cheese. It would be three weeks before Christmas with the family. Too hard to wait. He had to push on and get a salable produce. Future income depended on it…cheese being the most dependable product that was continuous. So…what next?

Maybe he'd go ahead with the milking of yesterday, and today he'd add to the starter that had already soured and make a small wheel of cheese, testing what Ma said about adding the flavor herbs to the milk. How much? He hadn't talked with Ma about that. Seems he'd be on his own if he started now.

All right. Half batch and add one tablespoon each of garlic, onion, parsley and dill. He'd already decided to add more salt. Cheese was supposed to be salty…at least where he lived.

He needed to drag up more wood for the stove. Time consuming. He needed an alternative heat source. That new little stove he saw in town…the one that burned kerosene? *Hmmm, have to think on that.* Of course, it'd be handy in the summer, not having to fire up the iron stove and make the shack so hot.

And there was that girl with the strawberry blossom complexion. Maybe he'd set out a few strawberry plants, just for the early, beautiful blossoms to remind him of her. NO! What he needed was to keep his mind OFF her and ON his business. *Wayne…for sakes alive…can't you…?* But seemingly he couldn't.

Boring business, right now, with a lot of questions. *Stop bellyaching, Wayne. You got questions to think on.*

Back to the cheese. He was so lucky to have that huge cave. Cool in the summer and not bad in the winter. Well, it wasn't that he was lucky, actually. It was the cave that had made him part with his hard-earned cash. For what he wanted to do, he HAD to have a cave, and they were too hard to build of the size he needed.

Back to the cheese. For lunch he'd heat up the yeast bread rolls and melt a slab of the good, but not good enough, cheese. He was of the opinion it would taste different on the yeast bread, rather than a biscuit. Also heated.

Maybe have another idea. *Sure to…*he promised himself. Lennie would be home in five days. Now, what did that have to do with tasting the cheese…?

Lennie sorted the mail bags in the order of the small towns they would pass, and helped herself to an apple, which was part of the lunch the railway provided. Very good apple. The seeds piled up on the counter beside the stool provided for guards. Those little black things made trees. Sort of magic, huh! *Say, I wonder…*so she slipped the seeds into her pocket. If she remembered to take them out, maybe....

Oh, come on, Lennie. Where would you plant them, anyway? But then she got a mental picture of Chigger Ridge. Groups of trees needed for goat protection. Beautiful spring blossoms. *Maybe Wayne...*

WAKE UP, Lennie. You got Middleburg comin' up and where is their bag? You know how heavy their bag always is?

Leon came into the stockroom. Some jobs were easier with two. He was just finishing his apple when the whistle sounded for Middleburg. Funny thing about Middleburg. There were no houses in any direction, so how did they have so much mail and so many packages?

"Leon, don't throw away the apple seeds. I want them."

"Whatever for...?"

"Not sure, really. Just sort of an idea."

The obliging young man picked the seeds from the core and handed them over. What she wanted with them was none of his business, and besides, he was too busy worrying about what Cassie was doing.

The Mountaineer slowed down for the Middleburg mail, and Leon pulled their loaded bag in through the window. A trickle of iciness fell from his hands. "Snow! Just look at that!" And he displayed the soft layer of whiteness on the stiff, oiled canvas bag.

"Snow? For a fact! Well it is December, remember."

Wayne switched the buggy for the sled and aimed Bessie toward the woodlot. There should be some dry windfall sticks for a quick fire. He shivered in his sheepskin-lined Macannaw top coat and rubbed his hands together. He really wanted to get at the cheese, but the trouble with this job, when he tried to do one thing, something else always had to be done first.

How in the world did Ma do it...and have time to help him or anyone who needed it? Hmmm, how would Lennie work out with this crazy idea he had? He'd never really told her everything. She seemed to like Chigger Ridge, but he figured it was because of the long view of the railroad rails.

It was time to break out the ax and bring down some of his large oaks. He needed the wood, and the goats would like the green shoots the stump would make next year. But when he'd get to it, he had no idea. Wood cutting took a surprising amount of time on the end of an ax handle....

Cheese. McCafferty's just served cold slices. Wonder if being hot made a difference...and could he convince them? Maybe better wait until he talked with them about the goat meat. Too many new things at once...and all that. Mustn't scare them off. It was a trouble he had with his mind. It kept working on some better way of doing something and the world didn't always agree with him. Or maybe it just wasn't ready for something new.

A shivering sprinkle of moisture sifted down his coat collar. He looked up at a squirrel racing across a small limb. "Snow! Well, it's time for it. Some on, Bessie, we'll pick up what's handy and get back to the barn."

Bessie swiveled her ears at 'barn.' Sounded good to her, so she whickered an agreement through her rubbery lips. With nothing else interesting to look at, she watched as the human gathered and piled sticks on the sled. She rippled her skin and shook off the flakes that were melting when they landed on her back.

"Ok, Bessie. Let's go."

Bessie also recognized 'go' and turned around, working her way between the trees and pulling back up the hill to a warm barn.

DECEMBER 1912

So thoughtful of Lennie's Grandad to allow him to pick her up. Of course, Wayne was forced to insist that he probably had a trip there, anyway. Most of the time it was true.

He stood on the platform with a few others and waited for the Mountaineer. The whistles had died away, and now the rails sang and vibrated as the iron wheels had begun to brake. With a final mild screech, the Iron Pony was headed into the 'barn.'

Lennie was first to debark, and she searched for his face and smiled, but turned and watched as each passenger put a foot on the iron step. Her hands were poised to assist if needed. Her handsome coworker was lifting bags and suitcases to the cart.

So beautiful. Red curls framing the band on her cap, cheeks tinted from the chilly west wind. Finally everyone had stepped down and she came to him. She had to sign out, but then she would be his. At least for the almost an hour it would take to get her home.

He'd shown the miniature wooden train to her Granddad, who had examined it with interest. Yes, he'd take charge, and have it on display when her next break came. December 20.

It took a while for the conversation to start. She began to prime his attention for an update on Chigger Ridge, but what was there to tell? Failure on the cheese…it was just not unique enough to create interest.

Why would she be interested in the amount of wood he needed for the winter…or how drafty the shed was? He'd known it was not suitable for winter but where had the time gone? Had intended to do better, but hadn't. Story of his life.

She chatted about this and that on the trip that she thought might interest him. Some of it did.

If either of them had been tuned in to the gossip grapevine that grew and thrived on the mountains of northern Arkansas, they would have heard from others who had plenty to talk about. Some of it was even true.

CHRISTMAS ON THE FIREFLY

It was finally January third, 1913.

Wayne Johnson, weary from the last two weeks, had decided it would never come, but now it was here. And he could go to Mountaineer depot and pick up the one who put courage into his life.

Of course, that was a lot to expect of one person, and a not very big person at that. Nevertheless, at 4:00 o'clock PM, he could wait on the platform at the depot for Lennie. After a moment in the office to sign in and leave her journal, she would be his…at least for the hour plus, that he would have her beside him in the buggy.

Once more.

For some reason he had been concerned about her, being that the Firefly headed for Little Rock. It was in a way that he had never been particularly concerned with her in the Mountaineer on the way to Memphis. Nothing he could put his finger on…so he laid it onto his loneliness…though how could he possibly be lonely with all he had going on?

He waited patiently until 4:00, and then became antsy. The Frisco family of locomotives were mostly on time. Finally, he asked the stationmaster. "Yes, they had heard from the Firefly and it was rolling." So what did that mean? Maybe rolling over on its side? Maybe upside down?

What was the problem, he wondered. The stationmaster, if he knew, was not inclined to share the information with the young man…other than, yes, it was a bit late. No, he could not give a new estimate of arrival. Yes, all the crew members were alive and breathing.

So the distraught young man paced. Most of those meeting the Firefly had long since taken a seat and some had managed to doze the minutes away. Sensible, actually, but Wayne could not bend his knees to sit down, opting rather to keep walking as though his steps could bring her closer. And sooner.

The clock hands moved to five, six, seven…and on to midnight. Again he racked up the courage to approach the stationmaster. Again he received no satisfaction or estimated time of arrival, other than a dispirited reply. "Young man, I realize you are anxious about the Firefly, but truly, I can tell you nothing except that all passengers and crew are safe and moving this way."

With an attempt to swallow the lump in his throat, what could he do but walk away…and continue to pace the floor like a caged jungle beast. It was at 1:37 AM that a distant whistle was heard. Wayne rushed to the tracks and could feel the wonderful vibration indicating the locomotive was within five miles and moving on its own power.

The north wind whipped the flaps of his jacket and tore roaringly past his uncovered ears. She was coming! Safe and breathing, he had been assured.

Minutes later came the reassuring whistle, and he'd never heard a more welcome sound. Then he could hear the powerful thrust of the drivers and the rails shivered in anticipation. Chips of cinders and flintstone gravel blew in the wind, burning his neck and ears but he felt it not.

With eyes glued the door, he was rewarded by the sight of black shoes and stockings, and the flare of a skirt. She made a quick look around, fastened her eyes momentarily on his face, lifted her hand in a finger wave and turned her back. As others stepped wearily down onto the cast iron step, she stood, hands ready to give assistance when needed.

She stepped over to the door and lifted down a child of about three, wrapped like a little mummy against the cold. Then reached a hand to balance a young mother with a packed bag on her arm and a bundle against her shoulder.

She reached forward and took the bulky traveling bag from an elderly woman whose steps seemed shaky. With her other hand, Lennie guided the trembling foot to the solid step and reached for her groping hand. He barely heard the trembling, old voice, "Thank you, dearie. Thank you so much."

He couldn't see Lennie's smile, but he knew it was there.

It seemed forever that passenger after passenger descended, some of them helping each other. Silently...determinedly... marching into the depot.

A bundled young man had been scooping bags and bundles onto the station cart. He apparently finished and closed the door. Dusting his hands in a farewell, he approached Lennie. A few words and he disappeared into the locomotive. Lennie turned and headed toward Wayne. Finally.

He extended a hand for assistance and welcome, but she walked into his arms. *Glory be! Thank you, Lord!* After a brief hug, she pushed away lifting her journal for him to see. He knew the score. She had to sign out and deliver her account of the trip.

Following her, he waited at the door until she reappeared. Her first words, "Let's go home." That seemed good enough to him. He had successfully retrieved his precious jewel from the snout...yeah, perhaps from the belly of the monster Iron Pony, still popping and crackling with cooling metal on the tracks.

She climbed aboard…with assistance…and settled heavily onto the bench, allowing herself to be covered and tucked into the numerous quilts. That, in itself, was not usual.

He told Bessie to "Move out" and she did, hooves sparking against the flint of the station yard. An hour and a half, with luck, and he would reach Chigger Ridge. He allowed his mind a minute to think of stopping with her, but pushed it aside. She would have parents and Grandad, if not waiting up, at least awake…and her parents' house would be warm with a soft bed. Well worth the extra twenty minutes of travel.

Besides, where would he put her…in the cold shed?

They rode in silence. A glance at her face showed the shine of her open eyes reflected in the light from the lanterns lighting Bessie's way. Something told him that if she wanted to talk, she would. She'd never been shy that way.

It was almost 4:00 when he finally reached her door. "Lennie, my dear, would you stay under the quilts until I arouse someone to the door? I'm concerned to get you into the warm without being chilled." In the lantern light she nodded.

Then he found the courage to ask, "Will I get to see you this time?"

Another nod. "Come early on Thursday and then take me back. We'll have time." The young man felt his heart leap at the gift. A day with her. And then he realized it might not be a joyful day. No matter.

He knocked at the door…a light appeared at the window. A lamp…still lit…was being brought to the parlor. Pa burst through the door. "Is she…?" He couldn't form the words he felt.

"She's good. I'll bring her in."

She allowed him to lift her down, as though her feet might not hold her up, and he guided her along the path, handing her over to her Pa at the door. "She's terribly tired. Tell her I'll see her in two days, ready to bring her back to the depot." And he turned around and was gone.

Bessie registered mild disapproval, but moved on in the direction she knew was her stable. And a scoop of chopped corn, if she was lucky. She was. Her master poured the corn into the feed box, shut the stable door against the wind and ran to his shack. Without bothering to heat the stove, he crawled into a tunnel of tossed quilts and shivered himself to sleep.

He awoke to the bleat of the goats locked in the corral. They cared not that he had had a horrible day and night and hardly 2 hours of sleep. It was now 6:00 and they deserved to be relieved of their full udders of milk. It had been in their 'contract' with the humans who took away their babies. The babies could have relieved the problem in short shrift.

Babies during the day…corral at night. The nannies demanded to be milked so they could start their day. The long hair flowing around their bodies was an insulated blanket of semi-hollow strands…the perfect insulation.

Wayne rolled from the bed and stepped into his icy boots. He was fully dressed from last night, and he bundled into his sheep-skin lined Macannaw and pushed through the door. With numb, icy fingers he removed the milk from the aching udders into the five gallon bucket made of shining steel.

Life goes on, Wayne. Dreams are not always easily filled. Sometimes they turn into nightmares. What did you expect, anyway? And then he grinned at the flash of memory brought back an incident on his sixth birthday. Ma was always good at doing something fun and unexpected, and he'd never forget the excitement caused when Ma put on the huge kettle she used for popping corn.

When the sound in the kettle had the amount of racket she desired, she simply removed the lid from the pan, and stood back. For the next almost 5 minutes, fluffy balls shot forth from the kettle bouncing off the ceiling, the floor, the birthday cake on the table, and nestling on the heads of his brothers and his sister. Shrieking with laughter, they leaped at the flying popcorn attempting to catch something.

Ma was laughing at the top of her voice, and shouted above the chatter, "Save what you catch! The one with the most gets the first piece of cake!"

The decibels of laughter increased exponentially. Wayne, the youngest, reached high for his share, and felt the hand of Ma at his pocket, slipping in a handful of the warm popcorn. He turned, but she stepped quickly away, pretending to catch the flying corn. She did, however, give him an exaggerated wink.

When the product of the contest was counted, his siblings were amazed that he had so many grains. Ma gave her own explanation, "Well, he was closest to the floor and had more time to see the grains falling." It was almost true, of course, and it had been a secret between them through the years.

Turning the goats loose and brushing Bessie with the curry comb to bring up her circulation, he carried dry sticks into his shack. Stacking them in the firebox, he stirred into the ashes for the few buried live coals. It would take a half an hour, at best, before he could bear to take off his Macannaw. He settled into his only chair and opened the door of his oven. Poking his feet into it, he stretched his toes into the delicious warmth.

It was then that he remembered it had been a month since he had made a wheel of his herb-flavored cheese. He had promised himself that would be the time he would taste it.

Poking his hardly-warm feet back into the icy depth of his winter shoes, he trudged to the cave. Stepping through the door, he was once again amazed how warm it seemed, compared to the outside. Maybe he should move his bed in here? Naw, he'd just stay in the shack and freeze. Likely he deserved it.

Lighting the candle, he made his way to the shelves and the cheeses that had not quite made the grade. From the herb flavored wheel, he sliced a generous chunk. Texture good. Cutable with a knife, and curds melded together tightly. That was necessary for putting in sandwiches. So he cut three slices, each almost a half an inch wide.

Hurried back to the shack and it almost seemed warm. Splitting two of his latest gift of biscuits, he cut the cheese to fit the halves, and put the pieces in the oven. Now for the coffee. Garden tea was cheaper and more abundant, but today was definitely a 'coffee' day.

An interesting aroma began to arise from the oven. Sliding out the pan, he saw the crumbs on the biscuit edges had begun to brown. Shoving the pan back, he told himself, just a minute more...and maybe the coffee will be ready. It was. He lifted an uncomfortably warm biscuit in his fingers and crunched through the browned edge.

He chewed, startled, as though a bucket of ice water had been dumped on his head. It was DELICIOUS! The edges of the cheese had semi-melted into the bread. The aroma was as enticing as ice cream on a hot day. He'd done it! He and Ma had done it!

Wait…was this a good and perfect gift? Of course, so it would have come from above. He looked up through the rough beams of his shack and closed his eyes. *Thank you, Lord. You took Ma's idea and my persistent stubborness, and you gave us this gift!*

He consumed the four half biscuits and three cups of coffee. *Time's up, Wayne, you got stuff to do.* Lunch would be easy. More biscuits and more cheese.

He shouldered his ax and chisel and carrying his saw and a bottle of water, he headed to the nearest timbered area he intended to thin. Trees down, limbs to burn, logs for more goat shelters, and next spring the goats would have the new little leaves to nibble from the stump sprouts.

Excitement gave him a massive boost of energy, and he worked steadily until 2:00 in the afternoon. Amazing what a tiny success can do, he told himself.

Opening a jar of Ma's canned tomatoes, he poured them in the kettle. Crumbled biscuits would thicken it. Not his favorite food, but was nutritious and available. Also warming. Waiting for it to simmer, he laid eyes on the last slice of cheese. Hmmmm…well, no better time to try it.

Slicing the cheese into strips, he lowered them into the bubbling red liquid, turning it to smooth pink. Then in went the biscuit pieces. It smelled heavenly…or he was terribly hungry. Likely both.

He took a bite. Another. And after the third bite he looked up at the ceiling beams once more. "Look at that, Lord! You and Ma and me…we done it again. We couldn't'a done it without you. Now, when I tell old man McCafferty about it, I could use your help again. I've never tried to sell nothin', before. Leastwise nothin' as important as this."

Then, his childhood teaching came back to him. "I know, Lord, You never died for my sins before, either…until You did."

While his meal settled, he reached for a pencil and scratch paper. He needed an advertisement for the Wishbone Cryer, if he could talk Mr. McCafferty into using his product. He toyed with several wordings, and decided to give it a little more thought. Now that the cheese problem might be over…surely an idea would follow.

The acts of living…bringing wood, sorting goats, filling water troughs and scooping tracked-in dirt from his shack used up the day.

At 8:00 AM the next day he was at the Marshalls. She'd said to come early…so was this late enough?

Seemed OK, and he was served a slab of frosted cake while he waited for her to gather her things together. Beautiful. The red curls that had been fluffed out everywhere, now behaved under the hat, showing only around the edges. Gold buttons on her jacket shone, and shoes were shiny black. Handing him her coat, she indicated it was time. Slipping it on, she kissed Grandad and Mama, and patted Papa on the shoulder. "Love you all," she announced as a farewell.

The winter sun shone brightly, without much warmth, but the side flaps on the buggy took care of that. For the hour plus that it took Bessie to make the trip, they chatted about this and that… pleasant, but not very productive. Did she remember how upset she had been?

But when they reached Wishbone, there were two things to do. Wayne needed to see if the Wishbone Cryer knew where to get advertising stickers. They did. And Lennie needed stockings, the only thing the job did not provide.

Then they found the diner. Seated, she looked at Wayne. "I don't know. I may talk a long time."

Wayne nodded. "Then I'll need to furnish you a lot of hot chocolate."

"It started alright at first," she began. "There was Howard Campbell and Jake Moreland, and I hadn't seen neither of 'em. Right off, they handed me the journal, sayin' my writin' was surely better'n theirs.

"We had eight cars and 178 people, eleven of 'em under a year old. We always keep that separate, and that means how many milk cans we take…you know, those little cans that need water to make 'em real milk? They're a lot handier than the jars we used to use. We put in cases'a crackers and sliced rattrap cheese, like always.

"We were down past Fayetteville when the engineer saw waving flags and thought it was just kids. It really was just a kid, but he meant business. We slowed down and he ran to the door. He told us his little brother was just around the corner… case we didn't stop. The fellows and I pocketed guns and stood ready.

"Then up on the hillside'a the tracks was a man with a red shirt on a pole. We ground to a stop again and he said there was a tree down on the track just around the blind corner. Said we'd been throwed off the track if we didn't stop…and we would'a. It took our fellows 20 minutes on the two-man saw to cut chunks out's that trunk and get 'em off the track. Foot and a half thick it was. Oak. Engineer just couldn't thank that man enough, but he just shrugged it off."

Here she grinned. "He pointed over at a spot of plowed field and said if we'd got throwed off the track and in his field, he'd have to work over the whole field again after we got pulled outta it. And we'd'a broke up his stone fence."

Then back to the serious frown. "We had to straighten part'a the track, but we were goin' again. We had to get on the Marconi and tap out a message the Torch to hang back on the sidin' 'cause we were late. Torch had 12 cars'a cotton so it didn't matter too much to be held up. We had people.

"Then we had a water stop at a town called Fort Smith, and headed on, but we got a leak in our boiler, and couldn't keep enough water in to make steam. Had to keep stoppin' at the rivers and streams. Took a lotta time, and Howie and Jake carried water. I had to stay with the people, all 178 of 'em, and a lotta of 'em gettin' cranky. Everybody wantin' somethin' and one little girl screamed that she couldn't weewee in that noisy hole, and she wouldn't use the little potty. She screamed and hollered until she didn't need it anymore, and I mopped up the floor.

"We stopped at some depot, I forgot the name, but they had a machine that made new seams in the boiler, but we lost an hour and a half there. We were just about gettin' on the track of the Shootin' Star that comes outta Little Rock straight to Memphis.

211

"They ain't part'a our family…but they had'a wait 20 minutes till we got over the trestle that's just one locomotive wide.I'm reckonin' they wasn't likin' it too much. They had people, too.

"We were gettin' low on crackers and on drinkin' water, but we finally limped into Little Rock, and the fellows and I had a whole eight cars that were filthy. They said to me if I'd just clean the sticky off the seats, they'd get the floors and I should take a nap. Said I needed to sleep. There'd be a lot to do goin' back. We'd have two crowded passenger cars and 10 boxcars'a cotton bales.

"Howie got pulled for a local run when a guard come down with the measles. He done had 'em, he thought. I woke up and Jake went to bed while the switchin' got done. The local brought up the cotton that was goin' north, and we got hitched on.

"We pulled out in the night so's we'd be past where we'd meet the Torch comin' back with six cars'a people. We waited more'n a hour and finally heard the Torch had run off the track just past a place called Mountainburg. It's in what is called the Boston Range'a mountains, and the whole track is built on bends and cut-away's where they've dug out the side of a mountain to lay the track.

"Word was, they hit a rock slide that damaged a wheel and when the track took the next bend, the engine shot right off the rails into a corn field full'a stubble. Pulled the coal car and two passenger cars off with it, and them still hooked onto the cars that were still on the track.

"So we eased on up knowin' we'd be meetin' the Torch, and when we got there, they had two liftin' jacks on the twisted couplin' but it was sprung. They was needin' to cut it loose so it could be pulled on off the tracks. They'd emptied the people from the leanin' cars and put 'em in the others, and finally the jacks got high enough that the couplin' cracked and let the engine and two cars fall over and the cars on the track straighten up, but the cuplin' was still twisted.

"It took a lot'a bangin' to get it almost straight. Bangin' took time.

"Meanwhile we had to BACK UP to the last waterin' cutoff and leave our cotton cars on the track. We came back, and managed to hook onto the front of the cars and pull them back so's a tractor could come down the track to pull the turned-over cars up.

"We pulled into a local place and got turned around and came back and pulled the passengers on back to Little Rock. Took four hours, and then we took our people and the Torch's people and sidled around the tractor by usin' a sidin' that was under water from a recent storm. Like to'a scared the be-jabbers outta all'a us.

"We had a new supply'a crackers and cheese and water now, and got ourselves to Fayetteville without any more problems, we thought. We had a baby with a fever, but we gave the ma wet cloths to try to help. Then we saw the baby was broke out with what smelled like measles. They stink somethin' fierce.

"Fayetteville didn't have no engine to help but hooked on two more passenger cars to us that was needed somewhere, and we gave one to the mother of the baby with the measles and her other children. The other folks were getting' nervous about their own youngens. Didn't blame 'em.

"All the way on, Jake and me, we were runnin' from one end to the other with screamin' children, worried mothers and fellows tryin' to get away from all the noise. We should'a stocked up on more candy. Didn't think on it at the time.

"We pulled into Bentonville and sent two cars on north on the Screamin' Eagle, and one east on the Mountaineer. Don't know what happened to the rest.

"We'd waited two hours for the Mountaineer to bring us eight coal cars and we hooked 'em on with our one passenger car. We finally got on the rails, and I made Jake go to sleep. I was too nervous to sit. Kept worryin' about the measles. They can be fierce, and they're highly catchin'.'"

Here, Lennie picked up her empty cup and looked at Wayne. He took the cup to the counter and brought it back full. This story might take several cups.

"When we got down past some place called Winslow, there was a little creek called Mulberry, I think, and there'd been a storm up north. River came up and washed out around a tree stump, carried it down river and backed up the water makin' it worse. Wind blew a gale and the stump hit a leg'a the water tank tower, and it dumped over, all the water washin' out all at once and loosened two of the wooden ties lettin' the rail sag over on one side. Would'a really sagged if we'd run on over it…not knowin'. Could'a threw us. We saw the flagman, and braked, barely stoppin' soon enough.

"The locals had gathered around and brought rocks, but couldn't lift the ties to get the rocks under so we could go over, 'cause they didn't have no liftin' jacks and the mud was so deep. Brakeman set up our jacks and they got that fixed, but we needed water and there wasn't none.

"We Marconied on ahead for our borrowed engine, Nighthawk, to hold up while we took on water outta the flooded creek. The neighbors had brought buckets and little kids had cans and kettles and they brought water. Jake climbed the ladder and the brakeman handed the water up. Took two hours for enough water to get a full head'a steam.

"We Marconied the Nighthawk to ease on down to Alma so's we'd get past 'em. We told 'em don't count on takin' on water at Winslow and slow down to get past the mud till a road crew can get at that track and make it stronger.

"We got our coal and one car'a passengers off at Little Rock, and hooked onto six passenger cars and seven boxcars'a cotton bales. We'd picked up Howie, and him breakin' out and red as a beet. We got a loan of James Jones from the Hotshot, takin' cotton to Memphis. We'd allowed we'd send James on the Mountaineer to get back to his home family once we got north again.

"We left one cotton car in Fort Smith and took on two passenger cars. Twenty-three children under a year old. Too many. I loaded on more milk cans and a whole crate'a boxes'a candy. No knowin' what I was gonna run into.

"First off, we quarantined Howie and his measles to the stockroom, the other fellows and I knew we'd had 'em, but Howie really got sick. We got really worried about 'im, but there wasn't nothin' we could do. We were awfully busy.

"We left Howie off at Fayetteville and they put 'im in the hospital. Jake and James both tried to nap, but couldn't get settled. It gets that way. When we needed rest the worst, it was the hardest to get to sleep.

"We was just out'a Fayetteville goin' north, climbin' up on a little rise, and saw a single car comin' down the next rise, straight at us. We tried to stop, hopin' we didn't make sparks on the rails. Don't know if we did. But the loose car came to the bridge in the valley and tipped off in the river, neat as you please, leavin' the track free. We hoped the bridge hadn't been messed up, 'cause we had to go over it in any case. Signalman said talk was goin' on back and forth on the Marconi but it wasn't none of it for us. Somethin' else must'a been goin' on with the others. We tried to put it outta our minds.

"But then it was a hour later and dark was comin' on. Our lights went out and our boiler started actin' up. Again. Little kids started screamin', so I lit a candle and walked from one end to the other, a'singin'.

"It came on full dark. We Marconied that we was stoppin' at a river to put on more water, and we didn't have locals to help. Some'a the men passengers helped, with James liftin' water and Jake a'pourin' in the boiler. It took a while, I think about forty five minutes. I got it wrote down, but I was so tired, I'm not sure what my journal looks like.

"I went all that time without clean clothes that I hadn't slept in, and had holes in my stockings. The fellows weren't no better, all of us smellin' like a pig sty. The holes in my stockin's started makin' blisters so I took 'em off. I lost my hairpins, but Jake knew how to braid. His sister taught him. So he braided me up and tied it in a knot so it'd stay under my cap.

"I don't know the engineer we finally ended up with, but when we got five miles from Eureka Springs he told 'em to lay onto the whistle. With our luck, there might be no one awake otherwise. Babies were too tired to cry, and youngens didn't want no more candy. Fellows had firm chins and tired eyes and very muddy shoes.

"So when we pulled in, and I saw you a'waitin' and us over eight hours late, I could'a cried for bein' happy but I didn't have the energy, and besides, the passengers had to get off first, and there were all those little kids....

"Since I left you before Christmas, I been to Little Rock and back three times in ten days. Twice we could'a de-railed if it hadn't been for locals. James wasn't as tired as Jake and me, but he had to go on with the Mountaineer back to Memphis to meet up with the

Shootin' Star. Shootin' Star couldn't wait long. Had ta get goin' so's to clear the track for the Hobo...."

She paused, drained the chocolate, cold now, and looked squarely into Wayne's eyes. "And that's what happened. At least as much as I remember. Good thing I had the journal or the officials'd never have believed it all."

Jake refilled the chocolate. She'd been talking for over two hours. He asked, "Did you tell your family all this?"

The blue eyes sprung open in alarm. "Oh, no! Not ever! There wasn't nothin' they could do to help and I still had to make a run. Mountaineer, this time. Back with Leon, I think."

So Wayne had his answer. She would stay with the train and the dream, leaving him with the goats, the cheese and the long goat hair. Well, she did what she did, and if it was not enough for him, he needed to look around. Perish the thought! He'd take what she could give, and make it enough.

One thing for sure, she was tough, and knowing his circumstances and dream, it was going to take some toughness... that is, if they ever got together. Had to look at it that way. There might still be a chance.

By now, she was a veteran, according to the railway. She would become twenty, likely somewhere between Memphis and Wishbone...or maybe on the Screaming Eagle flying north. Plain to see she hadn't had enough of hard work and danger.

He waited with her until the Mountaineer pulled in and transferred his eight boxcars of coal to the repaired Firefly. Jake would handle the Firefly security by himself until Fayetteville where he would pick up passengers and a young fellow named Conner Upright as a trainee.

But no matter. Lennie was back on the Mountaineer, and she would be whistling past Willow Bluff and flinging out the mail sack. Like usual.

It was during the month of February that Wayne and Lennie both received invitations to wedding parties. Both invitations were laid aside in favor goat cheese and a pocket full of candy for a restless child.

FETA CHEESE AT MC CAFFERTY'S CORNER

Wayne had seven long-haired nannies milking heavily. Could'a beeen milked both morning and night, but he couldn't quite fit in the time. Evening milking was left to the young goats who could be taken off grass. Didn't have time for anything...but the extra milk was putting the little creatures in tip top butchering shape.

Especially the little bucks. He hadn't figured yet how many females to keep, but he was facing another problem. He needed help. Giving it a lot of sleepless nights of thinking, he decided he would have to advertise.

If he could get together a cabin, there'd be someone...maybe an older single man, who would like a place to stay in return for milking and another chore or two. If that happened, Wayne'd like to raise his milkers to twelve or fifteen. More cheese.

First, though, he had to assure a market for the cheese. If it wasn't McCafferty's, then he'd likely have to go on to Eureka springs. That'd take a day. Each way. Also the cost of transport by train.

So the weak winter sun struggled over Echo Mountain with Wayne staring up in his cold dark room at the place where the ceiling should be. He had finally managed the courage to move his feet from the bed (somewhat warm) to his work boots (icy cold) and build up a fire for food. There were moments like this when he considered whether starving in bed might be a desirable option.

His stubbornness finally forced him to move his feet from under the pile of quilts and into the shoes. He cringed at their icyness just as the Mountaineer blew its 'animal' whistle, hoping to clear the tracks around the wide bend.

Lennie. It would be so easy if she was there beside him, but he shoved it from his mind. It had become patently obvious that two persons could not walk together if they were going in opposite directions, and he knew the strength of a dream. His own was the reason he was cold, tired and miserable.

A few live coals remained under the cover of ashes. Good. A handful of twigs brought them to life, and he sacrificed three of his precious dry logs. He put a kettle over the infant blaze and a scoop of expensive coffee grounds were tossed in.

Oatmeal. Heavily buttered. Three eggs (from Ma's hens) were boiling down in the coffee turning their shells dark brown. Three of ma's biscuits were split and laying on the top of the other burner cover.

The nannies were bleating pathetically. Full udders were painful, and the cold meant nothing to them. The human in the shed had obviously turned off his ears. The bleating must be raised a few decibels to get his attention...so it was.

Breakfast past and shoes warmed, minimally, the 'human' shouldered his milk buckets and joined the goats. This milking would fill his last available vat. Need to buy more vats. How long was the money going to last?

Bowing his head toward the long-haired flanks of the animal put him in a perfect position to think of the Power above. How was one to ask God for help with the milking...cold...fence building... butchering...etc....? Especially when the only answer to his prayer would be to cut back on the dream, and he couldn't.

"...God shall supply all your needs...." The promise in the Book came flooding into his mind, along with several others along the same line. OK, God. What do I do...?

And as he emerged from the cave after clamping the lid on the vat, here came the answer. Pa seldom offered advice or interfered in any way, but here he was.

"Pa...!"

"Hello, Son. Ma made me come over to see if you were still alive. Also, she had these two leftover raisin pies."

"Come on in, pa. I still got coffee...I think."

Pa blew the steam from the cup and peered at his youngest son. "Pardon my sayin' it, son, but you look totally gone. Wore out. Things come pilin' in on you...?

Silence was the answer.

"Well, I'm fixin' to break your own rule. I ain't really interferin', just makin' a suggestion. After all, you're still my son. There's times a body can't see the forest for the trees and I think that's where you live. Right in the thick'a the forest."

From the pocket of his Macannaw he pulled a wrinkled sheet of paper. "There are some things that are not humanly possible workin' at alone. You gotta have help. Look here at this paper. To my reckonin', you need a milk man. Single with another source of money. I've sorta been askin' around and here's what I come to.

"If you had a nice, tight cabin…maybe 16 feet square…you could advertise for help. Tight cabin. No rent. All the milk and cheese he could use. Access to the woods for hunting and a garden spot. All this in return for 5 hours of work a day…milkin' and maybe herdin' the goats. Gossip tells me you'd get a response. 'Course, you'd need to make changes to what I said you'd need. Only you know that. I was thinkin' that bein' tied to the udder'a them bleatin' nannies was cutin' into your day, keepin' you from doin' anything else."

Wayne had sliced into one of the pies and was hoisting a generous slice to his mouth. Pie for breakfast…what luxury. Spicy meat, raisins and honey. Pa just about said it all…for a fact. He watched as pa spread out the sheet of paper and put it before him. There, outlined in pencil, was a cabin. Crude but very easy to visualize.

"Now, Pa, when did you do this?"

"About a month ago."

There in his mind came the verse '…for your Father knoweth what things you need before you ask Him…." There was Pa…and the other Father. Of course. Positively uncanny how memorized verses came to mind 15 years later.

Pa went on, "Now that money you earned down at Turners Sawmill must be gettin' low, but I know it isn't gone, with you still here tryin' to manage. So if you was to buy the dimension lumber I'd manage to haul it over here if they'd bring it to my house. Mine bein' closer. If I got the foundation laid out, your brothers'd likely give you a half a day to get the roof gables up. Then I'd do the rest." He waited while his youngest son studied the paper.

Then he added, "Ma says she'd got extra's on everything but the iron stove. Might have to buy that."

Wayne studied the cabin. Say, wouldn't he love to have that for himself, but the wisdom of it made sense. It would take a good cabin to get decent help, and for himself he would want something a lot bigger. It would just have to wait.

"Yeah, Pa. I'd really appreciate it." Then a grin…. "If the fellows could help, I could pay them in cheese. I ain't even got a market yet!"

"Good idea. They'd go for it in a minute."

Wayne looked longingly at the pie, but decided to save the rest of it. Raisin pie got better with age. Everyone knew that. If he could keep from nibbling on it.

Then Pa, again. "Now, Son, not meanin' to put ideas in your head, but have you got some'a that cheese all ready, now?"

At Wayne's nod, he continued. "Then you need to get on in to McCafferty's right now with a sample. It may take a hard-headed Irishman a week or two to make up his mind that you have a good thing. I've got Jasper out there and he's sufferin' for a good run. Ride on over with a sample and pick up more vats. Ma said you'd need 'em."

Hmmm, now how would she have known that? Had he mentioned it? Didn't remember it, if he did.

Pa again. "I'll just take Bessie back home, and we'll swap back when it's handy. Now, Ma has a sign made to tack on the tree at the Junction. Be quicker'n the Cryer, Ma thought, and it'd attract locals…not someone too far away.

"I could go tack it up, and ride on down to Turner's and get an estimate on this cabin…if you agree. Right now catches me at a good time. Just layin' around gettin' fat."

It was a lot to take in, after the discouraging morning he had experienced, but it seemed like the sun just popped out from behind a cloud.

"Sure, Pa. I'd appreciate it."

The older man nodded agreeably. "I'm thinkin' you got the butcherin' all figured out. Young goat ain't like a hog or a steer."

"Yeah, Pa. Even got the pulley in the tree to hang the meat over night. Just waitin' for time."

"You're gonna get some, now." And Pa was gone. Jasper was snorting and nosing around for dry grass. Wayne dreaded the trip with everything that was within him. He was a worker and a planner…not a salesman.

With a sigh, he cut a slab of the cheese. Six inch diameter and eight inches long. Make about a dozen hefty sandwiches, he figured.

Wrapping it in brown butcher paper, he put it in the side saddle and headed toward Washbone. Thanks to Pa a'pushin' him, he'd get his answer now and know what to count on.

Jasper tossed his magnificent brown head and snorted his readiness to be on the way. The human on his back paid little attention as he broke into a distance-eating canter. Pulling wagons or buggies was a drudge, but a human on his back…now that was a pleasure on a day as nippy with cold as this one.

While they moved along the road that skirted the railway, the Mountaineer whistle blasted, and the donkey's tail of smoke appeared around the bend. Four passenger cars and eight boxcars. The boxcars rattled like they were empty…likely going for coal.

Wayne swallowed hard and turned his head away, though he usually watched as the darkened windows flew past. It was with mixed discouragement and relief that he let Lennie fly by on the wings of her own dream. It was clear he was not really anything to her but a ride home after her shift, and she was not ready to include him in her own dreams.

Best he look away and plan the way he would butcher and process the meat the way Ma had suggested.

Before the door to the sandwich shop, he drew in a deep breath and exhaled, though it didn't seem to help a lot. The old man who ruled the shop with an iron hand sat by the window, a steaming mug before him. Perfect timing.

"Mr. McCafferty…? Nippy day out there, but sunny."

The old man turned a head and just looked at Wayne with a total lack of expression.

Wayne moved toward him, and asked. "Could I possibly leave a sample of my new product? It's feta cheese from goats who came from Finland. Bred special for this kind'a cheese. Folks out my way say it has a good taste…a little different from what folks round here are used to. I'm going to have a supply of it in a couple of months, and thought I'd leave a free sample with you…if I could."

Wayne noticed the distant expression change with the word 'free.' So far, so good. He placed the wrapped bundle on the table beside the old man.

"I have some chores here in town, and a full day planned, so I can't stay but you wouldn't need me here to see if you like it. My ma thinks it brings up the flavor of the herbs better when it's been toasted under a flame…but you'd know that already."

Expression guardedly interested. Time to leave.

"Good day to you, Mr. McCafferty. I'll be checking around in a day or two…maybe three. I'm in the process of gearing up into full production, and I'd prefer not to have to go on to Eureka Springs." Then something just popped into this mind.

"I was thinkin' of maybe wanting just two places in Wishbone…maybe a retail café like yours, and later on, maybe Wilkerson's market. No more than that. My product will be a specialty, I'm thinkin', and if this works out, I will be havin' a meat product for makin' chile. One that can be left on the shelf until needed."

With a bright smile and a two-fingered salute, he turned and left, quietly closing the door behind him. Not one word had escaped the wrinkled face of the old Irishman.

Wayne grinned to himself as he headed toward the hardware store for the vats. Throwing out the hint of the meat was just a gift from his thoughts. Maybe the angels. Might make the old man curious.

THINKING TO DO

Lennie had not been watching when the Mountaineer sailed noisily by the man on the horse. She had, instead, made the last check of her passengers and perched on a stool in the stock room. She had actually parted with a dime of her earnings for a tablet on white, unlined sheets of paper, and another two cents for a No. 2 pencil.

She had not, for the last year, given much thought to her salary as it has been building up on the books of the BNSF railway. A salary had not been an important part of her dream. It was there, of course, and she could check on it when she wanted to, but mostly she didn't. The Railway furnished so much of her expense there was very little to buy.

Stockings, of course. If she could have used men's socks, they would have been free. Shoes they furnished. Handkerchiefs were furnished, and she had developed a liking for the huge, blue and white checked squares of soft fabric. And there were hairpins, of course, not furnished.

But this time she had drawn a whole dollar. Quite a lot, but she needed to have a bit of change just in case....

She had hired on for $8.00 a week, regardless of her schedule. After her month of 'training' she was raised to $10.00 a week. She knew it was a wonderful amount...even the young men with wives could see the advantage of something so permanent that supplied so many things.

Leon had bragged on his Cassie. He had installed her in a two-room cabin on the eastern hill surrounding the town. Cassie did not want Leon's money to stay on the books. She wanted it where she could keep track of it...right there in the Bank/Real Estate Office.

Leon had said that Cassie could squeeze a nickel so tight the buffalo hollered. She also searched for bargains where he would never have thought. She was saving for a bigger house, one that they would buy and not rent, and then there might be a baby.

But for Lennie, the Railway books were clearly the answer for safe-keeping. She could draw what she wanted any day as the railway was always open. So, other than stockings and hairpins, there was little she needed, and there was that thought that niggled within her brain that there would be an important 'something' someday. Even now she had no inkling as to what it would be.

But she wanted the tablet. The thread of feminity within her was alive and well even while she worked with young men and the various train crews. She had taken the tablet home with her, and, for some reason, had measured the size of her room...also the windows and ceiling height. Seemed important, somehow.

She also studied the pattern of the curtains that had decorated her room from the first time she could remember. Baskets of flowers. Most of them blue and a blue ribbon was tied on the basket handle. Between the flower baskets were butterflies of every size, shape and color, but mostly yellow. She wondered, absently, if there had been a choice of fabric when Mama had bought the yard-goods for the curtain. No matter. It all belonged to Papa and Mama, anyway.

So she sat on the stool with the pencil and a ruler straight edge. She made a square the size of her room, one inch equaling four feet. Looking at the square, she saw it was too small, so she re-drew it with one inch equaling two feet.

Much better. She studied it, placing the furniture there…in her mind. Nice thing about a mind, she could switch the furniture around in a minute and without a bit of effort and just the use of the rubber eraser. And pictures on the wall. Of course.

Her favorite wall decoration was the shelf Grandad had made for her train, the gift from Wayne. She stared out the window at the scenery rushing by. Such a nice fellow, Wayne. He was as dependable as the sun coming up every day. But he really bit off a lot with his dream. Sounded good, when he talked about it, which wasn't often. Seemed he never needed help.

Those goats! That buck kept climbing on the shed where he was existing, and Wayne was afraid he'd punch through the roof with his hooves. Sounded reasonable. Who knew when Wayne would be able to get a real house, but she had not a doubt that he would get there. Someday. He seemed to have unending patience.

She mentally climbed back aboard the Mountaineer. The scenery flew past, and occasional there would appear a mountain cabin, or a cluster of houses, likely family members, wanting to be close. There was that one house that she liked to see. It was just past Berryville, and looked out over the valley and the railway.

Made of stone, it was, with a porch all the way across the front. The porch pillars shone white as sheets on the line when they went by on a sunny morning. But there was also the two storied house with a balcony and windows all across the front. She liked that one as well. Maybe even better,

Then the familiar Mountaineer whistle sounded and jolted Lennie from her reverie. In a second the flowered curtains and the house on the bluff with the white pillars were erased from her mind like a puff of smoke in a windstorm.

Mail bags! Time to be on the job.

Leon had been manning the mail drops, and it was time for the tour from the coal car to the caboose, eyes searching for anything wrong or out of place, looking at every passenger unobtrusively from the 'corner of the eye,' so to speak.

A wrinkled claw of a hand reached out to her. "Miss, could I bother you for a cup of water. The doctor told me to take one of these, and it's time." In the shaking palm, he held a pressed tablet about the side of a horse pill. Oh, the poor fellow.

She was back in a flash with a cup of water, and insisted on holding it while he drank, hopefully to save his clothes from a soaking. Digging a hand in her pocket, she came with a cellophane wrapped mint. "Try this, sir. Maybe take away the taste. Could I unwrap it for you…?"

She could, and she remembered to thank him for the privilege of helping him. Company rule for the railway. Politeness and helpfulness beyond what was expected.

And the husky baby had sucked his bottle dry and was protesting loudly. Simple to take care of. It seemed almost a sin to take the money when so much of the job was so easy.

Money. She couldn't say exactly how much she had on the books, but it was over $500.00. Seemed incredible, along with a touch of unreality. Such a lot of money belonging to one person! But she had not the urge to let her thoughts dwell on it… just a thought in passing.

No one in her family ever mentioned the money she must have, and no one asked her what she was going to do with it. If they had, she couldn't have answered with any degree certainty.

While jogging back to Chigger Ridge (no chiggers still about, eggs must be dormant) a thought entered Wayne's head. Now that he had actually contacted Mr. McCafferty, he needed to hedge his salesmanship with a plan "B." Ma had said, and he had listened with interest, there was a certain kind of kettle that cooked under pressure and it took a lot less time and attention. Ma thought, though she wasn't sure, that there was one that could accept at least two half-gallon jars. Time to think of the goat meat, and that cooker might be the answer.

Ma had said that one of the ladies with a huge family had mentioned that her children saved and bought her one for Christmas because she was required to can in such large jars, and they took an extra hour to process…the hour that she did not have. Pressure canner, it was called. If it was available, Eureka Springs would have it.

He'd think about it, and maybe catch the Mountaineer over to see it. But before he got back to Chigger Ridge, that thought was overridden by one that said if such a thing was available, it would be impossible to get it home on horseback. It would take a buggy and a trip over there. Something to think on, anyway.

But the more he thought, the more he knew he'd do it. He had only to leave the goats out of the corral and the kids would take care of the milking. At this point, the milk was not that valuable, and the pressure canner would be.

Immediately after the morning milking, he hitched the buggy to Jasper and added a half a wheel of cheese, as he had for McCafferty. Stopped for a second at his parents' house…maybe Ma wanted something. She didn't, but she loaded him up with sandwiches enough to last two days.

"No way they could spoil in this cold," Ma assured him with a chuckle. Good old Ma! She so greatly wanted him to succeed with his project…his dream…He'd really lucked out with her.

It killed the better part of a day to get up to Ridge Road and down to the larger city of Eureka Springs. It was said that if it couldn't be gotten in Eureka, you didn't really need it. And the more he thought on it, he NEEDED that cooker, or he would be tied to the stove for days at a time to assure the meat sealed properly. Too much work went into it to chance losing it, and it was something he would need for years…if things worked right. Sometimes he felt as though he was pulling a string of boxcars and none of the couplings were hooked. Cars and problems going every which of a way.

Where would he go with the cheese? Many places came to mind, but the diner in the hotel seemed to tower above them. It was the preferred stop for festive occasions and for a place that was always open. They specialized in certain fish, so why would they not always specialize in feta cheese?

His cheese. Of course it may not be necessary to acquire them as a customer, but still he had that as part of his sales package. Folks should get to know about it.

And when he finally headed back up to Ridge Road toward Burnt Tree Junction, he rested easy in his mind. The canner in the back seat would easily hold three jars…the huge half a gallon ones. Also, the manager at the diner was intrigued and gladly accepted the free sample. They were always interested in new products, he was assured.

Even with Flora plodding alongside, Jasper was getting worked down and was content to walk…and to hang his head and blow his lungs when he had a chance. Ridge Road was created from hills and valleys.

Pa had already accepted the first load of dimension lumber from Turner's. That would be the floor joist. It'd keep him busy for a few days.

Wayne hid his weariness behind his excitement. Something was being done and wasn't he blessed with his parents?

While Pa was on the premises, Wayne attempted to butcher the first goat. He'd helped numerous times, but…well, it seemed right to have Pa near on the right time.

And the meat. He cut the pieces and boiled them down in one of the new vats. When the correct shrinkage had occurred, and the baseball sized pieces were tender, he packed them into three of the large jars, filling in the spaces with broth.

So now onward to the stove. The canner made a disturbing racket with its steam, and Wayne was a bit nervous. What if the whole thing blew up, taking his shack, such as it was, along with it? But no matter. The petcock jiggled merrily as he watched the pressure rise, then he timed it.

Forty-five minutes, and let it cool for an hour. That's what the directions said. He gently lifted the petcock. Nothing happened but a small swoosh of the last bit of steam. He waited another half an hour and lifted (with the handy little lifter) and the first jar came out. Lid sealed tightly, like Ma said it should be.

He set the jar on the warm part of the stove and stood back. It looked exactly like Ma's jars, except twice as big. One of the baby goats had filled three jars with enough for a meal for himself left over. This was indeed a big day, and he looked upward toward his patched ceiling and gave thanks. He had no strength for words.

He went to bed exhausted…mostly from nerves but his last thought was, say, Ma can use this canner for her beef. It would hold seven of her jars. It took a chunk out of his savings, but the cabin took more. Scary, actually. Some money was going to have to start coming the other way soon.

He timed his visit to McCafferty's to Lennie and the Mountaineer. It would chug and huff its way in just after dark, bringing her home. It would be cold, but they'd make it home. He still had Jasper, and he was a tough mule and did not seem bothered by the cold. They'd make it.

At the café, he wandered in as though he was not as tense as a bow string. "How are you, Mr. McCafferty? Think we'll get a little snow?"

No answer.

"I had business over in Eureka yesterday. Breeze was right brisk up on the Ridge. Needed to go, though. Warmed up in the hotel diner. They put on a good feed there, if a fellow's real hungry. Even thought they might be interested in the cheese, once I got goin'."

The crotchity old man just stared. Finally, "Harrumph! Case you're workin' up to it, I have a place bringin' me cheese regular. I been their customer fer years."

Wayne swallowed quickly and plastered on a smile. "That's good to know, Mr. McCafferty. The truth is, I already knew that. I just thought you bein' almost a neighbor, you'd what to know what all was around. Likely it'd stretch my capacity, anyway. My wheels are six inches around to a little over a foot long. Likely be more'n you could sell, anyway. By my figgerin' there'd be at least 24 slices. With a slicer like yours, it'd maybe make 30. That's a lotta cheese to be stuck with."

Silence.

"The diner, now, with the trade they got…anyway, I just came in for a bowl'a chile."

Mr. Macafferty yelled to the 'help' for service, and wondered, "How much was you sellin' that cheese for, anyway?"

Wayne crumbled crackers in his steaming chile and blew on the first bite. "Good chile. My ma makes hers with goat meat from a young kid, times she can get it. I'm gonna be havin' it real regular for her.

"Now that cheese. I'd only let it go by the total wheel and I'll be gettin' $2.00 each. Good chance that'd be more'n you want to pay, you already havin' a good source for the unflavored kind." He scooped another bite into his mouth, and commented, "Nothin' quite like chile on a cold day."

He finished the chile down to the last smidgen and stood up, "Well, Mr. McCafferty, been nice talkin' with you. See you later." And he headed for the door.

The grouchy old voice called, "Wait! Next time you're in, you can bring me a wheel'a that cheese."

Acting surprised, Wayne turned. "Are you sure, Mr. Macafferty? High priced as it is?"

"Young man, don't stand there and tell me what I can pay for. You just bring me a wheel…no, make it two. I've run this place longer'n you've been breathin'. Reckon I can make up my own mind."

"Yes, sir, Mr. McCafferty! Whatever you say. It'll likely be three days, but I'll be comin' in anyway, and I'll put it on the load."

Easing out the door, he took a breath of the frigid air. Gonna be cold goin' home. Good thing he had tight flaps on the buggy. Walking to the Mountaineer depot he felt so weak in the knees he wondered how his wobbly legs were holding him up.

Doin' a sellin' job sure took somethin' outta a fellow, he told himself by way of consolation. And at that moment the air was filled with the whistle of the Mountaineer. On time. Welcome sound, for sure.

He tucked Lennie into the quilts and wedged a pillow behind her back. They were not ten minutes down the road until she was asleep. The lanterns shone through the windshield on her beautiful face…flushed by the cold air. Skin the color of strawberry blossoms. Gonna have to plant some of those.

"Get on up there, Jasper. We're right along behind you."

And Jasper got!

HIRED MAN

Silas Cantrell had known about the 'short stick' all his life. Whoever drew it, even though it was not his fault, was passed over for whatever favor was going on. He had experienced it enough to know it well.

That was back when he was a youngen, but now, when he was becoming stooped and gray, why was the short stick rule still in effect?

Youngest in his family meant older siblings were in school when the diphtheria went around. Two weeks later they were dead. Ma died a year later. Pa said the baby took her, and Silas spent years of wondering before he learned how a tiny baby could kill a grown woman.

He and Pa went to Pa's parents to live. Ma didn't have no folks… they said. Silas never did figure how that could have happened. Then Pa got himself killed in the saw mill. Wasn't enough of him left to bury, they said.

Now Silas was permanently with his grandparents. Big Papa was a weaver. He wove split willow limbs and turned them into beautiful furniture. His settees were so strong they lasted a lifetime, even if left in the yard in the rain. He had a special way, but he failed to tell Silas what it was before he died from an infected knife wound.

Big Ma cried herself to death, the neighbors said.

So once more Silas got the short stick. Alone, now.

One thing, however, was that Big Pa had been teaching him the only thing he knew, and Silas was learning fast. He had not graduated to creating a settee, but stools, chairs and small tables were something he did well.

Then he met Daisy and wonder of wonders, she liked him. They were happy for 12 years, still hoping for a baby. But when the baby finally made an appearance, he lost them both. Together. That was when the devastation his pa had felt became real to him.

So now he was a forty-five-year-old man.

While selling his wickerware in Berryville, he met Christine. Lovely lady with a little three year old girl. Amazingly, Christine had agreed to marry him. He took her to the house left him by Big Pa and happily began to create wickerware with a flare. Ideas came in his head in his sleep, it seemed, and he was fierce to leave the bed to try them. Most of the time they worked.

Still, no babies came to him and Christine, but little Marcie was a joy...until she became fifteen and met Asher. They left together to go east to the big River where he would work as a stevedore. Big strong fellow, he was.

Christine cried herself to death, they said. It seemed that Silas' love was not enough to keep her alive, and a winter bout of the influenza took her to a better place...he hoped.

Short stick again.

But what was there to do with one's life except rise up in the mornings and do what one did best. The wickerware that he had no heart to sell began to pile up.

It was on the first of January, 1912, that he decided he'd had enough. Got his bucket of disappointments full...as folks were wont to call it. He loaded his product on his wagon and attached his horse. He'd pull out in the morning and leave word in town for someone to sell his land.

It was in the night that Sandy, his part-collie, began to bark and leap at the front door. Silas pulled himself from the bed and opened it.

There on the porch lay Marcie...at least it must be her. Beside her was a bundle wrapped in a scrap of blanket. The bundle was screaming with indignation, red faced and wet with tears. Wet elsewhere as well.

Sandy sniffed at Marcie and snorted. Not good. Silas felt her pulse. Faint. He pulled her into the room and put a pillow under her head. Her eyes never opened.

He picked up the bundle and took it to the kitchen table. He unwrapped the ragged blankets and found a baby boy...maybe six months old. Well, Silas had milk and babies needed milk. He was going to sell the goat in town, but instead he stripped her almost-dry udder and brought the milk into the house.

No nursing bottle. He poured the milk into a cup and lifted the baby to his lap. The little fellow fought the hard against rim of the cup but hunger finally won out. He slurped and sucked, allowing drool to soak his clothing. A jolly good mess.

Silas went back to the girl on the living room floor and felt her pulse. Nothing. Gone. On further examination, he saw the blood soaked coat. Her arm had been…shot? Now how could that have happened? And how had she gotten to the house with only one arm to carry the baby?

So many questions and no answers. No way to get answers. No matter, that was just the way his life went. Why should he expect something different? So now, just as he was leaving, he suddenly had two problems. What to do with Marcie and how to feed her little boy. And he didn't even know the baby's name.

Marcie first. He took his spade from the barn wall and walked out into the pasture. Selecting a small space among the cedar trees, he began to dig. Yes, he could take her to town and she would be buried properly, but he had the baby to contend with.

Short stick again.

He put the unfortunate girl on the sled and pulled her to the makeshift grave. He spread a blanket and put her on it, folding her hands across her chest. Such a pretty girl…she had been. He allowed himself the present of shedding a pair of tears for what might have been, and then he folded the blanket over her.

There were words that should be said, but he could think of none. He looked up through the cedars where a pair of bluebirds were scolding him to leave. They wanted access to their babies in the nest…and would Silas please leave….

The man spoke to the spot of blue sky. "You'd know better'n me what happened. You'd know I'm doin' the best I can, and I can use a little help with that baby. If you could see your way clear…."

Later, thinking on that moment, he wondered why it did not occur to him to take the baby to the authorities in Berryville. They'd have found him a home, but Silas did not even think of it…let alone decide to do it. He had always just taken what came his way and moved on. Dealing with circumstances as he found them. Or as they found him.

Obviously, he could not leave as he had planned. He unpacked his belongings and put the horse back in the pasture. He milked the goat as thoroughly as possible to try to eek out the supply…until he could make a better decision.

Another goat, maybe, or there were stores that had foods for babies. He could take the loaded furniture on to town and sell it.

Buy…what…? What do babies need, and how old is the little fellow? If he looked for help, the world outside his life would then decide that a sixty-one-year-old man was not capable of raising a baby. If that was true, then why was the baby in his house? It only made sense…until it didn't.

The little fellow was crying again. Wet and hungry. So he needed diapers and food, and more clothing. A better, baby-sized blanket to replace the faded and torn scrap he came in with.

He made a fire and put on the kettle with a half a dozen potatoes. It was a start. He had eggs…it helped to sell a farm with chickens in residence. He took ten of the eggs from the nest.

Eggs, boiled and mashed with milk? That was fed to baby chickens that had no ma…so why not a human?

Name. If Marcie'd only told him the baby's name. He held the baby by the window and studied his face. Stephen. He had a solid chin and firm bones. He would be built like his papa surely.

"So, Stephen, are you ready to eat?" The wide, brown eyes seemed to understand…and he was certainly ready. He was currently gnawing his toothless mouth on his knuckles. Slurping hungrily.

Silas hoisted him to a shoulder while he peeled a boiled potato with one hand. Mashed and soupy with milk, he lifted a tiny bite to Stephen's mouth. Stephen seemed ready for anything, and dealt with this strange substance with determination and a small amount of skill. Another bite and another. Very good.

Potatoes for breakfast, and eggs for lunch. It had to work. This must not be permitted to be a 'short stick.' Never had the 'short stick' been his fault, and up to now he'd had no opportunity to lengthen it. This time he did. He would keep this little bundle and hope he could do the right thing. They had something in common…the little fellow had gotten the short stick as well.

Things worked satisfactorily until he used up the willow switches he had, and the trip to gather more meant a trip to the fast flowing Kings River…a campout…and a wade into the water to get the best switches. To make the trip worthwhile, it needed to last two or three days. How was that to happen with Stephen who seemed to require constant attention…as any toddler would?

But Silas was accustomed to dealing with whatever came at him, and this one was facing him now. He bravely packed his tent, bedding, food in the way of potatoes and eggs. Tying the new goat to the wagon, he set out. The trip would take about an hour. He'd gather as fast as he could, and come home. Another hour. That would make about four hours. With luck.

At the river he parked the wagon in a grove of trees and settled almost two-year-old Stephen in the tent. As he headed to the river, the child toddled after him or screamed. Had to do something. Finally, to actually get enough switches to make the trip somewhat worthwhile, he tied a rope to one chubby leg and the other end to a tree. Stephen was securely tethered.

Rushing to the water, he waded in and slashed wildly at the spring sprouts, piling them on the bank, while attempting to ignore the agonized screaming from the trees.

He had a sizeable pile accumulated, and stood looking at it, trying to catch his breath. Glancing up at the sun, he realized the child might be getting hungry, and then maybe he'd nap.

But when he looked in the trees, there was no Stephen. Silas felt his heart leap into his throat, taking his breath away. Holding to the wagon bed, he pulled himself into his senses. Gone! The little fellow was gone, and he…Silas…had let it happen. *Dear Lord… what do I do…?*

Then he heard a familiar crow of glee. Stephen always loudly announced any new experience. Dashing toward the noise, he saw Stephen standing in the shallow water holding to a slender willow switch and pulling with all his small might. Seeing Silas running toward him, he laughed happily and said, "Tree! My tree!"

As Silas' terror settled into his chest, he slowed to a walk. "Son, are you helpin' Papa?"

"Help!" he squealed. It was one of the new words he had learned to say, but not exactly what it meant. He pulled at the tree and slid down into the mud of the bank. With his bottom squarely down in the water, he still held to the immature switch…too small to be of use. Silas, however, reached out and severed the stem, leaving the leafy end in the child's chubby fist.

"Help...?" he questioned his papa. He really liked to be sure of new words.

"Yes, Son. You are good help." But his firm lips would rather tell the child Papa was scared out of his 'bee-jabbers.' Taking him to the wagon, he changed the muddy clothing, and packed up the camping gear. Retrieving the rope from the tree, he saw that the granny knot had been carefully loosened by two-year-old fingers. Imagine that! There was a good chance he could make a weaver out of that boy, and pass on the only skill he had.

Guiding the horse through the trees, goat trailing behind, Silas relived the last hours. Pride, concern and doubt braided themselves securely together within the depth of his being. Clearly he had reached the point that something had to be done.

He had enough willow switches to last about a month, during which time he would decide. First he would make a trip to Eureka Springs with the products he now had...mostly small stools loved by children. He'd look around, and maybe there would be an answer

He'd sell his land. He certainly did not need forty acres that had no willows. He needed about five acres near a river...but how to find something so specific for his own particular and unique need?

He crossed the bridge over the Kings River, shivering over what could have happened. Truly, a fellow in his sixties had no business with a toddler who was going to be an active little boy. Maybe he'd take a room in Eureka Springs...or maybe Wishbone Hollow. He should be able to figure it all out before the switches were used up.

He'd sell what was on the wagon, and then go back and put the house up for sale. Climbing out of the Kings River valley was a long and tiring pull. At the top on Ridge Road he saw some patches of spring green and by now the horse could use a rest. He had a long way to go.

Silas guided the animal to the left and unhitched him. No one would begrudge him a little grass for the horse, and a place to rest at the tables nearby. And fix himself and the boy some food.

Stephen was overjoyed to be out of the constraints of the wagon, flitting here and there and laughing at the birds...and sometimes at nothing. Such a happy child! But he had to be watched every minute.

While following his 'son' around, he saw the sign tree. He'd heard of it, but hadn't seen it. There were several notices tacked to the trunk, and for something to do, he read them all.

This and that for sale. Funeral for so-and-so. Wedding party next Saturday.

Man needing handyman help. Cabin furnished, 5 hours work daily. All the milk and cheese he could use would be furnished, along with a woodland for hunting and a river with catfish and brem.

Directions were printed below. Hmmm, well...? Why not! Couldn't hurt to check it out. And while he was considering that, a man rode up on a horse. Seemed he had a sign to put on the tree.

After a greeting, the man looked at the tree. Well, well! His sign was still there. One couldn't count on signs not being stolen, and he had a replacement ready.

Silas approached. "That there sign yours?"

After receiving a nod, he asked, "Where at is that place?"

The man with the sign was interested. "Are you lookin' for a place?"

"Could be. That river have them little willow sprouts in it?"

"Afraid it does. Have to thin 'em out every so often. Belongs to my son and he needs the water flowin' for the goats. They're what has to have the four hours milkin' amd another'n for other stuff. I'm helpin' 'im finish up the cabin. Be ready in another week, maybe ten days."

"Mister, me...I make wicker furniture and I'd be glad to relieve your son of them sprouts, if I had a place there for my little boy. Don't mind milkin' goats, neither. Milk and cheese'd be good for the boy."

Wayne's pa bit his lip and gazed out over the bluff at Blue Lake. What was the likelihood...? "How about this. You could come talk with my boy that'd be hirein' you... 'course the cabin won't be ready yet."

"Won't matter. I gotta go back 'cross the river and sell my place. Good place. It'll sell good. I was gonna do that, anyway, bein' ready for a move. Needed a place to get willows and havin' no one to watch over the boy. Cabin'd be good for a start...anyway. He might let me put on a porch to work in...?"

The other man wrestled with his feelings of relief. How were the chances he'd come by just now, with the fellow here, and needing those pesky willows that clogged up the mountain streams. "Say, fellow, you take this here sign with you, and come see us. If you find you don't want the deal, you decide, and we'll put the sign up again."

"It's a deal. My name's Silas, and this here boy is Stephen. We'll be there and we'll just put up our tent 'tilst the cabin gets ready."

With a handshake and a swap of signs, the men parted ways, both puzzled over the way things work out at times. Poor Silas had the most trouble with it. He knew exactly how to deal with the short stick, but here was maybe a long one. How could he bring himself to believe it was real?

They re-crossed Kings River, and Steven squealed with delight and pointed, "Help…?"

Silas nodded. "That's water. It's a river."

"Water!" And he pounded excitedly on 'Papa's' back with both strong arms.

Silas smiled smugly to himself with all the pride afforded to the child of his heart, if not his blood.

SPRING ON CHIGGER RIDGE

March brings the green grass. True, it came up mainly in sheltered places but it does wonders for baby goats and the human spirit. The cheese maker finally warmed up enough to see some sense in his life.

At times it seemed as though he was someone who was expected to learn to swim by being tossed into the watering tower of the Mountaineer. Too deep to stand and no hand holds.

It was not that the problems were unexpected, but more that they came on faster than he had expected, partly brought on by his own success and impatience. He had not intended to keep all the female babies, but when it came to butchering his best asset, he found he couldn't do it.

He'd rather not be bothered by sheering and marketing the hair so soon, but the poor animals suffered too greatly from the Arkansas summer heat and milk production decreased. So he now had more than a dozen burlap sacks of hair hanging in the shed…

and was facing at least half that many more in a couple of months. He had put off butchering the baby males because taking the raw meat into Wishbone would have been impossible…timewise. But Ma's suggestion had eliminated that. He could just store the jars until a trip was made.

And speaking of trips, he had rather tied himself to the two trips to be made every ten days for Lennie. He didn't have to, of course, but her Grandad was so old, and….

Face it. However slowly his plans for the future seemed, he was reluctant…no, too stubborn…to turn loose of his tenuous hold on Lennie's time. True, at least a third of her departures and arrivals were in late evening or barely after midnight. So he lost a night's sleep as well.

On the other hand, if he made them, Lennie was at least at home when morning came, and could spend more time with her family. And he was back in his shack when the sun came up on his myriad of duties.

And the relationship. Was it plugging along evenly…or maybe declining? It was a worry, every time he allowed himself a minute to worry, but no answer seemed in sight.

So now it was spring and Silas and 'son' had been installed. Wayne had pictured a stooped and bearded old widower to whom the five hours of work were the extent of his energy. Instead, he had Silas who was excited to be there, and the milking chore was tossed off as so much nothing.

He was gray-haired, of course, but slim and strong, bright eyed and laughing, and stepped along spritely, followed by the robust little fellow. He had not confided as to his family situation, nor did Wayne ask…or even care. Silas had hardly moved in before he requested to enclose half the large porch making a room about eight by 10. Putting in another door, he had a room where he could tuck in his wood-burning cook stove and its supply of dry wood.

In the summer, he could merely open a window and close a door and leave the heat of cooking outside. The low gabled roof of the attic was six foot in the center making room for two full sized sleeping pads…or a couple hammocks if desired. Hammocks were cooler in the summer.

Inventive. Wayne liked him even more as the pile of willow switches were now garnered from the creek. The 'hired man' seemed to be settling in for a long time with only the initial expense of the lumber.

One problem down.

Next problem? He had located another buck of the same breed as the male he had purchased from Finland. It was in residence in Hot Springs, a town down to the south and almost to Little Rock. He'd decided he'd need a crate for Old Fellow, his goat, and would accompany it to Hot Springs on the Firefly. He'd be picked up by the owner of Oscar, the other goat, and swap out.

He was looking good on paper now that Silas was here to tend to the milking.

When he had returned Lennie to Wishbone after loading on the two wheels of cheese, he dropped in at McCafferty's Corner. Just for a 'casual chat.' He'd ordered chile again, and the old man commented on the prospect of canned meat delivered.

Wayne, learning some of the ways of selling, tossed off the question by stating, "Oh, that's just my ma's idea. She's always got somethin' she wants to do, and if she had a jar'a the meat settin' handy, she'd got a dozen things to do with it. Chile bein' one of the best. Soaks them beans and chops that meat into shreds and tosses it in with onions…spicin' it up at the end. Nothin' to it, and she can decide on the moment to do it." He faced the old Irishman with a casual smile.

"Well, Mr. McCafferty, that was a good lunch. I'll be runnin' along and…."

But the old man butted in. "Young man, what's the price on a half gallon'a that meat?"

Acting surprised, Wayne turned, "Oh, I was just makin' talk. You got a good set up here, butcher knowin' to keep you in mind, and you havin' help to go get it. Bound to be better for you. I was just…."

"SIT DOWN, young man. Listen to me. I don't need you tellin' me what I need and don't need. You put a price on that jar'a meat, or get on outta here."

Whereupon, Wayne smiled agreeably. "Sure thing, Mr. McCafferty. My price is without the jar, lessen I charge fifty cents more. The meat is $2.00, just like the cheese…makin' $2.50. But if that jar gets returned to me, there ain't no charge for the next one. That fifty cents is what I pay for jars, and I sure hate to be keep orderin' 'em. My hope'd be to drop off a jar or maybe two or three, and pick up the empties. There'd be a charge only on the first jar."

Mr. McCafferty was acquainted with sales pitches. "Remember, young man, I can add and subtract. Why don't you drop off a couple of jars on your next trip. I'd buy the jars and that would be $5.00. Right? Then if I don't like it, you could buy back the jars for a dollar. Understand?"

"Yes sir, Mr. McCafferty. I can add too, and I thank you. Fact is, I have a couple of jars in my buggy that I was headin' on up the street with. I could let you have them, and make that other delivery later."

"Do that. Bring 'em on in here."

And Wayne did. Then he walked away with a smug smile on his face and the pleasant weight of five silver dollars in his pocket. Once the old man saw the ease of the canned jars, he'd be a customer. Sure to be.

He'd really like to take a sample of the cheese up to Wilkerson's Market but he'd wait. Maybe McCafferty's Corner could take it all. He did a right smart business on workman's lunches.

Lennie sat on her stool and watched the scenery fly past the window. It had become a habit to have her notebook open, even when she had nothing to write. She had measured her parents' house from end to end and sideways, and marked off the position of the rooms.

Then scribbling it out, she kept the shell and positioned the rooms differently. Bigger parlor with real places for a group, rather than just for 'Sunday company' or someone selling something.

Soft stuffed settee. Maybe two of them opposite in the room. Lamps on the wall. There never seemed to be enough lamps at her parents' house and homework had seemed to end up on the kitchen table, though not until the dishes were removed. No matter! It was just fun to having something to think about other than the house up on the bluff with white porch pillars.

Leon came through for the mop. "Someone waited too long to go to the 'out house.'" He grinned tolerantly.

Lennie left the tablet and the window. "I'll do it. You need to be asleep."

He handed over the mop. "Thanks." Tumbling into his cot, he sighed and fell asleep. It was a neat trick that had to be learned, or they just wouldn't survive on their schedule.

Lennie lined up the mail bags and made a trip to the back. They had three passenger cars, and would pick up two more to take on to Berryville plus their baggage car and caboose. Also, there would be four empties to return to the Hobo Express (maybe she'd get to wave at Joe) and take on coal to go south on the Firefly.

Coal south…on the Firefly. Cotton north on the Eagle to the clothing mills up that way. That had been going on all winter. The Burlington Northern family of locomotives had been very busy. Word was that there were several new guards being interviewed. They needed them. On days off, that left only one guard on the Mountaineer, a lot of the time. Also, on the Screaming Eagle.

She had the mail for Willow Bluff ready to throw. She'd come around the wide curve that circled Chigger Ridge. No one in sight. She sighed wearily. What had happened with herself and Wayne? There was a time that they couldn't talk fast enough when they were together…now there were silences, discussions of the weather, or she napped on the pile of pillows.

It was almost like they were walking in opposite directions… or maybe just going the same direction but on opposite sides of the mountain. Like the morning side of the mountain that also had a twilight side of the hill and the inhabitants never met. Another sigh, and the Mountaineer rumbled through the small communities and whistled at the bends.

Dipped down to Kings River and crossed on the wonderful steel bridge. Safety bolsters on each side of the bridge to protect it against collations of any sort. Accidental or on purpose.

The change in the vibration woke Leon from his two hour nap. Sitting up and rubbing sleep from his eyes was an action well known to the guards. Worked well.

Leaving the cubby, he was aware of the new passenger cars taken on at Morrisville, and from habit, he turned toward the caboose. The baggage car was packed with suitcases and a few small crates and packages. He took in, without actually think of it, the size and number of the wooden boxes. Hmmm. Well, the local law enforcement must be stocking up on ammo.

On to the caboose, and a look around. The sound of the rails became different when they left the bridge. Interesting how one learned to tell by the vibration and rumble of the drivers where one was…forest, hills, valley, up hill or down hill…and the Kings River Bridge had a 'solid' sound if indeed a sound could seem to be strong and solid.

By the end of the bridge there stood a pair of wagons with horses in harness. Maybe it was three wagons, but he didn't get a really good look. He did hear a different sound. An ominous sound. Dread shivers passed from his scalp down his arms. Sort of a dizzy sensation…what in the tarnatin was wrong with him? Coming down with something…? For goodness sake, why was he feeling like he was going backward…and down hill?

He turned to the window and stared out, and saw he actually WAS going backward. Trees and clouds were zipping past going the wrong way. The caboose took a wobble and a jerk. Without the train to stabilize it, that is what would surely happen. Leon swallowed hard, grabbed something he hoped was solid enough to hold him, and watched.

Everything seemed to take long minutes to happen, but were actually just seconds. When the caboose finally hit the bolster of the bridge, it split at the corner of impact, and laid over. All loose contents of the cabin flew out of the broken part, including the security guard himself.

In seconds it had happened. Flying through the steelworks overhead, he collided with a bar that flung him away from the track but into the water. The icy liquid was somewhat welcome, for a moment. Water could be escaped from…and not as hard as stones. He was a good swimmer.

Then the pain attacked him with the stab of a sword plunging through his left leg. As if in sympathy, his right arm seemed to be on fire, and in horror a glance showed a reddening of the water.

The force of the water was carrying him under the bridge with determined speed. Grabbing a pillar he moved to the upstream side to stop the flow, looked above the water and heard excited screaming and scrambling.

Help coming…Wonderful! But it was not to be. It seemed the baggage car had followed the caboose down hill, and the Mountaineer could be heard retreating in the distance. In an instant, his mind cleared.

HOLD UP! That's what it had to be!

Jagged pains shot up from his leg and fiery stabs from his arm, and he was shivering from the water. He started to try to swim to shore but the noisy sound was the gleeful cries of the thieves as they carried wooden crates to the wagons. Suitcases and other baggage were strewn about…and ignored.

It was the ammo they were after, but how did they get the car to separate from the train? It was obvious that they'd expected this to happen. They were waiting in exactly the right place.

So what was he to do? Of course the Mountaineer would have known by now what must have happened, and someone would come…but when? As it was, he raised up as high as he could and counted. Nine persons, he thought, and three wagons. If they headed through the woods, they would leave a good trail to follow.

Not only that, the crates were heavy…took two men to carry… so they'd have to be stored somewhere close. Cave…? Surely, but what was the rest of their plan?

He heard their noisy chatter as they boarded the wagons and urged the horses against the load. They obviously had no idea anyone was about, and would likely not be in a great hurry.

One good thing, though. With them gone, he could work toward getting out of the water and seeing what his condition was. Not good, for certain.

The vegetation of the bank was only about twelve feet away, but with the pain it seemed at least a mile. The agony and uncertainty of swimming with one leg and one arm was daunting, but there was no other way. At one point the current whipped him away and downstream, but crashed him into a pillar on the downstream side of the bridge.

It was closer to the bank, and there were willow sprouts. With his teeth and his left arm, he levered himself toward the weedy edge of the river, and pulled himself up.

The cold water had seemingly staunched the bleeding damage to his arm, but when he seated himself on the bank, his worst fears were confirmed. Leg broke. Two places, he decided.

Well, so now…He was cold, and it would be night before help came. What all had he learned about times like this? Prepare to live. That was first. He tried to pull himself backward but the arm began to bleed again. How much blood could be lost and still live…? There seemed to be a lot of red on his sleeve.

From his pocket he pulled a sodden handkerchief and with the help of his teeth, he opened the wet folds. Twisting twice around just below his shoulder he was able to tighten the makeshift tourniquet and tuck the ends under. The friction of the wet cloth seemed to hold itself in place.

The leg. Every inch he moved sent violent pains all the way up his side and his pants leg was sodden with red.…

Still, he must somehow get across the track to the ruined caboose for protection. That…or the baggage car. Maybe there'd be something in the wreckage to splint his leg.

Lennie felt the nudge through the cars as the caboose separated, and face pressed to a window, she caught a glimpse of the runaway car just as the Mountaineer rounded a bend.

Dashing to the engine, she shouted. "Lost the caboose in the river!"

The cab crew already knew there was trouble and were on the Marconi to Berryville. "Send rescue to Kings River Bridge. Runaway caboose and baggage car. Passengers presumed safe."

Then Lennie did the next best thing. Find Leon and be ready for additional trouble. It would be almost an hour before Berryville, and trouble could happen in bunches. Security guards should be ready for anything.

The local law was stationed near the river, and the sheriff was accustomed to emergencies. Posse together and on the way within an hour and a half and headed toward the bridge on fresh mounts.

Lennie searched the cars without success, and Leon's cubby was empty. Only one thing could have happened…and obviously had. He was back there in the wreckage. *Oh, dear Lord…help us!*

Leon moved by virtually walking backward on his buttocks, an inch at a time, and dragging his left leg unward with his right hand pulling on his sodden pant leg. The pain was excruciating. He wanted to lay back and give over to the nothingness of a blackout, but instead screamed orders to his mind.

"You will NOT give up. Leg…you just go ahead and hurt if you have to but we're gonna live…you and me. Head…don't you go dizzy me. Don't you let me pass out on the track. A B C D E F G…." He shouted the alphabet over and over.

Both cars had been flung clear of the track…as had obviously been planned by the thieves. Darkness was falling, and in the dimness he saw the wreckage from the baggage car. Closer…just a little farther….

When he reached the first bag, it seemed a milestone. He barely had strength in his right arm to open the catch. Ladies underwear, he knew instantly, from the floral aroma that arose.

Laying it aside, he felt for the most sold, man-like suitcase. Maybe a coat. But no, only shoes and ties. Left arm back on the ground, he lay his hand on a…stick? No! It moved! He couldn't have gotten away if he had to, but he remained breathlessly still. Let it crawl off. No need to fight for territory.

After what seemed an eternity, he put his left arm back again. EEK! The thing was still there… and it was still and hard. Hmmm… just a walking cane.

Well, it had felt like a snake. But hey! If he could just find another one, he'd have a splint…of sorts. And those neckties back there with the shoes. By now the moon had appeared. Bright and encouraging, but not much light down here under trees in the valley.

Canes were a popular item for traveling men, and were not permitted in the cars. Of course there would more canes, and there were. Back to the neckties. Putting the canes on each side of his leg, he poked, with great effort and pain and one hand, three neckties under his leg and the canes and pulled them tight. If the neckties had not been so long, he'd never gotten the end in his teeth to hold them. Pulling them tight, he had reason to be grateful he had not lost teeth in the wreck.

So now, find a place to wait. The splint did not help much on the pain, but did keep his leg straight.Maybe avoid bone chips and splinters. Leaning one suitcase up against the other, he formed a back to lean against. Momentary comfort.

The moon had made considerable progress across the sky before the sound of men and horses. He heard the hooves cross the track, every sound being more wonderful than music.

"HERE! I'm over here! HELP…!"

Voice shouted back, incredulously, "I hear a voice! Stop, everybody!"

Leon gathered strength. "I'm here in the suitcases."

"Hold on, fellow. We're comin'." The sheriff made his way stepping through the suitcases. With luck, the voice would be one of the robbers, injured. "Are you hurt?"

"Sure am. I was in the caboose."

"No lie? Hold on…I see you. Come on over, fellows, bring a light."

With four carbide lanterns around him, Leon sat and gazed upward. Humans! They looked wonderful. The sheriff came closer and looked at the makeshift splint.

"Hmmm, Security Guard! Well, friend, we gotta go follow this trail but I'm leavin' Eb here to stay with you and keep the varmints away with his lantern. Quick as we can, we'll get a way to get you out. You bein' a guard, you understand, don't you? But you done good with the splint and we'll be back soon, one way or the tuther."

The sheriff swung onto the horse and disappeared, "All the rest'a you come on." The quiet of the night thundered from the hooves…maybe eight or ten husky animals.

Eb settled down beside him on another suitcase. "Friend, how'd a thing like this happen?"

Leon had the answer. "Suddenly! Very, very quickly."

True to his word, the sheriff was back. Behind him came a wagon full of something. Hmmm, people.

"What we're thinkin' is, we got these fellows tied back to back and they ain't in no mood to fight, tanked up like they are. I'm thinkin' we can move 'em to the back'a the wagon and put you and Eb in front. He'll drive you out of here. Fellows, find somethin' we can put him on to lift 'im in the wagon. Flat board or somethin'."

Kneeling down by Leon, he sympathized, "You hangin' in there, friend? Wish we could do better by ya, but Eb, here, he'll get you out. The boys and me, we gotta go back and guard the ammo till help gets here."

Leon could only mutter, "Thanks! Thanks a lot!"

A flat part of the caboose door was put beside the suitcase and, with all the care they could manage, moved him to it. At this point, relief almost outweighed the pain. It was actually the numbness that concerned him most. Scary, it was.

Hanging onto the sides of the wagon with his left hand to minimize the jiggles, he rode up out of the valley onto a road. The moon had lowered behind the trees, and the dark silhouette of limbs made a lacework on the horizon.

It was a scene that stamped itself in Leon's mind until he drew his last breath at age seventy-six. Until that birthday was reached, every time he saw moonlight through trees, there it was. The pain… the cold…the fright…the relief…and the actual pleasure of the jiggling wagon that took him to help…every moment of it remained like it was just happening.

Within minutes upon the Mountaineer reaching Berryville, the whole cause of the derailment was known. The 'appropriate' coupling had been filed.

Hidden from immediate view, the metal had been skillfully rasped at the point that would receive the most force as the Mountaineer pulled up from the valley of Kings River. Whoever created this disaster knew exactly what he was doing. It was the duty of the security to check every coupling on every trip and Lennie had not checked the newly attached cars. Neither had Leon.

Leon had been attending to the baggage and Lennie was assisting the passengers. There was a schedule to meet at Berryville and the Mountaineer had been 'assured' that the security check had been done. No matter that the rule was broken to keep a schedule. Each guard was responsible for his own cars, no matter what was told to him.

Lennie gritted her teeth and clenched her fists in anger and irritation that she had been ordered to 'hurry up' and get the passengers aboard. It was totally unfair! But when she saw where the rasping had occurred and how skillfully it had been hidden, she knew that in the dark, as it often was for a departure, she, herself, might have missed it. Lesson learned. Very important lesson learned.

The best part was when the voice on the Marconi advised Mountaineer that the 'guard had been rescued and was hospitalized, and most of the baggage had been recovered. More details to follow...."

Later prognosis advised that an arm muscle had been severely damaged and required extensive repair, and his leg had been broken above and below the knee. Leon would be 6 weeks on crutches, and likely a month more before he could be on duty.

So Lennie was alone. That was frowned on. In Memphis they were able to 'borrow' Joe from the Hobo that was there on a two day layover. The only bright spot for Lennie was to be again working with her trainer but at what cost?

But then, no one had promised her an easy job.

GARFIELD SLONE, EX-GROCER

There was a sudden need for a conference of the heads of the railway family.

Mr. Hackett, who reigned over the Wishbone depot, the Mountaineer's home port, was ordered onto the next transportation to Fayetteville. Mr. Smithfield had grumbled about trouble coming in threes, though the other two of the 'troubles' had not actually happened. Yet.

The current problem centered on the basic and continuing effort of keeping young men on the job.

The fellows, themselves, were not the largest problem. They mostly enjoyed the activity and a ten-day tour was nothing...unless they were courting the girl of their dreams. Turned out their dreams became nightmares when the young lady decided ten days of her youth (and 'looking' time) was too great a price to pay for waiting... and wasting her youthful beauty.

For the most part, marriage did not provide an answer. Bills and babies and loneliness heaped up on the brides demanding an onboard fellow when the problems occurred at home.

The four men gathered around the table and coffee was served. Danish rolls graced the center of the table and various sheets of paper decorated the perimeter.

Mr. Smithfield, the elder, began (with an irritated scowl), "Seems to me it'd be time to pay off the young man and let 'im go. Two and a half, maybe three, months off, and bein' short of guards."

Mr. Canter blew back the coffee steam and took a sip. Anything to kill a moment of time.

Mr. Hackett, hands jittery from nerves, cleared his throat. "I'd really hate to see that young man go. He...."

Mr. Smithfield butted in, "Let's be real. We got three fellows in the bullpen, haven't we? One of 'em was goin' to the Firefly to make three for them. Just send the next best one on over to the Mountaineer."

Mr. Canter found his tongue. "But sir, the Firefly has a very long route and turn-around. Allowin' for emergencies and days off, that route really needs four guards assigned and available. Gettin' through the Boston Mountain Range is notably dangerous from several directions, road hazard and hold-up. Next fellow up is Kendall Summers, bein' the next marksman. The other thing is, he lives in Greenland just south'a here. Mountaineer would be way off track for him."

Mr. Smithfield growled, "We don't pamper guards. They go where they're sent."

Under his breath, Mr. Canter muttered, "Or they quit."

"What was that you said?" demanded the old man.

LOVE AND A LOCOMOTIVE

Mr. Stuart, the youngest of the four, though being the 'boss' so to speak, sensed a quarrel. He offered, "Don't we have the young fellow from Blue Eye, up on the Missouri border? How is he doin'?"

Mr. Hackett managed courage to speak. "He's excellent, just his weapons skill. Barely passed on the second trial. We've got 'im in a trainng program for the next two weeks. If someone could wait that long…?"

"How come he can't shoot, being 22 years old? How's a trainin' program gonna help 'im if bein' 22 wasn't enough?"

Mr. Hacket, again. "It was his pa, sir. He wanted the boy to take over the family grocery store. The young man tried it for years, and it just didn't fit. Always wanted on the train."

Then Mr. Stuart. "Wasn't the injured fellow workin' with Miss Marshall?"

Rapid nod from Mr. Hacket. "Yes, sir. We got a little help from the Eagle for days off."

"They why'n't we put young Slone with her? He could pick up his accuracy on his days off."

Mr. Canter brought up, "But that ain't in the rules. What if a problem came up and he wasn't ready?"

Small silence. Then Mr. Stuart, whose word held the most weight, helped himself to a Danish and took a bite. "As I see it, we could bend the rules or change them. They're our rules, remember. Someone filin' the coupling wasn't in the rules, and no one seems to know who demanded Miss Marshall to omit her final check. I'm thinkin' that lady can handle whatever problem they might have, and we can get the service of him in the meantime. "

He lifted his coffee and took a drink. The problem had been settled and the other three knew it. Garfield (call me Gar) would be assigned to the Mountaineer on its next stopover at home port. Mr. Stuart was not through.

"Now the injured young man, Leon…was that his name? Hackett, how was he workin' out?"

Mr. Hackett brightened. It was so pleasant to be asked a question that he could actually answer. "Oh, very good, sir. With him we will have no girlfriend/wife problem. He married his girlfriend and she's happy with his salary, job and schedule. Savin' money on his pay, she is, and doin' a bit of work on the side. Savin' for a house. She likes havin' three whole days in a row with him there, not just every Sunday or something."

Mr. Stuart nodded his understanding. "Then we'll plan on keepin' 'im on. Either way, we're on the hook for his hospital. Three months' pay'll be nothin' beside trainin' another fellow…the way we go through 'em.

"So, is there anything else to discuss?"

There didn't seem to be. Ridding the plate of the last of the rolls, the men adjourned. Mr. Hackett followed Mr. Stuart and when out of hearing, whispered, "Sure do thank you! I was afraid I might lose that girl with this happenin'. She'll be good to train Garfield, and she won't be with us forever…but she's a winner while we got 'er."

Mr. Stuart clapped Mr. Hackett on the shoulder with a friendly fist. "Nothin' to it, friend. Nothin' to it at all. Let me know how it works out."

"Sure thing, sir!"

Mr. Hackett left Fayetteville with a smile on his face. It was going to be a pleasure to notify Miss Lennie Marshall.

"Miss Marshall, I called you in to compliment on your good work, and the way you handled the accident. Your early notification possibly saved your buddy's life and certainly a lot of valuable baggage.

"Now, for the other thing…."

Lennie drew in a breath, feeling her shoulder's tighten from tension. Here it comes. 'Passing' on an unsafe coupling was just about the worst thing a guard could do.

The man continued, "Leon will be moved to Eureka Springs for recuperation. They think it'll be about three months total before he could be on full duty. We WILL get him back, but you need someone in the meantime. We're short in two places, and with him off, that makes three. So you will be gettin' a trainee."

"Trainee…sir…?"

"Yes. I made it known that with you would be the best place for him. He excelled in every way except with weapons, but it is mainly because he was not allowed to grow up with fire power as most Arkansas boys have.

"He's comin' along, though, and he'll practice on his days off. His name is Garfield Slone, and he's from Blue Eye, on the Missouri border. He reminded me somewhat of you. He wasn't lookin' for a job when he come here…he had one. He was lookin' for THIS job. I'm thinkin' he'll fit in well. You'll see him tomorrow when you come in." The man smiled in her direction.

Actually, a pleased smile. It was very disconcerting. Lennie couldn't bear for something to hover over her that might eventually fall in on her. Apparently she still had her job…at least until the new fellow was trained. But that coupling…?

"Was there somethin' more, Miss Marshall?

"Uh, well, there was that accident. The…."

The man nodded. "Oh, yes! I should have told you, but I didn't think it was important to you. They found who did the filing of the couplin' and he was one of us. He ain't no longer, though. The law has 'im for passing on the inspection. That was enough to fire 'im, but he has the whole derail and robbin' on 'im, too. Had nothin' to do with you. That's up to the law.

"Incidentally, with you bein' a trainer, that puts you in for the top salary three months early. Enjoy it…and don't do no worryin'. Go have fun and we'll see you later. I think your young man's a'waitin'."

She swallowed the lump in her throat and wilted into relaxation. "Yes, sir. I think you, sir, and I'll do my best."

A trainer? Really! Hmmmm….

ON WITH THE DREAMS

Wayne, acting on pure and brave faith, had invested in one dozen of the huge canning jars, themselves creating a buggy load, and picked up a few other necessary items. He heard the whistle of the Mountaineer as it passed the five-mile marker.

He shook his head in wonder that the tiny toot-toot whistle could carry five whole miles, flowing over mountains, rivers and canyons and still have its shorts and longs distinguishable. He sauntered on down to the depot as it was pulling in.

Lennie stepped down, and motioned him forward. She had never done that before. In a stage whisper, she informed him, "Wayne, if you got somethin' to do, I'm gonna be a bit late. Gotta have a conference with Mr. Hacker." And she turned toward the door ready with help.

Thus dismissed, Wayne decided he'd check in at McCafferty's. Could use a bite of chile, anyway.

The grouchy owner nodded and continued to busy himself with papers. Wayne picked up his chile and took a seat across the room. In keeping with his new education as a salesman, he was NOT going to bring up the subject or ask the old man if he liked it. He occupied his mind as to what was wrong with Lennie. He knew her well enough to know there was something.

Finishing the chile, he stood to go, and the old man turned to him, wearing his accustomed scowl.

"Young man, sit over here."

Wayne did as commanded. So here it came. Oh, well, the diner in Eureka showed good interest. He waited.

"Got those jars ready." Wherewith, he reached beneath the desk and produced two jars, shiny clean.

"Now you can bring me four of these jars when you come back down here." Short and brisk. Was it impossible for him to be pleasant…even for a minute, maybe?

Surprised, Wayne decided to test his hearing. "Four jars, sir?"

The man raised his hand and extended his four spread fingers, as though illustrating to a small child. "Yes, I said four of them. The cook back there thought of somethin' else to use 'em for. Reckon I can take about six a month…maybe eight, if you got 'em."

"Yes sir. Thank you for your business, sir."

Wayne picked up the jars and left, one under each arm. He'd have given a lot to have asked what were the other things the meat would be used for, but he didn't. It could be easy enough to just drop in later and check out new items on the menu.

So, alright. That took care of the meat and maybe the cheese, at least for now. He certainly had enough of the product to produce it. Now he could concentrate on wondering what was the concern with Lennie. Putting the jars with those already in the buggy, he settled himself in the depot to wait. Didn't wait long.

She stepped through the door, scanned the room to locate him, then advanced, her lips firm and in a straight line. Wayne watched, he knew that expression. It meant conflicted thoughts, and not necessarily bad. Well, there'd be plenty of time if she chose to share whatever it was.

It was pleasant to be traveling in the daytime on a bright, early spring day. Lennie settled back, and seemed interested in the birds, or something. At one point, Wayne had to stop and adjust the packing to stop the jitter and jingle of the jars against each other. Lennie turned to watch.

She commented, "Looks like business is comin' on."

Wonderful opening, but he wasn't going to fall for it. If he got started on all the good things of the last week, he'd still be talking when they rode past Chigger Ridge. Something was bothering her and he had a right to know what it was.

"Seems like it," he answered, without elaborating. After a pregnant pause, he turned to her, "How was your last trip?"

Surprisingly, her response was brief. "You really wantin' to know?"

He turned to her, somewhat startled. "Sure do, or I wouldn't'a asked." He smiled to soften the words. "I got a feelin' it was a lot more interesting than mine."

A few more trees and birds went past before she spoke. "Worst thing was I like to'a got my buddy killed. You ain't heard'a the robbery over past Berryville?"

"Robbery! The train was held up?"

"Uh, no. More like cut apart. One'a the couplins' got filed down and we lost the caboose and baggage car, almost in the river. Leon was in there checkin' for the next mail drop. Cars almost went in the Kings, but Leon did. Landed in the water."

She now had his attention. "Hurt 'im?"

"Cut his arm and broke his leg in two places. He'll be off for maybe three months."

"Hmmm. Then who will be with you?"

"Got a new fellow from over to Blue Eye. He's been bonin' up on his weapons, but they'll move him up with me."

"Just like that? He can't shoot, and he'll be with you?"

Lennie nodded, and faced him with her best tightly clamped lips, a firm straight line. "It's me that'll be trainin' 'im. The bosses got themselves in sort of a tight. We was short already, and now with Leon out...."

Wayne tried to think of something appropriate. "I guess accidents happen. I'm just glad it wasn't you that got hurt."

A few birds, trees and fence posts went by.

"Yeah, so am I, but it was me that got him hurt."

"You...? How come?"

"I should'a checked the couplin'. I checked outta Wishbone, but we stopped in Berryville and took on two cars. I didn't check after the two cars got hooked on again. I was told we were so far behind, for me to go on ahead and take care'a the passengers, since we were behind schedule, and Leon was loadin' on supplies."

"But you were told...."

"Yeah, but I shouldn't'a listened. I was supposed to check every couplin'. It'd'a been hard to see, the way it was filed, but the fact is I didn't even look. They found who did it, and he was the one that brought me the message that checkin' had been done."

"I can't see how that was your fault. Did you get a... reprimand...or somethin'?"

"No, and that's the thing of it. I messed up, and yet I'm gonna take on a trainee that ain't been fully trained. It don't hardly make sense, and I can't get my head around it. Top of that, bein' a trainer makes me qualify for a pay raise."

A few more trees and fence posts. "So you still have your job?"

Just an observation. Statement of fact. Why did that not seem like good news to Wayne? He needed to say something else so he raked his brain for a further comment.

"So who's gonna guard the Mountaineer with Leon laid up and you on off time?"

"They pulled a fellow from the Firefly that needs the overtime, and the Eagle gets a fellow new like I do. Didn't hear if he could shoot or not. Did find out why Garfield ain't a good shot. His pa wanted him to be a grocery clerk, and didn't let 'im start early like other fellows."

"...uh, Garfield...?

"Yeah, that's the name'a the fellow I get. Garfield Slone. Pa owns a store in Blue Eye."

Wayne nodded. Just another of the names of the fellows who spent days and nights with Lennie. While he spent days and nights with the goats. Something about that wasn't quite right, somehow.

And Bessie trotted on past the land that led up to Chigger Ridge. He dropped her off at her parents' house and gave her a smiling goodbye. She smiled back and nodded. Her smile a tense, firm line of her rosy lips.

Something was dreadfully wrong, here, and he didn't see what he could do about it. The thing was, his dream was still as strong as it ever was, but the duties were rising and flying out of reach, much like the popcorn on his sixth birthday. He didn't have enough hands (time?) to catch it, and Ma couldn't help enough to make it work.

To make matters worse, here Lennie thought she messed up, and instead of a reprimand, she got a promotion. More money. Now what was that going to do to her feeling for the train? Good as she was on the job, and as much as they liked her, she could be staying there for the next ten years.

Following that dreary thought was, just where would he be in ten years...still in the shack and the cave? Eating Ma's biscuits? Likely.

Lennie, after greeting her parents, sauntered dispiritedly into her room and tossed her bag on her bed. There it lay, a bright blue lump on the softly faded, cozy, pieced quilt. Lennie had not actually pieced a quilt. She needed to do that...sometime. Didn't every girl...?

She dumped the bag's contents on the quilt and sorted out her soiled laundry of the last ten day. Underwear, stockings and hankies. She'd rub them out in the morning.

She picked up her notebook, and scooped all remaining items back in the bag which she hung on a hook behind the door. Notebook in hand, she went to the window and pushed aside the curtains. Something, almost alive inside her, pulled her to the outside...but not this outside.

Closing the curtains, she put the notebook on her dresser and stretched out on her bed. Weary. Bone tired. Now what was causing that?

She stared at her ceiling. Cobweb! There in the corner. Where did 'cobs' come from? She'd tear it down tomorrow with a broom.

And…what in the world did Wayne's ma want with all those gallon jars? Wayne hadn't seemed to want to be chatty about them. That was his privilege. Maybe he was tired as she was.

A long sigh. It didn't seem like she fitted inside her skin anymore. Restless. Now, when she should be wondering about her new partner, happy she had not been blamed for the derailment, concerned for Leon. But no.

Sitting up, she rubbed her eyes, arose and retrieved her notebook…pencil stuck in the spiral binding. What if her windows were a bit taller? That way, the curtains could start almost from the ceiling. They would be very attractive curtains, though she couldn't picture them at this moment.

Grandad. She needed to have a talk with him, and she needed him to go with her on a little trip that had been flitting around in her head. Flipping the page to her floorplan, she studied it critically, tipping her head this way and that. Would Grandad see in it what she thought she had drawn? Tomorrow she'd find out.

MORNING ON CHIGGER RIDGE

The rooster flew up to his post, flapped his wings and cut forth with his morning serenade. His 'Er..er..er..er..oooow' echoed out over the bluff. Nanny goats bleating their guts out. *Get up, Wayne.*

Then he glanced at the clock setting of top of the warming oven. Five-forty. Silas. Not time yet. *Have patience, nannies, you're twenty minutes too early.*

So Wayne settled back against the pillow. Just for a second. What was the top duty today? Probably butcher those goats. Two of them…? Or one today and one tomorrow. Cold as it was, he could do them both today, and be ready to put them in the jars tomorrow. Six jars, there would be…and four of them already sold. Maybe McCafferty would take all six? *No, Wayne, don't push it. The old codger wants to run his own show. If it works for him, he'll increase his order.*

Feet into cold shoes. Cheese on toasted biscuits. Could a fellow live on cheese and goat meat? Could do worse. Fire up the stove and get the coffee on.

Freshly tinted face surrounded by red curls. And she did look sharp in that blue uniform…though he had begun to hate the sight of it. And there was Gar…what, oh, Garfield Slone. What a name. Likely some handsome puff of nothing, and he'd be with Lennie day and night.

Oh, shut up, Wayne. You got stuff to do.

So did Lennie. She had something very important to do.

"Grandad, will you take me somewhere today? I need to do something and I need you along."

Now, what doting grandfather could resist that invitation? But what in the world were they doing heading down toward Turner's Saw Mill?

Silas drained the last from his coffee and set the mug on his table, smiling to himself as he often did these days. That short stick he had dealt with all his life had suddenly started to grow longer, and it was growing almost faster than he could manage it.

The little fellow just loved this house, with the animals, trees, rocks to play on and his interest in watching his 'father' twist, turn and bend the willow withes into interesting shapes like a chair that just fit him.

Small Stephen had become the pivot of Silas' life with pleasant duties whirling around him like satellites around a sun. The goats, for instance. Nothing to it. Sittin' down job…warm shed…soft udders to grip.

Deliver milk pails to the cave and his job was done. Less'n somethin' come up that the young man, his boss, needed a few minutes help.

Interesting young man, he is. Workin' hisself to death, though.

He glanced up at the clock. Six o'clock on the dot. *Here I come, nannies. You'll soon be in the pasture.* Then he remembered. The boss wanted a little help with the butcherin' goats. That'd mean fresh liver for himself and the kid for supper.

What a life! Somewhere to live, something to do, someone to love and plan for. That was all he'd ever wanted.

ENTER GARFIELD SLONE

His family name had started out to be something else, Pa had told him. A long name ending up with an 'i' that might be hard to pronounce. Someone on the boat to America had changed it. Slone seemed to work well.

That Garfield, though. Ma had insisted he be named after a president, and Mr. Garfield was the one Pa finally agreed to. It sounded important enough for his son, even though the poor man had been shot while in office.

Garfield's ma, the reader of the family, liked it that he was one of the log cabin presidents, born up north. Her parents' family had begun in a log cabin as did so many in northern wooded country, but when she had married the store keeper, her life was suddenly upgraded to a house build of dimension lumber.

With a name like Garfield, it would be only natural for it to be shortened to Gar. Being the only child of an older father, he received the best education the school and his mother could provide, and practical experience was received from his father.

Put in the store at age 14 to work a full day, he struggled with it for six years, though he stopped to listen every time the Shooting Star blasted its way through the little town of Blue Eye. Music to his ears. Pure music. There were the long and short blasts, and he had learned what they were. The very sound of the raucous blasts and the rattle of the rails caught him at the very bottom of his heart.

At age eight he had begged a ride and his mother had ridden with him to the Arkansas town of Eureka Springs. They had eaten pink ice cream and chocolate cookies and headed back. For the next years he had dreams of that magical day…and had constant daytime thoughts as he hoisted boxes of cans off the delivery dray, and heaved burlap sacks of grain from wagons that the store would sell for animal feed.

He served behind the counter, was taught how to be pleasant to the customers no matter how he felt. He learned how to figure bills and how to set the prices so just enough profit was made to make the business profitable.

"Have to set it just right, Son. We make it low as we can, but not so low we can't stay in business. If we aren't in business, a lot of folks would be hard put to get what they needed. So, here's what we do."

And Garfield did…but the whistle of the Shooting Star pulled his senses into another realm that consisted of riding the rumble of the drivers and feeling the vibration of the chug…chug…chug… that gently jerked the cars into line and fitted the hooks into their couplings, tight and snug.

When the sounds died out in the distance, he could again bow his head to the figures on the page, the cans in the boxes and the heavy sacks of wheat bran to make mash for chickens and hogs.

He managed his life, day by day, until his father, who had planned for and thought he was giving his son the key to a happy and secure life, finally had enough. Garfield was not happy in the store and obviously would never be. So he must be permitted to try his luck with the Frisco Line, and maybe he'd get to wave to him as he clattered through the town.

That is how Garfield Slone was almost ready to be a trainee guard when the derailment happened. Of course he couldn't fire a weapon with skill. Pa had taught him to aim at the robber, pull the trigger, and hope for the best.

But now he learned to take the weapon apart, oil it, fit it together, load it with 'persuader ammo' so he didn't need to kill unless it was them or him. He learned to aim with a steady hand and not be shaky, nervous or hesitant. He must be confident he'd hit what he aimed for, no matter how much practice it took.

And then, when he thought it would be another month or so before he could go on the job, he was to be put on the Arkansas train, the Mountaineer, to finish his training with a girl. Didn't Ma have fun with that one! Pa stroked his chin thoughtfully, but Garfield just couldn't wait. He didn't mind being trained by a girl…or a snowman or Santa Clause or maybe even an angel. He was now employed by the railway, and before he drew his last breath, he would be behind the controls running the whole metal monster. He knew that, but the train people had yet to find it out.

He smiled to himself as he made the solemn promise. He'd tried the store, but now he was going where he had always been meant to be.

And he appeared before his trainer. He greeted her with a wide smile. What a beauty she was, and he had thought she might be a cranky old so and so. They got acquainted on the gun range. Man alive! That girl was a crack shot. He nodded to himself as he promised he'd be just as good.

Lennie Marshall looked critically at her trainee. About five foot eleven, shoulders a bit broader than might be expected of a store clerk, and arms, showing from rolled up sleeves, were heavily muscled. Good. Black, black hair and eyes and a wide smile that said this was not just a job for him; it was THE job.

All good. Anyone could learn to shoot if they wanted to bad enough. And he'd like to be called 'Gar' if she didn't mind. 'Garfield' seemed too stuffy. She could only nod agreement.

He climbed the ladder to check for hobos. Checked the water and matched the supplies against the list. The baggage arrived on the cart and he grabbed up a pair of the larger suitcases. Lennie stopped him.

"Use the two-wheeler. We never lift when we can roll. Saves energy."

"Yes, Miss...ma'am...uh?

"Lennie is good enough. If others are around, it's Miss Marshall."

That taken care of, they were ready to board the passengers. That is, just as soon as they checked the floors (for cleanliness), the windows (for finger prints) and the cushions (for sharp objects and loose coins.)

The boiler was heating, and the first chuff of steam puffed out into the air. The first sudden jerk forward. The clang and the rattle, and another jerk. Lennie watched her trainee. A small, half-smile and a dreamy look in his black eyes. She nodded with understanding. He was smitten, purely and simply. Train fever. Leon had it as well.

She recognized the feeling and the expressions. A little boy with a new puppy...a girl with a new doll...a baby with a sucker...a lost child at the sight of his mother. Yes, he'd do well.

"Gar...!"

He startled into reality. They followed after the passengers onto the train. Through the window the depot was disappearing past them, and they were on the way.

"Gar...?"

"Uh…yes, Lennie…?"

"Here is the list of the towns to receive mail. Go to the baggage car and bring up the bags. We line them in the order of their need, because we have absolutely no time to waste. Throw and grab. It gets easier, though."

On the way back from Memphis they had picked up Leon from Berryville to be transported to the Eureka Springs hospital, and he would be able to convalesce at home.

Cassie, his wife, had come along for the transfer. With her along, there was no need for an accompanying hospital attendant. Lennie was curious to meet her.

If ever a ray of sunshine could be caught within a human girl, it was Cassie. Rosy cheeks, light brown hair pinned in wavy sausages all over the top of her head, held in place with a bright blue ribbon. Blue eyes, matched the ribbon. Laughing and happy to get her man back, even swathed in bandages and wearing a huge plaster cast.

Every minute she could, she chattered with Lennie. "I was wantin' so much to meet you. Leon said you didn't have no time for that, and I believed it. He don't have no time, either. But now he will. The railroad is going to pay him his wages until he gets back to work. Isn't that wonderful?"

Lennie could hardly nod before Cassie took off again. "I don't know if he told you, but I make things. Outta cloth, outta wax…I make really good perfumed candles. Sometimes I make things outta sticks, but my very favorite is clay. There's a special oven that makes rock outta clay, and when we can, we'll buy one. Then I can make things to sell in Eureka. Summer people buy anything."

Leon was right. Cassie was a jewel. She had her life figured out right down to the new oven. Lennie sensed a shiver of jealousy pass through her. It must be so good to know, for sure, what to do next.

There had been that trip to Turner's Saw Mill with Grandad, and she has shown her drawing to Simon. Yeah, well, they could make it. It might cost a lot. With all she wanted in built in, it would run up to…well, it'd be over $200.00.

Grandad had cringed at the amount.

And Simon had another question. Where at was she plannin' to put this building? That'd add to the expense if it was to be any distance away. Travel time and all.

With a sigh, she shook her head. Hadn't decided, really. Guessed she's need to look around a bit. Thanking Simon, they climbed into the buggy and Jasper pulled them up to Ridge Road.

Silence. Grandad was bursting with curiosity, and she would have gladly relieved him with answers, if she only had them. The price had not frightened her, but she mustn't tell Grandad. That would make him just that much more curious. What frightened her was that she had loaded up her hopes and dreams and started down the lane of her life, only to find the road barred by a heavy, metal gate. How does one open a gate that has no fastener or no hinges?

So there she was…and she had listened to Cassie all the way to Wishbone and waved to her and she left Cassie chattering and Leon asleep from medication. One thing was a small relief, though, she now knew her friend Leon was in good hands…the very best hands he could have imagined.

To say Grandad was curious would have been to put it too mildly. The old man's thoughts were in a whirl. Apparently the girl had not spoken to her parents about what was bothering her, or something would have been said by now.

Therefore, he knew he had been privy to a precious bit of Lennie's inner thoughts and confidences, but not enough to be of help. Knowing Lennie, the ride to Turners Saw Mill had not been a way to pass an afternoon. And he saw the acceptance of the cost without a flicker of emotion or surprise.

So, putting together what he knew, and subtracting what he wasn't sure of, then searching for a reason for what was left, Grandad did what he often did. When in doubt or searching for a decision, he turned to the animals.

Donning his jacket and cap, he wandered out to the horse meadow. Old Maybelle had, some time ago, been 'put out to pasture' but she raised her friendly face and watched his approach. Stems and grass blades drooped from her mouth as she chewed.

Granddad approached with extended hand, and Maybelle accepted the half a carrot, adding it to the grass in her mouth.

Grandad had always liked Maybelle, even more so now that they had both been 'put out to pasture,' so to speak. Fact was, though, being 'put out to pasture' gave both himself and the animal a lot of time.

Slipping a halter over her head, he adjusted the straps and hoisted himself aboard. He felt a shiver of pleasure pass through her loose skin, and she turned into the direction he guided.

Out to Willow Bluff and the train track. The answer just had to start there. On the way he could check in on that industrious young man now firmly engrossed in the goat business. Getting good at making that cheese. A real surprise. He'd dropped off a wheel of his cheese the last time he picked up Lennie.

Of the ways he thought Wayne Johnson might go, the goat business had not been in the running. Always did carve his own path, though, sometimes not the best way, but he was quick to see mistakes and correct them.

Back to Lennie. His thoughts had circled themselves so many times that they had virtually made a path in his mind. He was obviously missing something.

Passing by Chigger Ridge, he grinned tolerantly at the name on the sign. There, in the part of Willow Creek that flowed through Wayne's land, was the new fellow, the furniture maker. Gathering those willow sprouts, he was, with the little fellow trying to help.

On to the train track. Another hour and the Mountaineer would be rumbling past, noisily belching smoke as it revved up for the next hill. An hour. He'd just settle down to wait, and let Maybelle graze on a different bunch of grass.

The sketch that girl had. A lot of house there, and where was she planning to put it? Seemingly she didn't know. So why did she have it? What was the problem of leaving her money in the bank and keep it where it was until she knew for sure? Certainly there was no room on her pa's farm for another house…so, what was in her mind?

Since he had begun to live in his son's house, the old man had tried to stay out of anything that was not his business. A bit hard to do when you loved the people, and would like to have been a help. Somewhere.

So, where was that thing he was missing? Did it have something to do with Wayne? Very self-contained, should he try to find out?

Hmmm, well, did he dare? Of course he could stop in on Wayne's pa and share concerns, but maybe he shouldn't interfere. Or at least appear to be interfering. Maybe stop in on the young man himself.

Just neighborly, like.

The distant whistle blew and he could almost feel the toddler, Lennie, bouncing in his arms with excitement. On schedule, the whistle sounded to clear the tracks. The fluffy white mule's tail of steam floated above the trees and the huge locomotive rounded the corner. Iron pony, she'd named it.

Maybelle lifted her head and watched, chewing grass. Maybelle always took advantage of her surroundings. Hoisting himself aboard, he adjusted the reins. She turned as directed and headed up to Chigger Ridge.

He saw the neat cabin for the 'hired help' and moved on up to the hastily put together shack near the mouth of the very large cave. From this positon, there was still a small amount of the shiny track visible.

"Hey, there, Mr. Marshall!"

"Hello, Son. Thought I'd wander over to watch the Mountaineer roll past. Been there a lot of times with Lennie."

"'Speck you did, sir. Done that a lot's that myself. Come sit a spell. Time I was stoppin' for a cup of somethin' to get me goin' again."

"Don't mind if I do," Grandad accepted.

He heard about the goats, McCafferty's, the hired man, the amount of goat hair that was to be sheared and that he had found a market for it. Grandad learned that the shack was just a stopgap until he could get exactly what he wanted.

What did he exactly want? Well, he hadn't actually had the time to decide, with what there was to do. Had several ideas, just hadn't put them together...yet.

Grandad helped himself to another of Wayne's ma's cookies, and a picture descended before his eyes just like a revelation from heaven. There was Lennie's house, setting on Wayne's hill in view of the train track. Two halves of the peach. Two sides of an equation. Now what?

He tried to concentrate on Wayne's words as his mind grappled with what he had seen in a flash of thought. What...what should he do! Well, there was one thing.

He made a move to go, and Wayne responded. He certainly had things to do. Grandad could see that, and that was part of the answer. "Son, thought I'd mention. I got an errand to do over to Wishbone, and it'd be about the time Lennie comes in. You bein' so busy, I'll just go ahead to pick her up. You've been so good about it, and we appreciated it. And I know she liked havin' you pick her up, but she'll just have to put up with me." He chuckled to soften the statement.

Wayne looked surprised, but recovered nicely. "Yes sir, I've been busy but it wasn't no trouble to me. Glad to do it. Likely she'll be glad of a change, though."

Granddad nodded, smiled and swung aboard Maybelle. "Thanks for the coffee and the time. I'd like to hear more, later, so I'd like to come back."

"Any time, Mr. Marshall. I'm mostly here all the time."

Grandad moved way, his body swaying with the elderly gait of the old horse. Yes, he could plainly see the young man was there 'all the time.' And what was that statement that Lennie might like a change? Hmmm, well, he'd just have to play it out. That errand he had over in Wishbone was to haul his granddaughter back and find out what in the tarnation was going on in her mind? And her life?

THE TRIP HOME

The Mountaineer huffed its way into the depot, and Lennie stepped down. A frightfully handsome young man stepped down behind her. He wore the uniform of a Security Guard. Together they assisted the departure of the passengers.

When her foot had reached the iron step, she had cast her eyes about for Wayne, and instead had seen Grandad's waving hand. Grandad knew the score, so he went into the depot to find a place to sit.

Lennie frowned with concern. Hmmm, so what was going on? Something happen with Wayne? Well, she'd soon see. She signed out and left her trip journal, then met Grandad.

"Shall we go to McCafferty's for…somethin'?" he asked tentatively.

"Sure, Grandad, if you like."

They ordered sandwiches and tea, and settled themselves at the picnic type tables. Lennie looked up at the chalkboard menu. "Look, Grandad, they've got somethin' new. Toasted feta cheese sandwiches. That'd be Wayne's. We should'a ordered them."

"Still can." Grandad slid from his seat and approached the counter. "Believe I'll have one of the cheese sandwiches and one of those new 'spiced meat' ones."

"You wantin' to change your order?" That was frowned on and discouraged in every way possible.

"Oh, no. Just added to."

And he was seated again at the table. He turned brightly toward his pride and joy. "So…how did the new fellow do?"

"Really good, Grandad. He's born to it and it was a dream, like with me, only with him it'll be his whole life."

"And yours isn't." Statement. Something he wanted to learn.

"Oh, no, Grandad. It was just something I wanted to do. I like other things, too. Garfield had a good job with his pa, but it wasn't what he wanted. The train is. It wouldn't be a surprise to me if he ended up on the controls, some day. Not me."

That was a relief. Then came the sandwiches, all four of them. "Thought we'd see what those new ones were like," he explained.

Whereupon he sliced them in fourths and set one on her napkin. Then the other one. The cheese wafted a rich cheesy aroma and something else…maybe some kind of herb. The spiced meat was piled in the bun and it issued its own fragrant steam.

With a grin, she turned to the old man with the twinkle in his eyes. "Grandad! You knew about this! Wayne's been at it in a big way, hasn't he?" And she took a sample bite. Then, another.

"Grandad, Wayne's got a winner here, hasn't he?"

The old man nodded. "He might have, but he's a fellow stuck with little old 24 hour days. He's tryin' to hold the popcorn in the pan without a lid, like on his birthday. Ain't got hands enough. Livin' in a shack not fit for goats and got nothin' better in sight."

Something to think on. They ate in silence, Grandad studying her face when he thought he would not be noticed. There would be all the way home to talk. And then they were in the buggy, leftover sandwiches wrapped in a napkin.

Trees and fence posts moved steadily by. It was a beautiful April day, just a nippy little breeze playing with the newborn leaves on the trees. The time wouldn't get any better.

"Now Lennie, I've made a practice of mindin' my own business since your Grandma passed on. But what I'm thinkin' on right now has become my business. You invited me into it when you asked me to take you to the sawmill. You could'a took your ma, and she'd'a loved the trip.

"So here's what I see. You got a bee in your bonnet and I ain't sure what it is, but I don't want you stung. You got in your head what almost every girl'd like to have, but you don't know what to do with it. You did a lot'a figgerin' and plannin' and it all looks good. You got it all wrapped up and no place to put it. But you know that good land is hard to find.

"I been lookin' around and didn't see nothin' close enough for you but here was my idea. Haven't really talked to Wayne, but he's got that big farm, and he'll not ever use the whole of it...way he's goin'."

He glanced sidelong at the face within the red curls. He had her interest. "I was just thinkin' that if he'd like to sell you a little chunk, maybe ten acres of that bluff, then that drawin' of yours would perty much fit there. 'Course, there's a few other places that'd have a good view of the track, and likely there'd be one that that the owner'd like the extra cash for what they wasn't usin'."

Enough words for now.

Fence posts and trees went by. A doe stood stone still with a speckled fawn at her haunches. Statues. A turtle waddled past the wheels, totally oblivious to danger. New subject.

"Right fair tastin' sandwiches back there. That Wayne ain't really a salesman, but his dreams pushed on him so fast it chased away the fear. Plunged right in and made a good product. Gonna be a market big as he wants it, but he's got to have a little help. It's like that popcorn again."

No comment from his passenger. Her face a picture of thought, then, "Hired man ain't workin' out?"

"Oh, yes. Better than imagined, but that's just hired help. He needs help with himself and what he's got to do. Needs someone to share with him."

"I know that Grandad. The thing is, it can't be me. He ain't even got time to talk with me, and sure enough don't want me to know what he's doin'. I kind'a like what you said about getting' a piece of land. I'll think on it, and maybe you'll help me when I make up my mind. Thing is, I really can't do it alone, even if I have the money."

Grandad nodded. Enough words. "I agree that it'll take some thought. We'll work on it."

More trees and fence posts. "I might mention I got a stop to make at Chigger Ridge. Hope he's there. I need to bring another wheel of that cheese to your ma. She's thought up no end'a things to do with it."

Lennie was silent. Her face was a study of whirling thoughts.

Armed with the cheese, they were on the road again. Grandad saw what he was curious about. He almost had to fight with Wayne to take money for the cheese, and Wayne could hardly concentrate for watching Lennie, like a starving wolf looking through the wires of the chicken pen.

Enough words said. He had seen, among the cheeses, a kind he had not tried. Jars of dried herbs were lined up on a shelf, and shiny steel vats were upside down on a long work table. Must'a set him back a pretty penny. Wonder if his income is equaling his outgo… if not, it soon will be, if he just doesn't have a stroke from overwork.

He knew what he'd do tomorrow, and he would spend most of the night thinking how it could be done. He loved Wayne, and he loved Lennie, but there had to be something done. They were apparently not capable of seeing it on their own.

He presented the great wheel of cheese to his favorite daughter-in-law. With surprised eyebrows, she reminded, "But Papa, we've still got half a wheel left."

Granddad shrugged. "There'll be another one tomorrow. If you got too much, pass it around to the boys. They'll find a use for it."

Lennie watched her mom, surprised, and heard Grandad's explanation. Oh well, that was their concern. She had enough to think of without taking on something else.

A TRIP TO CHIGGER RIDGE

He found Wayne dragging firewood up from the woods.

"Need to get some of these trees down to make sprouts for the goats. Can use the firewood, anyway. Just have a hard time really gettin' at it. Can you stay for a cup'a coffee?"

Invitation seemed genuine. "It'd be my pleasure." Maybe he needed the sound of a human voice. Grandad was happy to oblige.

"Sure thing. Ma sent me three raisin pies and I've still got a pie and a half. She does a good job on them, and I'm mostly the one that eats 'em. One of my favorites for sure. Coffee'll heat in a minute." And it did.

He was right about Ma doing a good job. "Son, I come over for a sample of that new cheese, but I had another concern. I came by here last week and you were just full of things you wanted to do, with no time to do 'em, and I wondered if you'd have an answer to that problem before you were as old and gray as me."

Wayne lifted another bite of the pie. "Wonder that myself, Mr. Marshall. You got an answer for it?"

What more could he have asked! "Might have. Imaging yourself over to Blue Lake in a fishin' boat and it springs a leak. Course you got a bailin' bucket, and you can start bailing. That'd work...if you rowed hard and bailed fast enough and long enough, but when you got to shore, you'd still have a hole in your boat.

"Or you could use the plug you got right there in the boat and try to plug the leak. Then you could bail out and see an end to your hard labor."

Silence while he worked on the pie. Wayne slid another slice of pie onto his saucer. Didn't want him to leave. Looking for a more complete answer. "Can you tell me what that plug'd be...the one you say I got?"

"Sure thing, youngen. That girl knows you and will not be surprised to see you come for her. She will at least listen to what you way. That's a really good plug, and you'll know right away if it stops the leak."

Grandad nodded agreement with his last word, then continued. "Don't be surprised I know all that 'cause I got the same thing with Lennie. Leaky boat. I don't know about young folks these days. Got too much to do to spend time with each other. Two heads can be better than one, and four hands get a lot more done but not if they ain't workin' together. I look around these hills and see a passel'a girls that'd dearly love to help you hold that popcorn in the pan."

"'Speck so, Mr. Marshall."

"Then why in the tarnation are you wasting time in the woods with a choppin' ax when you should be pluggin' your leakin' row boat! If you don't get help, you're gonna end up with nothin' and wonder what you done wrong with your young years."

Silence. He topped off the coffee, and gave a dispirited sigh. As if on que, the Mountaineer sent forth the mournful blast and roared toward the bend.

Wayne looked at Grandad and jerked an elbow toward the sound. "What you're sayin' is true. The thing was, I sorta had my eyes on Lennie, and then saw the Mountaineer steal her away from me. Now, I might could'a fended off another fellow, but how could I fight off a train? Been over three years, and she's doin' so good... gettin' promotions and all. How'd she give that up long enough to be a help here?"

Clear and plain in the old man's ears were Lennie's words. "He ain't even got time to talk with me, and sure enough don't want to tell me what's goin' on." Granddad pressed his fork to the last of the flaky crust crumbs and transferred them to his mouth. Really fillin', raisin pie was. He might not be able to eat anything else for a week.

"Got a idea and a question. You ever find the time to talk to Lennie and see what she wants? The way I see it, you ain't seriously set your mind to courtin', and that'd be your job, not Lennie's. Fellows always got that part of it. Courtin' takes time and energy, just ask any married man. It takes time to find the plug to stop the leak in your boat, but saves time in the end.

"Now look at me…takin' up your valuable time and eatin' your ma's pies. Should be ashamed of myself, but I ain't. I like you… always have, and I recognize your problem. So if you'll just get me that cheese, the one where I thought I smelled dill. I'll just head on out." He donned his cap and stood, placing the two dollars on the table by his empty saucer.

Minutes later he swung up to Maybelle's back and reached for the cheese. "Good luck with the wood cuttin'."

The young man nodded. "Thanks for the words, Mr. Marshall. Wood cuttin'll have to wait. I do need that plug before I drown in my own sweat."

The old man rode off, a smile plastered within the wrinkles of his face. All the effort he had spent over the last hours with his highly worn 'Instruction Book' may have actually paid off. He had finally located, after much searching, the words he'd remembered. "Give instruction to a wise man and he will be wiser still; teach a just men and he will increase in learning."

It had been right there in Proverbs 9:9, so why was it so hard to find? Anyway, it could just prove to have been worth the time. And, with luck, tomorrow would be the day.

Wayne did a lot of thinking as the fields and fence posts went past his eyes. He even remembered the old fisherman saying, "What're you gonna do, man? Fish or cut bait?" Well, he'd cut enough bait, so now he'd see if it worked. Grandad was right about a lot of 'fish' in the brook. Seems to have come the time he'd have to pull one out.

A lot of words went through his mind, and he discarded them as they came. This test would have to be done without prior studying, but one thing he knew for sure. Before he returned to Chigger Ridge, he'd know, or at least have a good clue, to his next action.

He did his errands with half a mind on his actions. How do you prepare for an important test when you haven't read the book? And from what he'd heard, every girl in the world was a totally different book.

He was sitting in McCafferty's trying to ignore the liquid they called coffee when he heard the blast of the Mountaineer. Draining the dregs into his mouth, he stood, replaced his empty mug on the counter and strode out to meet his fate.

Lennie stepped down from the iron step, tiredness written all over her face. Should he actually bring this up now…or wait till she rested a bit? With a shrug and an intake of breath, he made up his mind. If she became his, there would be a lot of times she was done-in with weariness, and there would still have to be words. So just as well start now.

Catching his eye, she managed a smile and a finger-wave as she assisted the passengers when she could. Reaching for a baby, she was rewarded by a relieved smile from the mother who could now maneuver her feet, her skirt and her bags through the door and down the steps without tumbling. Then she was gone.

The doors closed and Lennie headed toward the office with her journal. He moved to the door, leaned against the wall and waited. She'd be through when she was through so fidgeting was useless.

Then she was back, and managed a smile for him…a smile that meant she was now ready to go home…not that she was over-joyed to see him. Wayne cast it from his mind…this was clearly the time to try the plug before his boat nosed into the undertow and was lost forever. If this was not the plug for him, then he needed to know it now.

Her bag and small suitcase stowed in the boot, herself settled in the comfortable seat among the cushions and afghans, she sighed and leaned back.

Wayne hoisted himself onto the padded seat and picked up the reins. He didn't asked her how was her trip…he didn't care. One thing was on his mind, and he'd now rid himself of it.

Passing about two fields and thirteen fence posts he began, and words poured forth like water from the downspout in a storm. Later, if he'd been asked what he actually said, he wouldn't have had a clue.

First she looked at him with polite interest, then with fascination mixed with a small amount of unbelief. She even touched her ear with a fingertip and gave a slight rub. Could words be coming through right? Did he know what he was saying?

Could this be the old-time-Wayne who had his next action planned and expected others to go with him…nor not…whichever they pleased. He'd still go forward, with or without a following. It was a thing she remembered from childhood play.

She sat up and turned toward him, intent on catching every word, and the words were coming out so fast and clear her understanding had to race to keep up. Not only that, she hardly had room for a word of her own during the whole way home.

They passed Chigger Ridge, and the herd of goats were wandering about, nipping this and that in the way of goats, and the kids were leaping about on springy feet.

He left it totally up to her as to whether she wanted a 'goodbye kiss.'

She did.

HOUSE ON THE BLUFF

It had been a wearying day, but it was now almost over. Miss Lennie wiped her tired, somewhat wrinkled hands on the softly-worn tea towel attached to the oven handle. She looked around the kitchen with the sweeping glance that always gave her pleasure. Small smile of thanks.

She strolled down from the north to the south of the house passing the well-appointed rooms on either side of the hall. All empty now, except for an occasional friend or family member passing through. Just as it should be. A young granddaughter was now the mistress, herself pleasantly rounded. Her young husband had a trip into Fayetteville, and she ably cared for the place. Just as the young Lennie would have.

The laughter and noisy clatter, the taunts and teasing and the rough-housing scuffles were gone. The book was closed on that chapter of her life. Living seemed to come that way…in chapters of a decade or so.

When she thought of it in that frame of mind, she pictured a shelf with school books, worn from use, and manuals telling how this thing or that thing could be constructed…used…or improved. All had their uses. Some of the mental 'books' covered many years, but there was that one exciting book that was completed in less than three years.

Yes, Mountaineer had its own recorded account on the shelf of her mind. The precarious beginning, the rumble of the wheels, the whine of machinery, the piercing whistle that had echoed from mountain to mountain.

And not to forget the fluffy, long muletail of steam, faint in the summer but highly viable in the winter. The length of it always indicating the amount of wind streaking over the hills or the lazy breeze in the summers. Sometimes with harsh outlines, sometimes soft as the fleece of a winter comforter.

But it never lasted more than a minute.

There was a time, back when Wayne had decided he must slow down and turn some of his work over to others, that he and Lennie took a trip to Memphis and back. A there-and-back turnaround, it would be called.

They'd climbed aboard in Wishbone depot. The step into the car was wide and padded against slippage, not just pierced iron. The door to the car folded into itself quietly and efficiently, its rubber seals shutting out every scraping sound or whiff of errant breeze.

The center aisle was carpeted in a thick pile. If a falling child happened…and how could it with the metal hand-holds…?, he could hardly hurt himself.

The chug and jerk that fastened the couplings between the cars no longer happened. The catches operated quietly, smoothly and with no possible way to fail. The windows had catches allowing an inch of cooling or a foot of fresh air…as the passenger preferred.

The nice leather seats were now plush, without the lovely leather smell. It smelled more of woodland and flowers. The pillows came in two sizes for either the resting of a head, or maybe the steadying of a spine.

Wayne, so often exhausted with living, leaned into the luxurious depth of the reclined seat and dozed contentedly. Lennie, by the window, sat bolt upright, her head a-buzz with memories, trying to gather into her mind how she felt.

The closest she came was at a school reunion, perhaps. The friends you knew so well, unless they were neighbors, were so different they seemed to be strangers. Young love, passed notes, shy glances and quick smiles that were remembered were replaced with weathered faces and calloused skin. And a knowing look.

Eyes, that you barely remembered, looked intensely into yours…searching for the 'old' you. Periods of time create massive changes.

The rumble of the iron pony's drivers was gone, sucked up somewhere in the plush carpet, no doubt. The whistle, instead of a startling blast, could scarcely be heard. The crackers and cheese were replaced with meals such as you might be served at a neighbor's house.

The Iron Pony was gone. He lived no more. His memories would now be retained in his own book on the bookshelf of Lennie's mind. The cover of the book was painted blue when the new blue pony was turned loose on the new steel rails.

It was an enjoyable trip. No doubt of that. But it was not a ride on the Iron Pony of her youth. Back in Wishbone, she stepped from the wide, padded step to a train yard of solid concrete, swept clean of cinders.

She knew, as one knows, that it was very near the time to write her later rhyme…the one that would be written from the viewpoint of a grown-up. The time was near, but not here yet.

Then, it was two years later, and Wayne had been taken to where he would never be tired. He wished he could take her along… he'd said…and she surely wished to go. They just couldn't figure out how that could happen. To commit a rash act would be a clear affront to the will of their Maker, who had His own timing.

So Wayne went and she stayed. Her time would come.

Today was a wonderful day. She made her way to the 'widow's walk' she had insisted be put on the new house. She was so certain the time was near for the later rhyme, she had brought her tablet and pencil along. They seemed to give her a bit of comfort.

She stood and looked over the railing at the fields and pastures well-tended by young Stephen Cantrell, though not so young anymore. It was so good that he stayed and loved the farm so well, and even better that one of her daughters had seen the solid young man he had grown into. They were grandparents, now, and little ones often romped on the pastures and tried to ride the baby goats.

It was just as she had seated herself in her rocker, the one that was kept on the 'widow's walk' balcony, that she heard the soft notes of the new, silver-topped locomotive. She pushed herself somewhat laboriously from the cushion of the rocker and made her way to the railing.

She stood, training her eyes on the spot beyond the trees where the Mountaineer would make its appearance. And there, beyond the new spring leaves, came the shining blue of the cars obediently following the sleek engine. No mulestail of steam. She put the pencil in the roomy pocket of her blue apron and waved.

No one would see her wave, of course, but the pony inside the train would know, just as the Iron Pony knew when small Lennie bounced in glee within Grandad's arms.

With a satisfied sigh, Miss Lennie seated herself.

The notes died away on the air, and Lennie took the pencil from her pocket. Opening her tablet to a fresh page, she wrote… scribing the words just as they came from her mind.

THE BOOKSHELF OF MY LIFE

I am the house I live in. It was given free to me.
The upkeep of this dwelling became my responsibility.
…Entirely up to me.
When I was born, I soon began to furnish it, and make it seem
To be the grand enclosure of my very fondest dream.
…The best that I can deem.
I furnished it with parents, friends, and teachers… then with a sigh

I sought about for other things. Searching, something
caught my eye,
...A locomotive thundered by.
What my house would look like, had I not seen the train,
And Iron Pony on the rails, to gallop in my brain.
...I surely can't maintain.
Its whistle was my music, its drivers sang my song.
The Iron Pony stole my heart and bade me come along.
...And how could that be wrong?
I tied my life together with two ribbons made of steel
It pulled my dream of life along like grinding of a wheel
...That's how it made me feel.
Time came I rode the Pony. My dreaming came awake
We spent our time together, living for each other's sake.
...A binding pack we make.
For years my pony romanced me. He was my own true
joy.
His box cars were my playhouse. His rails became my
toy.
...What else could I employ?
I cared for him in daylight, his headlamp lit my night.
His coal car was my heart beat, and it all had seemed so
right.
...Us, sharing every sight.

But then, so oft, as young love goes, his light began to
dim.
There was another love for me, not like my love for him.
...And it was not a whim.

The house I am took many turns, I cannot name them
all
But quite important to my life? The bookshelf on the
wall
...To help me to recall.
I put my life upon that shelf. Each minute, hour and day

Between its covers, I was safe, preserved in every way.
…What else can I say?
The children came, as children do, and each one had its place.
Each child's book stands on my shelf…not a spot to waste,
…And life pushed on in haste.
My second love stood by me, with tired hours, goats and cheese.
Two of us together…pleasures, pain and joy to seize
…This was no life of ease.
My Pony then rode rails of steel. His whistle tones were sweet.
His tinted windows softened light, his vents produced their heat.
…His carpets soft and neat.
We both grew old together. We went our separate ways.
No longer were we friendly as in past, romantic days.
…First love changes, but it stays.
My pony lives inside that train, so many boxcars long.
He knows he always has my heart. My hand waves high and long.
…He sings me his new song.

All I'd ever asked of life was given free to me.
Two loves were given me on earth, and one More Love I'll see
…When from this life I'm free.
For then I'll see my second love, who was so sad to leave
Me waiting, standing on the earth, to wait… and watch and grieve.
…No future dreams to weave.
Until I go, my Pony stands there on my bookshelf, new.
His cover is no longer black, but painted bright and blue.
…His trail of steam…just a memory too.

His whistle now no longer screams, but notes… resonant and deep,
Food stocked in his dining cars, his Pullman cars for sleep.
…His schedule he will keep.
My hair is silver…like his roof. My voice is softer… still…
I hear his love song on the air, as he creeps round the hill.
…I know I always will.
A time to laugh, a time to cry, that's what the wiseman said.
A time to work, a time a time to play, that leaves no time for dread.
…Life unwinds like a thread….
And so….

The pencil slipped from Lennie's withered hand.

It was her granddaughter, plumply round with her first, had climbed the steps to the balcony when Lennie did not answer the call to come down to supper.

She saw the tablet on Lennie's knee, laying there on the apron that was boxcar blue. The yellow pencil had slipped from her hand and lay on the balcony floor.

The silver hair lay resting against the padding of the old, comfortable rocker and her eyes were closed. Lennie Marshall Johnson was no longer at home behind blue eyes.

The granddaughter felt the lump form in her throat with the knowledge, and the moisture built up in her eyes with the sight. She picked up the notebook, turned and walked down the steps. She placed the notebook on the shelf with the carved locomotive and boxcars Grandad Wayne had bought for the young Lennie. She swallowed hard and walked away.

She called the menfolk in, and the silver hair, the blue eyes and the blue apron were brought gently down the steps, still seated on the old comfortable rocker.

A time to laugh, a time to cry, that's what the wise man said.* A time to work, a time to play. No time left to dread as live unwinds… just like a thread.

Then nothing is left but the empty spool.

She took her promised place beside the headstone, and the soft tones of Pony's whistle filtered through the new spring leaves of the trees. Goats lifted their heads, rapidly chewing their mouthful. Ears flicked.

Had they heard the Pony's goodbye whistle? Or had they felt a twinge of fall in the air?

> *"To everything there is a season, and a time to every purpose under the heaven. A time to be born, a time to die, a time to plant, and a time to pluck up that which is planted."*

- BONUS EXCERPT -

VOLUME TWO

The Ozark Mountains Historical Fiction Series

THE MIGHTY CEDAR

A FRIEND LOVETH AT ALL TIMES

JOANN KLUSMEYER

THE MIGHTY CEDAR

1

The old man on the bed groaned and shifted slightly on his bed in the dark room. The woman, though herself half asleep, responded in a reflex which had been perfected through the many years by his side.

"Marion? Are you all right, Marion?"

When she received no response, she arose and lighted the kerosene lamp beside the bed. Its light made shadows that deepened the creases and hollows of his face, giving his pale features a golden glow.

She placed a hand on his forehead. Not that she expected to learn anything about his condition from this touch, but it seemed the thing to do. It was what she had always done, and there was comfort for them both in this simple act. It was his need and her instant response. It said, "I'm here with you," and that act was its own comfort, be the malady a fever, or chills or just a bad day.

Yes, it was necessary to place her hand on his forehead.

The man did not acknowledge the hand. It had been a part of his life for nigh onto seventy years. To him, it had always meant that he was not alone, and if he was not alone, it meant that she was with him, and he had access to her strength as well as his own, and therefore, together, they had enough strength to go on.

The groan sounded again... actually, not a groan but a low moan. A cool cloth might give him ease. The kitchen was dark, and her own unsteadiness precluded the carrying of the oil lamp with her, so she lit the stub of a candle that was laying on the stand beside the lamp.

The match flared its flame and released its puff of sulfur odor. The candlewick caught the flame and the paraffin odor of the candle masked the sulfur of the match. She blew the flame from the matchstick she held in her wrinkled hand.

As she left the room, she walked by the tall mirror on the wall and caught a glimpse of her own face, its wrinkles highlighted in the candlelight. Again, as happened so often in her later years, she was momentarily startled into thinking, *How did I get into this old woman's body? I remember smooth, fair skin, dark curling hair, and steady footsteps. I remember them so well, but how did I get into this wrinkled old body?*

It was not stated as a concern, just a passing thought. A puzzling and surprising thought, but of no particular importance or consequence.

She set the candle on the table, and in its feeble light, she took a clean cloth from a drawer and moistened it in a pan of water. She did not really need the light of the candle at all. After more than sixty years of habit, she could have performed this duty with her eyes closed.

She brought the candle and the damp cloth back to the man's bedside. After blowing out the candle, she began to stroke the fevered forehead with the cool cloth. At her touch, the strained facial muscles relaxed.

"Esther?"

"I'm here, Marion."

"Let's take a walk up to the top of the bluff and watch the sunrise."

A game. A word game they had developed between them when the ability to climb to the top of the bluff was a thing of the past, but the memory of the sunrise was still vivid. He must be better to want to enter the little game.

"Sure, Marion. Just let me go change my slippers."

She waited. There was no responding remark, only another moan and a spell of erratic breathing. Her attention was caught by the sound. His words had been just a reflex, she decided, and she continued to stroke his head and to talk with the only other Presence in the room.

"I got'a thank You, Lord, for lettin' me stay here to tend to 'im in his last days. It was the one thing I felt confident You'd give me. I was always there when he needed someone. 'Member when I promised before You that I'd be doin' that?" She hesitated to add, 'till death do us part'.

She left the bedside to pull her comfortable old rocker nearer to him. The chair was not far away, but the weight of it took her strength and made her knees shaky. She sat down gratefully.

"Shouldn't be too much longer, Lord. Time and again, back through the past years, I thought it'd be me bein' the one first to go, but You pulled me through every ailment. Not wantin' to tell You Your business, Lord, but quick as he's gone, I'm ready to go. But it's whatever You want, and You know that, Lord."

She rocked back and forth as she looked at the black square of window behind the sheer curtain ruffles. No moon at all tonight. "Yea, though I walk through the valley," she quoted to herself to bring a bit of comfort. Her eyes were too dim to read, but the words from the Good Book committed to memory years ago had never failed her.

There had been many valleys along the way. She knew in her heart that this one would be the last one for her to walk beside her husband. "I appreciate You lettin' me be here, Lord. If I wasn't here, the takin' care'a him would fall on that precious little Jane Ann, and her with that new baby and all. She'd do it, though. For her granddad, she'd do whatever she could, but it's for me to do, and I thank You for leaving me here to do it."

Jane Ann, such a sweet child she was. She was around a lot when she was a tiny girl, and then other things came into her life. But here she was, back again, with that wonderful husband of hers, and she was helping him pastor the little church in River Bend.

It was the same little church that she and Marion had dreamed of and built and together had shepherded for more than twenty five years. They were years that had rolled past so quickly.

The old eyes closed, and the head eased onto the pillow on the back of the rocker, the pillow that was shaped to the exact size of her head. It was a pillow to dream on and relive old memories.

The years evaporated and the wrinkled skin disappeared. Her small, sturdy legs were smooth, and the tight curls bounced on her head. She slid from her bed in the cool, sod house located on the plains of Kansas, and when her tiny feet hit the thick, braided rug beside her bed, she leaped and bounded out the door, leaving it swinging on its leather hinges. Her exuberance propelled her into the golden Kansas sunshine.

"Come on, Esther. Let's go pick the flowers," came the voice of Louis, her brother just three years older than she. Her favorite brother, he was, and out of the ten of her mother's children, it was to him she felt the closest.

Together they ran, barefoot, across the rolling, grassy knolls to pick the morning's offering of wine-cup blossoms from the crawling green vine. The small, reddish-purple flower bowls of the plant petals glistened freshly in the morning sun.

With hands full of the fresh flowers, they raced back to the soddy to put them in the cracked cup that was set aside for that purpose.

The plains of Kansas were exciting and different from the woodlands of eastern Missouri, where she had been born. The train ride had brought them part of the way to the homestead claim in Kansas, and the covered wagon had finished the trip. It had all happened only months ago... at least not more than a year.

The happy scene played itself through her mind as she sat in the darkness, rocking quietly in the log cabin in central Arkansas. The little settlement called River Bend had been her home for a half a century. The tiny town was nestled among the hills within the sound of the noisy Tuscalara River, sometimes murmuring, often roaring, on its way to the Mississippi.

The scenes of childhood in her mind were still vivid, and she could even feel the coolness of the early morning soil against her small feet, though the sun would soon heat the baked earth to a searing hardness.

The family soddy in Kansas had been large, as soddies go, but still the beds had touched each other in their closeness, and from her own bed, crowded with sisters, she could thrust an exploring toe and touch the wood box beside the stove.

Their few changes of clothing were strung on the lines across the bed, and the doll she shared with her sisters hung on the wall by the cord around its neck. So many things she remembered.

She remembered happiness. There were inconveniences, to be sure, but she chose not to think of them.

Except sometimes. There were the driving rainstorms, dagger raindrops sheeting across the plains that caused water to flow into the sod house, creating a mud hole underfoot. Thick braided rugs were put into the mud to make a place, though soggy wet, where one could stand when absolutely necessary. Children spent rainy days on the bed, playing with their few toys or with string games on their fingers or re-reading the few books.

Overhead, a ceiling of tacked cheesecloth had been attached to keep spiders and other insects from dropping onto the bed or into the soup kettle. The ceiling of cheesecloth was washed when the sun came out and then put back. The rugs were also put outside as soon as the rain stopped. In this treeless prairie, the drying rack was a massive pile of deer antlers on which the clothing was spread. Or it might be a heap of tumbleweeds, having rotted themselves off at the base and been blown by the wind into mountains, coming to lodge against any solid structure.

She knew there was not precious wood to burn to cook the meals but that "hay cats", made of the prairie grass, tightly twisted, would supplement the buffalo chips that she and her brother gathered. She knew these things, but they did not worry her from inside her protected cocoon of childhood. Her mother took care of difficulties, as mothers do. All that Esther could remember of that period was the fun.

Kansas was a lot different from the land that surrounded her present cabin. Here, there were mountains, tall trees, bluffs, and wide, swift streams of water. There were vines that grew across the paths and small animals that hid in the bushes. So different.

In Kansas, her older brothers took the gun and a bag of shot and came back with rabbits or maybe a deer. Here, the rabbits came into the garden and ate your lettuce, and the deer nibbled the blossoms off the yard shrubs. So very different.

- END OF EXCERPT -

ADDITIONAL BOOK SERIES BY JOANN KLUSMEYER

The Great I Am Bible Story Series for Kids
6 books

The Young Pioneers Adventure Series for Kids
5 books

The Wentworth Triplets Mystery Series for Young Teens
3 books

Footsteps in the Canyon Adventure Series for Young Teens
4 books

Burnt Tree Junction: Historical Fiction for Adults
6 books

Ozark Mountains Historical Fiction Series for Adults
7 books

Taming the Wilderness Historical Fiction Series for Adults
7 books

The Sheltering Stones Historical Fiction Series for Adults
5 books

The Trilogy of Wishbone Hollow Historicial Fiction Series for Adults
3 books

www.ingramcontent.com/pod-product-compliance
Lightning Source LLC
Chambersburg PA
CBHW070444030726
47503CB00004B/891